The Island Home

by

Richard Archer

The Island Home
by Richard Archer

Copyright © 2024

All Rights reserved.

ISBN: 978-93-65789-67-6

Published by

DOUBLE 9 BOOKS

2/13-B, Ansari Road
Daryaganj, New Delhi – 110002
info@double9books.com
www.double9books.com
Tel. 011-40042856

ABOUT THE AUTHOR

Richard Archer was a 19th-century author known for his contributions to historical fiction and adventure literature. While specific details about his life are sparse, Archer's work reflects a deep engagement with themes of exploration and maritime life, indicative of his interest in the broader historical and cultural contexts of his time. Archer's most notable work, The Island Home, showcases his ability to weave compelling narratives set in exotic and isolated locales. His storytelling often involves detailed portrayals of adventure, survival, and personal discovery, reflecting the spirit of exploration prevalent in 19th-century literature. His novels typically focus on intricate family sagas and social dynamics, providing readers with a vivid sense of the era's cultural interactions and colonial influences. Through his writing, Archer contributes to the genre of historical fiction by combining engaging stories with thoughtful historical and cultural observations. His work not only entertains but also offers insights into the complexities of life in remote and adventurous settings, making him a notable figure in the realm of historical adventure literature.

CONTENTS

Chapter One
Introduction

"A wet sheet and a flowing sea,
 A breeze that follows fast,
That fills the white and rustling sail,
 And bends the gallant mast.
And bends the gallant mast, my boys,
 Our good ship sound and free,
The hollow oak our palace is,
 Our heritage the sea."

It is now some twenty years ago, that the goodly ship Washington, commanded by Mr Erskine, left the port of New York, on a trading voyage to the East Indian archipelago. With a select few good seamen, the owners had also placed on board some youths of their own families and immediate connections.

Having passed through the Straits of Magellan in safety, they were then on their way to Canton, where the young men were to be settled; and meanwhile the ship was to visit any of the isles in the Pacific Ocean that lay in their path. After some little delay on the part of the captain among the numerous groups of isles, the purpose of the voyage was frustrated by the events narrated in the volume. The extreme beauty of the wild loveliness of nature that these islets exhibited, tempted the young men, accompanied by Mr Frazer, one of the officers, to land on one that presented great charms of scenery, as well as having a convenient and easily accessible landing-place, and from that point the narrative commences.

It is not necessary for the elucidation of the narrative, to name more of the crew than those whose adventures are hereafter related by one of the party. The names of these castaways were John Browne, the son of a Glasgow merchant; William Morton, and Maximilian Adeler, of New York; Richard Archer, from Connecticut, the journalist; John Livingstone, from Massachusetts; Arthur Hamilton, whose parents had settled at Tahiti; and to them was joined Eiulo, prince of Tewa, in the South-Seas.

The narrative commences from the time of the party landing, and although in some parts prolix and unequal, being evidently from an unpractised hand, it bears all the characteristics of a boyish mind, and thus to a certain extent confirms its genuineness. The sayings and doings of the young adventurers are recorded with the minuteness that to older heads seems tedious. This disposition to dwell upon, and to attach importance to things comparatively trivial, is peculiar to the youthful mind, and marks that period of freshness, joyousness, and inexperience, when every thing is new, and possesses the power to surprise and to interest.

What became of the ship and crew we are not informed; but we may conclude, that insubordination would lead to neglect and carelessness, and that the vessel was wrecked and plundered by the native; and the wretched crew murdered or detained.

The South Pacific Ocean abounds with thousands of islands, of a vast many of which we have no account; but those mentioned in these pages appear to be the *Samoas*, the *Kingsmill*, and the *Feejee Groups* of islands, which lie nearly under the equator, and they are described by Captain Charles Wilkes, in his narrative of the United States Exploring Expedition between the years 1838 and 1842. These islands were all visited by the different vessels engaged in the expedition; many of them appear to be of volcanic formation, others are of coral origin; they are all characterised as possessing an exceedingly fertile soil; they abound with a picturesque beauty of scenery, and luxuriant vegetation, which excites the most painful feelings when we learn, that where nature has bestowed so much bounty, the inhabitants are, it is greatly to be feared, cannibals. In some two or three islands, a solitary white man was found, one of whom, Paddy Connell, (an Irishman, of course), a short, wrinkled old man, with a beard reaching to his middle, in a rich Milesian brogue, related his adventures during a forty years' residence at Ovolan, one of the Feejees. Paddy, with one hundred wives, and forty-eight children, and a vast quantity of other live stock, expressed his content and happiness, and a determination to die on the island. In other cases, the white men expressed an earnest desire to quit the island, and were received on board the expedition, to the great grief of their wives and connections.

The *Samoan Islands* are of volcanic structure, with coral reefs, and the harbours are generally within these reefs; and one of them was discovered by Commodore Byron in 1765, who reported it as destitute of inhabitants. Their character is variable, and during the winter months they have long and heavy rains, and destructive hurricanes sometimes occur. The air is generally moist, and light winds and calms during the summer, render vegetation luxuriant.

The woods in the interior of these islands are very thick, and are composed of large and fine trees; there are pandanus, palms, tree ferns, and a remarkable species of banyan, whose pendant branches take root to the number of thousands, forming steps of all dimensions, uniting to the main trunk, more than eight feet above the ground, and supporting a vast system of horizontal branches, spreading like an umbrella over the tops of other trees. The bread-fruit is the most abundant of all the trees, and grows to a very large size; the cocoa-nut, the wild orange, and the lime, are all to be found. Bamboos, wild sugar-cane, wild nutmeg, besides many others, only require cultivation. Caoutchouc, gum arabic, castor beans, ginger, orris root, and coffee, will in time be added to these productions. Lemons and sweet oranges have already been planted, and promise a large product.

Swine are abundant and cattle rapidly increasing. Poultry of all kinds is very plentiful, and fish are taken in abundance.

The beneficent effects of missionary labours are very evident amongst the Samoans; they are not now subject to wars, and for crimes they have punishment.

Their habits are regular; they rise with the sun, and after a meal, bathe and oil themselves, and then go to their occupations for the day; they eat at one o'clock, and again at eight, retiring to rest about nine. The men do all the hard work, even to cookery. The women are held in much consideration, and are treated with great kindness and attention. They take care of the house and children, prepare the food for cooking, and manufacture the mats, etcetera.

Their houses are carefully constructed, generally occupying eighteen months in building; the floor is paved with small round stones, and divisions or separate apartments formed. In some villages, broad walks and paths are kept in nice order. The females generally wear a kind of robe, similar to the poncho of the South Americans; and although not what may be termed pretty, they have some degree of bashfulness, which renders them interesting in appearance; when young, they are but little darker than a brunette, or South American Spaniard.

The entire population of the group is estimated at 60,000, of whom more than one-fourth have embraced Christianity, and it is understood that more than two-thirds of the population are favouring the progress of the gospel. Many thousands attend the schools of the missionaries, and the habit of reading is fast obliterating the original religion and superstitions of the race.

Of the *Kingsmill Group*, we possess a very sad account; one named Drummond's Island, which is of coral formation, is about thirty miles long, and about three-quarters of a mile in width. The island is covered with cocoa-nut and pandanus trees, but not a patch of grass was seen. The character of these islanders is of the most savage kind; their ferocity led to the belief that they are cannibals; one seaman of the expedition was carried off, and all attempts to rescue him were unavailing. Clad in coats of mail, and helmets made of the skin of a horny kind of fish, with weapons of the most frightful character, formed from the teeth of some of the voracious monsters of the deep, they appeared to the number of more than five hundred, prepared for resistance; their numbers continuing to increase. The officer in command, considered it both useless and dangerous to continue on the land. Failing to procure the desired end, prior to returning, the commanding officer determined to show the power of their arms, and having shot the leader of the savages dead, by a rocket and a volley, set their town, which was close to the beach, in flames; and the houses being formed of easily combustible material, a very short time sufficed to reduce the whole to ashes. The number of houses was supposed to be about three hundred.

The people appear to be under no control whatever, and possess little of the characteristic hospitality usually found among other savage tribes.

It was observed that their treatment of each other exhibited a great want of feeling; and in many instances their practices were indicative of the lowest state of barbarism. Their young girls are freely offered for sale by their fathers and brothers, and without concealment; and to drive a bargain is the principal object of their visits to a ship.

The *Kingsmill Group*, which consists of fifteen islands, are all of coral formation—every one appears a continuous grove of cocoa-nut and pandanus trees—they are all densely inhabited. From one of these islands, John Kirby, a deserter from an English whaler, was taken, who had resided there three years. He stated that the natives do sometimes eat human flesh; but their general food is fish. That these islands have been peopled at a period not very remote is tolerably certain, as the natives state that only a few generations back, the people were fewer than at present, and that then there were no wars.

The islanders of this group differ from other Polynesians, and they more nearly resemble the Malays. They are of a dark copper colour, are of middle size, well-made, and slender. Their hair is fine, black, and glossy—their beards and moustaches black, and fine as the hair of their heads. The average height of the men is five feet eight inches. The women are much smaller—they have delicate features, slight figures, and are generally pretty.

The *Feejee Group* excel all other islands of Polynesia in their luxuriant and picturesque beauty—they produce all kinds of tropical fruits and vegetables—the bread-fruit, of which there are nine kinds, flourishes in great perfection; the banana, cocoa-nut, and chestnut, the orange, the lemon, and the guava, the pine-apple, and the nutmeg, are all to be found; and the yam, which attains the length of above four feet, is the principal food of the inhabitants; besides these, the sugar-cane and turmeric are largely cultivated, and different varieties are found growing wild. Although the Feejeeans have made considerable progress in several useful arts, they are in many respects the most barbarous and savage race now existing upon the globe. Having had considerable intercourse with white men, some effect has been produced in their political condition, but it has had no effect in mitigating the ferocity of their character. Messrs Lythe and Hunt, missionaries at Vuna, one of the Feejees, have given a circumstantial account of a cannibal feast, for the preparation of which they were eye-witnesses. The missionaries having heard rumours that the king had sent for some men belonging to a refractory town not far from the capital, with the intention of killing them, and afterwards feasting on their bodies, they went to the old king to urge him to desist from so horrid and barbarous a repast, and warned him that a time would come when he would be punished for it. The king referred them to his son; but the savage propensities of the latter rendered it impossible for them to turn the savage from his barbarous purpose. They afterwards saw the bodies cut up and cooked. On two of these islands, however, the efforts of missionaries have been rewarded with some success; for the Reverend Mr Calvert, belonging to the Wesleyan society, assured the officers of the expedition, that in those islands heathenism was fast passing away, and that cannibalism was there extinct; but it must be observed that many of the residents on those two islands were Tongese, among whom it is well known the light of the gospel of Christ has long prevailed.

On one of those isles are five hot springs, the temperature of which is 200 degrees; the rocks in the neighbourhood is of volcanic creation — there is no smell of sulphur unless the head is held close to the water; but the water has a very strong bitter saline taste. These springs are used by the natives to boil their yams, which it does simply by putting them into the springs, and covering them with grass and leaves, and, although the water had scarcely any appearance of boiling before, rapid ebullition ensues. The yams are well done in fifteen minutes.

The population of the Feejee Group is supposed to be about 130,000. Their towns are all on the sea-shore, as the chief food is fish. The Feejeeans are very ingenious at canoe-building and carpentry, and, curious enough, the barber is a most important personage, as they take great pains and pride in dressing their hair. Their houses are from twenty to thirty feet in length, and about fifteen feet in height—all have fireplaces, as they cook their food, which is done in jars, very like an oil jar in form.

All these isles are girt by white encircling reefs, which, standing out at some distance from the shore, forms a natural harbour, so that when a vessel has once entered, it is as secure as in an artificial dock. There is generally but one entrance through the reef, and the difficulty of discovering it is well described by the Young Crusoes. Each one has its own peculiar beauty; but Ovolan exceeds all others; it is the highest, the most broken, and the most picturesque.

Having thus introduced our readers to the scene of these adventures, we proceed to give the narrative in the words of the journalist of the Young Castaways.

Chapter Two
The Tropical Island

A Cocoa-Palm — Views of Desert Island Life

"O had we some bright little isle of our own,
In the blue summer ocean, far-off and alone."

Wandering along the shore, (taking care to keep in sight of Mr Frazer, under whose convoy, in virtue of his double-barrelled fowling-piece, we considered ourselves), we came to a low and narrow point, running out a little way into the sea, the extremity of which was adorned by a stately group of cocoa-nut trees.

The spot seemed ill adapted to support vegetation of so magnificent a growth, and nothing less hardy than the cocoa-palm could have derived nourishment from such a soil. Several of these fine trees stood almost at the water's edge, springing from a bed of sand, mingled with black basaltic pebbles, and coarse fragments of shells and coral, where their roots were washed by every rising tide: yet their appearance was thrifty and flourishing, and they were thickly covered with close-packed bunches of tassel-like, straw-coloured blossoms, and loaded with fruit in various stages of growth.

Johnny cast a wistful glance at the compact clusters of nuts, nestling beneath the graceful tufts of long leaves that crowned each straight and tapering trunk; but he had so recently learned from experience, the hopelessness of undertaking to climb a cocoa-nut tree, that he was not at present disposed to renew the attempt. Max, however, who greatly valued himself upon his agility, and professed to be able to do any thing that could be done, in the way of climbing, manifested an intention to hazard his reputation by making the doubtful experiment. After looking carefully around, he selected for the attempt, a young tree near the shore, growing at a considerable inclination from the perpendicular; and clasping it firmly, he slowly commenced climbing, or rather creeping, along the slanting trunk, while Johnny watched the operation from below, with an interest as intense as if the fate of empires depended upon the result.

Max, who evidently considered his character at stake, and who climbed for "glory," rather than for cocoa-nuts, proceeded with caution and perseverance. Once he partly lost his hold, and swung round to the under side of the trunk, but by a resolute and vigorous effort he promptly recovered his position, and finally succeeded in establishing himself quite comfortably among the enormous leaves that drooped from the top of the tree. Here he seemed disposed to rest for a while, after his arduous and triumphant exertions, and he sat, looking complacently down upon us from his elevated position, without making any attempt to secure the fruit which hung within his reach in abundant clusters.

"Hurrah!" cried Johnny, capering about and clapping his hands with glee, as soon as this much desired consummation was attained, "Now, Max, pitch down the nuts!"

Having teased Johnny, and enjoyed the impatience caused by the tantalising deliberation of his own movements, Max detached two entire clusters of nuts from the tree, which furnished us an abundant supply.

Selecting a pleasant spot beside the beach, we sat down to discuss the cocoa-nuts at our leisure, which occupied us some little time. Upon looking round, after we had finished, we discovered that our convoy had disappeared, and Johnny, whose imagination was continually haunted by visionary savages and cannibals, manifested considerable uneasiness upon finding that we were alone.

As the sun was already low in the west, and we supposed that the party engaged in getting wood had, in all probability, finished their work, we concluded to return, and to wait for Mr Frazer, and the rest of the shore party at the boats, if we should not find them already there.

As we skirted the border of the grove, on our return, Johnny every now and then cast an uneasy glance towards its darkening recesses, as though expecting to see some wild animal, or a yelling troop of tattooed islanders rush out upon us. The forest commenced about two hundred yards from the beach, from which there was a gradual ascent and was composed of a greater variety of trees than I had observed on the other islands of a similar size at which we had previously landed. Arthur called our attention to a singular and picturesque group of Tournefortias, in the midst of which, like a patriarch surrounded by his family, stood one of uncommon size, and covered with a species of fern, which gave it a striking and remarkable appearance. The group covered a little knoll, that crowned a piece of rising ground, advanced a short distance beyond the edge of the forest. It was a favourable spot for a survey of the scene around us. The sun, now hastening to his setting, was tingeing all the western ocean with a rich vermilion glow.

The smooth white beach before us, upon which the long-rolling waves broke in even succession, retired in a graceful curve to the right and was broken on the left by the wooded point already mentioned.

As you looked inland, the undulating surface of the island, rising gradually from the shore, and covered with the wild and luxuriant vegetation of the tropics, delighted the eye by its beauty and variety. The noble Bread-fruit tree—its arching branches clothed with its peculiarly rich and glossy foliage; the elegantly shaped Casuarina, the luxuriant Pandanus, and the Palms, with their stately trunks, and green crests of nodding leaves, imparted to the scene a character of oriental beauty.

"Why do they call so lovely a spot as this a desert island, I wonder?" exclaimed Johnny, after gazing around him a few moments in silence.

"Did you ever hear of a desert island that wasn't a lovely spot!" answered Max. "Why, your regular desert island should combine the richest productions of the temperate, torrid, and frigid zones—a choice selection of the fruits, flowers, vegetables, and animal; of Europe, Asia, and Africa. This would by no means come up to the average standard. I doubt if you could find upon it so much as a goat or a poll-parrot much less an 'ónager,' a buffalo, or a boa-constrictor, some of which at least are indispensable to a desert island of any respectability."

"Why, then, do they call such delightful places desert islands!" repeated Johnny. "I always thought a desert was a barren wilderness, where there was nothing to be seen but sand, and rocks, and Arabs."

"I believe they are more properly called *desolate* islands," said Arthur; "and that seems proper enough; for even this island with all its beauty, is supposed to be uninhabited, and it would be a very lonely and *desolate* home. Would you like to live here, Johnny, like Robinson Crusoe, or the Swiss family?"

"Not all alone, like Robinson Crusoe. O no! that would be horrible; but I think we might all of us together live here beautifully a little while, if we had plenty of provisions, and plenty of arms to defend ourselves against the savages; and then of course we should want a house to live in, too."

"Nonsense," said Max, "what should we want of provisions?—the sea is full of fish, and the forest of birds; the trees are loaded with fruit; there are oysters and other shell-fish in the bays, and no doubt there are various roots, good for food, to be had by digging for them. As to a house, we might sleep very comfortably, in such weather as this, under these Tournefortias, and never so much as think of taking cold; or we could soon build a servicable hut, which would be proof against sun and rain, of the trunks and boughs of trees, with a thatch of palm-leaves for a roof. Then in regard to arms, of course, if it should be our fate to set up for desert islanders, we should be well supplied in that line. I never heard of any one, from Robinson Crusoe down, being cast away on a desert island, without a good store of guns, pistols, cutlasses, etcetera, etcetera. Such a thing would be contrary to all precedent, and is not for a moment to be dreamed of."

"But we haven't any arms," said Johnny, "except those old rusty cutlasses that Spot put into the yawl, and if we should be cast away, or left here, for instance, where should we get them from?"

"O, but we are not cast away yet," replied Max. "This is the way the thing always happens. When people are cast away, it is in a ship, of course."

"Why, yes; I suppose so," said Johnny, rather doubtfully. "Well—the ship is always abundantly supplied with every thing necessary to a desert island life; she is driven ashore; the castaways—the future desert islanders— by dint of wonderful good fortune, get safely to land; the rest of course are all drowned, and so disposed of; then, in due time, the ship goes to pieces, and every thing needful is washed ashore and secured by the islanders— that's the regular course of things—isn't it, Arthur!"

"Yes, I believe it is, according to the story-books, which are the standard sources of information on the subject."

"Or sometimes," pursued Max, "the ship gets comfortably wedged in between two convenient rocks, (which seem to have been designed for that special purpose), so that the castaways can go out to it on a raft, or float of some kind, and carry off every thing they want—and singularly enough, although the vessel is always on the point of going to pieces, that catastrophe never takes place, until every thing which can be of any use is secured."

"Do you suppose, Arthur," inquired Johnny, "that there are many uninhabited islands, that have never been discovered!"

"There are believed to be a great many of them," answered Arthur, "and it is supposed that new ones are constantly being formed by the labours of the coral insect. A bare ledge of coral first appears, just at the surface; it arrests floating substances, weeds, trees, etcetera; soon the sea-birds begin to resort there; by the decay of vegetable and animal matter a thin soil gradually covers the foundation of coral; a cocoa-nut is drifted upon it by the winds, or the currents of the sea; it takes root, springs up, its fruit ripens and falls, and in a few years the whole new-formed island is covered with waving groves."

"Mr Frazer says he has no doubt that these seas swarm with such islands, and that many of them have never been discovered," said Max; besides, here's poetry for it:—

"'O many are the beauteous isles,
  Unseen by human eye,
That sleeping 'mid the Ocean smiles,
  In happy silence lie.
The ship may pass them in the night,
Nor the sailors know what lovely sight
  Is sleeping on the main;'

"But this poetical testimony will make Arthur doubt the fact altogether."

"Not exactly," answered Arthur, "though I am free to admit that without Mr Frazer's opinion to back it your poetical testimony would not go very far with me."

"Hark! There go Mr Frazer's two barrels," cried Max, as two reports in quick succession were heard, coming apparently from the grove, in the direction of the spring; "he has probably come across a couple of 'rare specimens,' to be added to his stuffed collection."

Chapter Three
The Alarm and the Conflict

The Mutineers—The Race for Life—The Coral Ledge—A Final Effort—A Brief Warning—The Strange Sail

"Now bend the straining rowers to their oars;
Fast the light shallops leave the lessening shores,
No rival crews in emulous sport contend,
But life and death upon the event depend."

The next moment we were startled by a quick, fierce shout, followed immediately by a long, piercing, and distressful cry, proceeding from the same quarter from which the reports of fire-arms had been heard; and before we had time to conjecture the cause or meaning of these frightful sounds, Morton bounded like a deer from the grove, about a hundred yards from the spot where we were standing, and ran swiftly towards us, crying out— "To the boats! for your lives to the boats!"

Our first thought was, that the party at the spring had been attacked and massacred by the natives. Arthur seized Johnny by one hand, and motioned to me to take the other, which I did, and without stopping to demand any explanations, we started at a rapid pace, in the direction of the yawl, Max taking the lead—Arthur and myself, dragging Johnny between us, coming next, and Morton a few paces behind us, bringing up the rear. It took but a few moments to enable us to reach the spot where the yawl lay, hauled up upon the beach. There was no one in her, or in sight, except Browne, who was comfortably stretched out near the boat sound asleep, with an open book lying beside him.

Morton aroused the sleeper by a violent shake. "Now, then," cried he, "let us get the boat into the water; the tide is down, and the yawl is heavy; we shall want all the strength we can muster."

By a united effort we got the yawl to the edge of the surf.

Browne, though not yet thoroughly awake, could not but observe our pale faces and excited appearance, and gazing from one to another in a bewildered manner, he asked what was the matter; but no one made any answer. Morton lifted Johnny into the boat and asked the rest of us to get in, except Arthur, saying that they two would push her through the surf.

"Hold!" cried Arthur, "let us not be too fast; some of the others may escape the savages, and they will naturally run this way—we must not leave them to be murdered."

"There are no savages in the case," answered Morton, "and there is no time to be lost; the men have killed the first officer, and Mr Frazer, too, I fear; and they will take the ship and commit more murders, unless we can get there before them, to warn those on board."

This was more horrible than any thing that we had anticipated; but we had no time to dwell upon it: the sound of oars rattling in the row-locks, was heard from beyond the point.

"There are the mutineers!" cried Morton; "but I think that we have the advantage of them; they must pull round yonder point, which will make at least a quarter of a mile's difference in the distance to the ship."

"There is no use in trying to get to the ship before them," said Max, "the long-boat pulls eight oars, and there are men enough to fill her."

"There *is* use in trying; it would be shameful *not* to try; if they pull most oars, ours is the lightest boat," answered Morton with vehemence.

"It us out of the question," said Browne; "see, is there any hope that we can succeed?" and he pointed to the bow of the long-boat just appearing from behind the point.

"O, but this is not right!—Browne! Max! in the name of all that is honourable, let us make the attempt," urged Morton, laying a hand in an imploring manner on the arm of each. "Shall we let them take the ship and murder our friends, without an effort to warn them of their danger? You, Arthur, are for making the attempt, I know—this delay is wrong: the time is precious."

"Yes, let us try it," said Arthur, glancing rapidly from the long-boat to the ship, "if we fail, no harm is done, except that we incur the anger of the mutineers. I, for one, am willing to take the risk."

Max sprang into the boat, and seized an oar without another word.

"*You* know well, that I am willing to share any danger with the rest, and that it was not the danger that made me hesitate," said Browne, laying his hand on Morton's shoulder, and looking earnestly into his face; and then, in his usual deliberate manner, he followed Max's example.

Morton, Arthur, and myself now pushed the boat into the surf and sprang in. At Arthur's request, I took the rudder; he and Morton seized the two remaining oars, and the four commenced pulling with a degree of coolness and vigour, that would not have disgraced older and more practised oarsmen. As I saw the manner in which they bent to their work, and the progress we were making, I began to think our chance of reaching the ship before the crew of the long-boat, by no means desperate.

Morton, in spite of his slender figure and youthful appearance, which his fresh, ruddy complexion, blue eyes, and brown curling locks, rendered almost effeminate, possessed extraordinary strength, and indomitable energy.

Browne, though his rather heavy frame and breadth of shoulders gave him the appearance of greater strength than he actually possessed, was undoubtedly capable, when aroused, of more powerful temporary exertion than any other of our number; though in point of activity and endurance, he would scarcely equal Morton or Arthur. Max, too, was vigorous and active, and, when stimulated by danger or emulation, was capable of powerful effort. Arthur, though of slight and delicate frame, was compact and well knit, and his coolness, judgment and resolution, enabled him to dispose of his strength to the best advantage. All were animated by that high and generous spirit which is of greater value in an emergency than any amount of mere physical strength; a spirit which often stimulates the feeble to efforts as surprising to him who puts them forth, as to those who witness them.

Browne had the bow-oar, and putting his whole force into every stroke, was pulling like a giant. Morton, who was on the same side, handled his oar with less excitement and effort but with greater precision and equal efficiency. It was plain that these two were pulling Max and Arthur round, and turning the boat from her course; and as I had not yet succeeded in shipping the rudder, which was rendered difficult by the rising and falling of the boat, and the sudden impulse she received from every stroke, I requested Browne and Morton to pull more gently. Just as I had succeeded in getting the rudder hung, the crew of the long-boat seemed to have first observed us. They had cleared the point to the southward, and we were, perhaps, a hundred yards nearer the long point, beyond which we could see the masts of the ship, and on doubling which, we should be almost within hail of her. The latter point, was probably a little more than half a mile distant from us, and towards the head of it, both boats were steering. The long-boat was pulling eight oars, and Luerson, the man who had had the difficulty with the first officer at the Kingsmill Islands, was at the helm. As soon as he observed us, he appeared to speak to the crew of his boat, and they commenced pulling with greater vigour than before. He then hailed us,—"Holloa, lads! where's Frazer? Are you going to leave him on the island!"

We pulled on in silence.

"He is looking for you now, somewhere along shore; he left us, just below the point, to find you; you had better pull back and bring him off."

"All a trick," said Morton; "don't waste any breath with them;" and we bent to the oars with new energy.

"The young scamps mean to give the alarm," I could hear Luerson mutter with an oath, as he surveyed, for a moment, the interval between the two boats, and then the distance to the point.

"There's no use of mincing matters, my lads," he cried, standing up in the stem; "we have knocked the first officer on the head, and served some of those who didn't approve of the proceeding in the same way; and now we are going to take the ship."

"We know it, and intend to prevent you," cried Morton, panting with the violence of his exertions.

"Unship your oars till we pass you, and you shall not be hurt," pursued Luerson in the same breath; "pull another stroke at them, and I will serve you like your friend, Frazer, and he lies at the spring with his throat slit!"

The ruffian's design, in this savage threat, was doubtless to terrify us into submission; or, at least, so to appal and agitate us, as to make our exertions more confused and feeble. In this last calculation he may have been partially correct, for the threat was fearful, and the danger imminent; the harsh, deep tones of his voice, with the ferocious determination of his manner, sent a thrill of horror to every heart. More than this, he could not effect; there was not a craven spirit among our number.

"Steadily!" said Arthur, in a low, collected tone; "less than five minutes will bring us within hail of the ship."

But the minutes seemed hours, amid such tremendous exertions, and such intense anxiety. The sweat streamed from the faces of the rowers; they gasped and panted for breath; the swollen veins stood out on their foreheads.

"Perhaps," cried Luerson, after a pause, "perhaps there is some one in that boat who desires to save his life; whoever drops his oar shall not be harmed; the rest die."

A scornful laugh from Morton was the only answer to this tempting offer.

Luerson now stooped for a moment and seemed to be groping for something in the bottom of the boat. When he rose, it was with a musket or fowling-piece in his hands, which he cocked, and, coming forward to the bow, levelled towards us.

"Once more," he cried, "and once for all, drop your oars, or I fire among you."

"I don't believe it is loaded," said Arthur, "or he would have used it sooner."

"I think it is Frazer's gun," said Morton, "and he fired both barrels before they murdered him; there has been no time to reload it."

The event showed the truth of these suspicions; for, upon seeing that his threat produced no effect, Luerson resumed his seat in the bows, the helm having been given to one of the men not at the oars.

We were now close upon the point, and, as I glanced from our pursuers to the ship, I began to breathe more freely. They had gained upon us; but it was inch by inch, and the goal was now at hand. The long-boat, though pulling eight oars, and those of greater length than ours, was a clumsier boat than the yawl, and at present heavily loaded; we had almost held our own with them thus far.

But now Luerson sprang up once more in the bow of the long-boat, and presented towards us the weapon with which he had a moment before threatened us; and this time it was no idle menace. A puff of smoke rose from the muzzle of the piece, and, just as the sharp report reached our ears, Browne uttered a quick exclamation of pain, and let fall his oar.

For a moment all was confusion and alarm; but Browne, who had seized his oar again almost instantly, declared that he was not hurt; that the ball had merely grazed the skin of his arm; and he attempted to recommence rowing; before, however, he had pulled half-a-dozen strokes, his right hand was covered with the blood which streamed down his arm.

I now insisted on taking his oar, and he took my place at the helm.

While this change was being effected, our pursuers gained upon us perceptibly. Every moment was precious. Luerson urged his men to greater efforts; the turning point of the struggle was now at hand, and the excitement became terrible.

"Steer close in; it will save something in distance," gasped Morton, almost choking for breath.

"Not too close," panted Arthur; "don't get us aground."

"There is no danger of that," answered Morton, "it is deep, off the point."

Almost as he spoke, a sharp, grating sound was heard, beneath the bottom of the boat, and our progress was arrested with a suddenness that threw Max and myself from our seats. We were upon a ledge of coral, which at a time of less excitement we could scarcely have failed to have observed and avoided, from the manner in which the sea broke upon it.

A shout of mingled exultation and derision, as they witnessed this disaster, greeted us from the long-boat, which was ploughing through the water, but a little way behind us, and some twenty yards further out from the shore.

"It is all up," said Morton, bitterly, dropping his oar.

"Back water! Her stern still swings free," cried Arthur, "the next swell will lift her clear."

We got as far aft as possible, to lighten the bows; a huge wave broke upon the ledge, and drenched us with spray, but the yawl still grated upon the coral.

Luerson probably deemed himself secure of a more convenient opportunity, at no distant period, to wreak his vengeance upon us: at any rate there was no time for it now; he merely menaced us with his clenched fist, as they swept by. Almost at the same moment a great sea came rolling smoothly in, and, as our oars dipped to back water, we floated free: then a few vigorous strokes carried us to a safe distance from the treacherous shoal.

"One effort more!" cried Arthur, as the mutineers disappeared behind the point; "we are not yet too late to give them a warning, though it will be but a short one."

Again we bent to the oars, and in a moment we too had doubled the point, and were in the wake of the long-boat. The ship lay directly before us, and within long hailing distance.

"Now, comrades, let us shout together, and try to make them understand their danger," said Browne, standing up in the stern.

"A dozen strokes more," said Arthur, "and we can do it with more certain success."

Luerson merely glanced back at us, as he once more heard the dash of our oars; but he took no farther notice of us: the crisis was too close at hand.

On board the ship all seemed quiet. Some of the men were gathered together on the starboard bow, apparently engaged in fishing; they did not seem to notice the approach of the boats.

"Now, then!" cried Arthur, at length, unshipping his oar, and springing to his feet, "one united effort to attract their attention—all together—now, then!" and we sent up a cry that echoed wildly across the water, and startled the idlers congregated at the bows, who came running to the side of the vessel nearest us.

"We have got their attention; now hail them," said Arthur, turning to Browne, who had a deep powerful voice; "tell them not to let the long-boat board them."

Browne put his hands to his mouth, and in tones that could have been distinctly heard twice the distance, shouted— "Look-out for the long-boat— don't let them board you—the men have killed the first officer, and want to take the ship!" From the stir and confusion that followed, it was clear that the warning was understood.

But the mutineers were now scarcely twenty yards from the vessel, towards which they were ploughing their way with unabated speed. The next moment they were under her bows; just as their oars flew into the air, we could hear a deep voice from the deck, sternly ordering them to "keep off," and I thought that I could distinguish Captain Erskine standing near the bowsprit.

The mutineers gave no heed to the order; several of them sprang into the chains, and Luerson among the rest. A fierce, though unequal struggle, at once commenced. The captain, armed with a weapon which he wielded with both hands, and which I took to be a capstan-bar, struck right and left among the boarders as they attempted to gain the deck, and one, at least, of them, fell back with a heavy plunge into the water. But the captain seemed to be almost unsupported; and the mutineers had nearly all reached the deck, and were pressing upon him.

"Oh, but this is a cruel sight!" said Browne, turning away with a shudder. "Comrades, can we do nothing more?"

Morton, who had been groping beneath the sail in the bottom of the boat now dragged forth the cutlasses which Spot had insisted on placing there when we went ashore.

"Here are arms!" he exclaimed, "we are not such boys, but that we can take a part in what is going on—let us pull to the ship!"

The Alarm.

"What say you!" cried Arthur, glancing inquiringly from one to another; "we can't, perhaps, do much, but shall we sit here and see Mr Erskine murdered, without *trying* to help him!"

"Friends, let us to the ship!" cried Browne, with deep emotion, "I am ready."

"And I!" gasped Max, pale with excitement, "we can but be killed."

Can we hope to turn the scale of this unequal strife? shall we do more than arrive at the scene of conflict in time to experience the vengeance of the victorious mutineers?—such were the thoughts that flew hurriedly through my mind. I was entirely unaccustomed to scenes of violence and bloodshed, and my head swam, and my heart sickened, as I gazed at the confused conflict raging on the vessel's deck, and heard the shouts and cries of the combatants. Yet I felt an inward recoil against the baseness of sitting an idle spectator of such a struggle. A glance at the lion-hearted Erskine still maintaining the unequal fight, was an appeal to every noble and generous feeling: it nerved me for the attempt, and though I trembled as I grasped an oar, it was with excitement and eagerness, not with fear.

The yawl had hardly received the first impulse in the direction of the ship, when the report of fire-arms was heard.

"Merciful heavens!" cried Morton, "the captain is down! that fiend Luerson has shot him!"

The figure which I had taken for that of Mr Erskine, was no longer to be distinguished among the combatants, some person was now dragged to the side of the ship towards us, and thrown overboard; he sunk after a feeble struggle; a triumphant shout followed, and then two men were seen running up the rigging.

"There goes poor Spot up to the foretop," said Max, pointing to one of the figures in the rigging; "he can only gain time at the best but it can't be that they'll kill him in cold blood."

"Luerson is just the man to do it," answered Morton; "the faithful fellow has stood by the captain, and that will seal his fate—look! it is as I said," and I could see some one pointing, what was doubtless Mr Frazer's fowling-piece, at the figure in the foretop. A parley seemed to follow; as the result of which, the fugitive came down and surrendered himself. The struggle now appeared to be over, and quiet was once more restored.

So rapidly had these events passed, and so stunning was their effect, that it was some moments before we could collect our thoughts, or fully realise our situation; and we sat, silent and bewildered, gazing toward the ship.

Max was the first to break silence; "And now, what's to be done?" he said, "as to going aboard, that is of course out of the question: the ship is no longer our home."

"I don't know what we can do," said Morton, "except to pull ashore, and stand the chance of being taken off by some vessel, before we starve."

"Here is something better," cried Max eagerly, pointing out to sea; and, looking in the direction indicated, we saw a large ship, with all her sails set, steering directly for us, or so nearly so, as to make it apparent that if she held on her present course, she must pass very near to us. Had we not been entirely engrossed by what was taking place immediately around us, we could not have failed to have seen her sooner, as she must have been in sight a considerable time.

"They have already seen her on board," said Morton, "and that accounts for their great hurry in getting up anchor; they don't feel like being neighbourly just now, with strange vessels."

In fact, there was every indication on board of our own ship, of haste, and eagerness to be gone. While some of the men were at the capstan, getting up the anchor, others were busy in the rigging, and sail after sail was rapidly spread to the breeze, so that by the time the anchor was at the bows, the ship began to move slowly through the water.

"They don't seem to consider us of much account anyway," said Max, "they are going without so much as saying good-bye."

"They may know more of the stranger than we do," said Arthur, "they have glasses on board; if she should be an American man-of-war, their hurry is easily explained."

"I can't help believing that they see or suspect more, in regard to her, than appears to us," said Morton, "or they would not fail to make an attempt to recover the yawl."

"It is rapidly getting dark," said Arthur, "and I think we had better put up the sail, and steer for the stranger."

"Right," said Morton, "for she may possibly tack before she sees us."

Morton and myself proceeded to step the mast, and rig the sail; meantime, Arthur got Browne's coat off, and examined and bandaged the wound on his arm, which had been bleeding all the while profusely; he pronounced it to be but a trifling hurt. A breeze from the south-east had sprung up at sunset, and we now had a free wind to fill our sail, as we steered directly out to sea to meet the stranger, which was still at too great a distance to make it probable that we had been seen by her people.

It was with a feeling of anxiety and uneasiness, that I saw the faint twilight fading away, with the suddenness usual in those latitudes, and the darkness gathering rapidly round us. Already the east was wrapped in gloom, and only a faint streak of light along the western horizon marked the spot where the sun had so recently disappeared.

"How suddenly the night has come upon us," said Arthur, who had been peering through the dusk toward the approaching vessel, in anxious silence; "O, for twenty minutes more of daylight! I fear that she is about tacking."

This announcement filled us all with dismay, and every eye was strained towards her with intense and painful interest.

Meantime, the breeze had freshened somewhat and we now had rather more of it than we desired, as our little boat was but poorly fitted to navigate the open ocean in rough weather. Johnny began to manifest some alarm, as we were tossed like a chip from wave to wave, and occasionally deluged with spray, by a sea bursting with a rude shock over our bow. I had not even in the violent storm of the preceding week, experienced such a sense of insecurity, such a feeling of helplessness, as now, when the actual danger was comparatively slight. The waves seemed tenfold larger and more threatening than when viewed from the deck of a large vessel. As we sunk into the trough of the sea, our horizon was contracted to the breadth of half-a-dozen yards, and we entirely lost sight of the land, and of both ships.

But it was evident that we were moving through the water with considerable velocity, and there was encouragement in that, for we felt confident that if the stranger should hold on her present course but a little longer, we should be on board of her before our safety would be seriously endangered by the increasing breeze.

If, however, she were really tacking, our situation would indeed be critical. A very few moments put a period to our suspense by confirming Arthur's opinion, and our worst fears; the stranger had altered her course, her yards were braced round, and she was standing further out to sea. Still, however, there would have been a possibility of reaching her, but for the failure of light, for she had not so far changed her course, but that she would have to pass a point, which we could probably gain before her. But now, it was with difficulty, and only by means of the cloud of canvass she carried, that we could distinguish her through the momently deepening gloom; and with sinking hearts we relinquished the last hopes connected with her. Soon she entirely vanished from our sight, and when we gazed anxiously around the narrow horizon that now bounded our vision, sky and water alone met our view.

Chapter Four
At Sea

A Night of Gloom—Morton's Narrative—Visionary
Terrors—An Alarming Discovery

"O'er the deep! o'er the deep!
Where the whale, and the shark, and the sword-fish
sleep."

Even in open day, the distance of a few miles would be sufficient to sink the low shores of the island; and now that night had so suddenly overtaken us, it might be quite near, without our being able to distinguish it.

We were even uncertain, and divided in opinion, as to the direction in which it lay—so completely were we bewildered. The night was one of deep and utter gloom. There was no moon; and not a single star shed its feeble light over the wilderness of agitated waters, upon which our little boat was tossing. Heavy, low-hanging clouds, covered the sky; but soon, even these could no longer be distinguished; a cold, damp mist, dense, and almost palpable to the touch, crept over the ocean, and enveloped us so closely, that it was impossible to see clearly from one end of the yawl to the other.

The wind, however, instead of freshening, as we had feared, died gradually away. For this, we had reason to be thankful; for though our situation that night seemed dismal enough, yet how much more fearful would it have been, if the rage of the elements, and danger of immediate destruction, had been added to the other circumstances of terror by which we were surrounded?

As it was, however, the sea having gone down, we supposed ourselves to be in no great or pressing peril. Though miserably uncomfortable, and somewhat agitated and anxious, we yet confidently expected that the light of morning would show us the land again.

The terrible and exciting scenes through which we had so recently passed, had completely exhausted us, and we were too much overwhelmed by the suddenness of our calamity, and the novel situation in which we now found ourselves, to be greatly disposed to talk. Johnny sobbed himself asleep in Arthur's arms; and even Max's usual spirits seemed now to have quite forsaken him. After the mast had been unstepped, and such preparations as our circumstances permitted were made, for passing the night comfortably, Morton related all that he knew of what had taken place on shore, previous to the alarm which he had given.

I repeat the narrative as nearly as possible in his own words, not perhaps altogether as he related it on that night, for the circumstances were not then favourable to a full and orderly account, but partly as I afterwards, in various conversations, gathered the particulars from him.

"You recollect," said he, "that we separated at the boats; Mr Frazer and the rest of you, going along the shore towards the point, leaving Browne declaiming Byron's Address to the Ocean, from the top of a coral block, with myself and the breakers for an audience. Shortly afterwards, I strolled off towards the interior, and left Browne lying on the sand, with his pocket Shakespeare, where we found him, when we reached the boats. I kept on inland, until the forest became so dense, and was so overgrown with tangled vines and creeping plants, that I could penetrate no farther in that direction. In endeavouring to return, I got bewildered, and at length fairly lost, having no clear notion as to the direction of the beach. The groves were so thick and dark as to shut out the light almost entirely; and I could not get a glimpse of the sun so as to fix the points of the compass. At last I came to an opening, large enough to let in the light, and show which way the shadows fell. Knowing that we had landed on the west side of the island, I could now select my course without hesitation. It was getting late in the afternoon, and I walked as fast as the nature of the ground would allow, until I unexpectedly found myself at the edge of the grove, east of the spring where the men were at work filling the breakers. The moment I came in sight of them, I perceived that something unusual was taking place. The first officer and Luerson were standing opposite each other, and the men, pausing from their work, were looking on. As I inferred, Mr Nichol had given some order, which Luerson had refused to obey. Both looked excited, but no words passed between them after I reached the place. There was a pause of nearly a minute, when Mr Nichol advanced as if to lay hands on Luerson, and the latter struck him a blow with his cooper's mallet, which he held in his hand, and knocked him down. Before he had time to rise, Atoâ, the Sandwich Islander, sprang upon him, and stabbed him twice with his belt-knife. All this passed so rapidly, that no one had a chance to interfere—"

"Hark!" said Browne, interrupting the narration, "what noise is that? It sounds like the breaking of the surf upon the shore."

But the rest of us could distinguish no sound except the washing of the waves against the boat. The eye was of no assistance in deciding whether we were near the shore or not, as it was impossible to penetrate the murky darkness, a yard in any direction.

"We must be vigilant," said Arthur, "the land cannot be far-off, and we may be drifted upon it before morning."

After listening for some moments in anxious silence, we became satisfied that Browne had been mistaken, and Morton proceeded.

"Just as Atoâ sprang upon Mr Nichol and stabbed him, Mr Knight, who was the first to recover his presence of mind, seized the murderer, and wrenched the knife from his hand, at the same time calling on the men to secure Luerson; but no one stirred to do so. A part seemed confused and undecided; while others appeared to me to have been fully prepared for what had taken place. One man stepped forward near Luerson, and declared in a brutal and excited manner, that 'Nichol was a bloody tyrant, and had got what he deserved, and that no man could blame Luerson for taking his revenge, after being treated as he had been.' For a moment all was clamour and confusion; then Luerson approached Mr Knight in a threatening manner, and bade him loose Atoâ, instead of which, he held his prisoner firmly with one hand, and warning Luerson off with the other, called on the men to stand by their officers. Just at this moment, Mr Frazer, with his gun on his shoulder, came out of the grove from the side toward the shore, and to him Mr Knight eagerly appealed for assistance in securing the murderers of Mr Nichol. Pointing from the bleeding corpse at his feet, to Luerson, he said— 'There is the ringleader—shoot him through the head at once, and that will finish the matter—otherwise we shall all be murdered—fire, I will answer for the act?'

"Frazer seemed to comprehend the situation of things at a glance. With great presence of mind, he stepped back a pace, and bringing his gun to his shoulder, called on Luerson to throw down his weapon, and surrender himself, declaring that he would shoot the first man who lifted a hand to assist him. His manner was such as to leave no doubt of his sincerity, or his resolution. The men had no fire-arms, and were staggered by the suddenness of the thing; they stood hesitating and undecided. Mr Knight seized this as a favourable moment, and advanced upon Luerson, with the intention of securing him, and the islander was thus left free. At this moment I observed the man who had denounced Mr Nichol, and justified Luerson, stealing round behind Frazer. I called out to him at the top of my voice to warn him; but he did not seem to hear. I looked for something which might serve me for a weapon; but there was nothing, not so much as a broken bough within reach, and in another instant, the whole thing was over. As Knight grappled with Luerson, he dropped the knife which he had wrested from Atoâ, his intention evidently being to secure, and not to kill him.

"Atoâ immediately leaped forward and seized the knife, and had his arm already raised to stab Mr Knight in the back, when Frazer shot him dead. At almost the same instant, Luerson struck Mr Knight a tremendous blow on the head with his mallet, which felled him to the earth, stunned and lifeless. He next rushed upon Frazer, who had fairly covered him with the muzzle of his piece, and would inevitably have shot him, but just as he pulled the trigger, the man whom I had seen creeping round behind him, sprang upon him, and deranged his aim; two or three of the others, who had stood looking on, taking no part in the affair, now interposed, and by their assistance Frazer was overpowered and secured. Whether they murdered him or not, as Luerson afterwards declared, I do not know. As soon as the struggle was over, the man who had seconded Luerson so actively throughout, (the tall dark man who goes by the name of 'the Boatswain,') shouted out, 'Now, then, for the ship!' 'Yes, for the ship!' cried Luerson, 'though this has not come about just as was arranged, and has been hurried on sooner than we expected; it is as well so as any way, and must be followed up. There's no one aboard but the captain, and four or five men and boys, all told: the landsmen are all ashore, scattered over the island. We can take her without risk—and then for a merry life at the islands!'

"This revealed the designs of the mutineers, and I determined to anticipate them if possible. As I started for the beach I was observed, and they hailed me; but without paying any attention to their shouts, I ran as fast, at least, as I ever ran before, until I came out of the forest, near where you were standing."

From the words of Luerson which Morton had heard, it was clear that the mutiny had not been a sudden and unpremeditated act; and we had no doubt that it had grown out of the difficulties at the Kingsmills, between him and the unfortunate Mr Nichol.

It was quite late before we felt any disposition to sleep; but notwithstanding the excitement and the discomforts of our situation, we began at length to experience the effects of the fatigue and anxiety which we had undergone, and bestowing ourselves as conveniently as possible about the boat, which furnished but slender accommodations for such a number, we bade each other the accustomed "good night," and one by one dropped asleep.

Knowing that we could not be far from land, and aware of our liability to be drifted ashore during the night, it had been decided to maintain a watch. Arthur, Morton, and I had agreed to divide the time between us as accurately as possible, and to relieve one another in turn. The first watch fell to Arthur, the last to me, and, after exacting a promise from Morton, that he would not fail to awaken me when it was fairly my turn, I laid down upon the ceiling planks, close against the side of the boat between which, and Browne, who was next me, there was barely room to squeeze myself.

It was a dreary night. The air was damp, and even chilly. The weltering of the waves upon the outside of the thin plank against which my head was pressed, made a dismal kind of music, and suggested vividly how frail was the only barrier that separated us from the wide, dark waste of waters, below and around.

The heavy, dirge-like swell of the ocean, though soothing, in the regularity and monotony of its sluggish motion, sounded inexpressibly mournful.

The gloom of the night, and the tragic scenes of the day, seemed to give character to my dreams, for they were dark and hideous, and so terribly vivid, that I several times awoke strangely agitated.

At one time I saw Luerson, with a countenance of supernatural malignity, and the expression of a fiend, murdering poor Frazer. At another, our boat seemed drawn by some irresistible, but unseen power, to the verge of a yawning abyss, and began to descend between green-glancing walls of water, to vast depths, where undescribed sea-monsters, never seen upon the surface, glided about in an obscurity that increased their hideousness. Suddenly the feeble light that streamed down into the gulf through the green translucent sea, seemed to be cut off; the liquid walls closed above our heads; and we were whirled away, with the sound of rushing waters, and in utter darkness.

All this was vague and confused, and consisted of the usual "stuff that dreams are made of." What followed, was wonderfully vivid and real: every thing was as distinct as a picture, and it has left an indelible impression upon my mind; there was something about it far more awful than all the half-defined shapes and images of terror that preceded it.

I seemed to be all alone, in our little boat, in the midst of the sea. It was night—and what a night! not a breath of wind rippled the glassy waters. There was no moon, but the sky was cloudless, and the stars were out, in solemn and mysterious beauty. Every thing seemed preternaturally still, and I felt oppressed by a strange sense of loneliness; I looked round in vain for some familiar object, the sight of which might afford me relief. But far, far as the eye could reach, to the last verge of the horizon, where the gleaming sapphire vault closed down upon the sea, stretched one wide, desolate, unbroken expanse. I seemed to be isolated and cut off from all living things:

"Alone—alone, all, all alone!
Alone on the wide, wide sea;
So lonely 'twas, that God himself
Scarce seemed there to be."

And there was something in this feeling, and in the universal, death-like silence, that was unutterably awful. I tried to pray—to think of God as present even there—to think of Him as "Our Father"—as caring for and loving his creatures—and thus to escape the desolating sense of loneliness that oppressed me. But it was in vain; I could not pray: there was something in the scene that mocked at faith, and seemed in harmony with the dreary creed of the atheist. The horrible idea of a godless universe came upon me, bidding me relinquish, as a fond illusion, the belief in a Heavenly Father,—

"Who sees with equal eye, as Lord of all,
A hero perish, or a sparrow fall."

Language cannot express the desolation of that thought.

Then the scene changed once more. We were again on board the ship, and in the power of the enraged mutineers, about to suffer whatever their vengeance might impel them to inflict. Poor Spot was swinging, a livid corpse, at one of the yard-arms. Browne was bound to the main-mast, while Luerson and his fiendish crew were exhausting their ingenuity in torturing him. The peculiar expression of his mild, open countenance, distorted by pain, went to my heart, and the sound of that familiar and friendly voice, now hoarse and broken, and quivering with agony, thrilled me with horror. As he besought his tormentors to kill him at once, I thought that I kneeled to Luerson, and seconded the entreaty—the greatest favour that could be hoped from him. The rest of us were doomed to walk the plank. Morton was stern and silent; Max pale and sorrowful; his arm was round my neck, and he murmured that life was sweet, and that it was a hard and terrible thing to die—to die so! Arthur, calm and collected, cheered and encouraged us; and his face seemed like the face of an angel, as he spoke sweetly and solemnly, of the goodness and the love of God, and bade us put our whole trust and hope in Christ our Saviour. His earnest words and serene look, soothed and strengthened us; we also became calm and almost resigned. There was no abject fear, no useless cries, or supplications to our foes for mercy; but the solemn sense of the awfulness of death, was mingled with a sweet and sustaining faith in God, and Christ, and Immortality. Hand in hand, like brothers, we were preparing to take the fearful plunge—when I started and awoke.

Even the recollection of our real situation was insufficient to impair the deep sense of relief which I experienced. My first impulse was to thank God that these were but dreams; and if I had obeyed the next, I should have embraced heartily each of my slumbering companions; for in the first confusion of thought and feeling, my emotions were very much what they would naturally have been, had the scenes of visionary terror, in which we seemed to have just participated together, been real.

Morton was at his post, and I spoke to him, scarcely knowing or caring what I said. All I wanted, was to hear his voice, to revive the sense of companionship, and so escape the painful impressions which even yet clung to me.

He said that he had just commenced his watch, Arthur having called him but a few moments before. The night was still lowering and overcast, but there was less wind and sea than when I first laid down. I proposed to relieve him at once, but he felt no greater inclination to sleep than myself and we watched together until morning. The two or three hours immediately before dawn seemed terribly long. Just as the first grey light appeared in the east, Arthur joined us. A dense volume of vapour which rested upon the water, and contributed to the obscurity in which we were enveloped, now gathered slowly into masses, and floated upward as the day advanced, gradually clearing the prospect; and we kept looking out for the island, in the momentary expectation of seeing it loom up before us through the mist. But when, as the light increased, and the fog rolled away, the boundaries of our vision rapidly enlarged, and still no land could be seen, we began to feel seriously alarmed. A short period of intense and painful anxiety followed, during which we continued alternately gazing, and waiting for more light, and again straining our aching eyes in every direction, and still in vain.

At last it became evident that we had in some manner drifted completely away from the island. The appalling conviction could no longer be resisted. There we were, lost and helpless, on the open ocean, in our chip of a boat, without provisions for a single day, or, to speak more definitely, without a morsel of bread or a drop of water.

Chapter Five
The Consultation

Out of Sight of Land—Slender Resources—What's to be done?

"How rapidly, how rapidly, we ride along the sea!
The morning is all sunshine, the wind is blowing free;
The billows are all sparkling, and bounding in the light,
Like creatures in whose sunny veins, the blood is running
bright."

Morton alone still refused to relinquish the hope, that by broad daylight, we should yet be able to make out the island. He persisted in pronouncing it wholly incredible that we had made during the night, a distance sufficient to sink the land, which was but three or four miles off at the utmost, when we were overtaken by darkness; he could not understand, he said, how such a thing was possible.

Arthur accounted for it, by supposing that we had got into the track of one of the ocean currents that exist in those seas, especially among the islands, many of which run at the rate of from two to three miles an hour.

This seemed the more probable, from the fact, that we were to the west of the island, when we lost sight of it, and that the great equatorial current, which traverses the Pacific and Indian oceans, has a prevailing westerly course, though among the more extensive groups and clusters of islands, it is so often deflected hither and thither, by the obstacles which it encounters, or turned upon itself, in eddies or counter-currents, that no certain calculations can be made respecting it. Morton, however, did not consider this supposition sufficient to explain the difficulty.

"I should judge," said he, "that in a clear day, such an island might be seen fifteen or twenty miles, and we cannot have drifted so great a distance."

"It might perhaps be seen," said Arthur, "as far as that, from the mast-head of a ship, or even from her deck, but not from a small boat hardly raised above the surface of the water. At our present level, eight or ten miles would be enough to sink it completely."

At length, when it was broad day, and from the appearance of the eastern sky, the sun was just about to rise, Morton stepped the mast and climbed to the top, in the hope that from that additional elevation, slight as it was, he might catch a glimpse of land. There was by this time light enough, as he admitted, to see any thing that could be seen at all, and after making a deliberate survey of our whole horizon, he was fully convinced that we had drifted completely away from the island. "I give it up," he said, as he slid down the mast, "we are at sea, beyond all question."

Presently Max awoke. He cast a quick, surprised look around, and at first seemed greatly shocked. He speedily recovered himself, however, and after another, and closer, scrutiny of the horizon, thought that he detected an appearance like that of land in the south. For a moment there was again the flutter of excited hope, as every eye was turned eagerly in that direction; but it soon subsided. A brief examination satisfied us all, that what we saw, was but a low bank of clouds lying against the sky.

"This really begins to look serious," said I; "what are we to do?"

"It strikes me," replied Morton, "that we are pretty much relieved from the necessity of considering that question; our only part for the present seems to be a passive one."

"I can't fully persuade myself that this is real," said Max; "it half seems like an ugly dream, from which we should awake by-and-by, and draw a long breath at the relief of finding it no more than a dream."

"We are miserably provisioned for a sea voyage," said Morton; "but I believe the breaker is half full of water; without that we should indeed be badly off."

"There is not a drop in it," said Arthur, shaking his head, and he lifted the breaker and shook it lightly—it was quite empty.

He now proceeded to force open the locker, in the hope of finding them something that might be serviceable to us; but its entire contents consisted of a coil of fine rope, some pieces of rope-yarn, an empty quart-bottle, and an old and battered hatchet-head.

Meanwhile, Browne, without a trace of anxiety upon his upturned countenance, and Johnny, who nestled close beside him, continued to sleep soundly, in happy unconsciousness of our alarming situation.

"Nothing ever interferes with the soundness of Browne's sleep, or the vigour of his appetite," said Max, contemplating his placid slumbers with admiration. "I should be puzzled to decide whether sleeping, eating, or dramatic recitation, is his forte; it certainly lies between the three."

"Poor fellow!" said Morton, "from present appearances, and the state of our supplies, he will have to take it all out in sleeping, for some time to come, as it is to be presumed he'll hardly feel like spouting."

"One would think that what happened yesterday, and the condition of things as we left them last night, would be enough to disturb one's nerves somewhat; yet you see how little it affects him—and I now predict that the first thing he will say on opening his eye; will be about the means of breaking his long fast."

"I don't understand how you can go on in that strain, Max," said Arthur, looking up in a surprised manner, and shaking his head disapprovingly.

"Why, I was merely endeavouring to do my share towards keeping our spirits up; but I suppose any spirits got up under the present circumstances, must be somewhat forced, and as my motives don't seem to be properly appreciated, I will renounce the unprofitable attempt."

The sun rose in a clear sky, and gave promise of a hot day. There was, however, a cool and refreshing breeze, that scattered the spray from the foaming ridges of the waves, and occasionally showered us, not unpleasantly, with the fine liquid particles. A sea, breaking over our bow, dashed a bucket-full of water into Browne's face, and abruptly disturbed his slumbers.

"Good morning, comrades!" said he, sitting up, and looking about him with a perplexed and bewildered air. "But how is this? Ah! I recollect it all now. So then, we are really out of sight of land!"

"There is no longer any doubt of that," said Arthur, "and it is now time for us to decide what we shall do—our chance of falling in with a ship will be quite as good, and that of reaching land will of course be much better, if, instead of drifting like a log upon the water, we put up our sail, and steer in almost any direction; though I think there is a choice."

"Of course there is a choice," said Morton; "the island *cannot* be at any great distance; and the probability of our being able to find it again is so much greater than that of making any other land, that we ought to steer in the direction in which we have good reason to think it lies—that is, to the east."

"The wind, for the last twelve hours, has been pretty nearly south," observed Arthur, "and has probably had some effect upon our position; we had better, therefore, steer a little south of east, which, with this breeze, will be easy sailing."

To this all assented, and the sail was hoisted, and the boat's head put in the direction agreed upon, each of us, except Johnny, sailing and steering her in turn. There was quite as much wind as our little craft could sail with to advantage, and without danger. As it filled her bit of canvass, she careered before it, leaping and plunging from wave to wave, in a manner that sometimes seemed perilous. The bright sky above us, the blue sea gleaming in the light of morning, over which we sped; the dry, clear atmosphere, (now that the sun was up, and the mist dissipated), the fresh breeze, without which we must have suffered intensely from the heat; together with our rapid and bounding motion, had an exhilarating effect, in spite of the gloomy anticipations that suggested themselves.

"After all," said Max, "why need we take such a dismal view of the matter? We have a fine staunch little boat, a good breeze, and islands all around us. Besides, we are in the very track of the bêche de mer, and sandal-wood traders. It would be strange indeed, if we should fail to meet some of them soon. In fact, if it were not for thinking of poor Frazer, and of the horrible events of yesterday, (which, to be sure, are enough to make one sad), I should be disposed to look upon the whole affair; as a sort of holiday adventure—something to tell of when we get home, and to talk over pleasantly together twenty years hence."

"If we had a breaker of water, and a keg of biscuit," said Morton, "and could then be assured of fair weather for a week, I might be able to take that view of it; as it is, I confess, that to me, it has any thing but the aspect of a holiday adventure."

When Johnny awoke, Arthur endeavoured to soothe his alarm, by explaining to him that we had strong hopes of being able to reach the island again, and mentioning the various circumstances which rendered such a hope reasonable. The little fellow, did not, however, seem to be as much troubled as might have been expected. He either reposed implicit confidence in the resources, or the fortunes, of his companions, or else, did not at all realise the perils to which we were exposed. But this could not last long.

That which I knew Arthur had been painfully anticipating, came at last. Johnny, who had been asking Morton a multitude of questions as to the events of the previous day, suddenly said that he was very thirsty, and asked in the most unsuspecting manner for a drink of water. When he learned that the breaker was empty, and that we had not so much as a drop of water with us, some notion of our actual situation seemed to dawn upon him, and he became, all at once, grave and silent.

Hour after hour dragged slowly on, until the sun was in the zenith, with no change for the better in our affairs. It was now clear that we must give up the hope of reaching the island which we had left, for it was certain that we had sailed farther since morning than the boat could possibly have been drifted during the night, by the wind, or the current, or both combined. Our calculations at the outset must therefore have been erroneous, and we had not been sailing in the right direction. If so, it was too late to correct the mistake; we could not regain our starting-point, in order to steer from it another course. We now held a second consultation.

Although we had but a general notion of our geographical position, we knew that we were in the neighbourhood of scattered groups of low coral islands. From the Kingsmills we were to have sailed directly for Canton, and Max, Morton, and myself, would, before now, in all probability, have commenced our employment in the American factory there, but for Captain Erskine's sudden resolution to take the responsibility of returning to the Samoan Group, with the double object of rescuing the crew of the wrecked barque, and completing his cargo, which, according to the information received from the master of the whaler, there would be no difficulty in doing. From Upolu, we had steered a north-westerly course, and it was on the fourth or fifth day after leaving it, that we had reached the island where the mutiny took place, and which Mr Erskine claimed as a discovery of his own. Its latitude and longitude had of course been calculated, but none of us learned the result, or at any rate remembered it. We knew only, that we were at no great distance from the Kingsmills, and probably to the south-west of them.

Arthur was confident, from conversations had with Mr Frazer, and from the impressions left on his mind by his last examination of the charts, that an extensive cluster of low islands, scattered over several degrees of latitude, lay just to the south-east of us.

It was accordingly determined to continue our present course as long as the wind should permit, which there was reason to fear might be but a short time, as easterly winds are the prevailing ones within the tropics, as near the line as we supposed ourselves to be.

Chapter Six
The Calm

The Second Watch—An Evil Omen—The
White Shark—A Breakfast Lost

"All in a hot and copper sky,
The bloody sun, at noon,
Right up above the mast did stand,
No bigger than the moon."

During the remainder of the day the wind continued fair, and we held on our course, steering by the sun, and keeping a vigilant look-out in every direction. But the night set in, and we had yet seen no appearance of land, no speck in the distance which could be mistaken for a sail, not even a wandering sea-bird or a school of flying-fish—nothing to break the dead monotony of the briny waste we were traversing. As I sat at the helm, taking my turn in sailing the boat, and watched the sun go down, and saw the darkness gathering over the sea, a feeling nearly akin to despair took possession of me. In vain I strove to take an encouraging and hopeful view of our circumstances. The time within which relief must come, in order to be effectual, was so short, that I could not help feeling that the probabilities were strongly against us. I could not shut my eyes to the fact, that dangers, imminent and real, such as we had read and talked of, without ever half realising or dreaming that they could one day fall to our own lot, now pressed upon us, and threatened us close at hand. I knew that those fearful tales of shipwreck and starvation, were only too true—that men, lost at sea like ourselves, had pined day after day, without a morsel of food or a drop of water, until they had escaped, in stupor or delirium, all consciousness of suffering. And worse even than this—too horrible to be thought or spoken of—I knew something of the dreadful and disgusting expedients to prolong life, which have sometimes been resorted to by famishing wretches. I had read how the pangs of hunger, and the still fiercer torments of thirst, had seemed to work a dire change even in kind and generous natures, making men wolfish, so that they slew and fed upon each other. Now, all that was most revolting and inhuman, in what I had heard or read of such things, rose vividly before me, and I shuddered at the growing probability that experiences like these might be reserved for us. "Why not for us," I thought, "as well as for the many others, the records of whose terrible fate I have perused with scarcely more emotion than would be excited by a tale of imaginary suffering; and the still greater number whose story has never been recorded? We have already been conducted many steps on this fearful path, and no laws of nature will be stayed, no ordinary rules of God's dealing violated, on our behalf. No inevitable necessity requires the complexion of our future, to correspond and harmonise with that of our past lives. This feeling, which seems to assure me that such things cannot happen to us, is but one of the cheats and illusions of a shrinking and self-pitying spirit. All the memories that cluster about a happy childhood, all the sweet associations of home and kindred, afford no guarantee against the new and bitter experiences which seem about to open up upon us."

Such were the thoughts that began to disquiet my own mind. As to my companions, Morton seemed less anxious and excited than any of the others. During the evening he speculated in a cool matter-of-fact manner, upon our chances of reaching an island, or meeting a ship, before being reduced to the last extremity. He spoke of the number of traders that frequent the islands, for tortoise-shell, mother-of-pearl, sandal-wood, bêche de mer, etcetera; the whalers that come in pursuit of the cachelot, or sperm-whale; the vessels that resort there for fruit, or supplies of wood and water; the vast number of islands scattered through these seas; from all which he finally concluded, that the chances were largely in our favour. If, however, we should fail of immediate relief in this shape, he thought it probable that we should have opportunities of catching fish, or sea-birds, and so prolonging life for many days. He talked the whole matter over in such a calm, sober, unexcited manner, furnishing facts and reasons for every opinion, that I felt some confidence in his conclusions.

Browne, though quite composed and self-possessed, had, from the moment when he discovered that we were out of sight of land, taken the most serious view of our situation. He seemed to have made up his mind for the worst, and was abstracted, and indisposed to converse. I knew that the anxiety which Arthur evinced, was not mainly on his own account. It did not withdraw his attention from what was passing, or diminish his interest in it. Far from being gloomy or abstracted, he was active and watchful, and spoke with heartiness and cheerfulness. His mental disquietude only appeared, in a certain softness and tremor of his voice, especially when speaking to Johnny, who, as the night drew on, asked him over and over again, at short intervals, "Don't you think, Arthur, that we shall certainly find land to-morrow?" This was truly distressing.

As to Max, his feelings rose and fell capriciously, and without any apparent cause; he was sanguine or depressed, not from a consideration of all our circumstances, and a favourable or unfavourable conclusion drawn therefrom; but according as this view or that, for the moment, impressed his mind. He rendered no reasons for his hopes or his fears. At one moment, you would judge from his manner and conversation that we were indeed out upon some "holy day excursion," with no serious danger impending over us; the next, without any thing to account for the change, he would appear miserably depressed and wretched.

Soon after sunset the moon rose—pale and dim at first, but shining out with a clearer and brighter radiance, as the darkness increased. The wind held steadily from the same quarter, and it was determined to continue through the night, the arrangement for taking charge of the sailing of the boat, in turn. Browne and Max insisted on sharing between themselves the watch for the entire night, saying that they had taken no part in that of the one previous, and that it would be useless to divide the twelve hours of darkness into more than two watches. This was finally agreed upon, the wind being so moderate that the same person could steer the yawl and manage the sail without difficulty.

Before lying down, I requested Max, who took the first turn, to awake me at the same time with Browne, a part of whose watch I intended to share. I fell asleep, looking up at the moon, and the light clouds sailing across the sky, and listening to the motion of the water beneath the boat. At first I slumbered lightly, without losing a sort of dreamy consciousness, so that I heard Max humming over to himself fragments of tunes, and odd verses of old songs, and even knew when he shifted his position in the stern, from one side to the other. At length I must have fallen into a deep sleep: I do not know how long it had lasted, (it seemed to me but a short time), when I was aroused by an exclamation, from Max, as I at first supposed; but on sitting up I saw that Browne was at the helm, while Max was sleeping at my side. On perceiving that I was awake, Browne, from whom the exclamation had proceeded, pointed to something in the water, just astern. Following the direction of his finger with my eye, I saw, just beneath the surface, a large ghastly-looking white shark, gliding stealthily along, and apparently following the boat. Browne said that he had first noticed it about half an hour before, since which time it had steadily followed us, occasionally making a leisurely circuit round the boat, and then dropping astern again. A moment ago, having fallen into a doze at the helm, and awaking with a start, he found himself leaning over the gunwale, and the shark just at his elbow. This had startled him, and caused the sudden exclamation by which I had been aroused. I shuddered at his narrow escape, and I acknowledge that the sight of this hideous and formidable creature, stealing along in our wake, and manifesting an intention to keep us company, caused me some uneasy sensations. He swam with his dorsal fin almost at the surface, and his broad nose scarcely three feet from the rudder. His colour rendered him distinctly visible.

The White Shark.

"What a spectre of a fish it is," said Browne, "with his pallid, corpse-like skin, and noiseless motion; he has no resemblance to any of the rest of his kind, that I have ever seen. You know what the sailors would say, if they should see him dogging us in this way; Old Crosstrees, or Spot, would shake their heads ominously, and set us down as a doomed company."

"Aside from any such superstitious notions, he is an unpleasant and dangerous neighbour, and we must be circumspect while he is prowling about."

"It certainly won't do to doze at the helm," resumed Browne; "I consider that I have just now had a really narrow escape. I was leaning quite over the gunwale; a lurch of the boat would have thrown me overboard, and then there would have been no chance for me."

There would not, in fact, have been the shadow of a chance.

"Even as it was," resumed he, "if this hideous-looking monster had been as active and vigilant as some of his tribe, it would have fared badly with me. I have heard of their seizing persons standing on the shore, where the water was deep enough to let them swim close in; and Spot tells of a messmate of his, on one of his voyages in a whaler, who was carried off, while standing entirely out of water, on the carcass of a whale, which he was assisting in cutting up, as it lay alongside the ship. The shark threw himself upon the carcass, five or six yards from where the man was busy;—worked himself slowly along the slippery surface, until within reach of his victim; knocked him off into the water, and then sliding off himself, seized and devoured him."

Picking my way carefully among the sleepers, who covered the bottom of the yawl, I sat down beside Browne in the stern, intending to share the remainder of his watch. It was now long past midnight; fragments of light clouds were scattered over the sky, frequently obscuring the moon; and the few stars that were visible, twinkled faintly with a cold and distant light. The Southern Cross, by far the most brilliant constellation of that hemisphere, was conspicuous among the clusters of feebler luminaries. Well has it been called "the glory of the southern skies." Near the zenith, and second only to the Cross in brilliancy, appeared the Northern Crown, consisting of seven large stars, so disposed as to form the outline of two-thirds of an oval. Of the familiar constellations of the northern hemisphere, scarcely one was visible, except Orion, and the Pleiades.

At length the moon descended behind a bank of silvery clouds, piled up along the horizon. The partial obscurity that ensued, only added to the grandeur of the midnight scene, as we sat gazing silently abroad upon the confused mass of swelling waters, stretching away into the gloom. But if the scene was grand, it was also desolate; we two were perhaps the only human beings, for many hundreds of miles, who looked forth upon it. Our companions were wrapped in unconsciousness, and their deep and regular breathing attested the soundness of their slumbers. As the light failed more and more, and the shadows deepened, the sea began to assume a beautiful and striking appearance, gleaming in places with a bluish lambent light, and exhibiting, where the water was most agitated, large luminous patches. Thin waves of flame curled over our bow, and whenever a sea broke upon it, it seemed as though the boat was plunging through surges of fire. A long brilliant line, thickly strewn on each side, with little globules of the colour of burning coals, marked our wake.

But the shark, which still followed close behind our keel, presented by far the most singular and striking spectacle. He seemed to be surrounded by a luminous medium; and his nose, his dorsal and side fins, and his tail, each had attached to them slender jets of phosphoric fire. Towards morning this brilliant appearance began to fade, and soon vanished altogether. By this time I found it difficult to keep my eyes open longer, and leaving Browne to finish his watch alone, I resumed my place on the ceiling planks, and in spite of the hardness of my bed, which caused every bone in my body to ache, soon slept soundly. When I again awoke, it was long after sunrise, and we were lying completely becalmed. A school of large fish were pursuing their gambols at a short distance, and Browne was rowing cautiously toward them, while Arthur and Morton stood prepared to attack them with their cutlasses as soon as we should get within striking distance. We had got almost among them, and were just beginning to congratulate ourselves upon their apparent indifference to our approach, when they all at once scattered in every direction, with manifest signs of terror. The cause of this sudden movement was not long concealed; a brace of sharks rose in their very midst; one was visible but for a moment as he rolled over to seize his prey; the other, less successful in securing a victim, shot past us, like an arrow, in pursuit of a large division of the fugitives. Soon after, both of them were seen playing around the boat. They belonged to the species known as the tiger shark, and bore no resemblance to our ghastly visitor of the preceding evening. By the consternation which their sudden appearance had produced among the lesser fishes, they had in all probability robbed us of our breakfast. Morton, with his characteristic enterprise, suggested an attack upon one of them by way of reprisals; but before any measures for that purpose could be taken, they disappeared, leaving us with no other resource than to await our fate with such patience and resignation as we could command. The wind having entirely failed, there was nothing that we could do to change our situation—absolutely nothing. This forced inaction, with no occupation for mind or body, no object of effort, contributed to enhance whatever was painful in our condition, by leaving us to brood over it. The dead calm which had fallen upon the sea, seemed all that was necessary to complete our misery. We were all stiff and sore, from the exceedingly uncomfortable sleeping accommodations of the last two nights; but this was a comparatively trifling evil. Johnny had a severe cold, his eyes were inflamed and bloodshot, and he exhibited also strong symptoms of fever. Nevertheless, silent and uncomplaining, he came and sat down quietly by the side of Arthur in the stern.

As the day advanced, the heat became dreadful. We had not suffered much from it the day before, on account of the fresh breeze which had prevailed; but now, not a breath of air was stirring, and the glassy sea reflected back upon us the scorching rays of the sun, with increased intensity. Towards noon, it exceeded any thing I had ever experienced. The whole arch of the heavens glowed with a hot and coppery glare. It seemed as though instead of one sun, there were ten thousand, covering all the sky, and blending their rays into a broad canopy of fire. The air was like that of an oven: the water had no coolness, no refreshing quality; it was tepid and stagnant: no living thing was to be seen near the surface, for life could not be sustained there; and the fishes, great and small, kept themselves in the cooler depths, far below. Almost stifled by the heat, we began to experience the first real and extreme suffering that most of us had ever known. At Arthur's suggestion, we disengaged the now useless sail from the mast, and contrived a kind of awning, by fastening two of the oars upright in the boat, with the mast extending between them, throwing the sail over the latter, and securing the ends to the gunwales. This, although it could not protect us from the sultry and suffocating air, warded off the blistering beams of the sun, and during the greater part of the day, we lay crouched beneath it, a miserable company; one or another of us crawling out occasionally, to take a survey. Towards the close of the afternoon, my sufferings from thirst grew absolutely intolerable, and amounted to torment. My blood became fevered; my brain seemed on fire; my shrunk and shrivelled tongue, was like a dry stick in my mouth. The countenances of my companions, their bloodshot eyes, and cracked and swollen lips, shewed what they were undergoing. Johnny lay in the bottom of the boat with his eyes shut enduring all, with as much fortitude as the rest of us, except that now and then a half suppressed moan escaped him.

It was quite clear that relief, in order to be of any avail, must be speedy.

Chapter Seven
A Change

A Welcome Peril—The Albatross And their
Prey—A Tropical Thunder-Storm

"Eternal Providence, exceeding thought,
Where none appears, can make itself a way."

While lying crouched under the sail, almost gasping for breath, near the middle, as I suppose, of that terrible afternoon, I all at once became sensible of a perceptible cooling of the atmosphere, and a sudden decrease of light. Looking out to discover the cause of this change, I perceived that the sky was overcast, and that a light, unsteady breeze from the north-west had sprung up. Knowing that within the tropics, and near the line, winds from that quarter frequently precede a storm, and that great extremes of heat are often succeeded by violent gales, I observed, with apprehension, dark masses of clouds gathering in the north. It would not require a tempest to insure our destruction; for our little craft could not live a moment, even in such a gale as would be attended by no danger to a staunch ship with plenty of sea room.

The temperature had fallen many degrees, though the wind was still moderate and unsteady, ranging from west to north-east. The sun was completely obscured, so that the awning was no longer needed, and we pulled it down, in order the more fully to enjoy the breeze, and the delicious coolness of the darkened atmosphere, to the gratefulness of which, not even our awakening apprehensions could render us insensible.

While observing the strange appearance of the sky, and like preparations for a storm which seemed to be going on in the north and west, Morton espied a troop of Flying-fish a hundred yards or so to windward. Fluttering feebly a short distance in the air, they would drop into the sea, soon emerging, however, for a fresh flight; thus, alternately swimming and flying, they were steadily approaching; and from their rapid and confused motions, it was evident that they were hard pressed by some of the numerous and greedy persecutors of their helpless race; from whom they were struggling to escape. Presently, a glittering Albatross shot from the water, close in the tract of the fugitives, descending again in the graceful curve peculiar to his active and beautiful, but rapacious tribe. Another and another followed, their golden scales flashing in the light, as they leaped clear of the water, sometimes two or three together. We hastily made ready to attack both pursuers and pursued, the instant they should come within reach. The course of the chase brought them directly towards us, until the hunted fishes fell in a glittering shower, so near, that I feared they might pass under the boat before rising again; but they came to the surface close beside us, and as they fluttered into the air, we knocked down six or seven of them, and caught a number more, that dropped into the boat. Morton and Max, ambitious of larger game, devoted their attention to the Albatross, and slashed and thrust furiously, at such as came within reach of their cutlasses; which many of them did. Some darted under the boat, instead of sheering round it; and one enormous fellow, miscalculating in his haste our draught of water, must have scraped all the fins off his back against the keel, as he performed this manoeuvre; for the shock of the contact, caused the yawl to tremble from stem to stern. But such was the marvellous celerity of their movements, that though they came within easy striking distance, all the hostile demonstrations of Max and Morton proved futile.

The Flying-fish which had been taken, were divided and apportioned with scrupulous exactness, and devoured with very little ceremony. The only dressing or preparation bestowed upon them, consisted simply in stripping off the long shining pectoral fins, or wings, (they serve as both), without paying much attention to such trifling matters as scales, bones, and the lesser fins. Max, indeed, began to nibble rather fastidiously at first, at this raw food, which a minute before had been so full of life and activity; but his appetite improved as he proceeded, and he at last so far got the better of his scruples, as to leave nothing of his share except the tails, and very little even of those. Hunger, in fact, made this repast, which would have been revolting under ordinary circumstances, not only acceptable, but positively delicious.

Meantime, the dark mass of clouds in the north had extended itself, and drawn nearer to us. Another tempest seemed to be gathering in the west, while in the south, a violent thunder-storm appeared to be actually raging: the lightning in that quarter was vivid and almost incessant, but we could hear no thunder, the storm being still at a considerable distance.

Immediately around us all was yet comparatively calm, but the heavy clouds, gathering on three sides, seemed gradually converging towards a common centre; a short abrupt cross sea, began to form, and the water assumed a glistening inky hue. There was something peculiar and striking in the appearance of the clouds surrounding us; they seemed to rest upon the surface of the ocean, and towered upward like a dark wall to the skies. Their upper extremities were torn and irregular, and long narrow fragments, like giant arms, streamed out from the main body, and extended over us, as if beckoning each other to a nearer approach, and threatening to unite their gloomy array overhead, and shut out the light of day. As they drew nearer to one another, the lightning began to dart from cloud to cloud, while the most terrific peals of thunder that I have ever heard, rolled and reverberated on every side. We appeared to be surrounded by storms, some of which were very near, for the deep crash of the thunder, followed close upon the vivid lightnings that flashed in the south and west. Still the narrow space of sky directly overhead was clear, and the war of elements which was raging all around did not extend to our immediate neighbourhood. Against the dark sides of the cloudy pavilion that encompassed us, the sharp, zigzag lines of lightning, as they ran from the sky to the ocean, shone out with a blinding glare. A single half-hour had sufficed to change every thing about us. The brazen, burning sky, was transformed into a cold, clear expanse, of a bluish black. The sea, no longer stagnant and glassy, was fretted by short inky waves, with creamy crests, that gave it altogether a new aspect. The air was now fresh and cool, and the wind rising and falling fitfully, at one moment scarcely lifted our hair or stirred our garments, and the next, tore off the entire crests of waves, and scattered them over us in a shower of spray. For nearly an hour we remained apprehensive that the wind might increase to a gale. At the end of about that time, it came gradually round to the south-east, growing steady, but by no means violent, and the storms moved off in a westerly direction. One heavy cloud, as it slowly passed over toward that quarter, discharged a grateful shower of rain. We hastily spread the sail, and some of our garments, to gather the precious drops. The shower lasted only a few minutes, but during that time it rained briskly. I never shall forget my sensations as I stood with face upturned, while the big drops, more delicious than ambrosia, came pelting down. It was far better and more strengthening than food, or any medicine or cordial could have been, and seemed to infuse fresh life into us all. When it was over, we wrung out from the saturated canvass, and from our clothing, water enough to mitigate for the time, though by no means to satisfy, the raging thirst from which we had suffered so intensely.

Arthur had at first taken out of the locker the large bottle which had been found there, in the hope of being able to hoard up a small supply for the future; but there was not a drop of surplus for such a purpose, and he was obliged to put it back again empty as before.

Chapter Eight
Tokens of Land

The Centre of the Sphere — The Mysterious Sound — The Conflagration

"Thou glorious sea! before me gleaming,
   Oft wilt thou float in sunset pride,
   And often shall I hear in dreaming,
   Thy resonance at evening tide!"

At sunset every trace of the storms by which we had been so recently encompassed had vanished: the sky, except along the western horizon, was without a cloud: not a breath of wind ruffled the sea, and we lay once more completely becalmed.

This was our third night at sea; though to me, at least, it seemed that many days had passed since the mutiny and the immediately succeeding occurrences. It is a night which I shall not soon forget; the impression of its almost unearthly beauty is still fresh and vivid, and haunts me like a vision of fairy land. At this moment if I but close my eyes, the whole scene rises before me with the distinctness of a picture; though one would naturally suppose that persons situated as we then were, could scarcely have been in a state of mind congenial to the reception of such impressions.

The transition from early twilight to the darkness of night was beautiful beyond description. The array of clouds in the west just after sunset; their forms, arrangement, and colours; with the manner in which they blended and melted into one another, composed a spectacle, of the magnificence of which, neither language, nor the art of the painter, can convey any adequate idea. Along the edge of the horizon stretched a broad tract of the deepest crimson, reflecting far upon the waters, a light that gave them the appearance of an ocean of blood. Above this was a band of vivid flame colour: then one of a clear translucent green, perfectly peculiar, unlike that of any leaf or gem, and of surpassing delicacy and beauty. This gradually melted, through many fine gradations, into a sea of liquid amber, so soft and golden, that the first large stars of evening, floating in its transparent depths, could scarcely be distinguished, as they twinkled mildly, amid the flood of kindred radiance. A narrow streak of pearly blue bounded this amber sea with its islands of light, and divided it from the deeper blue of the wide vault above. During the earlier part of this glorious display, the eastern sky, as if in rivalry of the splendour of the opposite quarter of the heavens, was spanned by two concentric rainbows, describing complete semi-circles, with their bases resting upon the sea. In the smaller and interior bow, all the colours were beautifully distinct; in the outer and larger one, they were less brilliant, and arranged in an order the reverse of that which is usual, the violet being the lowest instead of the red. The rainbows vanished with the sun, and soon afterwards the fiery glow in the west began to fade. But the scene only changed its character, without losing any of its beauty. So smooth was the sea on that night that the whole dome of the sky, with every sailing cloudflake, and every star, was perfectly reflected in it. Until the moon rose, the line where the sky joined the ocean was indistinctly defined, and the two were so blended together, that we actually seemed suspended in the centre of a vast sphere; the heavens, instead of terminating at the horizon, extended, spangled with stars, on every side—below, as well as above, and around. The illusion was wonderfully perfect; you almost held your breath as you glanced downward, and could hardly refrain from starting nervously, so strong and bewildering was the appearance of hanging poised in empty space.

Johnny, who had been sitting for a long time with his hands supporting his head, and his elbows resting upon Arthur's knee, gazing out upon the ocean, suddenly looked up into his face, and said—

"Arthur, I want you to tell me truly—do you still believe that we shall be saved—do you hope so now, as you did yesterday, or do you think that we must perish!"

"Do you suppose that I would try to deceive you, Johnny," said Arthur, "that you ask me so earnestly to tell you truly?"

"No, but I feared you would not, perhaps, tell me the worst, thinking that I could not bear it: and I suspected to-night, that you spoke more cheerfully than you felt on my account. But I am not afraid, dear Arthur, to know the truth; and do not hide it from me! I will try to bear patiently, with you, and with the rest whatever comes upon us."

"I would not deceive you about such a matter, Johnny. I should not think it right, though you are so young. But I can know nothing certainly. We are in the hands of God. I have told you all the reasons we have to hope; we have the same reasons still. Only a few hours ago, the sea supplied us with food, and the clouds with drink: why may we not hope for future supplies according to our need? I think we yet have more reason to hope than to despair."

"Did you ever know, or hear of such a thing," inquired Johnny, after a pause, "as a company of boys, like us, starving at sea?"

"I do not remember that I have, under circumstances at all similar to ours," answered Arthur.

"It is too dreadful to believe! Is not God, our Father in heaven? He will not surely let us perish so miserably."

"*Yes*, Johnny," said Arthur gently, but earnestly, "God is our heavenly Father; but we must not make our belief in his love and goodness, a ground of confidence that any suffering, however terrible, shall not befall us. The young suffer and die, as well as the old; the good, as well as the bad. Not only the strong martyrs, who triumphed while they were tortured, but feeble old men, and little children, have been torn in pieces by wild beasts, or burned alive, or cast down precipices. And these things, that seemed so very hard to us, God has permitted. Yet he is good, and loves and cares for us as a father. This we must believe, and hold fast to, in spite of every thing that in our ignorance may seem to contradict it. If we feel as we ought, and as by his grace we may, we shall be able to trust all to him, with sweet resignation."

"But is it not very hard, dear Arthur, to be left to die so!—and God can save us so easily, if he will."

Arthur was deeply affected: the tears filled his eyes as he took Johnny upon his knee, and tried to explain to him how wrong and selfish it would be, to make our belief in the goodness of God, depend upon our rescue and preservation. It was a difficult task, perhaps an untimely one, as Max hinted. But Johnny gradually sobbed away his excitement, and became soothed and calm.

"Well," said he, after a while, drawing a long breath, and wiping away his tears, "I know one thing: whatever may happen, we will be kind and true to one another to the last, and never think of such inhuman things as I have read of shipwrecked people doing, when nearly dead with hunger, though we all starve together."

"Come to me, Johnny," cried Browne, with a faltering voice, "I must kiss you for those words. Yes, we will perish, if we must, like brothers, not sullenly, as if none had ever suffered evil before us. Weak and gentle spirits have borne without repining, sufferings as great as threaten us. Often has my mother told me the story of sweet Marjory Wilson, drowned in the Solway water, in the days of Claverhouse, because she met with her friends and kindred to worship God after their manner—and never could I listen to it without tears. Ah, what a spirit was there! She was but eighteen, and she could have saved her life by saying a few words. Life was as sweet to her as it is to us: she too had a home and friends and kindred, whom it must have been hard for the poor young thing to leave so suddenly and awfully. And yet she refused to speak those words—she chose to die rather. They took her out upon the sand where the tide was rising fast, and bound her to a stake. Soon the water came up to her face. She saw it go over the head of a poor old woman, whom they had tied farther out than herself. She saw her death struggles; she heard her gasp for breath, as she choked and strangled in the yellow waves. Ah! she must have had courage from the Lord, or that sight would have made her young heart fail. Once more, and for the last time, the king's officer asked her to make the promise never to attend a conventicle again. He urged it, for he pitied her youth and innocence. Her friends and neighbours begged her to save her life. 'O speak, dear Marjory!' they cried, 'and make the promise; it can't be wrong. Do it for our sakes, dear Marjory, and they will let you go!' But she would not save her life by doing what she had been taught to think was wrong; and while the swirling waves of the Solway were rising fast around her, she prayed to God, and kept singing fragments of psalms, till the water choked her voice—and so she perished. But, O friends! to know that such things have been; that spirits gentle and brave as this have lived, makes it easier to suffer courageously."

"Horrible!" exclaimed Max, "I seem to see all that you have so graphically told. But how stern and cruel the teachers who would sacrifice human life rather than abate their own sullen obstinacy, even in trifles—who could encourage this innocent but misguided girl, in her refusal to save her life by the harmless promise to attend a church instead of a conventicle."

Just as Browne was commencing an eager and indignant reply to Max's rash reflections upon the strictness of covenanting teachings, we were suddenly startled by a deep and solemn sound, which seemed to come from a distance. While we listened intently, it was several times repeated at short intervals of about fifteen seconds, each time more distinctly than before. It resembled somewhat, the deepest tones of a powerful organ, heard for an instant, and then abruptly stopped. Nothing was to be seen in the direction from which it seemed to proceed, but the sea glittering in the moonlight. Is it to be wondered at, if we listened with feelings, tinged with superstitious awe, to that strange sound, heard under such circumstances, and at such an hour? Johnny nestled closer to Arthur's side, and I thought that the faces of my companions grew visibly pale. Even Arthur looked perplexed and disturbed.

"What *can* that be?" said Morton, after a few minutes of almost breathless silence, during which we had listened in vain for its repetition.

"It is certainly very strange," said Arthur. "I never heard any thing at sea, at all like it, but once, and it is impossible that this can be what I then heard—but hark!" And again the same deep pealing sound was repeated several times, at shorter intervals, but more faintly than before; after continuing for a few minutes it ceased again.

"What was the sound which you speak of, as resembling this?" asked Morton, when all was silent once more.

"It was the cry of a kind of penguin, found at the Falkland Islands; when heard on shore it is harsh and loud; but a short distance at sea, and in the night, it has a pealing, solemn sound, like that which we have just heard."

"It must come from land in the neighbourhood," said Morton, "we can probably hear farther on such a night as this than we can distinguish land."

"Yes, sounds on the water, in calm still nights, when there is no wind, can be heard at great distances," said Arthur; "it is said that the 'All's well!' of the British sentinel at Gibraltar, is sometimes heard across the strait, on the African shore, a distance of thirteen miles. I have seen, at the Society Islands, native drums made of large hollow logs, which might perhaps, at a distance, sound like what we heard a moment ago. A Wesleyan missionary there, once told me of a great drum that he saw at the Tonga Islands, called the 'Tonga Toki,' which sounded like an immense gong, and could be heard from seven to ten miles."

"Why, I thought that *this* sounded like a gong," said Johnny, "perhaps we are near some island now; but what could they be drumming for so late in the night?"

"There would be nothing very unusual about that," said Arthur. "The Areoi Societies, which are extended over most of the larger inhabited islands in this part of the Pacific, sometimes hold their great celebrations, like the pow-wows, and war-dances, of our American Indians, in the night-time. At the Feejee Islands they have a strange ceremony called 'Tambo Nalanga,' which they celebrate at night, with the beating of drums, the blowing of conches, and a number of savage and cruel rites. Something or other of the same kind is observed at most of the islands, though under different names, and with slight variations."

While speculating in this way, and endeavouring to account for the noise which had startled us so much, we all at once became aware of an increasing light in the south, the 'Cross,' now half-way between the horizon and the zenith, enabling us to fix the points of the compass. As we gazed in that direction, the sky became strongly illuminated by a red glare, and an immense column of flame and smoke was seen shooting up in the distance. Nothing but the expanse of the ocean, splendidly illuminated, and glowing like a sea of fire, could be discerned by this light. Whether it was caused by a burning ship, at such a distance that nothing but the light of her conflagration was visible, or by a fire on some distant island, we could not determine. It was in the same quarter from which the sound had seemed to come.

Arthur was now of the opinion that we were in the neighbourhood of an inhabited island, or group, and that the light proceeded from the burning bêche-de-mer house of some successful trader, who had set fire to it, (as is their custom at the end of a prosperous season), to prevent it from falling into the hands of others in the same business.

We all grasped eagerly at this idea, for the probability that we were not only in the neighbourhood of land, but of a place where we should meet with Europeans, and have an opportunity of getting home, or perhaps to the places of our respective destination, was full of encouragement. In a very short time the conflagration was over, and a dark column of smoke, which marked the spot where it had raged, was lifted slowly into the air. We heard no more of the mysterious sound. None of the explanations suggested were so perfectly satisfactory, as to remove entirely the unpleasant impression which it had produced. Before lying down in our accustomed places, we made our usual arrangements as to the watch, unnecessary as it seemed, during the calm.

Chapter Nine
Dark Waters

Suffering and Delirium—The Midnight Bath—A Strange Peril

"Water, water, everywhere,
  And all the boards did shrink;
Water, water, everywhere—
  But not a drop to drink."

Several times in the course of the night, I was awakened by confused noises, like the blowing of porpoises, or the spouting of whales; but the sky had become overcast, and it had grown so dark, that on getting up and looking about, I could see nothing of the creatures producing these sounds. My slumbers were broken and uneasy, and in the morning I found myself suffering from a dull, heavy pain in the head, accompanied by a slight nausea, and a general feeling of languor and weakness. Even to get upon my feet required something of an effort, which I made, impelled rather by a dim, confused sense of duty, than by any spontaneous impulse or inclination: had I consulted inclination alone, I believe I should have remained passive, and let things take their course.

The occurrences of the last night had given rise to some faint expectation that by daylight we should discover land in sight to the southward, where we had seen the great light. But nothing was visible in that or any other quarter. Possessed by some hope of this kind, Arthur had been up, searching the horizon, since the first streak of day in the east. He showed me a large green branch which he had picked up as it floated near us. By the elegantly scolloped leaves, of a dark and glossy green, it was easily recognised as a branch of the bread-fruit tree; and from their bright, fresh colour, and the whiteness of the wood, where it had joined the trunk, it must have been torn off quite recently. The calm still continued. Immense schools of black-fish, or porpoises, or some similar species, could be seen about half a mile distant, passing westward, in an apparently endless line. The temporary beneficial effect of yesterday's scanty supply of food and drink, had passed away entirely, and all seemed to feel in a greater or less degree, the bodily pain and weakness, and the lassitude and indisposition to any kind of effort by which I was affected. To such an extent was this the case, that when Arthur proposed that we should row towards the school of fish in sight, and try to take some of them, the strongest disinclination to make any such attempt was evinced, and it was only after much argument and persuasion, and by direct personal appeals to us individually, that he overcame this strange torpor, and induced us to take to the oars.

On getting near enough to the objects of our pursuit to distinguish them plainly, we were sorry to find that they were Porpoises instead of black-fish, as we had at first supposed; the former being shy and timid, and much more difficult to approach than the latter; and so they proved at present. Still we persevered for a while; the hope of obtaining food having been once excited, we were almost as reluctant to abandon the attempt as we had been at first to commence it. But after half an hour's severe labour at the oars, we were obliged to give it up as quite hopeless, and soon afterward the last of the long column passed beyond pursuit, leaving us completely disheartened and worn out. The sail was again arranged so as to shelter us as much as possible from the sun, and Arthur commenced distributing the leaves and twigs of the bread-fruit branch, suggesting that some slight refreshment might perhaps be derived from chewing them. But they retained a saline taste from having been in the sea-water, and no one proceeded far with the experiment. Morton cut some small slips of leather from his boots, and began to chew them. He fancied that they afforded some nourishment, and recommended the rest of us to make a similar trial, which I believe we all did. Max almost immediately rejected with disgust the first morsel which he put into his mouth, saying that he must "starve a little longer before he could relish that." At noon the heat was more intense, if possible, than it had been the day before. Johnny was now in a high fever, accompanied by symptoms of an alarming character. It was distressing to witness his sufferings, and feel utterly unable to do any thing for him. Yet there was nothing that we could do—food and drink were the only medicines he needed, and these we could not give him. Towards the close of the afternoon he became delirious, and began to cry out violently and incessantly for water. His voice seemed to have changed, and could now scarcely be recognised. There was something very strange and horrible in the regular, unceasing cries which he uttered, and which sounded at times almost like the howlings of a brute. Arthur had made a sort of bed for him, to which each of us contributed such articles of clothing as could be spared. It was now necessary to watch him every moment and frequently to use force to keep him from getting overboard. At one time, having got to the side of the boat, before he could be prevented, he commenced dipping up the sea-water with his hand, and would have drunk it had he not been forcibly restrained. After this had lasted nearly two hours, he suddenly ceased his struggles and violent cries, and began to beg piteously for "a drink of water." This he continued for a considerable time, repeatedly asking Arthur to tell him *why* he could not have "just a little," since there was "such a plenty of it."

It is impossible to describe the horrible and sickening effect of all this upon us, in the state of utter physical prostration to which we had been gradually reduced. Browne and Arthur watched over Johnny with all the care and patient unwearying kindness that a mother could have shown; and they would not permit the rest of us to relieve them for a moment, or to share any part of their charge, painful and distressing as it was. Twice, when it became necessary to hold the little sufferer fast, to prevent him from getting over the gunwale, he spat fiercely in Arthur's face, struggling and crying out with frightful vehemence. But Browne's voice seemed to soothe and control him, and when Johnny spoke to him, it was gently, and in the language of entreaty. Towards night he became more quiet, and at last sunk into a kind of lethargy, breathing deeply and heavily, but neither speaking nor moving, except to turn from one side to the other, which he did at nearly regular intervals.

This change relieved us from the necessity of constantly watching and restraining him, but Arthur viewed it as an unfavourable and alarming symptom; he seemed now more completely depressed than I had ever before seen him, and to be overcome at last by grief, anxiety, and the horrors of our situation.

The heat did not abate in the least with the going down of the sun, but the night, though very close and sultry, was calm and beautiful, like the last. Soon after the moon rose, Max and Morton undressed, and bathed themselves in the sea. The smooth moonlit water looked so cool and inviting, that the rest of us soon followed their example, notwithstanding the danger from sharks. We were all good swimmers, but no one ventured far from the boat except Morton; I found that a few strokes quite exhausted me, and I was obliged to turn and cling to the gunwale. In fact, so great was the loss of strength which we had all suffered, that we came near perishing in a very singular and almost incredible manner: After having been in the water a sufficient time, as I thought, I discovered, on trying to get into the boat again, that I was utterly unable to do so, through sheer weakness. At the same time I observed Max making a similar attempt nearer the stern, with no better success. We were all in the water except Johnny; any difficulty in getting into the boat again had not been dreamed of; but I began now to feel seriously alarmed. My feet were drawn forcibly under the boat's bottom, and even to maintain my hold of the gunwale, as we rose and sunk with the swell, required an exhausting effort, which I knew I could not long continue. Arthur was swimming near the stern, holding on to the end of a rope, which he had cast over before coming in. By great exertion I raised myself so far as to be able to look over the gunwale, when I saw Browne in the same position directly opposite me.

"Can't you get into the boat!" I asked.

"Really, I don't think I can," said he, speaking like a person exhausted.

"I can't," added Max, faintly, "it is as much as I can do to maintain my hold." At this moment a voice was heard, calling out apparently from a distance, "Hilloa! where are you? Hilloa!" It was hoarse, strained, and distressed. Almost immediately the cry was repeated, much nearer at hand, as it seemed; and then, a third time, faint, and distant as at first. I was horror-stricken; the cry sounded strange and fearful, and I did not recognise the voice. Then it occurred to me that it must be Morton, who had swum out farther than the rest, and losing sight of the boat for a moment in the swell of the sea, had become bewildered and alarmed. This might easily happen; if but the length of a wave distant we should be invisible to him, unless both should chance to rise on the swell at the same time. The moon, too, had just passed behind a dark mass of cloud, and the sea lay in partial obscurity. I now heard Browne and Arthur shouting, in order, as I supposed, to guide Morton by the sound of their voices. I, too, called out as loudly as I was able. For a moment all was still again. Then I heard some one say, "There he is!" and a dark speck appeared on the crest of a wave a little to the right. At this moment the moon shone out brightly! and I saw that it was Morton, swimming toward us. He reached the boat panting and out of breath, and catching hold near me with an almost convulsive effort, remained some minutes without being able to speak a word. Arthur, who had observed Max's struggles to get into the yawl, now swam round to where Morton and I were hanging on, and taking hold also, his additional weight depressed the gunwale nearly to the water's edge, when he got his knee over it, and at last, by a sudden effort rolled into the boat. He then helped me to get in, and we two the rest.

Morton said that after swimming but a short distance from the boat, as he supposed, he found himself getting tired and very weak, and on turning, greatly to his surprise, could see nothing of us. In reality, however, there was nothing surprising in this, his face being on a level with the surface, and the boat with neither sail nor mast up, being much less in height than the long smooth swells. Perceiving how great was his danger, and becoming somewhat alarmed, he had called out in the manner described: when he heard us shouting in return, he was actually swimming *away* from us, and it was only by following the direction of our voices that he had at last reached the boat.

That night we kept no regular watch as we had hitherto done, or at least we made no arrangement for that purpose, though one or another of us was awake most of the time, watching Johnny, who continued, however, in the same deep lethargic slumber.

For my part, it was a long time before I could sleep at all. There was something in the fate that threatened us, more appalling than the terrors of death. The impressions produced by the ravings, and cries, and struggles, of our poor little fellow-sufferer were yet fresh, and they could not be effaced. All in vain I strove to control the workings of my morbidly excited imagination—I could not shut out the fearful thoughts and anticipations which the occurrences of the day so naturally and obviously suggested. The lapse of twenty-four hours might find us all reduced to the same helpless state, deprived of consciousness and reason. One after another must succumb to the fever and become delirious, until he who should last fall its victim, should find himself alone in the midst of his stricken and raving companions—alone retaining reason, no longer to be accounted a blessing, since it could only serve to make him sensible to all the accumulated horrors of his situation. I shuddered as I contemplated the possibility that I might be the most wretched one, the last of all to sink and perish. At length, I began to imagine that my mind was actually beginning to fail, and that I was becoming delirious. At first it was but a fearful suspicion. Soon, however, it took such strong possession of me, that I was compelled to relinquish all thought of sleep. Sitting up, I saw that Arthur was awake and by the side of Johnny. His face was upturned, and his hands clasped as if in prayer. I could see his lips move, and even the tears trickling from beneath his closed lids, for the moonlight fell upon his countenance. He did not observe me, and after a few moments he laid down again without speaking, and soon appeared to slumber like the rest.

Pressing my hands to my head, I leaned over the stern, my face almost touching the water. A current of cooler air was stirring close to the surface, as if it were the breathing of the sea, for there was no wind. How preternaturally still every thing seemed—what an intensity of silence! How softly the pale moonlight rested upon the water! A grand and solemn repose wrapped the heavens and the ocean—no sound beneath all that vast blue dome—

no motion, but the heaving of the long sluggish swell. Gradually I became calmer; the excitement and perturbation of my mind began to subside, and at length I felt as though I could sleep. As I resumed my place by the side of Browne, he moved, as if about to awake, and murmured indistinctly some broken sentences. From the words that escaped him, he was dreaming of that far-off home which he was to behold no more. In fancy he was wandering again by the banks of the Clyde, the scene of many a school-boy ramble. But it seemed as though the shadow of present realities darkened even his dreams, and he beheld these familiar haunts no longer in the joyous light of early days. "How strange it looks!" he muttered slowly, "how dark the river is—how deep and dark!—it seems to me it was not so *then*, Robert." Truly, companion in suffering, this is no falsely coloured dream of thine, for we have all come at last into deep and dark waters!

Chapter Ten
A Sail

The Cachelot and his Assailants—The Course—New Acquaintances

"Strange creatures round us sweep:
Strange things come up to look at us,
The monsters of the deep."

The first thought that flashed through my mind with returning consciousness, in the morning, was, "This is the last day for hope—unless relief comes to-day in some shape, we must perish." I was the first awake, and glancing at the faces of my companions lying about in the bottom of the boat, I could not help shuddering. They had a strange and unnatural look—a miserable expression of pain and weakness. All that was familiar and pleasant to look upon, had vanished from those sharpened and haggard features. Their closed eyes seemed singularly sunken; and their matted hair, sunburned skin, and soiled clothing, added something of wildness to the misery of their appearance.

Browne, who had slept beside me, was breathing hard, and started every now and then, as if in pain. Johnny slumbered so peacefully, and breathed so gently, that for a moment I was alarmed, and doubted whether he was breathing at all, until I stooped down and watched him closely. There were still no indications of a breeze. A school of whales was visible about a quarter of a mile to the westward, spouting and pursuing their unwieldy sport; but I took no interest in the sight, and leaning over the gunwale, commenced bathing my head and eyes with the sea-water. While thus engaged I was startled by seeing an enormous cachelot, (the sperm-whale), suddenly break the water within fifteen yards of the boat. Its head, which composed nearly a third of its entire bulk, seemed a mountain of flesh. A couple of small calves followed it, and came swimming playfully around us. For a minute or two, the cachelot floated quietly at the surface, where it had first appeared, throwing a slender jet of water, together with a large volume of spray and vapour into the air; then rolling over upon its side, it began to lash the sea with its broad and powerful tail, every stroke of which produced a sound like the report of a cannon. This roused the sleepers abruptly, and just as they sprang up, and began to look around in astonishment, for the cause of so startling a commotion, the creature cast its misshapen head downwards, and, throwing its immense flukes high into the air, disappeared. We watched anxiously to see where it would rise, conscious of the perils of such a neighbourhood, and that even a playful movement, a random sweep of the tail, while pursuing its gigantic pastime, would be sufficient to destroy us. It came to the surface at about the same distance as before, but on the opposite side of the boat, throwing itself half out of the water as it rose: again it commenced lashing the sea violently, as if in the mere wanton display of its terrible strength, until far around, the water was one wide sheet of foam. The calves still gambolled near us, chasing each other about and under the yawl, and we might easily have killed one of them, had we not been deterred by the almost certain consequences of arousing the fury of the old whale. Meantime, the entire school seemed to be edging down towards us. There was not a breath of air, and we had no means of getting out of the way of the danger to which we should be exposed, if among them, except by taking to the oars; and this, nothing short of the most pressing and immediate peril could induce us to do. But our attention was soon withdrawn from the herd, to the singular and alarming movements of the individual near us. Rushing along the surface for short distances, it threw itself several times half clear of the water, turning after each of these leaps, as abruptly as its unwieldy bulk would permit, and running a tilt with equal violence in the opposite direction. Once, it passed so near us, that I think I could have touched it with an oar, and we saw distinctly its small, dull eye, and the loose, wrinkled, folds of skin, about its tremendous jaws. For a minute afterwards, the boat rolled dangerously in the swell caused by the swift passage of so vast an object. Suddenly, after one of these abrupt turns, the monster headed directly towards us, and came rushing onward with fearful velocity, either not noticing us at all, or else mistaking the boat for some sea-creature, with which it designed to measure its strength. There was no time for any effort to avoid the danger; and even had there been, we were too much paralysed by its imminence, to make such an effort. The whale was scarcely twelve yards off—certainly not twenty. Behind it stretched a foaming wake, straight as an arrow. Its vast mountainous head ploughed up the waves like a ship's cutwater, piling high the foam and spray before it. To miss us was now a sheer impossibility and no earthly power could arrest the creature's career. Instant destruction appeared inevitable. I grew dizzy, and my head began to swim, while the thought flashed confusedly through my mind, that infinite wisdom had decreed that we must die, and this manner of perishing had been chosen in mercy, to spare us the prolonged horrors of starvation. What a multitude of incoherent thoughts and recollections crowded upon my mind in that moment of time! A thousand little incidents of my past life, disconnected and trivial—a shadowy throng of familiar scenes and faces, surged up before me, vividly as objects revealed for an instant by the glare of the lightning, in the gloom of a stormy night. Closing my eyes, I silently commended my soul to God, and was endeavouring to compose myself for the dreadful event when Morton sprang to his feet, and called hurriedly upon us to shout together. All seemed to catch his intention at once, and to perceive in it a gleam of hope; and standing up we raised our voices in a hoarse cry, that sounded strange and startling even to ourselves. Instantly, as it seemed, the whale drove almost perpendicularly downwards, but so great was its momentum, that its fluked tail cut the air within an oar's length of the boat as it disappeared.

Whether the shout we had uttered, caused the sudden plunge to which we owed our preservation, it is impossible to decide. Notwithstanding its bulk and power, the cachelot is said to be a timid creature, except when injured or enraged, and great caution has to be exercised by whalers in approaching them. Suddenly recollecting this, the thought of undertaking to scare the formidable monster, had suggested itself to Morton, and he had acted upon it in sheer desperation, impelled by the same instinct that causes a drowning man to catch even at a straw.

But, however obtained, our reprieve from danger was only momentary. The whale came to the surface at no great distance, and once more headed towards us. If frightened for an instant, it had quickly recovered from the panic, and now there was no mistaking the creature's purpose: it came on, exhibiting every mark of rage, and with jaws literally wide open. We felt that no device or effort of our own could be of any avail. We might as well hope to resist a tempest, or an earthquake, or the shock of a falling mountain, as that immense mass of matter, instinct with life and power, and apparently animated by brute fury.

Every hope had vanished, and I think that we were all in a great measure resigned to death, and fully expecting it when there came, (as it seemed to us, by actual miracle), a most wonderful interposition.

A dark, bulky mass, (in the utter bewilderment of the moment we noted nothing distinctly of its appearance), shot perpendicularly from the sea twenty feet into the air, and fell with a tremendous concussion, directly upon the whale's back. It must have been several tons in weight, and the blow inflicted was crushing. For a moment the whale seemed paralysed by the shock, and its vast frame quivered with agony; but recovering quickly, it rushed with open jaws upon its strange assailant which immediately dived, and both vanished. Very soon, the whale came to the surface again;

and now we became the witnesses of one of those singular and tremendous spectacles, of which the vast solitudes of the tropical seas are doubtless often the theatre, but which human eyes have rarely beheld.

The cachelot seemed to be attacked by two powerful confederates, acting in concert. The one assailed it from below, and continually drove it to the surface, while the other—the dark bulky object—repeated its singular attacks in precisely the same manner as at first, whenever any part of the gigantic frame of the whale was exposed, never once missing its mark, and inflicting blows, which one would think, singly sufficient to destroy any living creature. At times the conflict was carried on so near us, as to endanger our safety; and we could see all of the combatants with the utmost distinctness, though not at the same time. The first glimpse which we caught of the second antagonist of the whale, as it rose through the water to the attack, enabled us at once to identify it as that most fierce and formidable creature—the Pacific Sword-fish.

The other, as I now had an opportunity to observe, was a fish of full one third the length of the whale itself, and of enormous bulk in proportion; it was covered with a dark rough skin, in appearance not unlike that of an alligator. The cachelot rushed upon its foes alternately, and the one thus singled out invariably fled, until the other had an opportunity to come to its assistance; the sword-fish swimming around in a wide circle at the top of the water, when pursued, and the other diving when chased in its turn. If the whale followed the sword-fish to the surface, it was sure to receive a stunning blow from its leaping enemy; if it pursued the latter below, the sword-fish there attacked it fearlessly, and, as it appeared, successfully, forcing it quickly back to the top of the water.

Presently the battle began to recede from us, the whale evidently making towards the school, which was at no great distance; and strange as the sight was, we watched it with but a languid interest, as soon as our safety appeared to be no longer involved. The whale must have been badly hurt for the water which it threw up on coming to the surface and spouting, was tinged with blood. After this I saw no more of the sword-fish and his associate; they had probably abandoned the attack. As nearly as I can recollect, we did not, either during the progress of the fight, or after it was over, exchange a single word on the subject, so dumb and apathetic had we become. After a while the school of whales appeared to be moving off, and in half an hour more, we lost sight of them altogether.

All this while, Johnny had continued to sleep soundly, and his slumbers seemed more natural and refreshing than before. When at length he awoke, the delirium had ceased, and he was calm and gentle, but so weak that he could not sit up without being supported. After the disappearance of the whales, several hours passed, during which we lay under our awning without a word being spoken by any one. Throughout this day, the sea seemed to be alive with fish; myriads of them were to be seen in every direction; troops of agile and graceful dolphins; revolving black-fish, chased by ravenous sharks; leaping albatross, dazzling the eye with the flash of their golden scales, as they shot into the air for a moment; porpoises, bonito, flying-fish, and a hundred unknown kinds which I had never seen or heard of. At one time we were surrounded by an immense shoal of small fishes, about the size of mackerel, so densely crowded together that their backs presented an almost solid surface, on which it seemed as if one might walk dry-shod. None, however, came actually within our reach, and we made no effort to approach them.

From the time of our wonderful escape from being destroyed by the whale, until the occurrence which I am about to relate, I remember nothing distinctly—all seems vague and dream-like. I could not say with confidence, from my own knowledge, whether the interval consisted of several days, or of only a few feverish and half-delirious hours; nor whether the sights and sounds of which I have a confused recollection, were real, or imaginary. I think, however, that it must have been in the afternoon of the same day, (Arthur is confident that it was), that Morton came to me as I lay in the bottom of the boat in a state of utter desperation and self-abandonment and aroused me, saying in a hoarse and painful whisper, that there was a vessel in sight. Even this announcement hardly sufficed to overcome the stupor into which I had sunk, and it was with a reluctant effort, and a feeling akin to annoyance at being disturbed, that I sat up and looked around me. My eyes were so much inflamed that I could see nothing distinctly.

The first thing that I observed, was, that the calm was at an end. A breeze had sprung up, and was blowing gently but pretty steadily from the south. The surface of the sea was slightly ruffled, and its dead stagnant aspect, had given place to one of breezy freshness. In this change there was something reviving and strengthening. Far to the south, where Morton pointed out the vessel which he had discovered, I could just distinguish a white speck upon the water, which seemed more like the crest of a wave than any thing else. Morton had already called Arthur's attention to it, and he was watching it intently. Gradually it became more distinct, and in half an hour, I too, could make it out plainly, to be a small sailing vessel of some description. As she was coming directly down before the wind, there seemed to be no need of doing any thing to attract her attention. I now hastened to reanimate Max and Browne, by communicating to them the intelligence that relief was probably at hand. In three-quarters of an hour more, the strange sail was near enough to enable us to see that she was a large double canoe, such as is used by some of the islanders of the South Pacific, in their trading voyages. It had two masts, with large triangular mat-sails, and appeared to contain six or seven persons only, whom we supposed to be natives of some neighbouring island. As soon as they were within speaking distance, one of them, to our great astonishment hailed us in French. Arthur undertook to answer in the same language, when the other, probably perceiving that the French was not his native tongue, spoke to us in tolerable English, but with a strong French accent. It was easy to perceive, now that our attention was particularly called to him, that the spokesman was a European. Though almost naked like the rest, and elaborately tattooed upon the chest and shoulders, his light hair and beard, and florid though sun-burnt skin, sufficiently distinguished him from them. Of course the first thing with us, was to make known our wants, and to ask for food, and above all for water. As soon as they could bring the canoe near enough, the Frenchman watching his opportunity, reached out to us a large gourd containing water, of which we drank plentifully, passing it round several times. Arthur hastened to pour a little into Johnny's mouth, and the effect was astonishing: he seemed to revive almost instantaneously, and, sitting up, he seized the gourd himself and drank eagerly as long as Arthur would let him. The Frenchman next tossed us something wrapped in banana leaves, a thick, dark-coloured paste of some kind. It was enough that it was an article of food, and we devoured it without pausing for any very close examination, though its appearance was by no means inviting, and it had a crude and slightly acid taste. He threw us also several thin, hard cakes, similar in taste and colour to the other substance. Both were probably preparations of the bread-fruit, the latter being dried and hardened in the sun, or by fire. Ravenously hungry as we were, these supplies were divided and apportioned with the most scrupulous exactness. On finding that the natives were well supplied with water, having several large gourds full, we passed the calabash round again, until we had drained it dry, when they gave us another gourd. Meanwhile, though we were too busy to look about us much, the canoe's people watched us very narrowly, and in such a manner as to make me feel uneasy and doubtful as to their intentions, notwithstanding their kindness thus far. As soon as the first cravings of hunger and thirst were satisfied, I began to return their scrutiny, and I now observed that they differed in many respects from the Tahitians, and from all the other Polynesian tribes of which I knew any thing. Their complexion was a clear olive; their faces oval, with regular features; their hair straight and black; their eyes large, and the general expression of their countenances simple and pleasing, though there were several keen, crafty-looking faces among them. All were tattooed, more or less profusely, the chests of some resembling checker-boards, and others being ornamented with rosettes, and representations of various natural objects, as birds, fishes, trees, etcetera. Their only clothing consisted of the maro, a strip of tappa, or native cloth, tied round the loins. A wave happening to throw the boats nearly together, one of the natives caught hold of our gunwale at the stern, and another at the bow, and thus kept the canoe alongside.

They now began to cast searching glances at us, and at every thing in the yawl. I observed the Frenchman intently eyeing the handle of one of the cutlasses, which protruded from beneath a fold of canvass. He inquired eagerly whether we had any fire-arms, and seemed greatly disappointed to find that we had not. He next asked for tobacco, with no better success, which apparently surprised him very much, for he shrugged his shoulders, and raised his thick eyebrows with a doubtful and incredulous look. At this moment the gilt buttons upon Max's jacket seemed to strike the fancy of one of our new friends, and excited his cupidity to such a degree, that after fixing upon them a long and admiring gaze, he suddenly reached over and made a snatch at them. He got hold of one, and in trying to pull it off came very near jerking Max overboard. Morton, who was sitting next to Max, interfered, and caught the man by the arm, with a look and manner that made me fear he might do something imprudent. The savage, who was an athletic fellow, obstinately maintained his hold of Max's jacket, and casting a ferocious glance at Morton, snatched up a short, thick paddle, and brandished it over his head as if about to strike. Arthur appealed to the Frenchman to interpose, but before he could do so, one of the natives, a handsome boy, who was seated cross-legged upon a platform between the masts, spoke to the man in a raised voice, and with an air of authority, whereupon, to my surprise, he immediately dropped the paddle, and sullenly desisted from his attempt. This lad, who seemed to be so promptly obeyed, did not look to be more than thirteen or fourteen years of age. His voice was soft and girlish; he had a remarkably open and pleasing countenance, and surveyed us with an air of friendly interest, very different from the sinister and greedy looks of several of the others, including the Frenchman himself. In answer to the questions of the latter, Arthur told him that we were Americans, and related very briefly how we had come into our present situation. He then informed us in turn, that he had been cast away, some six years before, in a French barque engaged in the tortoise-shell traffic, upon an uninhabited island, about forty miles from the one where he and those with him, now lived. After remaining there for more than a year, he and his companions, having reason to believe that they were in the neighbourhood of a group occasionally visited by trading vessels, had set out in search of it, in a small boat. Their belief as to the existence and situation of these islands proved to be well founded; they had finally succeeded in reaching them, had been hospitably received and treated by the natives, among whom they had acquired considerable influence, but had as yet had no opportunity of returning home.

They were now, he said, on their return from a trading voyage to a neighbouring island, where they had just disposed of a cargo of mats and tappa, in exchange for baskets of native manufacture, and sharks' teeth. Having been becalmed all the preceding day and night, they feared that they had drifted out of their course, since, otherwise, they ought, after making full allowance for the calm, to have already reached their own island. He finished by assuring us, that we might calculate with confidence, upon enjoying perfect security and kind treatment among these people.

The conference being concluded, he directed us to put up our sail, and steer after the canoe; adding that he expected to reach the group before midnight if the wind held fair. He spoke with the air of one delivering a command, and evidently considered us entirely under his control. But of course we felt no disposition to object to what he directed. The fact, that the natives had treated him and his companions so well, was an encouragement to us, as affording some proof of their friendly and peaceful character, and we supposed that he could have no possible motive for using his influence to our prejudice. Even had there been any other course for us to choose, to escape perishing, we were in no condition to make any effectual opposition to the will of our new acquaintances.

> Note. This fish story has several rather astonishing features—at least to an inexperienced landsman. The sword-fish and thresher are said to seek and attack the right whale together; but a nautical friend, whom I have consulted on the subject, says he has never heard of their interfering with the cachelot, or sperm-whale, which would, he thinks, be very likely to make mince-meat of them both, should they be guilty of such temerity: the right whale uses no other weapon than his powerful tail; whereas the cachelot goes at an adversary with open jaws. Upon my inquiry whether threshers, "of several tons weight," and jumping "twenty feet into the air," were common, my friend the captain, seemed piqued at my implied scepticism as to marine monsters, and briefly made answer, that there were more strange creatures in the sea, than were dreamed of in my philosophy, and that "many an old sailor could give more real information on the subject, than all the natural history books in the world."

Chapter Eleven
A Catastrophe

The Whirling Columns—A Stupendous
Spectacle—We lose our New Friends

"Still round and round the fluid vortex flies,
Scattering dun night, and horror through the skies,
The swift volution and the enormous train
Let sages versed in Nature's lore explain;
The horrid apparition still draws nigh,
And white with foam the whirling surges fly."

The breeze was now steady, though gentle, and Max and Morton set to work rigging the sail, which for the last two days had served as an awning.

During our mutual inquiries and explanations, the Frenchman had kept the canoe close alongside of us; he now braced round the yard of his triangular sail, which had been shaking in the wind, and began to draw ahead. The young native who had interfered so effectually in Max's behalf, observing the eagerness with which we had devoured the doughy mass of pounded bread-fruit, tossed another cake of the same substance into the boat as we separated, which, when distributed, afforded a morsel or two to each of us. I had particularly observed this boy on the first approach of the canoe, from the circumstance of his occupying a small raised platform, or daïs, of wicker-work, covered with mats.

As our sail had been entirely disengaged from the mast and gaff, it was quite a piece of work to rig it again for service, and by the time this was effected, the canoe was some distance ahead of us: though she was far better adapted than the yawl for sailing with a light breeze, yet we nearly held our own with her, after once getting fairly under way.

When the wind first sprang up, the sky had become slightly overcast with broken masses of clouds, of a peculiar and unusual appearance. From the most considerable of these masses, radiated, as from a centre, long lines, like pencils of light, running in straight, regularly diverging rays, to the ocean.

We had been sailing in the wake of the canoe, perhaps half an hour, when I observed in the south-west a singularly shaped cloud, to which a dark column, extending downward to the sea, appeared to be attached. This column was quite narrow at the base, but enlarged as it rose, until just below the point of union with the cloud, it spread outward like a gothic pillar, diverging into arches as it meets the roof. I surveyed this strange spectacle for several minutes before its true character occurred to me. It was already observed by those in the canoe, and from their exclamations and gestures, they evidently viewed it with apprehension and dread.

It was moving slowly towards us, and we also watched, with feelings in which alarm began to predominate over curiosity and interest, the majestic approach of this vast body of water, (as we now perceived it to be), held by some secret power suspended between heaven and earth.

"It appears to be moving north before the wind," said Arthur, at length; "if it keeps on its present course, it will pass by, at a safe distance on our left."

This seemed probable; but we felt disposed to give it a still wider berth, and shifting the sail, we steered in a north-easterly direction. Scarcely had our sail filled on the new tack, when a cry of terror again drew attention to the canoe, and the natives were seen pointing to another water-spout, moving slowly round from the east to the north, and threatening to intercept us in the course we were pursuing. This, unlike the first, was a cylindrical column of water, of about the same diameter throughout its entire length, extending in a straight and unbroken line from the ocean to the heavens. Its upper extremity was lost amid a mass of clouds, in which I fancied I could perceive the effects of the gradual diffusion of the water drawn from the sea, as it wound its way upward with a rapid spiral motion, and poured into that elevated reservoir. As the process went on, the cloud grew darker, and seemed to stoop with its accumulating weight of waters.

Our position was fast becoming embarrassing and dangerous. We had changed our course to avoid the first water-spout and now we were confronted by another still nearer at hand.

For a moment all was confusion, indecision, and dismay.

"Quick! round with her head, and let her go right before the wind!" shouted Max hurriedly.

"That would be running directly into the danger," cried Morton, "they are both moving north, and approaching each other."

"Then let's pull down the sail, until they are at a safe distance."

"I would rather keep her under headway," said Arthur, "or how could we escape, if one of them should move down upon us!"

"What can we do, then?" exclaimed Max; "we can't sail in the teeth of the wind."

"I am for going about to the left again, and steering as near the wind as possible," said Arthur; "the one on that side is farthest north."

This was the course which the natives had already adopted, and they were now steering nearly south-west. We immediately followed their example, and the fore and aft rig of the yawl enabled us to sail nearer the wind than they could do.

In a few moments the funnel-shaped water-spout, which we had first seen, had passed off northward, and was at such a distance as to remove all apprehensions on account of it. Not so, however, with the second; for hardly had we tacked again, when, notwithstanding that we were to windward of it, it began to move rapidly towards us.

Its course was not direct and uniform, but it veered now to the right and now to the left, rendering it difficult for us to decide which way to steer in order to avoid it.

Arthur sat at the helm, pale, but quite calm and collected, his eyes steadfastly fixed on the advancing column, while Johnny crouched at his side, holding fast one of his hands in both his own. Morton held the sheet and stood ready to shift the sail, as the emergency might require.

Onward it came, towering to the skies, and darkening the ocean with its impending bulk; soon we could perceive the powerful agitation of the water far around its base, and within the vortex of its influence: a dense cloud of spray, thrown off in its rapid revolutions, enveloped its lower extremity: the rushing sound of the water as it was drawn upward, was also distinctly audible. And now it seemed to take a straight course for the canoe. The natives, with the exception of the boy, threw themselves down in the bottom of the boat in abject terror; it was, indeed, an appalling spectacle, and calculated to shake the stoutest heart, to see that vast mass of water, enough as it seemed, to swamp the navies of the world, suspended so strangely over them.

The Frenchman appeared to be endeavouring to get the natives to make some exertion, but in vain. He and the boy then seized a couple of paddles, and made a frantic effort to escape the threatened danger; but the whirling pillar was almost upon them, and it seemed as though they were devoted to certain destruction. The Frenchman now threw down his paddle, and sat with his hands folded on his breast, awaiting his fate. The boy, after speaking earnestly to his companion, who merely shook his head, stood up in the prow of the canoe, and casting one shuddering look at the dark column, he joined his hands above his head, and plunged into the sea. In a moment he came to the surface, and struck out vigorously towards us.

The canoe seemed already within the influence of the water-spout, and was drawn towards it with the violently agitated waters around its base. The Frenchman, unable longer to endure the awful sight bowed his head upon his hands; another moment, and he was lost to sight in the circle of mist and spray that enveloped the foot of the column; then a strong oscillation began to be visible in the body of the water-spout; it swayed heavily to and fro; the cloud at its apex seemed to stoop, and the whole mass broke and fell, with a noise that might have been heard for miles. The sea, far around, was crushed into smoothness by the shock; immediately where the vast pillar had stood, it boiled like a caldron; then a succession of waves, white with foam, came circling outward from the spot, extending even to us.

The native boy, who swam faster than we sailed, was already within forty or fifty yards of us, and we put about and steered for him: in a moment he was alongside, and Arthur, reaching out his hand, helped him into the boat.

The sea had now resumed its usual appearance, and every trace of the water-spout was gone, so that it was impossible to fix the spot where it had broken. Not a vestige of the canoe, or of her ill-fated company, was anywhere to be seen. We sailed backward and forward in the neighbourhood of the place, carefully scrutinising the surface in every direction, and traversing several times the spot, as nearly as we could determine it, where the canoe had last been seen: but our search was fruitless: the long billows swelled and subsided with their wonted regularity, and their rippled summits glittered as brightly in the sunshine as ever, but they revealed no trace of those whom they had so suddenly and remorselessly engulfed.

The water-spout which had first been seen, had disappeared, and a few heavy clouds in the zenith alone remained, as evidences of the terrific phenomenon which we had just witnessed.

Chapter Twelve
Our Island Home

The Illusion of the Golden Haze—The Wall of
breakers—A Struggle for Life—The Islet of Palms

"Keel never ploughed that lonely sea,
   That isle no human eye hath viewed;
   Around it still in tumult rude,
The surges everlastingly,
Burst on the coral-girded shore
With mighty bound and ceaseless roar;
A fresh unsullied work of God,
By human footstep yet untrod."

The native lad now seemed to be quite overwhelmed with grief. He had made no manifestations of it while we were endeavouring to discover some trace of his companions, but when at length we relinquished the attempt, and it became certain that they had all perished, he uttered a low, wailing cry, full of distress and anguish, and laying his head upon his hands, sobbed bitterly.

The Frenchman had told us that the island lay to the northward; and we now put the head of the boat in that direction, steering by the sun, which was just setting.

When the first violence of the boy's grief had somewhat abated, Arthur spoke to him gently, in the dialect of the Society Islands. He listened attentively, turning his large eyes upon Arthur's face with an expression of mingled timidity and interest and replied in a low, musical voice. They seemed to understand one another, and talked together for some time. The language spoken by the boy, differed so little, as Arthur told us, from that of the Tahitians, that he easily gathered the meaning of what he said. Upon being questioned as to the distance of the island, and the course which we must steer in order to reach it, he pointed to a bright star, just beginning to be visible in the north-east.

It is customary with the South-sea Islanders, before setting out on their long voyages, in which it is necessary to venture out of sight of land, to select some star by which to regulate their course in the night-time; this they call the "aveia," or guiding star of the voyage. They are thus enabled to sail from island to island, and from group to group, between which all intercourse would otherwise be impossible without a compass. The star now pointed out to us, had been fixed upon by the companions of the little islander, at the commencement of their ill-fated voyage, as marking the direction of the home which they were destined never to regain. Among other things, we learned from the boy, that his native island, which we were now endeavouring to reach, was the largest of a group of three, over all of which his father's authority, as chief or king, extended: that there were six whites living among them, who had arrived there many years before, with the one who had just perished, and had come from an uninhabited island to the southward, upon which they had been wrecked.

During the night the wind continued fair, and animated by the hopes to which the statements of the little native had given rise, we renewed our watch, which had lately been discontinued, and sailed steadily northward, cherishing a strong confidence that we should reach land before morning.

The second watch—from a little after midnight to dawn—fell to me. As it began to grow light I almost feared to look northward, dreading the shock of a fresh disappointment, that must consign us again to the benumbing apathy from which we had yesterday rallied.

There seemed to me to be something unusual in the atmosphere, that impeded, or rather confused and bewildered the sight; and when the sun rose, I had not made out anything like land. It was not mist or fog, for the air was dry, and there were already indications of a fiercely hot day, though it was yet fresh and cool. The sky above us, too, was perfectly clear, all the clouds seemed to have slid down to the horizon, along which a white army of them was marshalled, in rounded fleecy masses, like Alpine peaks towering one above another, or shining icebergs, pale and cold as those that drift in Arctic seas.

One by one my companions awoke to learn the failure, thus far, of all the sanguine expectations of the preceding evening. The native boy could suggest no reason why we had not reached the island, and when questioned on the subject, and told that we had steered all through the night by the "aveia," he merely shook his head with a bewildered and hopeless look. Max, on perceiving that we were still out of sight of land, threw himself down again in the bottom of the boat without speaking a word, where he remained with his eyes closed as if sleeping.

Arthur, after some further conversation with the little islander, came to the conclusion that in steering due north, we had not made sufficient allowance for the strong current setting westward; and he proposed that we should now sail directly east, to which no objection was made, most of us having at last come to feel that it could matter little what course we thenceforth steered. He accordingly took the direction of things into his own hands: the wind, which had moderated, was still from the west, and he put the boat before it, and lashed the helm. The peculiar appearance of the atmosphere still continued. During the morning a number of tropic birds flew by us, the first that we had seen since our separation from the ship. About noon, two noddies alighted on the gaff, and the little native climbed the mast after them; but though they are generally so tame, or so stupid, as to permit themselves to be approached and taken with the hand, these flew away before he could seize them. We hailed the appearance of these birds as a favourable omen, neither species being often seen at any considerable distance from land. It was, I suppose, about an hour after this, that happening to look back, I saw what appeared to be a high island, covered with tall groves of palms, some two miles distant. The elevated shores, and the green tops of the trees, were plainly visible; but just at the point where land and water met, there was a kind of hazy indistinctness in the view. We were sailing directly from it, and I could not understand how we had passed as near as we must have done without observing it. Browne, catching sight of it almost at the same time with myself, uttered an exclamation that quickly aroused the attention of the rest, and we all stood for a moment gazing, half incredulously, upon the land which seemed to have started up so suddenly out of the sea, in the very track which we had just passed over.

Arthur alone, appeared to be but little moved; he looked long and intently, without uttering a word.

"This is singular—very singular!" said Morton. "It seems as though we must have sailed over the *very* spot where it lies."

"Unless I am mistaken," said Arthur, "we have been going backward for some time past: we must be in a very powerful current, which is carrying us in a direction contrary to that in which we are heading: the wind is so light that this is not impossible."

"I believe you are right," said Morton, "I can account for it in no other way."

"We had better then pull down the sail, and take the benefit of the full force of the current," resumed Arthur: this was accordingly done, and the mast unstepped.

A short time passed, during which we appeared to be steadily drawing nearer to the land. The shore itself where it emerged from the ocean, we could not see with perfect distinctness: a fine, golden haze, like a visible atmosphere, waved and quivered before it, half veiling it from sight, and imparting to it an uncertain, though bright and dazzling aspect: but this appearance was confined to the lower part of the land; the bold shores and high groves were clearly defined.

"I trust we are not the subjects of some fearful illusion," said Browne, breaking a long silence, during which all eyes had been rivetted upon the island; "but there is something very strange about all this—it has an unearthly look."

As he spoke, the bright haze which floated over the sea near the surface, began to extend itself upward, and to grow denser and more impervious to the sight: the wooded shores became indistinct and dim, and seemed gradually receding in the distance, until the whole island, with its bold heights and waving groves, dissolved and melted away like a beautiful vision.

"What is this?" exclaimed Browne, in a voice of horror. "I should think, if I believed such things permitted, that evil spirits had power here on the lonely sea, and were sporting with our misery."

"It is a mirage," said Arthur quietly, "as I suspected from the first. But courage! though what we have seen was an optical illusion, there must be a real island in the distance beyond, of which this was the elevated and refracted image. It cannot, I think, be more than thirty or forty miles off, and the current is sweeping us steadily towards it."

"I suppose then," said Morton, "that we can do nothing better, than to trust ourselves entirely to this current which must in fact be a pretty powerful one—at least as rapid as the Gulf Stream."

"We can do nothing better until the wind changes," replied Arthur, cheerfully; "at present I am disposed to think we are doing very well, and fast approaching land."

But there was no change of the wind, and we continued hour after hour, apparently making no progress, but in reality, as we believed, drifting steadily westward. All through the day we maintained a vigilant watch, lest by any possibility we should miss sight of the island which Arthur was so confident we were approaching. Late in the afternoon we saw a flock of gannets, and some sooty tern; the gannets passing so near that we could hear the motion of their long twisted wings. Later still, a number of small reef-birds passed over head; all were flying westward. This confirmed Arthur in his belief of the proximity of land. "See," said he, "these little reef-birds are bound in the same direction with the others, and with ourselves; you may depend upon it, that the sea-fowl we have seen, are hastening homeward to their nests, on some not far distant shore."

So fully did I share this confidence, that I commenced a calculation as to the time at which we might expect to reach land. Assuming it to have been thirty miles distant at the time when we had seen its spectrum, by means of the refraction, arising from a peculiar state of the atmosphere; and estimating the rate of the current at three miles an hour, I came to the conclusion that we could not even come in sight of it until late at night; and it was therefore without any strong feeling of disappointment, that I saw the day fast drawing to a close, and nothing but sky and ocean yet visible.

The sun had already set, but the long tract of crimson and flame-coloured clouds that glowed in the horizon where he had disappeared, still reflected light enough to render it easy to distinguish objects in that quarter, when I was startled by a cry of joyful surprise from the native boy, who, shading his eyes with his hands, was looking intently westward. After a long and earnest gaze, he spoke eagerly to Arthur, who told us that the boy thought he saw his native island. Looking in the same direction, I could make out nothing. Arthur and Browne spoke of a brilliantly white line, narrow, but well-defined against the horizon, as being all that they could see. Morton, who was very keen-sighted, thought that he distinguished some dark object beyond the low white band seen by the others. As the light gradually failed, we lost sight of this appearance. It was some hours before the rising of the moon, which we awaited with anxiety. She was now at her full, and when at length she came up out of the sea, her disc, broad and red like a beamless sun, seemed to rest, dilated to preternatural size, upon the edge of the last wave that swelled against the horizon. As she ascended the sky, she shed over the ocean a flood of silvery light, less glaring, but almost as bright as that of day. The wonderful brilliancy of the moon and stars within the tropics, is one of the first things noted by the voyager. It may be owing to the great clearness and transparency of the atmosphere: but whatever the cause, their light is much more powerful than in higher latitudes, and they seem actually nearer, and of greater magnitude.

We now looked eagerly westward again; the snow-white line, of which the others had spoken, was by this time distinctly visible to me also, and beyond it, too plainly relieved against the clear blue of the sky, to admit of doubt or illusion, were the high outlines of a tropical island, clothed with verdure to its summit.

Again the little islander shouted joyously, and clasped his hands, while the tears streamed down his olive cheeks.

He recognised his native island, the smallest and most easterly of the three, of which his father was the chief. We should soon come in sight of the remaining two, he said, which were lower, and lay to the north and south of it; he explained that the appearance, like a low white line running along the base of the island, was caused by the surf, bursting upon a coral reef about a mile from the shore.

Here then, at last, was the land which we had at one time despaired of ever beholding again, and now we were well assured that it was no airy phantasm; yet strange as it may seem, our feelings were not those of unmingled joy.

A thousand vague apprehensions and surmises of evil, began to suggest themselves, as we approached this unknown shore, inhabited by savages, and under the dominion of a savage. We doubted not that we might depend upon the good-will, and friendly offices of the little native, but we felt at the same time, that the influence of one so young, might prove insufficient for our protection.

We were in some measure acquainted with the savage customs, the dark and cruel rites, that prevailed among the Polynesian races generally, and had often listened with horror, to the recital of what Arthur and his uncle had themselves seen, of their bloody superstitions, and abominable practices. As I looked into the faces of my companions, it was easy to perceive that they were possessed by anxious and gloomy thoughts.

Meanwhile, the current continued to sweep us steadily onward toward the shore, the outlines of which became every moment more distinct. Occasionally a cloud drifted athwart the moon, and cast a soft shade upon the sea, obscuring the view for a time; but when it had passed, the land seemed to have drawn perceptibly nearer during the interval. At length, when the night was far advanced, and the island was right before us, at the distance of scarcely a mile, the native lad, who had been gazing wistfully toward it for the last half-hour, uttered a plaintive cry of disappointment. He had looked long and anxiously, for the appearance of the two remaining islands of his father's group, but in vain; and now he yielded reluctantly to the conviction, that he had been deceived by the white line of surf, similar to that which bounded on one side his native island, and that he had never before seen the one which we were approaching. This discovery was a relief to me, and removed a weight of apprehension from my mind. The thought of being cast upon a desert and uninhabited shore, seemed less dreadful, than that of falling into the power of a tribe of savage islanders, even under circumstances which would probably secure us a friendly reception.

But now a strange and unforeseen difficulty presented itself. Between us and the island, stretched a barrier reef, running north and south, and curving westward; and appearing, as far as we could see, completely to surround it. Along the whole line of this reef the sea was breaking with such violence as to render all approach dangerous; neither could we espy any break or opening in it, through which to reach the shore. Towards this foaming barrier the current was rapidly bearing us, and we were too feeble to struggle long against its force. To permit ourselves to be carried upon the reef would be certain destruction, and our only hope of safety seemed to lie in discovering some inlet through it. Our true situation flashed upon me all at once; I had not before thought of the impossibility of receding. Glancing at Arthur, I caught his eye, and saw that he comprehended the full extent of the danger. "We are near enough to see any break in the reef," said he, "let us now take to the oars, and coast along it in search of one."

This was accordingly done. But it was not until we had pulled along the shore for some time, and found that in spite of our endeavours to preserve our distance from it, we were steadily forced nearer, that the rest seemed aware of the imminence of the danger.

"The current is carrying us among the breakers," exclaimed Morton, at length, "though we are heading rather away from the shore, we are getting closer every moment." This appalling fact was now apparent to all.

"The wind seems to have died away," said Browne, "at any rate there is not enough of it to help us: we must put about and pull out of the reach of this surf, or we are lost."

"How long do you suppose we can continue that?" said Arthur. "No, our only hope is in finding an entrance through the reef, and that speedily."

We now steered a little farther away, and strained at the oars, as those who struggle for life. Occasionally, when lifted on the crest of a wave, we caught a transient glimpse of a smooth expanse of water beyond the foaming line of surf, and extending from the inner edge of the reef, to the shore of the island. The tall tops of the palms bordering the beach, seemed scarcely a stone's throw distant and you could fancy that, but for the roar of the breakers, you might hear the rustling of their long, drooping leaves; but it only added to the horror of our situation, to see that safe and peaceful haven, so near, yet so inaccessible.

In some places the reef rose quite out of the water; in others, it was, in nautical phrase, "all awash;" but nowhere could we attempt a landing with safety. All the while, too, it was evident that in spite of our desperate exertions, we were being driven nearer and nearer the breakers. This kind of work had continued almost an hour, when our strength began to fail.

"There appears to be no use in this, comrades," said Browne, at last; "had we not better just let her go upon the reef, and take our chance of being able to get to the shore?"

"O, no!" exclaimed Arthur, earnestly, "that is too desperate."

"We shall be so completely exhausted that we shan't be able to make an effort for our lives, when at last we are carried into the surf," answered Browne, "and we must come to that sooner or later."

"I hope not—there is reason to hope not," rejoined Arthur, "but if so, we may as well be exhausted, as fresh; no strength will be of any avail; we shall be crushed and mangled upon the rocks; or if by any possibility some of us should reach the shore, what is to become of our poor, sick Johnny?"

"I will look after him," said Browne, "I will pledge myself that he shan't be lost, unless I am too."

"Let us hold out a few moments yet," implored Arthur; "I will take your oar; you are the only one who has not been relieved."

"No," said Browne, "you had better keep the helm; I can stand it a while longer, and I will pull until we are swept upon the reef; if you all think that the best plan."

It was barely possible that if we should now act as Browne proposed, we might be carried clear off the reef into the lagoon beyond, for we were opposite a sunken patch, upon which there was more water than at other places. Failing of this, the boat would inevitably be dashed to pieces; but still, if not bruised and disabled among the rocks, or carried back by the return waves, we might be able to reach the smooth water inside the reef, when it would be easy to swim ashore.

But to most of us, the attempt seemed too desperate to be thought of, except as a last resort; and we preferred to toil at the oars as long as our strength should last in the hope of discovering an inlet. Arthur, on whose skill and judgment we all relied, steered still farther out, and for a while we seemed to make head against the swell and the current.

For full half an hour longer, we kept up this severe struggle, that admitted not of an instant's pause or respite. But then our progress became almost imperceptible, and every stroke was made more feebly and laboriously than the last. I could hardly hold the oar in my stiffened fingers. Still no break was to be seen in the long line of surf which seemed to hem in the island, extending like a white wall, of uniform height, far as the eye could reach, on either hand. I had read of islands, like that of Eimeo, completely encircled by coral reefs, with but a single gateway by which they were accessible. What if this were such an one, and the only entrance, miles from the spot where we were toiling for our lives! The conviction that we must risk the chance of success in an attempt to land upon some ledge of the reef, was forcing itself upon all our minds, when Max, trembling with eagerness, pointed to what appeared to be an opening through the surf, nearly opposite us; there was a narrow space where the long waves, as they rolled towards the shore, did not seem to encounter the obstacle over which they broke with such violence on both sides of it, and the swell of the ocean met the placid waters of the lagoon, without any intervening barrier. Through this gap, the shore of the island could be seen, down to the water's edge.

Arthur hastily made a bundle of the mast and gaff, and placing it within Johnny's reach, told him to cling to it, in case of accident. Then, calling upon us to pull steadily, he steered directly for the inlet. As we neared it the noise of the surf became almost deafening: the huge rollers, as they thundered against the perpendicular wall of coral, rising abruptly from the depths of the sea, sent up a column of foam and spray, twelve or fifteen feet into the air. When just within the entrance, the spectacle was grand and appalling. But the danger, real or apparent, was soon over: with a firm hand, and steady eye, Arthur guided the boat along the centre of the narrow pass, and in a moment we had glided from the scene of fierce commotion without the reef, into one of perfect tranquillity and repose. A dozen strokes seemed to have placed us in a new world. Involuntarily we rested on our oars, and gazed around us in silence.

From the inner edge of the reef, to the broad white beach of the island, a space of perhaps half a mile, spread the clear expanse of the lagoon, smooth and unruffled as the surface of an inland lake. Half-way between the reef and the shore, were two fairy islets, the one scarcely a foot above the water, and covered with a green mantle of low shrubs; the other, larger and higher, and adorned by a group of graceful young cocoa-nuts.

The island itself was higher, and bolder in its outlines than is usual with those of coral formation, which are generally very low, and without any diversity of surface. Dense groves clothed that portion of it opposite to us, nearly to the beach, giving it at that hour, a somewhat gloomy and forbidding aspect.

As we surveyed this lovely, but silent and desolate landscape, the doubts and apprehensions which we had before experienced began once more to suggest themselves; but they were dissipated by the cheerful voice of Arthur, calling upon us to pull for the shore. He steered for the larger of the two islets, and when, as the boat grated upon the coral tops beside it, we threw down the oars, the strength which had hitherto sustained us, seemed suddenly to fail, and we could scarcely crawl ashore. The last scene of effort and danger, had taxed our powers to the uttermost, and now they gave way. I was so feeble, that I could hardly avoid sinking helplessly upon the sand. With one impulse we kneeled down and returned thanks to Him Who had preserved us through all the strange vicissitudes of the last few days. We next began to look round in search of such means of refreshment as the spot might afford.

The cocoa-palms upon the islet, though far from having attained their full growth, (few of them exceeding twelve feet in height), bore abundantly, and we easily procured as much of the fruit as we needed. Tearing off the outer husk, and punching a hole through the shell, which in the young nut is so soft that this can be done with the finger, we drank off the refreshing liquor with which it is filled; then breaking it open, the half-formed, jelly-like kernel, furnished a species of food most nutritious and agreeable, and probably the best adapted to our half-famished condition.

Hunger and thirst being appeased, our next care was to make some arrangement for passing the night more comfortably than could be done in the boat. Selecting a clear space in the centre of the group of young cocoa-nuts, we proceeded to make a rude tent, by fixing two of the oars upright in the ground,—tying the mast across their tops and throwing the sail over it, the ends being then fastened to the ground at a convenient distance on each side.

Finding that the bare ground would make a rather hard couch, though far less so than we had lately been accustomed to, Morton proposed that we should bring a load of leaves from the neighbouring shore to spread upon it. He and I accordingly rowed over to the mainland, and collected in the grove near the beech, a boatload of the clean dry foliage of the pandanus and hibiscus, which made excellent elastic beds. Johnny watched our departure as though he considered this an exceedingly rash and adventurous enterprise, and he seemed greatly relieved at our safe return. It was now past midnight, and after hauling the boat well up on the shore, we laid down side by side and were very soon asleep.

Chapter Thirteen
The Exploring Expedition

Eiulo—Pearl-Shell Beach—A Warlike Colony—An Invasion Repelled

"They linger there while weeks and months go by,
And hold their hope, tho' weeks and months are past;
And still at morning round the farthest sky,
And still at eve, their eager glance is cast,
If there they may behold the far-off mast
Arise, for which they have not ceased to pray."

For a number of days we remained upon the islet where we had first landed, seldom visiting even the adjacent shore. During this time we subsisted upon cocoa-nuts and a small species of shell-fish, resembling mussels, which we obtained in abundance from the ledges of the neighbouring reef, and which the little native told us, were used as a common article of food among his own people. We had reason to feel grateful that, while we were as feeble and incapable of exertion as we found ourselves for some days, food could be so readily procured. It was also fortunate that during this period the weather continued remarkably fine and mild, with no perceptible variations of temperature; for I have little doubt that in the reduced and exhausted condition in which we then were, and being without any effectual shelter, two or three days of bad weather would have cost some of us our lives. The nights were dry and mild, and no dew seemed to fall upon the islet: thanks to this genial weather, and to abundance of nourishing food, we began rapidly to recover strength.

Some time passed before we thought of making any attempt to penetrate or explore the island. We were, naturally, very reluctant to admit even to ourselves, the probability that our stay upon it was to be of any long duration; and we did not therefore feel as much interest in its character and resources as we should otherwise have done. All our thoughts and hopes ran in one channel. We looked for the coming of a ship to rescue us from our dreary position; and every morning and evening, at least, and generally many times a day, some one of us climbed into the tuft of an inclining palm, to take a careful survey of that portion of the ocean, which could be seen from our side of the island. The thought of acting in any respect as though the lonely spot where we now found ourselves was destined to be our permanent abode, was in fact too painful and repugnant to our feelings to be willingly entertained; we were content therefore, to provide for our daily wants as they arose, without anticipating or preparing for the future.

A few days passed in this unvaried and monotonous routine, seemed in reality a long period; recent occurrences began to assume the vagueness of things that had happened years ago. I remember particularly, that, in looking back at the dreadful scenes of the mutiny, and our subsequent sufferings at sea, the whole seemed unreal, and more like a horrible dream, than an actual part of our past experience.

We soon found that this inert and aimless mode of living—this state of passive expectation, while awaiting the occurrence of an event which we could do nothing to procure or hasten, was a most miserable one: though our physical strength was in a great measure recruited, there was no increase of cheerfulness. Except when engaged in procuring food, or making our daily surveys of the ocean, (which was all our occupation), we were dispirited and listless.

Arthur perceived the evil of this state of things, and set himself to devising a remedy.

We had been at the island about two weeks, when he proposed, one morning, that we should go over to the mainland and commence a search for water, making an excursion a little way into the interior, if it should prove necessary.

Max objected to this, saying that we had no need of water, since we could, without doubt, obtain cocoa-nut milk as long as we should be obliged to remain upon the island, and that by going into the interior, out of sight of the ocean, we might lose an opportunity of being rescued.

To this, Arthur replied, that the exclusive use of cocoa-nut milk was considered very unwholesome, and was supposed to be the cause of certain dropsical complaints, common among the natives of many of the Pacific islands; that beside; it was by no means certain that a supply of it could be obtained throughout the year. He finally suggested the possibility that our stay on the island might be longer than we anticipated, in which case its resources, and the means of subsistence which it afforded, would be matters of great interest to us. In regard to the danger which Max seemed chiefly to fear, he said that we should seldom altogether lose sight of the ocean, but might, on the contrary, obtain a wider view of it from other parts of the island. I warmly seconded Arthur's proposal, for I perceived the probable beneficial effects of effort, or occupation, of almost any kind. Morton also was decidedly in favour of it; and Johnny, who had recovered strength and spirits wonderfully within the last few days, was quite enthusiastic for the excursion. He calculated confidently upon our discovering a creek of fresh water, full of fishes and lobsters, and cited the history of the Swiss family Robinson, in support of the reasonableness of these expectations; declaring that for us part, he could not see why we might not count upon equal good fortune with them. Browne seemed indifferent about the matter. The little native, (whose name, upon Arthur's authority, I shall write "Eiulo," though "Iooloo," comes nearer to the sound, as he himself pronounced it), shared in Johnny's delight in prospect of the expedition; indeed, the two had already become the best friends in the world, notwithstanding the difficulty of communicating with one another, and seemed to harmonise in every thing. The excursion was accordingly determined upon, and this being so, there was nothing to prevent our setting out at once.

Morton proposed that, instead of undertaking to penetrate into the interior, we should keep along the shore to the northward, as by that means some idea might be gained of the extent of the island; and since any considerable spring or stream must find its way to the sea, we should also be more likely to discover water, than by pursuing the other course. Along the southern shore, the land was lower and less uneven than in the opposite direction, and held forth a slighter prospect of springs or streams. The difficulty of holding a straight course through the forest, where we should be without any means of ascertaining the points of the compass, was a consideration of great weight, and Morton's plan was at last adopted, as being upon the whole the best.

The sun was not more than half an hour high, when we pushed off from the shore of the islet, and rowed over towards the mainland. The morning was fine and clear, and either the fresh, bracing sea-air, or the stir and excitement of setting out upon our expedition, had an exhilarating influence, for we gradually became quite cheerful, and even animated; and the faces of my companions began to brighten up with more of the old familiar expression, than I had seen there for many a day.

The merest breath of a breeze just stirred the crisp leaves of the palms upon the neighbouring shore; the tiny wavelets rippled softly upon the snowy, shell-spangled beach, or, out in the lagoon, danced and sparkled in the sunlight; still further out and just beyond the barrier that fenced in this quiet and secluded scene from the open ocean, we could see the huge blue rollers with their foaming crests surging high into the air; and the heavy booming of the surf, as it thundered upon the reef, might be heard for miles around, amid the prevailing silence. Beyond this again, stretched away to the horizon, the blue, swelling arch of the ocean—a clear, deep, intense blue, contrasting beautifully with the paler blue of the sky, against which it was relieved, and with the emerald expanse of the lagoon.

Browne gazed about him with more interest than I had yet seen him manifest in any thing since we had reached the island. He inhaled the fresh morning air with the appearance of actual relish and enjoyment and at last, to my surprise, (for Max had accused him, not without some reason, of having been the most lugubrious of our party), he began to sing to a brisk and cheerful tune—

"O, happy days of hope and rest
    Shall dawn on sorrow's dreary night,
Though grief may be an evening guest,
    Yet joy shall come with morning light!
The light of smiles shall beam again,
    From lids that now o'erflow with tears,
And weary hours of woe and pain,
    Are earnests of serener years."

"Well," said he, as he finished his song, "this may be a desert island, but I will defy any one to gainsay that the morning is delicious, and the scene a right lovely one."

"I am glad you begin to wake up to it," said Morton, "it looks very much as it has at this hour for ten days past."

"No, no," protested Browne, "this bright, clear atmosphere makes a very great difference in the appearance of things: we have had no such mornings as this."

"I wish you could manage to enjoy it," said Max, "without missing every other stroke, and digging me so unmercifully in the back with your oar-handle; if you can't, I must ask you to change seats with me, and let me take the bow-oar."

"How natural and refreshing that sounds!" cried Morton, laughing; "it is a sure token that prospects are brightening, and serious dangers are over, when we find ourselves again in a condition to scold about trifles."

"It isn't such a trifle, to be thumped and mauled with the butt of an oar, as I have been all the while Browne was singing, and rhapsodising, and going into ecstasies about the beauty of the morning; which is just such another as we have had ever since we have been here; all the difference being in his feelings, which happen to be a shade or two less doleful than usual, and so cause things to look brighter."

"Perhaps you would have me believe," answered Browne, "that the sun will invariably shine when I chance to be in good spirits, and that a thunderstorm would be the natural consequence of my having a fit of the blues?"

"I should be sorry if that were the case," replied Max, "as we should then be sure to have a large average of bad weather."

"This excursion reminds me of our school-days," said Arthur; "it almost seems as though we were once more starting off together, on one of our Saturday rambles, as we have so often done on fine summer and autumn mornings at home."

"I think I shall never forget those forays through the woods," said Morton, "over hill and hollow, in search of nuts, or berries, or wild-grapes, or meadow-plums—the fishing and swimming in summer, the snowballing, and sledding, and skating, in winter! an innocent and happy set of urchins we were then!"

"Really," said Max, laughing, "to hear you one would suppose that we were now a conclave of venerable, grey-haired sages, scarcely able to remember the time when we were children, and so full of wisdom and experience, that we had long ago ceased to be 'innocent and happy.'"

"Without professing to be so wise or experienced, as to be very unhappy on that account," returned Morton, "I suppose I may say that I am old enough, and sufficiently changed since those days, to feel, as I now look back upon them with a sigh, their peculiar happiness, so unlike any thing that after-life affords."

"How singular it is," said Browne, "that you four who were playmates when children, should have happened to keep together so long."

"And still find ourselves together on an island in the Pacific Ocean, thousands of miles from home," added Arthur.

"After quitting school," continued Browne, "I never met with any of my comrades there. Of all the mates with whom I used on the Saturday half-holydays, to go gathering hips and haws, or angling in the Clyde, I have not since come in contact with one."

"It don't seem at all like Saturday to me," said Johnny, who for some minutes past had appeared to have something on his mind, as to the expediency of communicating which he was undecided; "I was afraid that it was Sunday, every thing is so still; but I hope it is not, for Arthur would not think it right to start upon an exploring expedition on Sunday, and so it would be put off."

"Truly," said Browne, "that is extremely flattering to the rest of us. Do you think we are all heathens, except Arthur? I, for one, have no notion of becoming a savage, because I am on a desert island; I shall go for maintaining the decencies of Christianity and civilisation."

"Does any one know what day it really is?" inquired Morton.

Max said he believed it was Monday. Arthur thought it was Wednesday, and added that he had memoranda, from which he had no doubt he could fix the day with certainty.

"It was on Friday," said Max, "that the mutiny took place, and that we got to sea in the boat."

"Yes," said Arthur, "and it was on Wednesday night, I think, five days afterwards, that we landed here."

"Five days!" cried Max. "Do you mean to say that we were but five days at sea before reaching the island?"

"I think that is all," replied Arthur, "though the time certainly seems much longer. Then, if my calculations are correct, we have been here just two weeks to-day, so that this is Wednesday. But," continued he, "as our heavenly Father has thus guided our little bark safe through this wilderness of waters, let us celebrate the day of our landing on this 'Canaan,' by making it our first Sabbath, and our grateful voices shall every seventh day, from this, be lifted up in praise and thanksgiving for the mercy thus vouchsafed to us."

While this conversation was going on, we reached the shore. Johnny scrambled eagerly to the bow, anxious to be the first to land, and he attained this object of his ambition, by jumping into the water nearly up to his waist, before the boat was fairly beached. Then, after gazing around him a moment with exclamations of wonder and admiration, he suddenly commenced running up and down the wide, firm beach, gathering shells, with as much zeal and earnestness, as though he was spending a holiday by the sea-side at home, and could tie up these pretty curiosities in his handkerchief, and run back with them in five minutes to his father's house. There was certainly some ground for Johnny's admiration; just at the spot where we had landed, the shore was thickly strewn, in a manner which I had never before seen equalled, with varieties of the most curious and beautiful shells. They were of all sizes, and of every conceivable shape and colour. The surfaces of some were smooth and highly polished; others were scolloped, or fluted, or marked with wave-like undulations. There were little rice and cowrie shells;

mottled tiger shells; spider shells, with their long, sharp spikes; immense conches, rough, and covered with great knobs on the outside, but smooth and rose-lipped within, and of many delicate hues. There were some that resembled gigantic snail shells, and others shaped like the cornucopias, used to hold sugar-plums for children. One species, the most remarkable of all, was composed of a substance, resembling mother-of-pearl, exquisitely beautiful, but very fragile, breaking easily, if you but set foot on one of them: they were changeable in colour, being of a dazzling white, a pearly blue, or a delicate pale green, as viewed in different lights. Scattered here and there, among these deserted tenements of various kinds of shell-fish, were the beautiful exuviae and skeletons of star-fish, and sea-eggs; while in the shallow water, numerous living specimens could be seen moving lazily about. Among these last, I noticed a couple of sea-porcupines, bristling with their long, fine, flexible quills, and an enormous conch crawling along the bottom with his house on his back, the locomotive power being entirely out of sight.

Johnny seemed for the moment to have forgotten every thing else, in the contemplation of these treasures; and it was not until Arthur reminded him that there was no one to remove or appropriate them, and that he could get as many as he wanted at any time, that he desisted from his work, and reluctantly consented to postpone making a collection for the present.

Having drawn the boat high up on the beach, and armed ourselves with a cutlass apiece, (Johnny taking possession of the longest one of the lot), we commenced our march along the shore, to the right, without further delay.

We had by this time scarcely a remaining doubt that the island was uninhabited. No palm-thatched huts occupied the open spaces, or crowned the little eminences that diversified its windward side; no wreaths of smoke could be seen rising above the tops of the groves; no canoes, full of tattooed savages, glided over the still waters within the reef; and no merry troops of bathers pursued their sports in the surf. There was nothing to impart life and animation to the scene, but the varied evolutions of the myriads of sea-fowl, continually swooping, and screaming around us. With this exception, a silence like that of the first Sabbath brooded over the island, which appeared as fresh, and as free from every trace of the presence of man, as if it had newly sprung into existence.

With the continued absence of every indication of inhabitants our feeling of security had increased to such an extent, that even Johnny ventured sometimes to straggle behind, or to run on before, and occasionally made a hasty incursion into the borders of the grove, though he took care never to be far out of sight or hearing of the main body. Soon after starting, we doubled a projecting promontory, and lost sight of the boat and the islet. The reef bent round to the north, preserving nearly a uniform distance from the shore, and was without any break or opening.

The forest in most places, extended nearly to the beach, and was composed chiefly of hibiscus, pandanus, and cocoa-nut trees, with here and there a large pisonia, close to the lagoon. One gigantic specimen of this last species, which we stopped a moment to admire, could not have been less than twenty feet in girth. Max, Morton, Arthur, and myself, could not quite span it, taking hold of hands, and Johnny had to join the ring, to make it complete. For several hours we continued our journey pretty steadily, encountering no living thing, except tern, gannets, and other sea-birds, and one troop of gaudy little paroquets, glittering in green, and orange, and crimson. These paroquets were the only land-birds we saw during the day. Max pronounced them "frights," because of their large hooked bills, and harsh discordant cries. They certainly gave Johnny, a terrible "fright," and indeed startled us all a little, by suddenly taking wing, with loud, hoarse screams, from a hibiscus, beneath which we were resting, without having observed that they were perched over our heads.

When it was near noon, and we had travelled, as we supposed, making allowance for delays and deviations, some six or eight miles, the character of the shore suddenly changed. The white, shelving beach, and the dense groves meeting it near the water, now disappeared, and were succeeded by an open strip of land, bordering the lagoon, strewed with huge, irregular fragments of coral rock, and seamed with gullies. The line of the forest here receded some distance from the shore, leaving a broad rounded point, embracing a large area of low and barren ground, covered thinly with a growth of stunted shrubs, and a few straggling, solitary looking trees. The lagoon was at this point quite shallow, and low rocks and coral patches appeared above the surface, at short distances apart, nearly to the centre of the channel. The reef opposite, was entirely under water, and its position was indicated only by a line of breakers. A large portion of the point, comprising several acres, was covered with the rude nests of various aquatic birds.

Many of these nests were occupied even at that hour, and the birds seemed in no wise alarmed, or even disturbed by our approach. When we came very close to any of them, they would survey us with an air half angry, and half inquisitive, stretching out their long necks; and screwing their heads from side to side, so as to obtain a view of us first with one eye, and then with the other; this seeming to be considered indispensable to a complete and satisfactory understanding of our character and intentions. After a thorough scrutiny, they would resume their former appearance of stupid indifference, as though we were creatures altogether too unimportant to merit further notice. They all, without exception, seemed perfectly tame and fearless, and quite ready to resent any infringement upon their rights.

Johnny, while inspecting too closely the nest of one of them, curiously constructed of long stiff reeds, resembling rods of steel, suddenly received, as a rebuke for his impertinence, a blow from the wing of the offended owner, which laid him sprawling upon his back.

Notwithstanding this severe lesson, the gentle and amiable aspect of a large white bird, so far reassured him, that he ventured to make some friendly advances, whereupon he got so severely pecked, that he at once gave up all further attempts at familiarity with any of them. This harsh treatment, in fact, so disgusted Johnny with the whole race of sea-birds, and so impaired his faith in their innocent and inoffensive looks, that he declared he would never have any thing more to do with them, "since that beautiful white bird had bitten him so savagely, when he only offered to stroke its neck."

Some of these birds were very large and strong: in several of the unoccupied nests I saw eggs, as large as those of the duck: they were of different colours some of them prettily speckled or mottled, but most were of an ash colour, or a whitish brown. Eiulo pointed out two kinds, which he said were highly prized for food, and which, as we afterwards found, were, in fact, nearly equal to the eggs of the domestic duck.

The heat had by this time become exceedingly uncomfortable, and we concluded to halt until it should abate a little, at the first convenient and pleasant spot. Leaving the shore, which, besides being unsheltered from the sun, was so rugged with crevices and gullies, and great irregular blocks of coral, as to be almost impassable, we entered the borders of the wood, and took a short cut across the point. Johnny, in imitation of the desert islanders of the story-books, desired to give appropriate names to all the interesting or remarkable localities with which we became acquainted. He had already christened the little island on which we had first landed, "Palm-Islet," and the spot upon the opposite shore, abounding in brilliant shells, had, from that circumstance, received the impromptu name of "Pearl-shell Beach." He now proposed to call the point, "Cape Desolation," from its waste and forbidding aspect; but finally fixed upon "Sea-bird's Point," as being more appropriate, the birds having, in fact, taken possession of nearly its entire area, which, judging from the warlike spirit they had displayed, they were likely to hold against all comers. Having crossed the point and reached the lagoon again, we found that the shore resumed its former character. The forest again extended nearly to the beach, but it was more open, and not so thickly wooded as before, and the trees were of a finer growth, and in much greater variety; many of them being of kinds unknown to any of us. We had not proceeded far, after regaining the beach, when we espied just such a resting-place as we were in search of.

Chapter Fourteen
Castle-Hill

The Noonday Halt—A Charming Resting-Place—Heathen Skill versus Civilisation and the Story-Books

"Beneath the tropic rays,
Where not a shadow breaks the boundless blaze,
Earth from her lap perennial verdure pours,
Ambrosial fruits, and amaranthine flowers."

A little way before us rose a smooth and gentle acclivity, crowned by a clump of majestic trees, which promised to afford a deeper and more grateful shade than any other spot in sight, and we accordingly made towards it. On a nearer approach it proved to be more elevated than had at first appeared, and in order to reach the top, we were obliged to scale a long series of natural terraces, almost as regular as though they had been the work of art. From this spot there was a fine view of the shore, the lagoon, and the ocean, to the north and west. The trees that covered the level space at the summit of the ascent, were varieties of a much larger growth than those generally found on the low alluvial strip of land bordering the lagoon. Conspicuous among them, were the majestic candle-nut, with its white leaves and orange-coloured blossoms; the inocarpus, a kind of tropical chestnut; and most magnificent and imposing of all, a stately tree, resembling the magnolia in its foliage and manner of growth, and thickly covered with large white flowers, edged with a delicate pink. The ground was level as a parlour floor, and free from brushwood or undergrowth of any kind, except a few long-leaved, fragrant ferns, and in places a thick carpet of flowering vines and creepers. The trees were stationed at such distances apart, as to compose a fine open grove, and yet close enough to unite in one rich mass of foliage overhead, impenetrable to the rays of the sun, and creating a sombre and almost gloomy shade, even during the fiercest glare of noonday. In one spot, a number of gigantic trees were grouped nearly in a circle. Their dense tops formed a leafy dome, through which not the smallest patch of sky was visible. Around their huge, but shapely, stems, which one might look upon as forming the pillars of a natural temple, a number of flowering parasites twined in luxuriant wreaths, and hung in festoons from the tower branches. A considerable space around the boles of some of these trees was completely covered by an elegant species of creeping plant with fine cut foliage of a delicate pea-green, and large clusters of scarlet blossoms, about which, swarms of brilliantly-coloured insects, of the butterfly tribe, were hovering.

"Here we may actually, and not figuratively, indulge in the luxury of 'reposing on the beds of flowers,'" said Max, throwing himself down at the foot of a towering candle-nut, amid a soft mass of this vegetable carpeting. All were sufficiently tired by the long march of the morning, to appreciate the luxury, and our entire company was soon stretched upon the ground, in attitudes in which comfort rather than grace, was consulted.

"What do you think of this, Johnny?" said Max, "it strikes me, as being quite romantic and like the story-books—almost up to the Arabian Nights. If the history of our adventures should ever be written, (and why shouldn't it be?) here's material for a *flowery* passage. Just see how this would sound, for instance:— 'And now our little band of toil-worn castaways,' (that's us), 'weary and faint with their wanderings through the desert, (that's Cape Desolation, or Sea-bird's Point, or whatever Johnny in his wisdom shall conclude to call it), arrived at a little oasis, (this is it), a green spot in the wilderness, blooming like the bowers of Paradise, where stretched at ease, upon beds of bright and odoriferous flowers, they reposed from the fatigues of their journey.' There, that sentence, I flatter myself is equal in harmony and effect, to the opening one in the history of Rasselas, Prince of Abyssinia—there's my idea of the style in which our adventures should be recorded."

As we had taken no refreshment since setting out in the morning, we now began to feel the need of it. At the edge of the eminence, on the southern side, grew several large cocoa-nut trees, fully three feet in diameter at the base, and rising to the height of seventy or eighty feet at the very least. Eiulo was the only one of our number, who would have dreamed of undertaking to climb either of them; he, however, after finding a young purau, and providing himself with a strip of the bark, fastened the ends about his ankles, and then firmly clasping the trunk of one of the trees with his hands and feet alternately, the latter being as wide apart as the ligature would permit, he vaulted rapidly and easily upward, and soon gained the dizzy height where the nuts grew. Once fairly perched in the tuft of the tree among the stems of the enormous leaves, where he looked scarcely larger than a monkey, he quickly supplied us with as many cocoa-nuts as we could put to present use. Loading ourselves with the fruit, we returned to our first resting-place, and after piling the nuts in a heap, reclined around it, after the manner of the ancients at their banquets, while we enjoyed our repast. Though all these nuts were gathered from the same tree, and, in fact, from the same cluster, some of them contained nothing but liquid, the kernel not having yet begun to form, and in these the milk was most abundant and delicious: in others, a soft, jelly-like, transparent pulp, delicate and well-flavoured, had commenced forming on the inner shell: in others, again, this pulp had become thicker and firmer, and more like the kernel of the imported nut, the milk having diminished in quantity, and lost in a great measure its agreeable taste.

Johnny, after having tried all the different varieties with the zeal of an epicure, declared that he was beginning to get sick of cocoa-nuts: he wondered whether we should have to live entirely on cocoa-nuts and shell-fish, and whether there was not some bread-fruit on the island.

"If there is," said Browne, "it will be of no use to us, unless we can find means to make a fire, and cook it."

"Make a fire!" cried Johnny, "that's easy enough—all we've got to do, is just to get two dry sticks and rub them together briskly for a few minutes. None of the shipwrecked people I ever read of, had any trouble about that."

"How lucky we are," cried Max, gravely, "in having some one with us, who has read all about all the desert islanders that have ever lived, and can tell us just what to do in an emergency! Please get a couple of those dry sticks which you speak of, Johnny, and show us how unfortunate castaways in our condition, are accustomed to kindle a fire."

Without seeming, in the simplicity of his heart, to suspect for a moment the perfect good faith and sincerity of Max's compliment, Johnny commenced casting about for some sticks or pieces of wood, with which to make the experiment. He soon found a fallen branch of the inocarpus, well baked by the sun, and which had long lost every particle of moisture. Breaking it into two pieces, he began to rub them together with great zeal, and apparently with perfect faith in the result: gradually he increased his exertions, manifesting a commendable perseverance, until the bark began to fly, and the perspiration to stream down his face; but still there was no fire nor any sign of it.

Meantime, Max encouraged him to proceed.

"Keep it a-going, Johnny!" he cried, "if you stop for half a second, you lose all your labour; only persevere, and you're sure to succeed; none of the shipwrecked people you ever read of had any trouble about it, you know."

But Johnny concluded that the sticks could not be of the right kind, and notwithstanding Max's exhortations, he at last gave up the attempt.

Morton, however, not discouraged by this unfortunate result, nor by Max's disposition to make fun of the experiment expressed a belief that the thing could be done, and after preparing the sticks by cutting away one of the rounded sides of each, he went to work with an earnestness and deliberation, that caused us to augur favourably of his success. After nearly ten minutes powerful and incessant friction, the sticks began to smoke, and Johnny, tossing his cap into the air, gave an exulting "Hurrah!"

But his rejoicing proved premature, for, though the wood fairly smoked, that was the utmost that could be attained, and Morton was obliged to desist, without having produced a flame.

Eiulo had been watching these proceedings with great interest; and he now intimated by signs that he would make a trial. Taking the sticks, he cut one of them to a point, with Arthur's knife, and made a small groove along the flat surface of the other, which he then placed with one end upon the ground, and the other against his breast, the grooved side being upwards. Placing the point of the first stick in the groove, he commenced moving it up and down along the second, pressing them hard together. The motion was at first slow and regular, but increased constantly in rapidity. By-and-bye the wood began to smoke again, and then Eiulo continued the operation with greater vigour than ever. At length a fine dust, which had collected at the lower extremity of the groove, actually took fire; Arthur quickly inserted the edge of a sun-dried cocoa-nut leaf in the tiny flame, and it was instantly in a blaze.

"Bravo!" shouted Max, "that's what I consider a decided triumph of heathenism over civilisation, and the story-books."

Morton now seized the sticks again, and imitating Eiulo's method of proceeding, succeeded in kindling them, though it took him a considerable time to do it: thus it was satisfactorily established, by actual experiment, that we could obtain a fire whenever we should want one.

The question was now raised, whether we should continue our exploration further that day, or remain where we were until the following morning; and as the heat was still very oppressive, and we were sufficiently tired already, the latter course was unanimously determined upon.

Johnny liked the spot which we occupied so well, that he proposed "building a hut" upon it, and making it our head-quarters, as long as we should have to stay on the island. It was certainly a pleasant site; and, commanding as it did a wide view of the ocean, vessels could be descried at a greater distance, and signalled with a surer prospect of attracting notice, than from any other locality yet known to us. From the wooded summit, the land descended on every side—towards the shore in a series of terraces—

towards the interior in one smooth and continuous slope, after which it again rose in a succession of densely wooded eminences, irregular and picturesque in their outlines, and each higher than the last as you proceeded inland; the farthest of them towering up in strong relief against the south-eastern sky. The various shades of the masses of different kinds of foliage with which these heights were clothed, from that of the pale-leaved candle-nut, to the sombre green of the bread-fruit groves, contributed greatly to the pleasing effect of the landscape. On the right, as you looked towards the ocean, lay the flat tract, occupied by the sea-fowl, and which Johnny had named after them. At nearly an equal distance on the left, the line of the beach was broken, by what appeared to be a small grove, or clump of trees, detached from the main forest, and planted directly on the line of the shore.

As we had concluded to suspend our explorations until the next day, every one was left to his own resources for the remainder of the afternoon. Johnny having set Morton at work, to make him a bow, "to shoot birds with," began to occupy himself in the very important task of finding an appropriate name for the height, which he finally concluded to call "Castle-Hill," from its regular shape and bold steep outlines. Max extended himself on his back in the coolest nook he could find, and spreading his handkerchief over his face, to protect it from the gaudy, but troublesome, winged insects which haunted the spot, forbade any one to disturb him on pain of his high displeasure. Arthur, taking Eiulo with him, proceeded upon a botanising tour about the neighbourhood, in the hope of making some discovery that might prove useful to us. For my own part, happening to think of the question which had been started in the morning, as to the day of the week, I began to make a retrospect of all that had taken place since the fearful night of the mutiny, and to endeavour to fix the order of subsequent events, so as to arrive at the number of days we had been at sea, and upon the island. In the course of these calculations, and while Browne and myself were discussing the matter, he suggested the want of pencil and paper. I found that the last leaf had been torn from my pocket-book, and the rest were in an equally destitute condition. In this strait, I remembered having heard Arthur describe the manner in which the native children had been taught to write in the missionary schools at Eimeo, the only materials used being plantain leaves and a pointed stick. I mentioned this to Browne, and we forthwith proceeded to experiment with different kinds of leaves, until at last we found a large heart-shaped one, which answered our purpose admirably; it was white, and soft as velvet on the under side, and marks made upon it with the rounded point of a small stick, were perfectly distinct, showing of a dark green colour upon a white ground.

Late in the afternoon, Arthur and Eiulo returned from their tour of examination, having made, as Arthur intimated, some discoveries, of which, in due time, we should all reap the benefit. Morton having found a tough and elastic kind of wood, had shaped a tolerable bow for Johnny, when it came to providing a string, the resources of both failed. The difficulty being made known to Eiulo, he volunteered to supply what was wanted, and went with Johnny and Morton into the adjoining forest to look for a certain kind of bark, from which to make the required cord.

"There!" said Arthur, when we were left alone together; "how capitally this excursion has worked. How differently things seem from what they did yesterday, when we were at the islet perfectly stagnant and stupid. One would not take us for the same people. Only let us always have something to do, something to interest and busy ourselves about, and we need not be very miserable, even on a desert island."

Chapter Fifteen
Camping Out

A Desperate Engagement—Johnny Discovers an "Oyster
Tree"—Vagrants, or Kings?—A Sleeping Prescription

"Travellers ne'er did lie,
Though fools at home condemn them: If in Naples,
I should report this now, would they believe me?"

About sunset we went down to the beach to bathe. The trees along the
shore were occupied by immense crowds of exemplary sea-fowl, whose
regular and primitive habits of life had sent them to roost at this early hour.
Notwithstanding their webbed feet, they managed to perch securely among
the branches, many of which were so heavily freighted, that they bent
almost to the ground beneath their load.

Finding a spot where the beach shelved off gradually into deep water,
with a smooth, firm bottom, free from shells and corallines, we had a
refreshing swim. Afterwards, strolling along the shore by myself, I found
a large fish, beautifully marked with alternate black and yellow bands, in a
shallow, fenced off from the lagoon at low water, by a coral ridge. The too
eager pursuit of some of the smaller tribe of fishes, had probably beguiled
him into this trap, where he had been left by the tide, to fall a victim, as
I confidently reckoned, to his own rapacity. All escape into deep water
seemed to be pretty effectually cut off and I looked upon him as already
the captive of my bow and spear; but fearing lest some of the others should
come up to share the glory of securing so splendid a prize, I forthwith set
about effecting his actual capture. Rolling my trowsers above my knees, I
waded into the water to drive him ashore; but I soon found that my task was
not going to prove by any means as easy as I had anticipated. My intended

victim was exceedingly vigorous and active, and as ferocious as a pike. He obstinately refused to be driven at all, and struggled and floundered as desperately as if he already had a vivid presentiment of the frying-pan, snapping viciously at my fingers whenever I undertook to lay hold of him. To add to the aggravating features of the case, he seemed to bristle all over with an inordinate and unreasonable quantity of sharp-pointed fins and spines, which must have been designed by nature as weapons of defence, since there were certainly more of them than any fish could use to advantage for swimming purposes. I began to suspect that I had caught a Tartar; but I had now gone too far to back out with credit: my self-respect wouldn't admit of the thought. So, taking a short breathing spell, I again advanced to the attack, somewhat encouraged by perceiving that my scaly antagonist seemed exhausted and distressed by his recent exertions. His mouth was wide open, and his gills quivered; but I was rather uncertain whether to regard this as a hostile demonstration, or a sign of pain and fatigue. However, at it we went; and, after getting my hands badly cut by some of the aforesaid bristling spines and fins, besides being drenched with water, and plastered all over with wet sand, which he splashed about in the struggle, I succeeded in seizing him firmly by the tail, and throwing him high and dry upon the beach. I then scooped out a hollow in the sand, a little above the tide-mark, and filling it with water, pushed him into it, thus securing him for the present.

Max, Morton, and Browne, who had been practising climbing cocoa-nut trees, at the edge of the wood, with very indifferent success, had witnessed, from a distance, the latter part of the "engagement," as Max facetiously called it; and they now came up to learn the particulars, and to inquire "whether it was a shark, or a young whale, that I had been having such a terrible time with." While they were admiring my captive, and jocosely condoling with me on the hard usage which I had received, the voice of Johnny, (who, accompanied by Eiulo, had ventured to stroll off in the direction of the point), was heard, raised to its highest pitch, as he shouted for us to "come and see something strange." But it seemed that his impatience would not permit him to await the result of his summons, for the next moment he came running towards us in a state of great excitement, and all out of breath, crying out that he had "found a tree covered with oysters," and he had no doubt, there were "lots more of them."

"A tree covered with *what*?" inquired Browne, dubiously.

"With oysters—with fine, large oysters!" cried Johnny, "just come and see for yourselves."

"Wonderful island! productive soil!" exclaimed Max, in mock admiration. "If oysters will take root, and grow here, I suppose pretty much any thing will: I believe I will plant my boots to-morrow: they may do for seed, and are good for nothing else any longer—don't you begin to think this must be an enchanted island, Johnny?"

"O, you may make fun of it, if you please; but it's true: and if you'll come with me, I'll shew you the trees."

"Well," said Browne, "I am ready for almost any thing in the way of the marvellous, since having seen a solid and substantial-looking island turn into a vapour, and vanish away before my very eyes. I shall be careful about doubting any thing, until I get back to some Christian country, where things go on regularly. For the present, I am in state of mind to believe in phoenixes and unicorns—and why not in oyster-trees? Who knows but we have happened upon a second Prospero's isle? Lead on, Johnny, and bring us to this wonderful tree." And Johnny started off accordingly, followed by Browne and Morton.

In a moment the latter was heard calling out, "I say, Max! do you understand conchology?"

"Yes, enough to tell a bivalve when I see one: should like to have a 'dozen fried' before me now."

"If a 'dozen raw' will answer, just step this way, and we'll accommodate you equal to Florence."

On hastening to the spot, all scepticism as to the "oysters growing on trees," was speedily removed. A row of mangroves lined the shore for some distance, each elevated upon its white pile of protruding and intertwisted roots. Attached to the branches of these trees, which overhung the water and drooped into it at high tide, were abundance of fair-sized oysters. Looking down into the water beneath the mangroves, I perceived the certain indications of an extensive and well-stocked oyster-bed. The bottom was thickly covered with them, in every stage of growth multitudes being scarcely larger than a sixpence. I could also see, through the shallow water, an immense number of little white specks, like drops of spermaceti, scattered about among them. It was evident, that here was an abundant and unfailing supply of these delicious shell-fish.

"With one impulse we kneeled down."

Browne broke off from one of the trees a large branch, having half a dozen oysters attached to it, with which he hastened to confront the unbelieving Max, and flourishing it in his face, demanded to know if he was "convinced now." Although constrained to admit that they *looked* very like oysters, Max seemed to consider the evidence of more than one of the senses necessary to afford satisfactory proof of so extraordinary a phenomenon, and accordingly proceeded to see how they tasted.

After opening one of the largest, (using his cutlass as an oyster-knife), and making the experiment with due deliberation, he announced himself perfectly satisfied.

By the time we had all sufficiently tasted the quality of the oysters, (which were really very good, and well-flavoured, notwithstanding the unusual position in which they were discovered), it had become quite dark. Though the evening was fine, there was not much light, the moon and stars glimmering faintly through a soft purple haze, which, as I had observed since we had been on the island, generally seemed to fill the atmosphere for a short time after sunset, and at a little later hour entirely disappeared. As we strolled back towards the foot of "Castle-Hill," Johnny suddenly looked up, and inquired, as if the thought had just occurred to him, where we were going to sleep.

"That's a pretty question to ask," said Browne, laughing, "it implies that we are common vagrants."

"So we are, strictly speaking," answered Max, "we have no regular means of living, and no fixed place of abode, and that I believe, makes us common vagrants, according to Webster."

"I should think our means of living were 'regular' enough to rescue us from the definition," replied Morton, "having been thus far, cocoa-nuts and mussels every day, and all day long, and nothing but cocoa-nuts and mussels. I am glad that there is now some prospect of a little more irregularity in future."

"As to our having no fixed habitation or place of abode," said Browne, "that does not arise from poverty, or lack of land—'the isle is all before us where to choose'—and we are now on a tour of observation through our extensive domains, in order to decide upon the finest spot for our head-quarters. Meantime, for a night or two, we shall have to be satisfied with 'a tent in the green wood, a home in the grove,' in other words, we shall have to 'camp out,' as the most renowned hunters and soldiers have frequently done before us. I'm sure there's no vagrancy in that."

"Why," cried Johnny, forgetting for the moment his anxiety on the score of our quarters for the night, "we are no more vagrants than Robinson Crusoe was:—

"'We are monarchs of all we survey,
And our realm there is none to dispute,'

"As he says of himself so that we are much more like kings than vagrants."

"And the sea-birds and fishes," said Max, "are to be considered as our subjects, I presume, since we have no man Friday, and no goats or poll-parrots to reign over."

"Yes," said Johnny, "I suppose so; there are enough of them too."

"And some very disloyal, rebellious, and stiff-necked ones among them," added Max, "who ought to be dealt with as traitors forthwith—that sturdy feathered rebel for instance, who not regarding the inviolability of the royal person, no longer ago than this morning laid one of our royal majesties sprawling upon his royal back."

"And that other scaly traitor," added Browne, "who perversely refused to come out of the water to be cooked, in accordance with the royal will, and who nearly bit off the sacred thumb of one of our majesties, in resisting the royal authority."

"Well, Johnny," said Max, "if we are not actually kings, we at any rate have some royal blood upon the island. Not to speak of myself, who am descended direct from 'Kaiser Maximilien,' here is Eiulo, who is a real prince, his father being King of the Cannibal Islands, or some other islands in these seas."

"I wish you wouldn't speak so of Eiulo's father," said Johnny, warmly, "he is not a cannibal, and I believe he is a very good man; I think his islands are near here, and if we should one day get there, he would treat us kindly, and let us go home whenever we should have an opportunity."

"Hilloa!" cried Max, "what has put all that into your head? What do you know about Eiulo's father, or his islands, or where they are?"

This sudden outburst of Johnny's surprised us all, with perhaps the exception of Arthur, and we listened with some interest, as he replied to Max's volley of questions.

"Oh, I have talked with Eiulo about it," he answered, "mostly by signs; and he has made me understand that he believes his home is not far distant—off in that direction, (pointing north), and that ships sometimes stop there; and so I have been thinking that if we could only find the way there, we should have some prospect of getting home at last."

Upon this we became silent and thoughtful; nothing further was said, until Johnny recurred to the question which he had started a few moments before, and again asked where we proposed to pass the night.

"Not in those gloomy woods, I hope," said he, "where it is so lonely, and the wind and the trees make such strange noises. I would rather sleep down here upon the shore; this nice dry, white sand, up where the water never comes, will make a very good bed."

Thus far, we had passed every night upon the islet, to which we had now become familiarised and accustomed. Its small extent, and separation from the mainland, gave it an air of security, which made us feel more at our ease there at night, than we could among the sombre and unexplored forests of the larger island, about which we as yet knew so little. Johnny's timidity was not therefore unnatural. Indeed, unless I am mistaken, none of us was, on this first night of our exploration, entirely free from a vague spirit of insecurity, and of liability to some unknown danger.

"That will hardly do, Johnny," said Browne, in answer to his suggestion about taking up our quarters for the night upon the shore, "a heap of dry pandanus leaves will make a much more comfortable bed than the hard sand. Thus I propose to arrange it—we will go up to the top of the hill where we rested to-day, and lodge there; our beds of leaves shall be all in a circle, and Johnny's shall be in the middle; and then he won't feel lonesome or afraid, for all the uncanny noises of the wind and the trees; knowing that he has good friends and true all around him, and particularly one stout John Browne, who is worth all the rest together, being a fair match for any thing in this part of the South-Seas!" and by way of raising Johnny's spirits, and inspiring him with the greater confidence in the prowess of his protector, he flourished his cutlass, and went scientifically through the broad-sword exercise, slashing and carving away at his imaginary antagonist, with a fierceness and vigour wonderful to behold, having lopped off an indefinite quantity of airy heads and limbs, be finished, by reciting with a bold and warlike air—

"Scots wha hae wi' Wallace bled!
Scots wham Bruce has aften led!" etcetera.

This demonstration seemed to produce the desired effect and Johnny soon became reassured, and quite reconciled to "camping out" in the woods.

The evening was so fine, and the gentle breeze setting in from the ocean was so cool and grateful, after the excessive heat of the day, that we continued for some time loitering along the shore. The sea was highly phosphorescent; that is, during the earlier part of the evening, and before the mist or haze before spoken of cleared up. The tiny wavelets, as they rippled upon the beach in rapid succession, sparkled with phosphoric fire, and out in the lagoon, wherever a coral patch rose to the surface, or the water was disturbed by any floating object, it gave forth a clear and brilliant light, and was studded by myriads of fiery dots and spangles.

At length Johnny began to complain of weariness, and we scaled the terraced hill, and gathering a large quantity of clean and well-dried leaves, arranged our beds as Browne had suggested, beneath the group of noble trees where we had taken our siesta at noon.

The novelty of our situation, long proved with me an effectual antidote to fatigue and drowsiness, and I lay looking up at the moon glimmering through the foliage of the trees, an hour after the rest seemed to be asleep.

Just as I was at last sinking into unconsciousness, Johnny, sitting up among the leaves in which he was half buried, inquired softly, "Max, are you awake!" I spoke to him, to let him know that he was not alone. "I can't get asleep," said he, "every thing looks so beautiful and so strange. It seems to me I never saw the moon and the stars so big and so bright."

"You must keep your eyes shut, and not look at the moon, if you want to get asleep."

"But the trees keep rustling so; just as if they were whispering softly to one another; and then the sound of the waves on the reef is so sad and mournful, that it sets me to thinking all sorts of strange things. I wonder whether there are any wild animals on the island!" I assured him that it was quite improbable, and that no dangerous animals of any kind were ever found on the islands of the Pacific. This, however, did not seem to satisfy him entirely, and I began to suspect that his mind was running on the jackalls, tiger-cats, and hyenas of the Swiss Family Robinson. A question or two which he presently asked, showed that I had guessed correctly, and I hastened to meet the difficulty, by reminding him that "their island, (if indeed it was an island at all, and not a part of the mainland), was situated near the coast of New Holland, from which animals might pass over to it by swimming."

"Why, I thought," said Johnny, "that there were no wild animals in New Holland, except kangaroos and opossums: my book of beasts, birds, and fishes, says so."

This was a fact in Natural History which I was not prepared to gainsay; especially when backed by so redoubtable an authority as "the book of beasts, birds, and fishes." For a moment I was taken all aback; but being loathe to give up my little companion a prey to imaginary jackalls, tiger-cats, and hyenas, I rallied again, resolved upon one more desperate effort for his deliverance.

"Well," said I, "the fact is, we don't know exactly where the Swiss Family Robinson's island really was—it is altogether uncertain. It may have been near Java, or Ceylon, or the coast of India, in which case, all those Asiatic beasts could easily have got there—that is, if the two places were close enough together. Now we know that we are somewhere in the middle of the Pacific, a vast distance from any continent, or any of the great Indian islands, so that large animals here are out of the question, unless they have taken a swim of a thousand miles or so."

This seemed to be pretty decisive; and I think it settled the jackalls, tiger-cats, and hyenas, effectually, for Johnny said no more on the subject, except to remark, that, even if they *could* swim that distance, they would stand a bad chance with the sharks and other sea-monsters; to which I added, as a final clincher, that in any event they would be sure to starve on the voyage, unless they should bring a large supply of provisions along. "Well," said he, after a minute's silence, "I'm not afraid of anything; but somehow or other I feel very wide awake to-night, and not in the least sleepy."

"Shut your eyes," said I, "and think of a great wheel, whirling round and round, with a regular and even motion, and never stopping, until you have counted it go round a hundred times."

Johnny laughed softly to himself, as though pleased with this device, and was quite still for a minute or two; then he spoke again.

"It has gone round a hundred times, but towards the end it got a-going dreadfully fast; it *would* go fast in spite of all I could do."

"Never mind the wheel, then," said I, "but think of the huge lazy swells in a calm, rising and falling, rising and falling, as they did when we lay rocking in the boat, all those long days and nights, out on the sea."

"Well, I'll try—but I don't believe it will be of any use."

"Don't look at the moon, and don't speak to me again—unless for something very particular—and now good night."

"Good night!" and he nestled down among his leaves again. In a very few minutes the deep and regular breathing of the little patient, proved the efficacy of my sleeping prescription, and announced that his troubles for that night were over.

Chapter Sixteen
Domestic Embarrassments

A Desert Island Breakfast—Persuasive Reasoning—
Romance and Reality—The Prince and Princess

"Now my co-mates, and brothers in exile,

Ha

Th

Mc

He

Th

An

The ne: ere stirring
early; and g my eyes,
was a busy ered round
a fire at a l interesting
operation. ory organs,
and on ap atter more
closely, I f dergoing a
somewhat be the chief
director an so roasting
in the emb appetising
odour refe

"Good arly ready;
and a breal a course of
cocoa-nut (is eyes will
open—to s. e of thanks
for our earl

The Island Breakfast.—'

The Island Home | 113

Morton and Browne at this moment emerged from their respective heaps of leaves, and, after rather more than the usual amount of yawning and stretching of limbs, came towards the fire.

"Fee, faw, fo, fum!" cried Morton, snuffing the agreeable smell of the cookery in progress, "I trust we're not too late for breakfast, and that there is something more than the savour of good victuals left."

"You are in good time," said Johnny, bustling about the fire with an air of official dignity, "the first bell hasn't rung yet."

"But why has Shakespeare such a long face?" said Max; "has camping out caused a reminiscence of rheumatism!"

"Bad dreams, horrible dreams!" answered Browne, shaking his head solemnly, "which came of lying staring at the moon last night, until I fell asleep:" — then throwing himself into an attitude, he commenced declaiming with a tragic air —

> "'O, I have passed a miserable night,
> So full of fearful dreams, of ugly sights,
> That as I am a Christian, faithful man,
> I would not pass another such a night
> Though 'twere to buy a world of happy days,
> So full of dismal terror was the time.'"

"Bravo!" cried Max, applauding furiously, "I like to see that; it's what I call coming out strong under discouraging circumstances. Here are we, six forlorn castaways, on a desert island, somewhere, (no one knows where), in the Pacific Ocean; and, instead of moping, and sulking, and bemoaning our hard fate, we wake up of a fine morning, quite bright and cheerful, and one of the six, (or seven, more correctly speaking), goes to work spouting Shakespeare, carrying us back to old times, and making us feel, (as Morton would say), like 'happy schoolboys again.'"

"What's all this?" cried Arthur, coming forward with a puzzled air, "what is Max making a speech about? has he taken the stump as a candidate for the presidency of the island?"

"He needn't do that," said Browne, "we're not going to have any presidents, or other republican trumpery here; I have formally taken possession of the island in the name of Victoria; and it is therefore a colony of Great Britain; I shall apply, at the first convenient opportunity, for letters patent, making me colonial governor."

"Tory, monarchist!" cried Max, "recant at once, or you sha'n't taste a mouthful of my breakfast."

"Do you think I'll sell my loyalty for a mess of pottage! No, I'm for a well-regulated monarchy: hurrah for Victoria!"

"Down with the Britisher!" cried Johnny, entering into the spirit of the scene, and tugging at Browne's coat-tails; "make him hurrah for the stars and stripes, or else don't give him any of our oysters!"

"You're surely not going back to the principles of the dark ages—you won't attack the right of private judgement, and persecute for opinion's sake."

"The right of private judgment, indeed!" answered Max, with great contempt. "I hold that no person can have a right, on any pretence whatever, to entertain erroneous opinions on important subjects, affecting the welfare of mankind. If a man does entertain such opinions, it is the duty of those who know better to convince him of the error by the most effectual arguments at their command. It is, therefore, my duty to open your eyes to the blessings of liberal institutions. I have here, (pointing towards the incipient breakfast), the most powerful means to assist and quicken your perception of the truth. Shall I not use those means?"

"The line of argument which you indicate is exceedingly forcible, (how delightfully those oysters smell!) I really think I begin to perceive some of the advantages of republicanism already."

"With the right of private judgment, properly understood," resumed Max, "I should be reluctant to interfere. You will, I presume, enjoy the exercise of so precious a privilege, even with a cocoa-nut breakfast, which you can probably obtain, by requesting Prince Eiulo to scale one of yonder tufted trees."

"How clear the matter becomes with a little reflection," observed Browne "(this camping out in the open air gives one a famous appetite). In fact your reasoning is almost irresistible, (that fish looks particularly nice), and really I begin to think I can safely profess myself a good republican— until after breakfast at any rate."

Max's culinary operations being at last completed, Johnny placed a huge shell to his lips, and sounded a long blast by way of announcement that breakfast was ready. The fish was served up in a fresh palm-leaf, and Johnny declared with much complacency, that not all the crockery-stores in New York, could furnish a platter of such royal dimensions. The leaves of the hibiscus, served admirably for plates; for knives and forks, we used the strong stalks, or central fibres, of cocoa-nut leaflet; which, with fingers in reserve for an emergency, answered at least as well as the chopsticks of the Chinese. Upon the whole, it cannot be denied that our table-service, simple as it was, has its advantages: it involved no necessity for any washing of dishes, no anxiety on the score of broken crockery, and we could indulge in the extravagance of a new dinner set every day, or even at every meal, for that matter, if so disposed.

The fish proved most excellent, resembling the striped bass in flavour and appearance: as to the oysters, they were unanimously voted equal to Shrewsburys.

"Ah!" sighed Max, "if we had now but a cup of coffee and a hot roll, those inestimable blessings of civilisation, we could almost forget that we are on a desert island."

"Wait until the bread-fruit ripens," said Arthur, "and we shall have a tolerably fair substitute for your 'hot rolls.' Eiulo will show us the most approved mode of preparing it, and we shall find it nearly equal to the wheaten loaf."

"All that Max seems to think about, is the eating," said Browne, swallowing the last remaining oyster, "but I begin to feel troubled about another matter: see, I am getting fairly out at the elbows, and neither 'coffee and rolls,' nor roast-beef and plum-pudding in indefinite quantities, would afford me any satisfaction, compared to the possession of a supply of clothing, or even a few changes of linen—in fact, comrades, what are we to do? There is danger that we shall all become savages: I begin to feel a loss of self-respect already."

"We shall have to go into the manufacturing business, I suppose," said Arthur. "I have often watched the whole process of making tappa, or native cloth, from the bark of the paper-mulberry; it is quite simple, and I have no doubt we can succeed in it; I have talked with Eiulo on the subject and find that he understands the process thoroughly."

"But are there any paper-mulberries on the island!" inquired Morton.

"I have not seen any," answered Arthur. "If there are none, the bark of the bread-fruit tree will answer nearly as well: the cloth made from it is as strong and durable, though not so fine."

"For the present, and before we go into home manufactures," said Max, "I advise Shakespeare, in order to avoid the loss of his remaining self-respect in consequence of wearing foul linen, to betake himself to the beach, wash his garments, and take a bath until they dry in the sun, which is the course I intend to pursue myself."

"And what are we going to do for shoes, I wonder!" said Johnny, "mine are badly cracked and torn, and nearly worn out: we shall all have to go barefoot!" and he looked aghast at the thought.

"We must kill a shark by-and-bye," said Arthur, "when we have nothing more pressing to do; and we can make leggins, or moccasins, from the skin."

"How these things kill the romance and poetry of desert island life!" said Max, "there's no romance about being out at the elbows, or being obliged to wear dirty linen—"

"Or in doing one's own washing in salt-water, and sitting naked while one's clothes are drying," interposed Browne, pathetically.

"Or in having your toes poke out at the end of your boots," added Morton, advancing his right foot in illustration.

"No! these are all stern realities," said Max, "cases not provided for in the story-books; how is it, Johnny, are there any precedents going to show how desert islanders do their washing and mending?"

"I think they generally saved heaps of clothes from the wreck," answered Johnny, gravely. "Robinson Crusoe brought off several chests, containing ever so many sailors' clothes of all sorts; whether there were any shoes or not, I don't remember: the Swiss family Robinson also obtained an abundance of such things from the wreck of their ship before it sunk; Philip Quarll made garments for himself from the skins of animals."

"But what are we to do? we havn't any wreck from which to supply ourselves with chests of clothing, with arms and ammunition, and stores of ship-biscuit and salt provisions. We're worse off it seems, than any of our predecessors. And since we are not supplied with the requisite capital and stock-in-trade for desert islanders, it is reasonable to infer that we are not destined to a Robinson Crusoe life, so that we may confidently expect to be taken off by some ship, in a short time."

As we were finishing our breakfast, a couple of tiny, fairy-like tern, came flying round us. They were very tame, and hovered smoothly over our heads, at the distance of sometimes but a few feet. Their plumage was snowy-white, and as they glided quietly around, peering curiously into our faces, you could almost fancy that there was the gleam of intelligence in their large eyes.

"O, what beautiful little birds!" cried Johnny, in great delight: "I wish I had some crumbs of bread for them."

"Who knows, Johnny," suggested Max, "but these strange little birds, as they seem to be, are no birds, after all, but an unfortunate prince and princess, who having incurred the resentment of some potent enchanter, have been transformed by his magical arts into their present shape, and banished to this desert island; and have now come to us for sympathy and assistance—see what a mournful expression there is in their mild dark eyes!" Johnny was pleased with the conceit, and the little tern were always afterwards known as the prince and princess. They frequently came hovering around us in the most friendly and fearless manner, when we were in that part of the island.

Chapter Seventeen
The Progress of Discovery

A Voice in the Woods—Vive Napoleon!—Calculating
the Longitude—The "Wild Frenchman's" Hat

Stephano. Hark! what sound is that?
Caliban. Art thou afeard, master?
Stephano. No, monster, not I.
Caliban. Be not afeard: the isle is full of noises.

Our failure to discover fresh water, or any indications of it, during yesterday's expedition, increased the anxiety which we felt on the subject and we determined to devote the day to a continuation of the search.

The base of Castle-Hill was skirted on the left and divided from the neighbouring forest by a deep gully, that had much the appearance of a dried-up water-course, and was probably a channel by which, in the rainy season, the water from the higher ground was conveyed to the sea. From the hill we could trace the course of the ravine, until it struck the beach, near the point where the small grove, before spoken of, seemed to spring up out of the lagoon. Our last evening's ramble along the shore had extended nearly to this spot and to avoid going over the same ground a second time, we struck into the ravine, and followed its course as it descended towards the beach.

Johnny every now and then, without any apparent object, unless to evince his entire superiority to any feeling of timidity, separated himself from the rest and disappeared for a time in the forest, generally returning with a specimen of some new plant or flower, or an account of some strange bird, or curious tree, which he had seen. From one of these adventurous excursions, he came rushing back; closely followed by Eiulo, both looking a good deal frightened, and, as soon as he had recovered breath sufficiently to be able to speak, he earnestly affirmed that he had heard a man call out to him in the wood. His statement was strange enough; he had found a twining plant, with a flower like a morning glory, and called loudly for Eiulo, who was a little way off, to come and see if it was the patara vine.

The root of this plant is a valuable and nutritious esculent, and Arthur had described the leaf and flower to us, in order that we might recognise it if met with. Immediately a harsh voice issued from a neighbouring thicket, uttering some words which he did not distinctly understand, but they were in French, and were something about Napoleon.

"In French!—and about Napoleon!" cried Arthur, in amazement. "Are you quite sure, Johnny, that you heard any words at all;—any thing more than a strange noise of some kind?"

But Johnny was positive;—he had heard the "Napoleon," as plainly as he ever heard any thing. There were only a few words—not more than two or three, but they were spoken very distinctly, and quite loud, as if the person were cheering; he could not be mistaken.

"Only two or three words," pursued Arthur, "would you know them again if you should hear them repeated?"

"Yes, I think I should."

"Was it 'Vive Napoleon!' that you heard?"

"Those are the very words!" cried Johnny; "they were spoken as plainly as you speak them, but in a rougher voice."

"Did you see any thing—did you look towards the thicket!"

"I saw something stir, but could not tell what it was. The voice was harsh and angry, and I was frightened, and ran away as fast as I could. I thought perhaps it was a wild man—some one who had been shipwrecked here many years ago, and lived alone in the woods until he had grown wild or mad."

Johnny was so positive in this singular story, that for a moment we hardly knew what to think of it. Eiulo too had heard the voice—the same harsh voice that Johnny described as issuing from the thicket. But the notion of any person amusing himself by shouting "Vive Napoleon!" in the forests of a solitary island in the Pacific, seemed so preposterous, that we could not help coming to the conclusion, that some sudden noise in the wood had seemed to Johnny's excited imagination like a human voice—though why he should fancy that it uttered those particular words—the words of a strange language, was a puzzle which we could not solve. We, however, turned into the forest, and Johnny pointed out the spot where he was standing when he heard the voice. There were the vines, with flowers like morning-glories; and there was the thicket whence, as he alleged, the sound had proceeded. We shouted aloud several times, but there was no response, except from a large bird that rose heavily into the air, uttering a discordant scream; and we were satisfied that it was this, or some similar sound, that had startled Johnny; in which conviction we dismissed the matter from our minds.

The flowering vine proved to be the patara, which Arthur had been so anxious to discover, and on digging it up, two roots, resembling large potatoes, were found attached to the stalk. Quite a number of these plants were scattered about the neighbourhood; enough, as Arthur said, to make a tolerable potato patch.

All this time Max was missing, having been some little distance in advance of the rest, when Johnny had raised his strange alarm. When we got back into the ravine, he was not in sight, but we had hardly resumed our progress towards the shore, when we heard him calling out that he had found water. At this announcement, our orderly march broke at once into a hasty scramble. Browne alone maintained his dignity, and came on at his usual elephantine pace, probably suspecting that the pretended discovery was a hoax. Morton and I raced along the hollow, "neck and neck," till we suddenly reached a point where there was an abrupt descent to the level of the shore. We were under too much headway to be able to stop, and jumping together down the steep bank, we narrowly missed alighting upon Max, as he lay extended on the ground, scooping up water with his hand, from the basin of a small pool. I came down close beside him, while Morton, sprang fairly over his head, and alighted with a great splash in the centre of the pool. I had barely time to roll out of the way, when the others, with the exception of Browne, came tumbling in their turn over the bank, which took them as much by surprise as it had us. Morton's lamentable figure, as he stood motionless in the midst of the pool, drenched with water, and with a great patch of black mud plastered over one eye, together with Max's look of consternation at his own narrow escape, were irresistibly ludicrous, and provoked a laugh, in which, after a moment, they both heartily joined.

"Very obliging of you, Morton," said Max, recovering his self-possession, "I wanted to see how deep it was, and you are a good enough measuring-stick; just stand still a minute, if you please."

"You have reason to feel obliged to me," answered Morton, extricating himself from the mud, "it was on your account solely that I got into this pickle. I had to choose between breaking your neck, as you lay right in my way, or jumping into this hole, and not having much time to deliberate, it isn't surprising if I came to a foolish conclusion."

"It would be less unfeeling," replied Max, "as well as more strictly according to the facts of the case, to say a hasty conclusion, which might be understood literally, and would then be literally correct."

The water, which we found to be good, though slightly brackish, was contained in a narrow pit situated in the centre of a circular hollow, or basin. It was not more than half full, but its sides showed a fresh and distinct water-mark, more than a foot above the present level. At the edge of the basin, a solitary palm shot upward its straight shaft, to the height of nearly a hundred feet; the long, fringed leaves drooping from the top, like a bunch of gigantic ostrich plumes, and overshadowing the well. It seemed difficult to account for this supply of fresh water in so unpromising a spot, and so near the sea-shore. I was at first inclined to think it nothing more than a reservoir of standing water, left by the last rains, which had filled not only the pit, but also the surrounding basin. The former being deep and narrow, evaporation would be very gradual, which might, I supposed, account for the small quantity still remaining.

"That can hardly be," said Arthur, when I suggested this explanation, "the spot is wholly unsheltered from the sun, except at noon, by this screen of palm-leaves, and if the entire hollow were filled with water this morning, there would not be a drop of moisture left in three days, unless the supply were renewed. Besides, the water is too fresh and sweet to have stood since the last rains."

"I should judge," said Morton, "that this spot is but little above the level of the lagoon, and if the bottom of the well here, is below that level at ebb tide, this supply of fresh water can be easily accounted for."

"The rise and fall of the tide here, does not seem to be more than eighteen inches, or two feet," said Max, "and as to the depth of the pit or well, as you call it, you ought to be able to speak with confidence, having so recently been to the bottom of it."

"There are wells on the low islands of the West Indies," said Morton, "which communicate with the sea, and rise and fall with the tide, the sea-water penetrating through the sand, and being distilled in its passage: and I think this is one of the same kind. Here is a recent water-mark, more than a foot above the present level. If I am right, we shall find that the tide is now low."

Arthur thrust a stick into the side of the well to mark the height of the water, while Johnny rushed furiously down to the beach, and in a moment came posting back with the announcement that the tide *was* low.

"Very well, so far," said Arthur, "it only remains to be seen, whether, when the tide has risen, there will be any corresponding rise here."

"And, meantime," suggested Browne, "let us refresh ourselves with a bath, before the sun gets higher; and we can also take the opportunity to give our under garments the benefit of an ablution, as Max has proposed."

No one can fully appreciate the luxury of sea-bathing who has not enjoyed it within the tropics.

The calm, transparent water, with the firm white beach and bottom, looked so deliciously cool and inviting, that the suggestion was adopted as soon as made; and the expedition with which the preliminaries were got through with, reminded me of those eager races to "the pond," on the letting out of the village school at home, of a hot summer afternoon, in which several of our present company had often been competitors for the honour of being "the first one in." Arthur warned us to beware of sharks, and to keep a vigilant look-out for "back fins," and our dread of those prowling and rapacious monsters, was a great drawback to the enjoyment of our bath. In all the feats and dexterities of the swimmer's art, Eiulo far outdid the rest of us, moving through the water with the ease, rapidity, and gracefulness of a fish. After one or two trials with him, in swimming under water, and diving for shells, even Max yielded the palm, declaring that he was ready to match himself against any land animal, but should for the future decline entering into a contest of that kind with amphibious creatures.

Eiulo thought that this swimming in smooth water was but indifferent sport and began to talk to Arthur with great animation, in his native tongue, about the pleasures of "faahee," or surf-bathing, and the exquisite fun of dodging the "manos," or sharks, among the rollers. Presently he struck out into the lagoon, and before we could guess his intention, he swam over to the reef, and, picking his way across it, plunged fearlessly among the breakers on the outside. He stayed, however, but a short time, and came back saying, that the "manos" were altogether too thick out there, and that a huge blue one, had come near seizing him in the surf, before he could catch a roller so as to land safely upon the reef. When blamed by Arthur for his rashness, he laughed, and promised that he would not incur the risk again. From his frightened looks when he got back, I guessed that he had not found "dodging the mano" such exquisite fun as he had anticipated.

Max presently desisted from swimming, in order, as he said, to "do his washing," consoling himself for the hardship of being obliged to do laundress' work, with the reflection that the necessity for such a task would soon cease, as our clothes being in constant use, without the benefit of a change, could not last long. Browne and I followed this example, and having spread our garments in the sun to dry, resumed our aquatic sports in the meantime. Arthur dressed himself and accompanied by Eiulo, left us, saying that he would rejoin us in an hour at the hill. The two proceeded a short distance along the shore to the right, and then turned into the forest to search, as we supposed, for plants, or roots, capable of being turned to useful account.

By the time our clothes were sufficiently dry to be put on, the tide had risen considerably, and on repairing to the well, we found the water several inches above Arthur's mark, thus confirming Morton's theory in regard to it. Though we should have been better pleased to have discovered a spring, yet there was no reason to doubt that here was an ample and permanent supply of fresh water.

As it was now getting towards noon, and the day was excessively hot, we returned to Castle-Hill, to enjoy the grateful shade of its cool, dark groves, and the breeze which was sure to play about its summit, if air was stirring any where. Max sought out a leafy bower of ferns and creepers, near the foot of the great candle-nut tree, where he stretched himself out and went to sleep. Johnny got his bow and arrows, and began to practise archery, by shooting at the large and gaudy insects hovering around the blossoms of the vines, and when, probably by accident, he carried away the wing of one of them at the distance of some six or seven yards, he boasted loudly of the exploit, and intimated that in case of a brush with any cannibals, his bow might be relied on to do some execution. Getting tired at length of his crusade against the butterflies, he expressed a wish to try his skill upon some larger game, but as nothing in the shape of a jackall or tiger-cat was obliging enough to make its appearance, he put aside his weapons with a sigh, and lying down near Max, was soon asleep. There was a drowsy influence in the profound quiet, and subdued light of the spot, to which I should soon have yielded but for Browne, who began to talk of Scottish scenes and legends, with sufficient interest to keep Morton and myself awake. It seemed strange enough, to lie there in that tropical forest, listening to an enthusiastic description of the rugged sublimity of the Trossachs, the romantic beauty of Loch Vennacher, Loch Katrine, and Loch Achray, or the lovely vale of Kelso, bosomed in green woods, with its placid streams, smooth lawns, and hazel-fringed dells.

About noon, Arthur and Eiulo made their appearance, emerging from the grove to the south-east of the hill, laden with roots, plants, strips of bark, etcetera. They had been looking for the auti, or paper-mulberry, but without success. Arthur had discovered a large and beautiful species of sweet-scented fern, with a tuberous root shaped like a sweet-potato, which he said was baked and eaten by the Society Islanders: he brought with him several entire specimens, root and all. The leaves were fragrant and elegantly shaped, and the roots were of a mottled brown and yellow. Eiulo carried in his hand an unripe bread-fruit—a splendid pea-green globe, nearly as big as his head. They had discovered a noble grove of this most valuable tree, at no great distance from the hill, but the fruit was not yet perfectly ripe. Johnny, who had awaked at the return of the absentees, was greatly delighted at these discoveries, and began to lament that he had not accompanied Arthur. He inquired very particularly as to the direction of the bread-fruit grove, as if cherishing the design of setting out at once to visit it; but Browne letting some thing drop about the voice in the woods, Johnny changed the subject, and saying that it must be nearly dinner-time, proposed to make a fire, and bake the fern roots, so as to test their quality. Upon hearing this, Max, whose slumbers had also been disturbed, raised his head for a moment and exclaimed so vehemently against the very mention of a fire, when we were already dissolving with heat, that nothing further was said about it.

"And now," said Arthur, after having given a full account of his discoveries, and answered all Johnny's questions, "I believe it is just noon, and while I think of it, I will try to ascertain our longitude."

"Ascertain our longitude!" exclaimed Browne, "pray, how do you propose to do that without instruments?"

"I know the longitude of the Kingsmill islands," answered Arthur, "and if I can find our distance east or west of them, of course, I have the longitude of this island."

"But there's the difficulty; how can you ascertain even whether we are to the east, or to the west of them?"

"In the first place, then, I have Kingsmill island time; my watch was last set, one day while we were there, just after Mr Frazer had taken an observation."

"Do you mean to say," inquired I with some interest, "that you have regularly wound up your watch every day since then, without once forgetting or neglecting it during all that has since occurred?"

"I did regularly, every night before sleeping; and during all the time that we were at sea in the boat, hardly a day passed that I did not note down some memoranda in my pocket-book."

"That now, is positively diabolical!" exclaimed Max, from his covert among the creepers, where he was completely invisible, except his heels, which were kicking in the air; "I wouldn't have believed, Arthur, that you were such a methodical, cold-blooded creature! I suppose now, that if I had tumbled overboard during that hideous time, and been gulped down by a shark, or if Shakespeare had starved to death, you would have made a regular memorandum of the event, in business-like style, and wound up your watch as usual. I think I see the entry in your pocket-book, thus: '1839, June 3rd—Mem. Max Adeler fell overboard this day, and was devoured by a shark—an amiable and interesting youth, though too much given to levity, and not prepared, I fear, for so unexpected a summons. June 5th—Mem. My worthy and estimable friend, John Browne, late of Glasgow, Scotland, died this day, from lack of necessary food. Threw him overboard. What startling monitions of the uncertainty of life!'"

"Peace, Kaiser Maximilien, peace!" cried Browne, "and let the Professor proceed to fix our longitude."

"The first thing," resumed Arthur, "is to plant a straight stick upright in the ground; when it casts no shadow east or west it is twelve o'clock *here*. My watch will then show what time it is at the Kingsmills: if it shows an earlier hour there, we must be east of them; if a later hour, then we are west of them."

"I think I understand that," said Johnny; "the next thing is to tell how far east or west we are."

"That is quite easy. There are, you know, three hundred and sixty degrees of longitude: the sun passes through them all—that is, round the globe in twenty-four hours. Then, of course, in one hour, it passes through fifteen degrees, and through one degree in four minutes; so that for every four minutes' difference of time, there will be a difference of longitude of one degree—that is, near the equator, about seventy miles."

"It must be very near noon now," said Johnny, running out into a patch of sunshine, where a small opening in the grove let in the light, "see! I have hardly any shadow at all."

Arthur planted a stick in the ground, and as soon as the shadow marked the hour of noon, looked at his watch, by which it was eighteen minutes after twelve.

"It would seem from this," said he, "that we are four degrees and a half, or over three hundred miles, west of the Kingsmills: it also appears that we are very near the line, but a little south of it, for the shadow inclines a little southward."

"It is all nonsense," cried Max, sitting up in the grass, "to pretend to ascertain where we are, in any such way as this. If your watch, (which you know is a miserable time-keeper), has lost or gained but twenty minutes since we left the Kingsmills, which is now nearly two months, then what becomes of your learned calculations about the difference of time, and of the longitude, and all that?"

Arthur laughed, and admitted that this grave impeachment of the character of his chronometer, was not entirely without foundation, and that in consequence, the strict accuracy of the results arrived at, could not be relied on.

"The only thing that we can be at all certain about in regard to our position," said Max, "is, that we are south of the line."

"How can that be?" inquired Browne, "the Pole-star is visible from here, or, at any rate, we saw it on the second or third night we were at sea in the boat."

"A part of the Great Bear can be seen," answered Arthur, "but not the north star, I think. I looked for it last night, and though I could see all the stars of the Dipper, the pointers were near the horizon, and the Pole-star below it. But even if visible, it would be no evidence that we are north of the equator, for I believe it can be seen from the fourth or fifth degree of south latitude."

"See now," said Browne, "what a pretty neighbourhood you are getting us into, with your wise calculations! If we are south of the line, and far west of the Kingsmills, we must be somewhere near the Bidera Sea, and the Mendana Archipelago, about which the young sailor Roby, who was always boasting of having sailed with the famous Captain Morell, used to tell us such wonderful stories."

"It is good ground," replied Arthur, "for one who wants to exercise a traveller's privilege, and recount marvels and prodigies, without fear of contradiction. Those seas are full of large islands, with countless numbers of smaller ones, and remain to this day almost unexplored. In fact, little more is now ascertained in regard to them, than was known two hundred and fifty years ago, soon after their discovery by the Spanish navigator Mendana; so that a man who pretends, as Roby does, to have gone over the ground himself, may tell pretty much what stories he pleases, without danger of any one being able to convict him of inaccuracy."

"What!" exclaimed Johnny, opening his eyes to their utmost extent, "do you suppose we are near those islands Jack Roby tells about, where the natives chew betel and lime out of a carbo-gourd, and sacrifice men to their idols, and tear out and devour the hearts of their enemies?"

"And where King Rogerogee lived," added Max, "(you remember him Johnny), the giant seven feet and a half high, who wore a paradise plume on his head, and a girdle of the claws and beaks of birds around his waist? Why, this may be the very island of Podee over which he reigned, and we ought not to be greatly surprised to see him look in upon us at any moment, with his paradise plume waving among the tops of the trees, and his spear, eighteen feet long, in his hand."

"Don't let Rogerogee disturb your dreams, Johnny," said Arthur, "if there is any such place as the island of Podee, which I very much doubt, it is, according to Roby's own account, but a few leagues to the east of Papua, and some twelve or thirteen hundred miles at least, west of us."

Max now got up, and after stretching himself, and giving three or four great yawns, came towards the spot where the rest of us were sitting; but after taking a few steps, he suddenly stopped, uttering an exclamation of surprise, and looking down at something in the grass at his feet. He then kicked a dark object out of a tall bunch of fern, towards us. It was an old beaver hat crushed flat, and covered with mildew and dirt. Robinson Crusoe was not more startled by the footprint in the sand, than were we at the sight of this unequivocal trace of civilised man. Arthur picked it up, and restoring it partially to its proper shape, examined the inside. On the lining of the crown appeared in gilt letters—

Pierre Baudin,
Chapelier,
Rue Richelieu, Numero 20
A Paris

"Here, then," said Max, "is an end of the notion that we are the first inhabitants of this island; it is clear that others have been, if they are not now upon it. Perhaps, Johnny, this is the hat of the man you heard talking French in the woods this morning."

"At any rate," said, Arthur, after a moment of thoughtful silence, "this must be the place where the Frenchman who perished in the water-spout and his companions, were cast away, and from which they afterwards reached Eiulo's island in a small boat. The well yonder is probably their work, and we may perhaps find other evidences of their stay here, when we come to explore the island more thoroughly."

Chapter Eighteen
About Tewa

A Dull Chapter, but Necessary—Wakatta and
Atollo—A Gentle Hint—Max as an Architect

"In the forest hollow roaring,
Hark! I hear a deepening sound,
Clouds rise thick with heavy lowering,
See! the horizon blackens round."

It must not be inferred from the occasional bursts of holiday humour in which we indulged, that we had become reconciled to our exile, and were now ready to subside into a state of indolent contentment satisfied with security from present danger, and the abundant means of subsistence which we had discovered.

Not even a tropical paradise, with its warm, glowing sky and balmy atmosphere, its "ambrosial fruits and amaranthine flowers," could charm us into oblivion of home, and those who made it dear; or diminish the bitterness of the thought of being cut off for ever from human intercourse, and of having all our plans of life deranged and frustrated. Though we did not brood continually over our unfortunate situation, we were far from being insensible to it. The loveliest island that ever reposed in undiscovered beauty, upon the bosom of the "blue summer ocean," though rich in all things necessary to supply every material want, must still have seemed to us but as a gilded and luxurious prison, from which we should never cease to sigh for an escape.

Arthur's conclusion, mentioned at the end of the last chapter, seemed in itself so probable, and was confirmed by so many circumstances, that it was readily adopted by us all; and believing that the party, of whose presence at one time upon the island the hat was an evidence, had left it years ago, the occurrence no longer appeared to possess any importance, and we dismissed it altogether from our thoughts.

Eiulo, when questioned on the subject of the white men living among his own people, repeated substantially his former statement, that they came from an island lying south of his father's, and distant from it less than a day's sail. It seemed, also, that before the arrival of the whites, an island lying in the direction from which they had come, had been known to some, at least, of the natives, and visited by them. In the course of the conversations which he had with Arthur, at various times, about his father's people and their affairs, Eiulo had often spoken of an old warrior, Wakatta by name, famous for his courage and great personal strength, of which he related many remarkable instances. Through two generations he had been the most devoted and valued friend of the family of his chief; and upon his wisdom, sagacity, and prowess, Eiulo's father and grandfather had relied in many an emergency, and seldom in vain. Formerly, the three islands were independent of each other, and were ruled by separate chiefs, who sometimes engaged in sanguinary wars among themselves, in most of which Wakatta had played a prominent part.

A great many moons ago, as Eiulo expressed it, the chiefs of the two smaller islands had united their forces against his grandfather, who was then chief of Tewa, the third and largest. To this enterprise they had been incited by Atollo, an uncle of Eiulo, and younger brother of the present chief, his father. This man was possessed of great ability, and his reputation as a warrior was second only to that of Wakatta, who was many years his senior, so that among those of his own age he was considered without an equal. But, though eminent for talent and courage, he seemed to be entirely destitute of principle or feeling; and impelled, as was supposed, by a spirit of unscrupulous ambition, (for no other motive could be assigned), this unnatural son plotted against the lives of his own father and elder brother. His designs being discovered, and fully exposed, he fled to one of the neighbouring islands, and sought the protection of its chief, his father's most formidable and inveterate enemy. Afterwards, by his address and energy, he succeeded in bringing about a league between the chiefs of the two smaller islands, for the purpose of an attack against Tewa, by their combined forces. The enterprise was planned with the greatest secrecy, and executed with equal skill and daring. At midnight, the allies set sail, in a fleet of war canoes, and two hours before dawn they had disembarked at Tewa, marched to the principal village, where the chief resided, and made all their dispositions for the attack, which was so totally unexpected, that it was crowned with complete success. Scarcely any resistance was made: the principal Tewan warriors were slain in their beds, or taken prisoners; and Eiulo's father and grandfather, with Wakatta, only saved their lives by fleeing to the mountains. Knowing that the strictest search would be made for them, and that if taken, instant death would be their doom; they stole forth from their lurking-place by night, repaired to the beach, and taking a large canoe, which they discovered there, set sail in her, steering boldly southward, in search of a considerable island which was believed to lie in that direction. Soon after sunrise they came in sight of land, but, on approaching it, they found that the surf was bursting with great fury upon a barrier reef, stretching between them and the shore; and it was not until they had coasted along it for many hours, that they succeeded in effecting a landing. Eiulo had heard both his father and Wakatta speak of the island as a singularly beautiful spot, nearly as large as Tewa, and abounding in bread-fruit and cocoa-nut trees. Here the fugitives remained for several months, until, becoming wearied of their solitary life, and possessed by an irresistible longing to revisit their homes, they came to the determination to venture back, and learn the state of things there, at every hazard. They accordingly set sail one day at noon, in order that they might reach their destination under cover of night, in which they succeeded.

Seeking a temporary place of concealment in the woods, they seized favourable opportunities to discover themselves to some friends on whom they could rely. They learned that the victorious allies had been guilty of the most intolerable cruelty towards the people of Tewa. Many of the prisoners had been slain, as sacrifices to the gods, and many more had been made slaves. Atollo had established himself as chief at the conquered island, and had gathered about him a band of the most ferocious and desperate men, who practised every species of cruelty and oppression upon the inhabitants. The latter, driven to the utmost verge of endurance, were now ready to incur any risk in an attempt to deliver themselves from a yoke so galling. They needed only a leader, and the experience and prowess of Wakatta, together with the presence of their ancient and rightful chief and his son, inspired them with confidence and courage. Gathering a small, but resolute, band of warriors, they awaited the favourable moment to strike a decisive blow; and then, emulating the secrecy and suddenness of Atollo's recent enterprise, they sallied forth at night, from their rendezvous in the forest and fell upon him and his adherents. Wakatta was unable to restrain the ferocity of his followers, excited by the insults and injuries they had suffered, and they killed on the spot all who fell into their hands, pausing to make no prisoners. Atollo, after fighting like a tiger, though almost alone, succeeded in making his escape with a few of his attendants. The victors promptly carried the war into the neighbouring islands, both of which were completely subdued, and afterwards remained under the sway of Eiulo's grandfather until his death, when the present chief succeeded. Atollo, after resisting as long as there remained the slightest prospect of success, had sought refuge among the recesses of the mountains, where he still lurked with a few outlaw followers, as desperate as himself. His father had forbidden any search for him, or any efforts for his capture to be made; and such was the dread inspired by his desperate courage, ferocity, and cunning, and such the superstitious terror with which he was generally regarded, that few felt any inclination to transgress this command, or to meddle in any way with him or his followers; and he was consequently left unmolested in his favourite haunts, among the wild and almost inaccessible precipices of the interior. In seasons of scarcity, his father had even caused supplies of food to be placed where they would be likely to fall in his way. Eiulo always shuddered when he spoke of this man. Once, when accompanied by a young playmate and an attendant, he had strayed a long way into the wood in search of wild-flowers, and had, without being aware of it, approached the region frequented by the outlaws, a spear had suddenly been hurled at him from an adjacent thicket, with so deadly a purpose, that it whistled past within a few inches of his side. As they fled in alarm, and were clambering hastily down a steep descent, a mass of rock was disengaged from the verge of an overhanging precipice, and came near crushing them all. Looking back, in their flight, they saw a wild figure, which the attendant recognised at once as that of Eiulo's uncle, stooping at the edge of the cliff, in the act of loosening another large stone. Notwithstanding this murderous attempt, the present chief of Tewa continued to pursue the same forbearing course which his father had adopted, and Atollo was still permitted to remain unmolested among his mountain fastnesses.

Eiulo, even before the discovery of the hat, had believed that we were upon the same island which his father had visited, as above related, and from which the whites had afterwards come. He was confident that by sailing northward, with a fair wind, we should reach Tewa in less than a day. Though generally cheerful, and overflowing with boyish spirits, there were times when it was apparent that he pined for his home; and, though he never directly urged it, he earnestly wished to have us make the attempt to reach his father's island in the yawl.

At length I began to suspect, from the constant and minute inquiries which Arthur made in relation to Tewa, and its people, their usages, habits, etcetera, that he was thinking seriously of some such attempt. He directed his inquiries particularly to the point whether the island was ever visited by ships. Eiulo remembered hearing his father speak of big canoes, without any outriggers, and whose masts were as high as a cocoa-nut-tree, having passed in sight of the island. He had heard, too, that a long while ago, one of these great vessels had got aground, upon a reef between Tewa and the adjacent island, and that the natives had gone off to her in their canoes, and some of them had ventured on board at the invitation of the strangers. Old Wakatta was one of these, and he had received a wonderful present from the white chief, which he had often exhibited to Eiulo, and which, from his description of it, appeared to be neither more nor less than a small looking-glass. The great canoe had, by throwing overboard a part of her cargo, got off from the reef at the rising of the tide, and resumed her voyage. It was pretty evident that the arrival of a European vessel at the islands, was an event of very rare occurrence, and in all probability the result of mere accident. Except that he steadily pursued inquiries of this kind, Arthur said nothing to show that he entertained the thought of such an undertaking as I suspected him to be revolving. Browne and Morton both had exaggerated notions of the cruelty and treachery of the "heathen native;" as the former called them, and would, I had no doubt, be strongly averse to any step calculated to place us in their power, unless it should also, in some way, increase our prospects of ultimately getting home.

For several days after the occurrences narrated in the last chapter, we remained at Castle-hill, making little excursions daily in various directions. Having now discovered a supply of fresh water, and abundant means of subsistence, it seemed as though there was at present nothing further for us to do, except to assist Arthur, as far as we could; in his preparations for manufacturing tappa. The weather was so genial, (except during the middle of the day, when the heat was frequently intolerable), that we felt no want of any other shelter than such as the grove afforded us. Generally, towards evening, a refreshing breeze set in from the sea, and lasted several hours. We experienced no bad effects from sleeping in the open air, and far from finding it a hardship, we soon came to consider it every way more pleasant, than to be cribbed and cabined within four close walls. There was something delightful, in dropping off into dreamland, listening to the whispering of the leaves above you, and catching glimpses through them, of a sky so deliciously blue, and stars so wonderfully bright. It seemed as though in this favoured spot, the fable of a perpetual summer was to be realised, and the whole circle of the year was to be crowned with the same freshness and verdure and beauty, the same profusion of fruits and flowers, which we had thus far enjoyed. But such expectations, if any of us were beguiled into entertaining them, were destined to be rudely dissipated. One hot afternoon, we were startled from a drowsy siesta in the grove, by a peal of thunder, such as is rarely heard in temperate climates, and on springing up and looking about us, we beheld above and around us, certain indications, which it would have been far more interesting and agreeable to contemplate from beneath the shelter of a snug and comfortable dwelling. The wind moaned through the bending tree-tops; the face of the heavens was black as night, and the waters of the lagoon, and of the ocean, had darkened to a steely blue beneath their frown. Before we had fairly shaken off our drowsiness, another abrupt peal of thunder burst overhead, with a suddenness that seemed to jar the very clouds and shake the water out of them, for the rain began all at once to come down violently, in big drops, that rattled like hailstones upon the crisp leaves of the forest. The thunder appeared to have completed its office in giving the signal for the clouds to discharge their contents, and we heard it no more. For a time, the dense foliage of the large tree under which we gathered, completely sheltered us; but soon the moisture began to drip slowly from the lower leaves, and occasionally fell in sudden showers, as the branches were shaken by the wind.

At length, the ground became thoroughly saturated, shallow puddles formed in every little hollow or depression, and there was the prospect of a most miserable night if the storm should continue. Happily, this did not prove to be the case; in about an hour after we had been aroused by the first thunder peal, the clouds dispersed almost as suddenly as they had gathered; the sun shone forth brightly; the trees and the grass sparkled with raindrops, lustrous as diamonds, and the whole landscape smiled in fresher beauty than ever.

This little occurrence, however, served as a seasonable hint to recall to our minds the importance of contriving some kind of a dwelling to afford us shelter in bad weather, and we resolved to lose no time in setting about it. Accordingly, the day following that of the thunder shower, as soon as we had returned from the beach, after taking our regular morning swim, Arthur called a council, to deliberate and determine upon the matter of house-building. The first thing was to fix upon a site; the only objection to the level space at the top of the hill, was its elevated position, exposing it to the full force of the violent winds which prevail at certain periods of the tropical year. But on that side from which the strongest winds blow, the spot was protected by still higher land towards the interior, and the fine trees of various kinds and sizes, (some of them evidently the growth of many years), among which could be seen no prostrate trunks, showed, as we thought, that nothing was to be feared from that source.

We, therefore, selected a smooth, open space, near the edge of the terrace, commanding a view of the sea, through a vista of noble trees. Max insisted, that, inasmuch as with our limited architectural resources we could not make our house of more than one storey, we ought to build in "cottage style," and make up for deficiency in height, by spreading over a large surface. He then proceeded to mark out a ground-plan, upon a scale that would have been shockingly extravagant, had we been in a part of the world where the price of building-lots was to be taken into consideration. A parallelogram, nearly forty feet long by twenty-five in width, the narrower side fronting the sea, was the plan of the main building. This was to be flanked by two wings, each some sixteen feet square, which would serve to strengthen and support the principal structure. "Upon this model," Max complacently observed, "he intended one of these days to build his country-seat, near Mount Merino, on the Hudson: meantime, we were welcome to the benefit of the idea."

"Really, we're greatly obliged to you, Max," said Browne, "for helping us so generously through with the most difficult part of the business. All that we now want in order to finish it at once, is merely a few loads of joist, plank, pine-boards, shingles, and window-sash; a supply of nails, a set of carpenter's tools, and a couple of carpenters to use them."

"Of course," rejoined Max, "we shall want a supply of building materials, tools, etcetera, and I am expecting them along daily. We have now been here several weeks, and it is quite time, in the natural and regular course of things, and according to the uniform experience of people situated as we are, for a ship heavily laden, (say in our case), with lumber and hardware, to be driven upon our shores in the midst of a terrible storm, (yesterday when it began to thunder I thought it was at hand). The ship will come driving upon the reef—the crew will take to the boats, but no boat can live in such a sea, and notwithstanding our humane and daring efforts to assist them, all perish among the breakers—that is to say, all except the carpenter—whom I rescue, by plunging into the raging flood and dragging him ashore by the hair, just as he is about sinking for the third time."

"Nobly done!" said Browne, "but couldn't you at the same time manage to save a drowning washerwoman? she would be as great an acquisition as the carpenter, in my mind."

"At length," resumed Max, "the storm abates—the sea becomes smooth—we go out in the yawl to the stranded vessel, where she lies upon a coral patch, and bring off, in two boat loads, the carpenter's chest, a keg of gunpowder, a blunderbuss, seven muskets, fourteen pairs of pistols, and a bag of doubloons, (think of that, Johnny!) That very night the wind rises again: the surf breaks the wreck to pieces, and washes the fragments ashore, and in the morning the sea is strewn far and wide with floating spars, and bales, and barrels; and the reef is covered for miles with 'joist, plank, pine-boards, shingles, window-sash,' and whatever other trifling conveniences are requisite for building my cottage. This is what Johnny and I confidently calculate upon."

"In the meantime," said Arthur, "in case by any unfortunate accident your ship should fail to arrive in time to enable us to get the cottage up before the rains set in, I propose that we commence a less ambitious structure." He began to trace upon the ground with a pointed stick, the oval outline of what he called a 'Tihitian faré.' "But even for my faré," he added, "we shall need the means of cutting down a number of good-sized trees."

"Of which we are entirely destitute," said Max, with an air of triumph, "and I don't see but that we shall have to wait for my ship after all."

"Not so," answered Arthur, "for I think that two or three of the cutlasses may be converted into tolerable saws, with which, by dint of a little patience, we can get out as many posts and rafters as will be requisite for the frame of our building, though I admit it will be tedious work."

Johnny heaved a profound sigh at the prospect of the difficulties that lay in the way of his pet project of house-building, and wished that "that old magician who built the castle with a thousand windows for Aladdin, in a single night, would only be clever enough to lend us his assistance." But upon second thought, he concluded that there would be "no fun" in having our house ready-made for us, and magnanimously declared that if he had the wonderful lamp in his hands that minute, with full power to summon up the obedient genius, and set him to work, he would not do it.

"I hope you would make him supply us with a few good axes, Johnny, at least," said Browne.

But Johnny was disposed to be very self-denying and high-minded; he did not think he ought to do it; we should take a great deal more pleasure in our house if we made it ourselves, without any magical assistance of any kind.

"Now, that you mention axes," said Morton, "it occurs to me that there is an old hatchet-head among the rubbish in the locker of the yawl, and though it is a good deal battered and worn, it could be fitted with a handle and made useful."

We all now remembered having seen it, though no one had before thought of it. Arthur suggested that we should make an excursion to Palm-Islet as soon as the heat of the day was over, and the sea-breeze had set in, for the purpose of getting the hatchet, and bringing the boat round to the side of the island where we intended to fix our residence, as we might have occasion for its use. "We can get there before dark," said he, "and pass the night once more at our old quarters on the little island; then we can row back in the fresh of the morning, before sunrise, and be ready to commence our building in earnest."

Chapter Nineteen
The Coral Reef

Johnny and the Chama—Amateur Pearl-Diving—A
Shark Blockade—Culinary Genius

"Down in the depths of the lonely sea,
I work at my mystic masonry;
I've crusted the plants of the deep with stone,
And given them colouring not their own;
And now o'er the ocean fields they spread
Their fan-like branches of white and red:
Oh! who can fashion a work like me,
The mason of God, in the boundless sea."

Late in the afternoon, when the slanting beams of the sun began to lose
their fierceness, and the heat was tempered by the breeze setting in from
the ocean, we descended to the beach, and set out for the eastern side of the
island, in accordance with Arthur's suggestion, mentioned at the close of
the last chapter. As we made our way across Sea-bird's Point, the clamorous
cries of the gannets, raising their harsh voices to the highest pitch, in angry
remonstrance against this invasion of their domain, were almost deafening.
They might well be alarmed for the safety of their nests—or rather of their
eggs, which they lay upon the bare ground, without any attempt at a nest—
for they strewed the whole point so thickly that it was no easy matter to pick
one's way without treading upon them at every alternate step. In nearly
every tree were to be seen the rude nests of the frigate-bird, built of a few
coarse sticks; and numbers of the birds themselves, with their singular
blood-red pouches inflated to the utmost extent, were flying in from the sea.
The large sooty tern, the graceful tropic bird, and the spruce, fierce-looking
man-of-war's hawk, with his crimson bill, and black flashing eye, flew
familiarly around us, frequently coming so near, that we could easily have
knocked them down with our cutlasses, had we been inclined to abuse, so
wantonly, the confidence which they seemed to repose in us.

When half-way across the point, I came suddenly upon a magnificent male tropic bird, sitting in his nest behind a tussock of tall, reedy grass. He did not offer to quit his post, even when the others approached very near, and paused to admire him; being apparently engaged, in the absence of his mate, in attending to certain domestic duties, generally supposed to belong more appropriately to her. He was somewhat larger than a pigeon, and was a very beautiful bird, though not so brilliantly coloured as several other species of sea-fowl. His plumage, soft and lustrous as satin, was of a delicate pearly grey, except the long middle-feathers of the tail, which were of a pale red, and projected full a foot and a half beyond the rest. He manifested not the slightest fear, even when Johnny stooped and stroked his glossy coat. Just as we left the spot, the partner of this exemplary bird arrived, and hastened to relieve him from duty, giving him notice to quit, by two or three quick, impatient chirps, and a playful peck upon the head, whereupon he resigned his place, into which the other immediately settled, with a soft, complacent, cooing note, as expressive of perfect content as the purring of a well-fed tabby, stretched cosily upon the earth-rug before a cheerful winter evening fire. This transfer was effected so quickly, that Johnny was baffled in an ill-bred attempt which he made to pry into the domestic concerns of the affectionate pair, and he could not get even a transient glimpse of the contents of the nest.

Without permitting ourselves to be tempted into any further deviation or delay, we kept steadily along the beach, until we arrived, a little before sunset, at the spot where the yawl lay, drawn up on the sand, opposite the islet.

Max declared that after our long march, we ought to have a supper consisting of something more substantial than cocoa-nuts, and proposed that we should pull over to the reef, and procure some shell-fish, which proposition meeting with general approval, we got the boat into the water, and in five minutes reached the inside of the ledge, and landed upon it at a point about a quarter of a mile from the opening through which we had first entered the lagoon. In this place, it was some fifteen or twenty yards in width, and consisted of a seamed and broken flat of dead coral, elevated but slightly above the level of the sea. Though there was no wind, and had been none during the day, the mighty billows of the open ocean came rolling in upon the outer edge of the reef with their accustomed violence. The action of the trade-winds is upon the whole so steady and uniform, that when it does cease for short periods, its effects continue, and upon the windward side of these coral-belted islands, there are breakers that never cease to rage, even in the calmest weather. No sight could be more grand and imposing, than that of these enormous waves encountering the reef. One of them would sometimes extend along it a mile, or a mile and a half, in an unbroken line. As it sweeps onward, with a slow and majestic movement towering up, like a dark-blue mountain, it seems as if nothing could resist its power, and you almost tremble lest the solid barrier upon which you stand should be hurled from its foundations. It meets the curving line of the reef with a tremendous concussion, and thus suddenly arrested by the parapet of coral, reared from the depths of the sea, it rises at once, throughout its entire length, to the height of twelve or fifteen feet perpendicularly, and stands for a moment as if congealed in its progress; then breaking with a hollow roar, it falls in a deluge of foam and spray, filling all the seams and crevices, and marking their course in lines of white upon the dark ground of the ledge. Not the least striking feature of the spectacle, was the multitude of fishes, of all shapes, colours, and sizes, that could be seen suspended in the face of this liquid wall, the very moment before it fell. How they escaped being thrown upon the reef seemed inexplicable, but they darted hither and thither at the very edge of the roller, with the greatest apparent ease and security, and almost invariably turned sea-ward just in time to save themselves. Occasionally, however, some careless or unskilful individual, not sufficiently versed in this perilous kind of navigation, suffered shipwreck, and was left gasping and floundering upon the coral.

While thus engaged in watching the bursting of the waves upon the reef, I suddenly heard Johnny at a little distance calling out lustily for help, and hastening to the spot, I found him in one of the yawning crevices of the coral rock, up to his neck in water, and struggling violently to get out, in which he seemed to meet with opposition from some object in the hole.

"Something has got me by the feet," he cried, as soon as he saw me; "it is an enormous oyster, or a shell-fish of some kind, and it pinches dreadfully."

I looked down into the water, and saw what in fact, seemed to be a gigantic shell-fish, gripping both his legs: it retained its hold so tenaciously, that I found I could not extricate him, and when Arthur came up, as he did in a moment, it was as much as we could both do, to lift him and his singular captor, which still clung obstinately to him, out of the crevice. We were then obliged to pry open the shells with our cutlasses before we could release him.

Arthur pronounced this extraordinary shell-fish, to be a specimen of the "Chama Gigas." The shells were nearly three feet in length, and curiously marked and clouded. Johnny had slipped from the slimy edge of the chasm, and happened to fall fairly into the expanded jaws of the chama, which, had instantly closed upon him. If the water had been deeper, the consequences might have been serious, as there are instances of persons being drowned, by having their feet caught in the vice-like grip of this formidable bivalve.

Not far from the scene of Johnny's mishap, was a green spot upon the reef, where a group of young trees seemed to spring up out of the bare coral. On approaching the place, we found that a little island, about the size of Palm-islet was there in process of formation. Notwithstanding the exposed and barren character of the locality, and the scantiness of the soil, which was not anywhere a foot in depth. It was covered with a thrifty vegetation, among which were several well-grown-palms, a group of young casuarinas, and some ferns and tournefortias. Nor was this embryo islet destitute of inhabitants. The trees were at this hour filled with aquatic birds, and I observed among them one remarkable species, long-bodied, and slender, like swallows, with red bills and feet, white breast, and slate-coloured wings; these, instead of perching, like the rest of their feathered associates, upon the trees, nestled in the concavity of the long palm-leaves, far enough from the stem, to be rocked gently by the undulating motion of the leaf, which a breath of wind, or the slightest stirring of the birds in these swinging nets was sufficient to produce. But by far the most numerous and singular portion of the population of the islet, consisted of a species of large land-crab, inhabiting burrows hollowed out beneath the roots of the trees. Great numbers of them appeared to be bathing or sporting in the shallow water on the lagoon side of the islet, but, at sight of us, they scrambled off to their burrows with a degree of agility that could hardly have been expected from such clumsy-looking creatures. Owing partly to this unlooked-for rapidity of locomotion, and partly to a natural shyness and hesitation which we felt about handling them rashly, (their pincer-like jaws, with half a dozen pairs of which each individual seemed to be provided, having a rather formidable appearance), they escaped before we could capture even a specimen. Johnny forthwith posted himself in ambush among a bunch of fern, and riveting his eyes upon one of the burrows at the foot of a young cocoa-nut tree, waited impatiently for the crabs to venture forth once more. In a few moments a patriarchal-looking old fellow emerged cautiously from the hole, and was presently followed by several more. Johnny prudently delayed any hostile movement, until they should get far enough from their place of security to enable him to cut off their retreat; and, in the meantime, I was greatly amused and interested in observing the ingenious method in which the patriarch commenced operating upon a cocoa-nut which had fallen to the ground near his den.

Managing his complicated apparatus of claws with surprising dexterity, he seized the nut, and stripped off the outer husk in a twinkling; then setting it upon one end, he began to hammer away at the orifices through which the stalk and root of the future tree make their way when the nut germinates. Having at length removed the filling up of these orifices, he inserted a claw, and actually split the strong inner shell, dividing it neatly into halves. At this stage of the proceedings, half a dozen greedy neighbours, who had been looking on, without offering a helping claw, shuffled nimbly forward to share the spoil, and it was curious to see how quickly they cleaned out the shell, leaving not a particle of the kernel. Johnny seized this as a favourable moment for a sally, and rushed forth cutlass in hand, having adopted the discreet resolution of disabling them, by lopping off those formidable claws, before coming to close quarters. The sally, however, was premature, and proved entirely unsuccessful, for the crabs backed and sidled into their burrows with such expedition, that the last of them disappeared before their assailant could get within reach. Leaving Johnny to renew his ambuscade, if so disposed, I proceeded along the reef, and found Max and Browne bathing for the second time that day. They had discovered a charming place for the purpose, where a kind of oval basin was formed by the lagoon setting into the inside of the reef. The water was deep and clear, so that there was no danger of wounding the feet by means of shells or corals. Max had discovered what he supposed to be an enormous pearl-oyster, attached to a wall of coral, at the depth of five or six fathoms, and they were diving for it alternately. Both succeeded in reaching it, but it adhered so firmly to the rock by its strong beard, that neither of the amateur pearl-divers could tear it off, and getting soon exhausted and out of breath, they abandoned the attempt.

The submarine scenery of the lagoon was in this spot unusually varied and beautiful, and the basin formed a bath, fit for the Nereids themselves. Numbers of different kinds of shell-fish were attached to the coral branches, or wedged into their interstices. Others were feeding, and reflected the brightest colours with every motion. Purple mullet, variegated rock-fish, and small ray-fish, were darting about near the bottom. Another species of mullet, of a splendid changeable blue and green, seemed to be feeding upon the little polyps protruding from the coral tops. Shells, sea-plants, coral, and fishes, and the slightest movement of the latter, even to the vibration of a tiny fin! or the gentle opening of the gills in respiration, could be seen with perfect distinctness in this transparent medium. But what chiefly attracted attention, was the gay tints, and curious shapes, of the innumerable zoophytes, or "flower animals," springing up from the sides and bottom of the basin, and unfolding their living leaves above their limestone trunks or stems which encased them. Blue, red, pink, orange, purple, and green, were among the colours, and the variety of patterns seemed absolutely endless: they mimicked, in their manner of growth, the foliage of trees, the spreading antlers of the stag, globes, columns, stars, feathery plumes, trailing vines, and all the wildest and most graceful forms of terrestrial vegetation. Nothing was wanting to complete this submarine shrubbery, even to the minutest details; there were mosses, and ferns, and lichens, and spreading shrubs, and branching trees; bunches of slender thread-like stems, swaying gently with the motion of the water, might, (except for their pale, purplish, tint), pass for rushes, or tussocks of reedy grass; and it required no effort of the imagination to see fancifully shaped wild-flowers in the numerous varieties of actiniae, or sea anemones, many of which bore the closest resemblance to wood-pinks, asters, and carnations. The imitations of these flowers were in some cases wonderfully perfect, even to their delicate petals, which were represented by the slender, fringe-like tentacles of the living polyp, protruding from its cell. Besides these counterparts of land vegetation, there were waving sea-fans, solid masses of sponge-coral, clubs of Hercules, madrepores, like elegantly-formed vases filled with flowers, dome-like groups of astraeae, studded with green and purple spangles, and a thousand other shapes, so fantastic and peculiar, that they can be likened to no other objects in nature.

Johnny having got tired of lying in wait for the crabs, came to watch the swimmers and search for shells. In the course of frequent beach excursions with Mr Frazer, he had picked up the names, and chief distinguishing characteristics of the principal genera of marine shells, in consequence of which he had at length come to regard himself as quite a conchologist, and was ambitious of making a "collection," like other naturalists, in which design Arthur encouraged and assisted him.

Joining me, where I was lying upon a flat ledge, peering down into the basin, he presently espied a Triton's trumpet, more than a foot in length, in some five fathoms of water, and pointing it out to Max, he begged him to dive for it, earnestly assuring him that he had never seen so fine a specimen of the "Murex Tritonica." But the latter very decidedly declined sacrificing his breath in the cause of science, declaring that he had completely exhausted himself by his exertions in pearl-diving.

Eiulo coming up at the moment with a number of shell-fish which he had obtained, Johnny appealed to him for aid, and not in vain, for as soon as the much-coveted shell was pointed out to him, he threw off his wrapper, and plunging into the water, almost instantly returned with it. Max now showed him the supposed pearl-oyster, and challenged him to make an attempt to bring it up. Eiulo laughed, and nodded his acceptance of the challenge: after pausing a moment to take breath, he dived perpendicularly downward, reaching the shell easily with a few strokes, and made one or two vigorous but ineffectual jerks at it; then, just as I thought him about to give it up, and ascend again, he grasped it with both hands, brought his feet under him, and bracing himself firmly against the wall of coral, he wrenched it off, and bore the prize in triumph to the surface. It proved to be a pearl-oyster, as Max had supposed, and on being opened was found to contain eleven seed-pearls. Eiulo presented the shell and its contents to Johnny, who seemed to value the former, quite as much as the latter, and presently ran off in search of Arthur, to inquire whether it should properly be classed with the "genus ostrea," or the "genus mytilus."

After watching the swimmers a little longer, I strolled along the reef, in the direction which Johnny had taken in pursuit of Arthur, stopping occasionally to watch the bursting of a wave of uncommon magnitude, or to examine some of the interesting objects that were strewn with such profusion in every direction, and which rendered that barren ledge so choice a spot for the studies of the naturalist. Some ten or fifteen minutes had been thus employed, and it was beginning to grow dark, so that Arthur and Johnny, whom I had not yet overtaken, could be but just distinguished, like two specks in the distance, when I heard the powerful voice of Browne, raised in a loud and prolonged halloo. Pausing to listen, I soon heard the cry repeated, in a manner that showed as I thought, that something unusual had taken place. Hastening back, I found that Max and Browne had swum off to a coral knoll, in the lagoon, a stone's throw from the reef, and dared not venture back, being closely blockaded by a large fish swimming about near the spot, which they supposed to be a shark. They called loudly for me to come after them in the boat, and to lose no time about it, as there was water enough on the knoll, to enable a shark, if tolerably enterprising, to reach them where they stood. Though it was rapidly getting dark, there was still sufficient light to enable me to distinguish an enormous fish of some kind, cruising back and forth, with the regularity of a sentinel on duty, between the reef, and the shallow where Max and Browne were standing up to their knees in water. The case appeared to admit of no delay, and jumping into the boat, I pulled over to the coral patch with all possible speed, passing the fish close enough to see that it was in fact a large shark, and he proved also to be an exceedingly fierce and ravenous one. It almost seemed as though he understood my errand, for he followed, or rather attended me, closely, keeping so near the bow of the boat that it was with great difficulty and some danger, that I at length got the blockaded swimmers aboard. When this was effected, his disappointment and consequent bad temper were quite apparent; he swam round and round the boat in the most disturbed and agitated manner as we returned, making a variety of savage demonstrations, and finally going so far as to snap spitefully at the oars, which he did not discontinue, until Browne had two or three times rapped him smartly over the nose. After landing in safety, Max pelted him with shells and pieces of coral rock, until he finally swam off.

Meantime, Arthur and Johnny had returned from their wandering along the reef; the latter had come across another colony of crabs, and had succeeded in capturing three of them, or rather two and a half, for having, as he fondly imagined, disabled one enormous fellow by hacking him in two with his cutlass, the one half had scrambled into the hole, while Johnny was securing the other.

We now placed the chama shells, the crabs, and other shell-fish, together with Johnny's specimens, to which he had added a splendid madrepore vase, in the boat, and as soon as the swimmers were dressed, we pulled over to Palm-islet. Here we arranged a tent in the same manner as we had done on the memorable night when we first reached these shores. Max then kindled a fire, and prepared to cook our supper. The shell-fish were easily managed by placing them upon the embers, but the crabs, which it was necessary to boil, and which were of the size of small lobsters, presented a more difficult case. Max's culinary genius, however, stimulated by a keen appetite, eventually triumphed over every obstacle. He procured a number of stones, which he heated in the fire; then filling one of the deep and rounded chama shells with water, he proceeded to drop the heated stones into it, using a couple of sticks as a pair of tongs. This process he continued until the water boiled, when he remorselessly plunged the unhappy crabs therein, and from time to time dropped in more of the heated stones, until the cookery was complete.

Chapter Twenty
Arthur's Story

Browne on "The Knightly Character"—Rokóa—
The Cannibal Island of Angatan

"This is no Grecian fable of fountains running wine,
Of hags with snaky tresses, and sailors turned to swine:
On yonder teeming island, under the noon day sun,
In sight of many people, these strange, dark deeds were
done."

Having made a hearty and satisfactory supper, and concluded the meal
with a draught of cocoa-nut milk, we sat down, like the patriarchs of old,
"in the door of our tent" facing the sea, to enjoy the freshness of the evening
breeze.

Johnny, after having settled it to his own entire satisfaction, that the
shell in which his pearls had been found, was properly a mussel, and not an
oyster; and having also, by Arthur's help, resolved his doubts and difficulties,
touching divers other knotty points in conchology; successively raised and
canvassed the grave and edifying questions—whether there actually were
such creatures as mermaids?—whether sea-serpents were indigenous to
the neighbourhood of Cape Cod and Massachusetts Bay?—whether the
narratives of ancient and modern voyagers, in regard to Krakens, and
gigantic Polypes, with feelers or arms as long as a ship's main-mast, had any
foundation in fact or were to be looked upon as sheer fabrications?—and,
finally, whether the hideous and revolting practice of cannibalism, really
prevailed among the inhabitants of certain groups of islands in the Pacific?

"This puts me in mind, Arthur," said Johnny, suddenly, while the last-
mentioned subject was under discussion, "of a promise you made during
the voyage, to tell me a story about a cannibal island upon which you were
once cast, and the adventures you met with there. This is a good time to tell
it: it is quite early, and the night so beautiful, that it would be a shame to

think of going to bed for two or three hours yet; for my part, I feel as though I could sit here all night without getting sleepy."

"A happy thought, Johnny," said Browne, "it will be the pleasantest possible way of passing the evening; therefore, Arthur, let us have the story."

"O yes, the story! let us have the cannibal story by all means!" cried Max, "this is just the hour, and the place, to tell it with effect. The dash of the surf upon the reef; the whispering of the night wind in the tree-tops; the tall black groves on the shore yonder, and the water lying blacker still in their shadow, will all harmonise admirably with the subject."

"I believe I did promise Johnny an account of an unintentional visit I once made to a place known as 'the Cannibal Island of Angatan,' and I have no objection to redeem my pledge now, if desired. I wish you to take notice, however, at the outset, in order to avoid raising false expectations, that I do not promise you a 'Cannibal Story'—how much my narrative deserves such a title, will appear when you have heard it."

The call for the story being quite eager and unanimous, Arthur settled himself into a comfortable position, and after giving one or two of those preliminary ahems, common to the whole fraternity of story-tellers from time immemorial, he proceeded as follows:—

Arthur's Story of the Cannibal Island of Angatan

"About a year and a half ago, and just before the time when I was to sail for the United States to complete my preparation for the seminary, I was induced to embark upon a voyage to the Palliser Islands, planned by a young chief of Eimeo, named Rokóa, and a Mr Barton, an American trader residing at the island. The object of the young chief in this expedition, was to ascertain the fate of an elder brother, who had sailed for Anaa, or Chain island, several months before, with the intention of returning immediately, but who had never since been heard from: that of Mr Barton, was to engage a number of Hao-divers, for a pearl-fishing voyage, contemplated by him in connection with another foreign trader. He did not himself embark with us; but his son, a young man, two or three years my senior, accompanied us instead, to make the necessary arrangements for engaging the divers, and also to purchase any mother-of-pearl, pearls, and tortoise-shell, which the natives might have to dispose of, at such places as we should visit. With a view to the latter purpose, he was provided with a supply of trinkets and cheap goods of various kinds, such as are used in this species of traffic. At the Society Islands, the natives had learned the fair value of their commodities, and would no longer exchange even their yams, bread-fruit, and cocoa-nuts, for beads, spangles, and fragments of looking-glasses; but among the smaller groups, lying farther to the eastward, where the intercourse with Europeans was comparatively infrequent, these, and similar articles, were still in great demand, the simple islanders readily giving rich shells, and valuable pearls, in barter for them. I accompanied the expedition, at the request of Rokóa, and with scarcely any other object than to gratify him; though I was made the bearer of letters, and some trifling presents to a Tahitian native missionary, who had recently gone to Hao, to labour there. I had long known both Rokóa and his brother, now supposed to be lost. The former was a remarkable and interesting character. He had accompanied my uncle and myself on a voyage to Hawaii, and visited with us the great volcano of Kilauea, on that island, said to be by far the grandest and most wonderful in the world, not excepting Vesuvius itself. In making the descent into the crater, and while endeavouring to reach what is called the Black Ledge, he saved my life at the imminent hazard of his own. It was upon that voyage, that I first became acquainted with him. We afterwards travelled together, through the most wild and inaccessible parts of the interior of Tahiti and Eimeo; and in the course of this intimacy, I discovered much in him to esteem and admire. There was in his character, such a union of gentleness and courage, such childlike openness of disposition, and such romantic fidelity to what he considered the obligations of friendship, as reminds me of young Edmund, in Johnny's favourite story of Asiauga's Knight. With a chivalrous daring, that could face the most appalling danger without a tremor, was united an almost feminine delicacy of character, truly remarkable in a savage."

"That," said Browne, "is the true ideal of the knightly character— courage, which nothing can daunt, but without roughness or ferocity even in the hour of mortal combat. The valour of the knight is a high sentiment of honour, devotion, loyalty; it is calm, gentle, beautiful, and is thus distinguished from the mere animal courage of the ruffian, which is brutal, fierce, and cruel."

"I think I shall like Rokóa," said Johnny, rubbing his hands together in token of satisfaction, "and I guess this is going to be an interesting story; there will be some fighting in it, I expect."

"Of course, there will be plenty of fighting," said Max, "or else what is the meaning of this preliminary flourish of trumpets, about Rokóa's chivalrous courage, and all that?"

"I once more give fair and timely notice, in order to prevent disappointment, that I am merely relating a sober narrative of facts, and not improvising one of Max's florid romances about Sooloo pirates, Spanish bandits, Italian bravos, or the robbers of the Hartz mountains."

"Or enchanted castles, captive princesses, valiant knights, fire-breathing dragons, and diabolical old magicians," added Browne, "which formed the staple of a highly edifying tale with which I overheard him entertaining Johnny the other afternoon at Castle-hill, as we were taking our siesta in the shade."

"And a capital story it was, too," said Johnny, "but go on, Arthur, please."

"Well, every thing being arranged for our voyage, we set sail in a large 'Vaa Motu,' or single canoe, furnished with a great outrigger, and manned by a crew of nine natives. Our cargo consisted of Barton's stock of goods for trading with the islanders, and a quantity of stained tappa, fine mats, shark's teeth, etcetera, which Rokóa had laid in for purposes of his own.

"The commencement of the voyage was pleasant and auspicious. We set out in the morning, with a fine westerly breeze, which is of rare occurrence in that latitude, and early in the afternoon we passed the high island of Meetia, just in sight to the southward, showing that we had made at least seventy miles, in about nine hours. The wind continued steady and fair, and the next day at sunset, we reached Anaa. Here we remained only long enough to enable Rokóa to obtain all the information to be had, that promised to throw any light upon the fate of his brother. All that could be learned was, that a canoe from Tahiti had touched here several months since, and after obtaining a supply of water, had immediately sailed for Motutunga, or Adventure Island, but from the description given us of the canoe, and of the number and appearance of her company, there was little reason to believe that this was the party with which Rokóa's brother had embarked. Barton being anxious to improve the favourable breeze, which still continued to blow with unwonted steadiness from such a quarter, we resumed our voyage, and steered eastward for Hao, on the day after our arrival at Anaa.

"That night the weather suddenly changed, and a storm arose, the wind blowing strongly from the south-west. Our crew became alarmed, and a part of them began to clamour to return to Anaa, which we might have done, by three or four hours' incessant paddling, in the teeth of the gale. Rokóa, however, believed that the weather would change again in the morning, and determined to continue on our course; we accordingly ran before the wind, with barely sufficient sail to keep the canoe steady, and enable us to steer her. The storm continued without intermission or abatement for the next twenty-four hours, contrary to Rokóa's prediction; and to avoid the danger of being swamped, we were obliged still to keep running before it. The second night, at sunset, the wind fell, and in the morning, the sea had become tolerably smooth, with only a moderate breeze blowing. But though the gale had ceased, the weather was still thick, and the sky so obscured by clouds that we could not see the sun, or even fix upon the quarter of the heavens in which he stood. Thus, those means upon which the natives are wont to rely for directing their course upon their long voyages, wholly failed us. The canoe was furnished with a small ship's compass, a present to Rokóa from the missionaries, but this had been broken, by one of our crew being thrown violently upon it during the storm, while Barton was consulting it. We did not get even a glimpse of the sun all that day; nor the next, until late in the afternoon, when it cleared beautifully, and for the first time since the loss of the compass, we were able to distinguish north from south, and east from west. We found that we had got completely 'turned round,' as the phrase is, and were heading due north; and we now put about, and steered in what we supposed to be the right direction. At dawn the next day, we were surprised to find ourselves in sight of a strange island, which none of us remembered having seen before. A remarkable looking black rock, resembling the hull of a large man-of-war, rose abruptly from the water about half a mile from the shore.

"Rokóa, who had sailed a great deal among the islands east of Tahiti, and had visited most of them, could form no conjecture in regard to the one now in sight. Presently some of our crew began to whisper mysteriously together, and the word was passed from one to another, that this was no other than the ill-famed island of Angatan. I knew that an island of that name, the subject of a thousand bug-bear stories, to which I had often incredulously listened, was said to lie somewhere to the north of Hao; but I had never met with any one who could give me any definite and satisfactory information respecting it.

"According to general report, its inhabitants were cannibals, and were in the habit of murdering and devouring all who were so unfortunate as to be cast upon their shores, or who had the hardihood or temerity voluntarily to land upon them. It was also said, that the island had never been visited by white men; and, owing to the popular belief in regard to the ferocious and warlike character of its people, it is certain that the natives of the neighbouring groups could not, as a general thing, be induced by any consideration to engage in a voyage having this reputed cannibal island for its destination; voyages of this kind having been sometimes contemplated, but never to my knowledge actually undertaken.

"Among the other marvellous reports concerning Angatan, was one, to the effect that its inhabitants were possessed of immense hoards of pearls and shell, of the value of which they were utterly ignorant.

"One of our crew, a garrulous Hao-man, and an inveterate boaster, declared that, about a year since, he had embarked for Angatan with a party of Chain Islanders, in a large double canoe, being tempted to incur the perils of the enterprise, by the prospect of the enormous gains that might be realised in trading with the natives, if a friendly intercourse could once be opened with them. They had succeeded in reaching the island; but scarcely had they set foot upon the shore, when they were attacked by a party of the inhabitants, who issued suddenly from the forest, and, disregarding all their friendly signs and gestures, fell upon them, and killed the greater part of their number, the rest making their escape with difficulty, and solely through the courage, presence of mind, and extraordinary exertions of the narrator, without which they must all infallibly have perished. He described the islanders as fierce, wild-looking men, of gigantic stature, armed with long spears, and heavy clubs set with sharks' teeth, and wearing little or no clothing; yet, strange to tell, around the necks of these almost naked savages were strings of the richest pearls, instead of the common ornaments of ovula-shells.

"Our veracious Hao-man, most solemnly asseverated the entire and literal truth of all these particulars, and declared that the island before us was the veritable cannibal Angatan, the singular black rock enabling him, as he said, to identify it beyond all doubt. To this story I was myself disposed to accord about the same degree of credit as to the adventures of Sinbad the Sailor; but it was easy to perceive that our crew, far from being so sceptical, were firm and unhesitating believers in Angatan, its man-eating giants, its treasures of pearl, and the whole catalogue of marvels current respecting it.

"I was the less inclined to repose any confidence in the man's declarations, because all the best accounts located Angatan far to the north of Hao and Amanu, while we had reason to believe that we were now to the south-west of them.

"Barton's curiosity and love of adventure, were stimulated by what he had heard; perhaps, also, the hints which had been dropped respecting rich shell and costly pearls, were not without their due share of influence, and he declared himself desirous of taking a closer look at this 'terra incognita,' respecting which such marvellous tales were current. Rokóa, too, no sooner heard the first whispered conjecture of the identity of the place before us with Angatan, than he resolved to land, notwithstanding the evident reluctance of the crew, and the open remonstrances and warnings of Sinbad. I suspected, I scarcely know why, that he cherished a vague hope of being able to gain here some clue to the fate of his missing brother. On approaching the shore, we found that a heavy surf broke upon it, but there was a good beach, and a landing could be effected without much difficulty. We accordingly took in our sail, and resorting to the paddles, made for what seemed to be a favourable spot. Soon after passing the black rock before alluded to, I observed several figures stealing along the shore, in the covert of a row of mangrove bushes, and apparently watching our movements. When we had reached the edge of the surf, and were preparing to dash through it, they came out of the thicket, and with threatening gestures warned us away. This created such a panic among our crew, that they could not be prevailed upon to paddle nearer. Rokóa stood up in the bow, and made such signs and gestures as are used to indicate peaceful and friendly intentions, while Barton displayed some of his most attractive-looking trinkets. The people on shore now seemed to confer together, and in a few moments, one of their number, who, from his stained tiputa of yellow and crimson, appeared to be a chief or person of consequence, came down to the water's edge, waving a green bough, and beckoning us to land. Our Sinbad pronounced this sudden apparent change in their disposition towards us, to be a treacherous pretence, designed to lure us ashore, in order that they might plunder, kill, and devour us; but, as he did not explain why, if such was their object, they should in the first place have menaced us as they had done, we gave little heed to his warnings. The party of natives did not seem greatly to outnumber us, and were not particularly formidable in their appearance. They were, as well as we could judge at such a distance, of no more than the ordinary stature. With the exception of the individual already referred to, in the gay tiputa, they wore nothing but the maro, and were armed with long spears. Nevertheless, our crew still refused to make any nearer approach, suspecting that more of the natives were lurking among the mangrove; ready to sally out upon us at the proper moment if we should venture to land.

"Rokóa, finding all attempts to overcome the cowardice of our men unavailing, took a few trinkets in his hand, and springing overboard, swam through the surf to the shore. The personage in the tiputa waited to receive him, continuing to wave the green branch, and to make amicable signs. Rokóa advanced, and greeted him in the Tahitian fashion, by rubbing faces. The two then walked together to the skirts of the wood, where the others still kept themselves, and Rokóa after distributing his trinkets, came down to the beach again, and beckoned us to come ashore, supposing that our crew might by this time be so far reassured as to venture it. Sinbad was about to remonstrate again, when Barton drew a pocket-pistol, with a pair of which he was provided, and threatened to shoot him, unless he kept quiet. This effectually silenced the croakings of the Hao-man, for the time at least and we finally induced some of the others to take to the paddles, and push through the surf to the spot where Rokóa awaited us. As soon as the canoe was beached, and we were all fairly ashore, the natives came forward, somewhat hastily, from the skirt of the wood, probably in the expectation of receiving further presents; but our men, mistaking this sudden advance for a hostile movement, laid hold of the canoe, and would have put her into the water again, had not Rokóa, armed with a heavy paddle, and backed by Barton with his pistols, interfered with so much decision and vigour, that their fears began to take a new direction and they came to the sensible conclusion, that they had better run the risk of being roasted and eaten by the cannibals, than encounter the far more immediate danger of having their heads broken by the club of their chief, or their bodies bored through by the pistol-balls of the young Papalangi.

"On the other hand, the leader of the party of natives spoke to them, and restrained their impatience; then, advancing before the rest, he waved his hand, and throwing himself into an oratorical attitude, made a little speech, thanking Rokóa for his gifts, and welcoming us to the island. The language which he spoke was a dialect of the Tahitian, differing from it so slightly that I had no difficulty in understanding what he said.

"When he had finished, Rokóa made an appropriate reply, according to the rules of Polynesian etiquette. He commenced by paying our gaudily-attired friend some florid compliments. He then gave a graphic account of our voyage, describing the storm which we had encountered in such terms, that our escape must have seemed little short of a miracle; and concluded by stating the manner in which we had been driven from our course, and finally reached the island. The natives listened attentively, and signified their sense of Rokóa's eloquence by frequent exclamations of 'Maitai! Maitai!' (good! good!) and by nodding their heads emphatically at the end of every sentence."

Chapter Twenty One
The Cannibal Village

The Marae and the Priest—Mowno at Home—
Cannibal Young Ladies—Olla and her Friends

"And there, with awful rites, the hoary priest,
Beside that moss-grown heathen altar stood,
His dusky form in magic cincture dressed,
And made the offering to his hideous god."

"So then," said Browne, interrupting Arthur's narrative, "these two parties of savages, instead of going to work, knocking each others' brains out, as one might naturally have expected, actually commenced entertaining one another with set speeches, very much like the mayor and aldermen of a city corporation receiving a deputation of visitors!"

"There is," replied Arthur, "an almost childish fondness of form and ceremony among all the Polynesian tribes, as is seen at their high feasts and festivals, their games, and religious rites. The chiefs and priests are in the habit of making little orations upon a variety of occasions, when this is expected of them. Formerly there existed in the Society Islands, a class of persons called Rautis, or orators of battle, whose exclusive business it was to exhort the people in time of war, and on the eve of an engagement. Even during the heat of conflict they mingled with the combatants, and strove to animate and inflame their courage, by recounting the exploits of their ancestors, and urging every motive calculated to excite desperate valour and contempt of death. Some very remarkable instances of the powerful effect produced by the eloquence of these Rautis are recorded, showing that they constituted a by no means useless or ineffective part of a native army. The islanders almost universally have a taste for oratory, by which they are easily affected; and they hold those who excel in it in high estimation."

"It would appear then," said Browne, "that they are not such utter heathens after all; I should never have given them credit for so much taste and sensibility."

"You see, Browne," said Max, "what advantages you will enjoy over the rest of us, when we get to Eiulo's island, as Johnny is confident we are destined to do, one of these days. You shall then astonish the simple inhabitants, with Pitt's reply to Walpole, or 'Now is the winter of our discontent,' and gain advancement in the state, by your oratorical gifts. Who knows but you may rise to be prime-minister, or chief Rauti, to his majesty the king!"

"Pray, let Arthur proceed with his story," said Morton, laughing, "I see that Johnny is beginning to grow impatient: he probably thinks it high time for the cannibals to be introduced, and the fighting to commence."

"Well," resumed Arthur, "as soon as the speech-making was over, the natives, who seemed thus far, quite friendly and inoffensive, came forward once more, and we all went through the ceremony of rubbing faces, with a great show of cordiality, though it was easy to perceive that our party were still under the influence of secret fears and misgivings.

"Barton and I, received more than our due proportion of these civilities, and from the wondering exclamations of our new acquaintances as they examined the articles which composed our dress, and their remarks to one another upon our complexion, I inferred that some of them at least, had never seen a white person before. Barton, in particular, attracted a large share of their attention, owing probably to a complexion rather florid, and uncommonly fair, notwithstanding a two years' residence within the tropics, which, together with his light hair and blue eyes, afforded a striking contrast to the tawny skins and long black elf-locks of the natives.

"The chief of the party, who had acted as spokesman, was called Mowno. He was a young man, with a handsome, boyish face, expressive of good-nature and indolence. Rokóa walked apart with him to make inquiries, as I had no doubt, connected with the subject of his brother's fate. Meanwhile Barton produced a piece of tortoise-shell, and some pearls, which he exhibited to the natives, asking whether they had any articles of the kind; but after carelessly looking at them, they shook their heads, and inquired what such things were good for; whereupon Barton, casting an annihilating glance at the disconcerted Sinbad, significantly demanded of him what had become of those necklaces of pearls, worn by the natives of Angatan, and whether these simple, inoffensive people, were the gigantic cannibals, about whom he had manufactured such enormous lies.

"After Mowno had concluded his conference with Rokóa, he led us to a large building near the beach, in a very ruinous and decayed state, and completely over-shadowed by aged tamanu-trees. It seemed, from its size and peculiar structure, to be a deserted marae, or native temple. He then sent away two of his people, who soon returned with several clusters of cocoa-nuts, and some bananas, for our refreshment. On learning that the supply of water which we had taken in for our voyage, was nearly exhausted, he informed us that there was no spring or stream, nearer than his village, which was some two miles inland, and promised to have a supply sent us during the day. They had come down to the shore, as we now learned, for the purpose of cutting mangrove roots, from which they make large and powerful bows, and the whole party soon left us at the marae, and proceeded to the beach; in about an hour we saw them depart inland, carrying fagots of these roots, without taking any further notice of us.

"It had fallen calm soon after sunrise, so that we could not for the present have resumed our voyage, had we been so inclined.

"About half an hour before noon, a number of the natives whom we had seen in the morning, again made their appearance, with several large calabashes of water, and a quantity of taro and bread-fruit for our use. Rokóa distributed among them some trifling presents, which they hastily concealed among the folds of their maros. A few moments afterwards Mowno himself emerged from the grove, attended by the remainder of the party we had seen in the morning. There was now a further distribution of presents, when I perceived the reason why the first comers had so hastily concealed the trifles which had been given them. All presents, no matter on whom bestowed, seemed to be regarded as the especial perquisites of the chief, and a youth, who acted as Mowno's personal attendant, presently went round among the others, collecting and taking possession of everything which he had seen them receive. This was submitted to without remonstrance, and apparently as a matter of course, though by no means cheerfully.

"Soon after this somewhat autocratic proceeding, Mowno turned abruptly to Barton, and saying that he must now return to the village, invited him to go with him to visit it. Barton appearing to hesitate, the chief pressed the matter so earnestly that his suspicions were aroused, and he peremptorily declined. Mowno's angry looks evinced his displeasure, and after walking about for a quarter of an hour in sullen silence, with very much the demeanour of a spoiled child thwarted in his whim, he at length made a similar request of me, letting drop at the same time, some expression to the effect that one of us *must* go with him. Fortunately Rokóa, whose high spirit would have taken instant offence at the least semblance of a threat, did not hear this. I saw plainly, that for some reason, the young chief had set his heart upon having either Barton or myself visit his village, and I suspected this was, in fact, the sole object of his return. I observed, also, that his party was somewhat more numerous, and much better armed than it had been in the morning, and I had no doubt that, rather than suffer himself to be baffled in his purpose, he would resort to force to accomplish it.

"After a moment's reflection, I was pretty well satisfied that I had nothing to fear from acceding to his request, believing, as I did, that I understood the motive of it. I thought, too, that a refusal would in all probability lead to an instant hostile collision between the natives and ourselves, and I finally resolved to accept, or more accurately speaking, to yield to, the invitation. Having come to this conclusion, I told Mowno that I would go with him, upon the condition that I should return before night, to which he readily assented, showing extreme satisfaction at having finally succeeded in his wishes. I gave no credit to the alleged cannibal propensities of the islanders, and was inclined from what I had already seen, to think much more favourably of them than the event justified. I supposed that the curiosity of the people of the village had been excited by the reports of those who had seen us in the morning, respecting the pale-faced strangers, and that Mowno's only object in insisting as he did, on having Barton or myself go with him, was to gratify some aged chief who was too infirm to come down to the shore to see us, or did not want to take the trouble of doing so."

"Well, was you right in your conjecture?" inquired Browne.

"Yes, partially at least; there was, I think, no unfriendly motive as far as Mowno was concerned. What designs others of the natives may have entertained I will not at present undertake to say. But instead of some superannuated chief, it was the curiosity of Mowno's young wife that was to be gratified. On hearing his account of the white strangers, she had despatched him forthwith back to the shore, to bring them to the village; which commission, it seemed, he was resolved faithfully to execute, at every hazard."

"Really," said Browne, "civilisation must have made some considerable progress in Angatan, if the savages there make such docile and complaisant husbands."

"This was not an ordinary case," replied Arthur; "in the first place, Mowno was an uncommonly good-natured sort of a savage; then he had a very pretty, persuasive little wife, and he had not yet been long enough married, to have entirely merged the zeal and devotion of the lover, in the easy indifference, and staid authority of the husband; but this is anticipating.

"When I informed Rokóa of the young chief's invitation, and my acceptance of it, he refused to consent to my going, except upon the condition that he should accompany me, and share whatever danger might attend the step. Mowno acquiesced in this arrangement, though I thought he didn't seem to be altogether pleased with it. Barton, also, on learning that

Rokóa and myself had concluded to go to the village, resolved to accompany us. Mowno was impatient to have us set out at once, and Rokóa having given some directions to the crew as to their conduct during our absence, we hastily made our preparations, and in a few moments after the matter had been decided upon, the whole party left the shore and entered the forest. A quarter of an hour's walk brought us to a flourishing bread-fruit plantation, which we passed through without seeing a single dwelling, or any indications of inhabitants. This was bounded by a wild ravine, crossing which, we entered a dense and gloomy grove, composed almost entirely of the sacred miro, and one other kind of tree, the branches of which sprang horizontally from the trunk in a series of whorls, one above another, twisting round from left to right, and clothed with broad leaves of so dark a green as to seem almost black. Near the centre of this grove, we came suddenly upon a large marae, built principally of loose stones, overgrown with moss and lichens. It was a spacious, uncovered inclosure, the front of which consisted of a strong bamboo fence, while the three remaining sides were of stone. Within the inclosure, at one side, was a small building, probably the priest's dwelling, and in the centre arose a solid pyramidal structure, on the terraced sides of which were ranged the misshapen figures of several gigantic idols. In front of this, and between four rude tumuli of broken coral, was a low platform, supported by stakes, and resembling the altars used for human sacrifices, during the ancient reign of heathenism in Tahiti. Beneath this platform, or altar, was a pile of human skulls; and suspended from the trees, were the shells of enormous turtles, and the skeletons of fishes. A hideous-looking old man, whom I supposed to be the priest, sat in the door of the small building, within the inclosure, and looking intently at me, made strange faces as we passed by. His skin was sallow, and singularly speckled, probably from some cutaneous disease; he had no eyebrows, and his eyes were small and glittering like those of a snake; in his countenance there was a mingled expression of cunning and cruelty that made me shudder. When we were nearest to him in passing, he struck himself violently on the breast, and cried out in a strong but dissonant voice, pointing with his long, skeleton fingers, towards the young chief:— 'Mowno, son of Maloa, rob not the servant of Oro of a priest's share!' so at least, I understood the words which he uttered; but the natives hurried on, without seeming to pay any attention to him."

"That would have frightened me mortally," interrupted Johnny. "I should have thought that they were going to make a cannibal feast of me, and that the wicked old priest was speaking for his share."

"Well, I confess that some notion of the sort flashed across my mind for a moment. The dark grove, the great idolatrous looking marae, with its heathen altar, and monstrous images; the pile of skulls; the hideous old man and his strange words; all tended to suggest vague but startling suspicions. But another glance at the open and friendly countenances of our guides reassured me. In answer to a question in regard to the building which we had just passed, Mowno said, with a natural and indifferent air, that it was the house of Oro, where a great solemnity was soon to be celebrated; and although I did not allude to the skulls, he added that they were a part of the remains of the priests, who had been buried within the inclosure, and which were now, in accordance with an established custom, placed beneath the altar. The dark wood was bounded by a charming valley, with a brook running through it, and I was glad to escape from its gloomy shade, into the cheerful light. We forded the shallow stream, which was so clear that every pebble in its gravelly bed was visible, and found ourselves at the foot of a long, green slope. Before us, lying partly in the valley, and straggling half-way up the ascent, was a pretty village. The neat and light-built native dwellings dotted the side of the slope, or peeped out from among embowering trees along the banks of the brook, in the most picturesque manner. The thatching of the cottages, bleached to an almost snowy-whiteness, offered a pleasing contrast to the surrounding verdure. Troops of children were pursuing their sports in every direction. Some were wading in the stream, sailing tiny boats, or actively spattering one another with water, a recreation which they could enjoy without any fear of that damage to clothing, which would have rendered it objectionable in more highly civilised communities. Others again, (many of them scarcely old enough to walk, as one would suppose), were swimming about in the deeper places, like amphibious creatures. Some were swinging on ropes of sennit, suspended from the branches of the trees, and a few were quietly sitting in the shade, making bouquets and wreaths of wild-flowers. Among them all, there was not a single deformed or sickly-looking child. I did not observe any grown persons, most of them probably being at that hour asleep in their houses. In passing through the village, our escort closed around us in such a manner as to screen us from observation, and we reached the top of the slope without seeming to have attracted notice. Here Mowno dismissed all his attendants except two, and we then struck into a fine avenue of well-grown trees, running along the crest of the hill, and leading to a large native house, of oval form, prettily situated upon a green knoll, and over-shadowed by wide-branching bread-fruit trees. This, Mowno informed us, was his dwelling. At a short distance from the house, beneath a fan-palm, was a group of young girls, so entirely absorbed in the congenial task of arranging one another's abundant tresses, and adorning themselves with flowers, that they did not observe our approach. Mowno seemed intent upon some playful surprise, and laughing softly to himself like a pleased child, he motioned us to hide ourselves in a thicket of young casuarinas. From our ambush he pointed out to us one of the group beneath the palm, having several white buds of the fragrant gardenia in her hair, and a garland of the rosa cinensis about her neck; when satisfied that he had drawn our attention to the right person, he gave us to understand, with an air of great complacency, that she was 'Olla,' his wife. While thus engaged, we were suddenly discovered, being betrayed by Mowno's gaudy tiputa, seen through the foliage by the quick eye of his better half, who immediately sprang up with a clear, ringing laugh, scattering a lapful of flowers upon the ground, and came running like a fawn towards him; the rest of us still keeping concealed. She was very pretty, graceful as a bird in every movement, and had a singularly pleasing expression of countenance.

"On witnessing the greeting which she bestowed upon Mowno, Barton whispered me that he ought to consider himself a happy savage, and to do him justice, he seemed to be of the same opinion himself. She commenced talking at once, with wonderful vivacity, pouring forth a continuous torrent of words, with little gushes of laughter interspersed here and there by way of punctuation, and making no longer or more frequent pauses than were absolutely necessary for the purpose of taking breath. Notwithstanding her amazing volubility, I could understand enough of what she said, to perceive that she was inquiring after 'the pale-faced youths,' and presently she appeared to be scolding her husband in a pretty lively strain, for having failed to bring them with him according to his promise. It was amusing to witness Mowno's ludicrous struggles to look grave, while he made feigned excuses, and explanations of our absence. His demeanour resembled more that of a boy, whose head has been turned by becoming, for the first time, the actual and uncontrolled owner of a watch, or a fowling-piece, than of a stern warrior, or savage chief. He could not, with all his efforts, maintain sufficient gravity and self-possession, to carry out the jest, poor as it was, which he had undertaken; but kept glancing towards our hiding-place, and finally, burst into a boisterous explosion of laughter; when Olla, peeping into the thicket, caught sight of us, and instantly darted away with a pretty half-scream, and rejoined her companions. Mowno now beckoned us forth, and we approached the group, whereupon they made a show of scampering off into the grove, but apparently thought better of it, and concluded to stand their ground. At first, they seemed actually afraid of Barton and myself, peeping cautiously at us over one another's shoulders from a safe distance. Presently, one, more enterprising than the rest, ventured so far as to reach out her hand, and touch Barton on the cheek, when, finding that no disastrous consequences immediately followed this act of temerity, they gradually laid aside their apprehensions, and pressing around us, soon became sufficiently familiar to try a variety of highly original and interesting experiments upon our complexion and clothing. These, though somewhat annoying, were accompanied by questions and observations so irresistibly ludicrous, that we soon found it entirely out of the question to preserve any sort of gravity, and as the whole troop always joined in our laughter without stopping to understand its cause, or instantly led off of themselves, upon the slightest provocation, the woods resounded with peals of merriment.

"One of these damsels, after examining Barton's fair skin, and flowing yellow locks, gravely communicated to a companion, her conviction that we had come from the moon. A second stoutly maintained our earthly origin, and attributed our paleness to the influence of some strange sickness; while a third, being of a sceptical and suspicious turn of mind, suddenly seized Barton by the wrist and spitting upon the skirt of her pareu, commenced scrubbing his hand with great vigour, to see whether the colours were fast. Our tight-fitting garments; too, seemed to puzzle them exceedingly, and we were listeners to an animated debate, upon the question whether they were a natural or an artificial covering; the young lady who upheld the theory of our lunar origin, inclining strongly to the opinion, that like the feathery coat of birds, our clothing was a part of ourselves. But the sagacity and penetration of the one who had endeavoured to wash the paint from Barton's hand, soon enabled her to discover the unsoundness of this doctrine, and, in order the more triumphantly to refute it, she insisted upon pulling off my jacket, and trying it on herself. Finding that nothing less would satisfy her, I resigned the garment, when having succeeded, with some assistance, in getting into it, and buttoning it up as far as was practicable, she snatched Barton's cap to complete her costume, and commenced parading up and down the avenue, the admiration and envy of her companions. I fully expected that Barton's coat would next be put in requisition, and he whispered me that he stood in momentary dread, lest the now awakened spirit of investigation and experiment, should prompt our new friends to still more embarrassing extremes.

"This, however, proved to be a groundless apprehension, for their curiosity was presently diverted into a new channel by Olla, who suddenly demanded to know my name. I accordingly repeated it, and she endeavoured several times to pronounce it after me, but without success. The 'th' seemed to constitute an insuperable difficulty, which, however, she finally evaded, by softening 'Arthur' into 'Artua,' and this, singularly enough, was what Rokóa had always been in the habit of calling me. He and Barton were now called upon for their names, and in return, we were favoured with the liquid and vowelly appellatives, by which our ingenuous and communicative acquaintances were respectively designated. Barton assumed the alias of Tom, which was straightway metamorphosed into 'Tomma.'

"While this exchange of names was going on, an old woman came from the house, and delivered some message to Olla, which from the repetition of the words 'poé, poé,' I conjectured to be a summons to dinner. Mowno leading the way, we now proceeded towards the dwelling. It was surrounded by a strong, but neat hedge of the ti-plant some three and a half feet high, with an ingeniously contrived wicker gate opposite the door. A path strewn with marine shells, and fragments of white coral, led from the gate to the door. The space within the inclosure was chiefly devoted to the cultivation of yams and other vegetables, but Olla showed me a little plot of ground, near the house, which she said was her own garden. It was tastefully arranged, and carefully kept, and a considerable variety of flowers, all of which she had herself transplanted from the woods, were there in full bloom. Most conspicuous among them was the native jasmine, and a species of wood-pink, both of which were fragrant. The building itself was a model of a native dwelling, and since we are to-morrow to try our own skill in house-building, I will endeavour to describe it. It was of an oval shape; the sides were inclosed with handsome mats, with spaces left for the admission of light and air. The roof was composed of a firm and durable thatch of pandanus leaves, strung upon small reeds, laid closely together, and overlapping one another from the eaves to the ridge-pole.

"From the inside, the appearance was the neatest and prettiest imaginable, the whiteness of the straight and slender rafters of peeled hibiscus, contrasting well with the ceiling of shining brown leaves which they sustained. The furniture of the house consisted of a number of large sleeping-mats, five or six carved wooden stools, and two narrow tables, or rather shelves, of wicker-work, fastened against the wall at opposite sides of the room. Upon one of these were arranged a number of calabashes, carved wooden dishes, cocoa-nut drinking-cups, and other domestic utensils. Upon the other was a native drum, several clubs and spears, a long vivo or native flute, and a hideous-looking wooden image with four arms and a bunch of red feathers fastened to what was doubtless meant for its head. The rafters were ornamented with braided and coloured cords wound round them, the ends of which hung down several feet, and sustained a number of weapons and various other articles suspended by them.

"At the farther end of the room, a woman was pounding taro, or bread-fruit, in a wooden mortar; another, apparently very old and infirm, was sitting upon a low stool near the wall, swaying her body slowly from side to side, and making a low, monotonous noise. I observed that Olla frequently looked towards the latter, with a mournful expression of countenance. When we first entered the house, she went and sat down by her side, and talked with her in a low tone, and when she turned away, her eyes were full of tears. The old woman did not evince any corresponding emotion, but muttered something feebly and indistinctly, as if replying to what Olla had said, of which I could distinguish the words, 'It is best, child; Malola is very old; she is sick and weak; she cannot work; it is time she should be buried out of the way.' I instantly suspected that this unhappy creature was to be destroyed by her own friends, on account of her age and infirmities, according to a most horrible and unnatural, but too prevalent custom. I had once been present at a scene of this kind, without the slightest possibility of successful interference, when a native woman had been strangled; her own son, pulling at one end of the tappa which encircled his mother's neck. In that case, the victim, instead of submitting quietly and willingly to her fate, (as is most usual), suddenly lost her courage at the moment of reaching the grave, beside which she was to be strangled, and opposed a frantic and desperate resistance to her murderers. Her heart-rending cries; her fearful struggles; and, more than all, the horrid indifference and cruelty of her executioners, have left upon my mind an indelible impression. I now resolved that if my suspicions proved just, I would make an earnest effort to prevent the repetition of so inhuman a deed, and from what I had already seen of the mild disposition of Mowno, I was inclined to believe that there was great hope of success in such an endeavour.

"Rokóa, on hearing the conversation above mentioned, had given me a significant glance, which sufficiently explained to me how he understood it. A very few moments sufficed to confirm my worst suspicions: I learned that the aged female who had spoken of herself as Malola, was Mowno's aunt and that she was, with her own full consent and approval, to be destroyed in a few days. From the manner in which Olla alluded to it, while I inferred that such acts were by no means uncommon among these people, I at the same time clearly perceived, that custom and education had not stifled or perverted in her gentle nature, at least, the ordinary feelings and impulses of humanity, and that she anticipated the deed with terror and loathing. I determined to watch for an opportunity to converse with Mowno, and discover, if possible, whether the cruel insensibility, implied in countenancing such a practice, could really be concealed beneath so smooth and pleasant an aspect.

"Meanwhile, the meal to which we had been summoned was spread under the shade trees beside the house. It consisted of baked fish, served up in banana leaves, roasted yams, poé-poé, a preparation of bread-fruit, and an excellent kind of pudding, made of cocoa-nut-pulp and taro. It was easy to perceive that Olla, with all her playfulness and girlish vivacity, was a notable housekeeper."

"Let me interrupt you a moment, to ask a single question," said Max. "Did you get the recipe for making that pudding from Mrs Mowno?—if so, please impart the same for the general good, and I will try my hand at it the first convenient opportunity."

"Heathen!" exclaimed Browne, "can you think of nothing but gormandising? Pray, Arthur, proceed."

"And bring on those cannibals forthwith," added Morton, "for unless you do so, Johnny will despair entirely of any fighting, and go to sleep."

Chapter Twenty Two
An Explosion

The Cannibals appreciate Music and Eloquence, but take Offence at the New Theology

"Then tumult rose, fierce rage, and wild affright."

"In the afternoon," resumed Arthur, "we went with our host and hostess, and our companions at dinner, to a grove on the banks of the stream—a place of general resort for the villagers during the latter part of every fine day. The younger people met there, to pursue a variety of sports and athletic exercises, and the older to gossip and look on. We had intended to return to the boat, as soon as the repast was over, and it would have been well had we done so. But our new friends insisted so strenuously upon our accompanying them to the grove, that we yielded at last to their playful importunities, so far as to consent to make a brief pause there on our way. We had gone but a short distance from the house, when a bird of about the size of a robin, flew down from a tree beneath which we were passing, and after circling several times around Olla's head, alighted on her finger, which she held out for it to perch upon. It was a young wood-pigeon, which she had found in the grove, when a callow half-fledged thing, the old bird having been captured or killed by some juvenile depredators. Taking pity on its orphan state, Olla had adopted and made a pet of it: it was now perfectly tame, and would come readily at her call of 'Lai-evi', (little captive), the name she had given it, attending her so closely as to be seldom during the day beyond the sound of her voice.

"On reaching the grove, we found quite a number of the natives, of all ages and of both sexes assembled, and though they soon began to gather about us with inquisitive looks, we were subjected to much less annoyance than might reasonably have been expected under the circumstances. We were neither crowded, nor jostled, nor even offensively stared at, the very children appearing to possess an innate delicacy and sense of propriety, (though it may have been timidity), which made them try to gratify their curiosity covertly, seizing those opportunities to peep at us, when they thought they were themselves unobserved.

"Barton, who possessed an enviable faculty of adapting himself to all sorts of people and circumstances, was in a few moments as much at home among the villagers as if he had lived for years in their midst. He gossiped with the old people, romped with the children, and chatted and frolicked with the prettiest and most lively of the dusky maidens, to the manifest disapprobation of several grim-looking young savages, who stalked about in sullen dignity watching these familiar proceedings of the handsome stranger, with rising jealousy and indignation.

"At length a bevy of laughing girls, in punishment for some impertinence with which they charged him, fell to pelting him with jasmine buds and pandanus cones, the latter of which, in mischievous hands, are capable of becoming rather formidable missiles. Foremost among the assailants were our fair acquaintances of the morning, and even Olla, forgetting her matronly station and dignity, joined zealously in the flowery warfare; which was maintained with such spirit, that Barton was at length obliged to beg for quarter, promising at the same time to 'make some music' for them, as a condition of the suspension of hostilities. This proposition, as soon as it was understood, seemed to afford the most extravagant delight; the shower of missiles ceased at once, and Barton was immediately surrounded by as attentive and breathlessly expectant an audience as artist could desire. Taking his stand upon a moss-covered fragment of rock, he drew an enormous Jew's-harp from his pocket, and handed it to me, gravely requesting me to 'accompany' him upon it, while he sang. Then, after clearing his throat, with quite a professional air, he commenced 'Hail Columbia,' and as he had a full, clear voice, and sang with great spirit, the performance was listened to with every mark of enjoyment, and was succeeded by rapturous applause.

"He next gave a solo on the Jew's-harp to the air of 'Yankee Doodle,' with brilliant and original variations, which likewise met with a flattering reception. But by far the greatest sensation was produced by 'Auld Lang syne,' which we sang together as a grand finale. The natives really seemed to feel the sentiment of the music, although Barton turned it into a burlesque by such an exaggerated pathos of tone and expression, and gesture, that I had much difficulty in getting through my part of the performance without laughing; but my vexation at being surprised into taking a part in such a piece of buffoonery, greatly helped me in resisting my sense of the ludicrous. At the end of every verse, Barton grasped my hand in the most demonstrative manner, and commenced shaking it vigorously, looking me all the while solemnly in the face, and shaking away through the entire chorus, thereby producing a number of quavers, which, though not set down in the music, greatly added to its pathetic character. After the last chorus, he spread open his arms, rushed forward, and gave me a stage embrace. This performance, including the pantomime, must have been of a very moving character, for when we had finished, I actually saw tears in the eyes of several of our audience. This evidence of the gentle and unsophisticated character of these simple people, affected me almost as much as our music had moved them, and I could not help thinking to how much better account such amiable impressibility was capable of being turned.

"Having thus performed his promise, Barton now insisted that we ought to be entertained in our turn with some music, and after a little persuasion, three young girls sang, or rather chaunted, several plaintive, but somewhat monotonous airs. Their voices, though neither strong nor clear, were soft and melodious, like the cooing of their native wood-pigeons. In vain we asked for something livelier and more spirited. Barton humming the tune of 'Yankee Doodle,' to make them the better understand what we wanted. All their melodies seemed to be of a slow and measured character, and those specimens which we heard, embraced a comparatively narrow range of notes.

"Just as the native girls finished singing, we were joined by a fresh party of eight or ten men, who came across the brook, and mingled with the others. I heard Barton say to Rokóa, 'There is the old priest again,' but on looking around I could not see him. The new-comers did not appear to be in the same holiday humour as the throng around us; they walked gravely about without joining in the general mirth and gaiety, and manifesting none of the curiosity in regard to ourselves, which the others had evinced. I, however, thought nothing of this at the time, supposing that they had been of the number of those whom we had seen in the morning by the sea-shore, although I did not recognise any of them.

"Presently, Olla and her companions commenced begging us for more music. One young lady in particular, (the same who had pronounced us to be inhabitants of the moon), pressed Barton with unceasing importunities, mingled with threats of a renewal of hostilities in case of non-compliance. Finding all attempts at excuse or evasion utterly unavailing, he suddenly snatched a wreath of yellow candle-nut-blossoms from the head of his tormentress, crowned himself therewith, and springing upon the top of the rock, assumed an oratorical attitude, and waved his hand, as if about to harangue the people. Then, while I was wondering what was to come next, he fixed his eye sternly upon a sinister looking man of middle-age, with the head-dress of an inferior chief, who was standing directly in front of him, and began to declaim in Latin, with great vehemence— 'Quo usque tandem abutere, Catilina, patientia nostrâ,' etcetera, which the audience seemed at first, to consider highly interesting and entertaining. As he proceeded, delivering the sounding sentences, 'ore rotundo,' and emphasising each thundering polysyllable with a fierce gesture of his clenched fist, I observed that the individual before mentioned, whom the orator seemed to have chosen to represent Catiline, and who, without understanding Latin, could very well perceive that there was something menacing and vituperative in the language addressed to him, began to look at first puzzled, and then incensed. He stole two or three hurried and uncertain glances at those behind and immediately around him, as if to assure himself whether this torrent of denunciation was not in fact directed against some other person; but when all doubt on this point seemed to have been resolved by the unequivocal demonstrations of the orator, his rigid features assumed an expression of such anger and ferocity, that I began to fear some violent outbreak of passion, and made several attempts by signs and gestures, to indicate to Barton the danger of pursuing so thoughtless and imprudent a pleasantry. But he either did not perceive my meaning, or else, felt rather flattered than alarmed, by the effect which his elocution seemed to produce upon Catiline, for he continued to pour out upon him the torrent of his oratory for several minutes longer, and it was not until his memory began evidently to fail him, that he concluded with a last emphatic invective accompanied by a sufficiently significant pantomime to convey some notion of its meaning, and bowing to his audience, leaped from the rostrum.

"This performance, seemed to afford even greater pleasure to the male part of the assembly, (with a few exceptions), than the previous musical entertainment had done, and they testified their approbation, by emphatic nods and shouts of applause.

"I now thought it time to terminate our visit, and return to the boat, and was about to speak to Rokóa on the subject, when Barton seized me by the arm, and pushed me towards the platform of rock.

"'Now, Arthur, it is your turn,' said he, 'you perceive what an effect my eloquence has produced on old Catiline, there: give him a lecture upon the sinfulness of indulging the vindictive passions, and exhort him to repentance.'

"The younger people pressed about me, and instigated and aided by Barton, they fairly forced me upon the rocky platform. Though by no means pleased at being obliged to take a part in a farce so little to my taste, and for which I possessed none of Barton's talent, I saw plainly that the shortest and least troublesome way, was to comply with their wishes, and I accordingly endeavoured to recall some fragment of prose or verse which might serve the present purpose. Supposing that English would be quite as intelligible and acceptable to them as Barton's Latin, I was just about to declaim those noble opening lines of Comus—

"'Before the starry threshold of Jove's Court,' etcetera.

"Which used to be a favourite of mine at school, when suddenly another impulse seized me.

"As I glanced around upon the circle of smiling, upturned countenances, I was struck by the docile and childlike expression of many of them. I thought of the sad and benighted condition of this simple people, without the knowledge of God, or the hope of immortality, given up, as it seemed, a helpless prey to the darkest and most cruel superstitions. I thought of the moss-grown marae in the dark wood, with its hideous idols, its piles of human bones, and its hoary priest—fit minister of such a religion. I remembered the aged woman at Mowno's house, and the frightful doom in reserve for her. I felt that perhaps to such impressible spirits, even a passing word, unskilfully and feebly spoken, might by God's blessing do good; and yielding to the impulse of the moment, instead of declaiming the verses from Comus, I began to speak to them in their own language, of those great truths, the most momentous for civilised or savage man to know, and the most deeply interesting to every thoughtful mind, of whatever degree of culture—truths so simple, that even these untutored children of nature could receive, and be made happy by them.

"In the plainest and simplest language I could command, and striving to adapt myself to their habits of thought, and to use those forms of expression most familiar to them, I announced the great doctrine of the existence of one God, the sole creator of the world, and the loving Father of all his creatures. I spoke of his power and his goodness, and told them that though invisible to our eyes, as the wind which stirred the tops of the palm-trees above them, he was ever near each one of us, hearing our words, seeing our actions, reading our thoughts, and caring for us continually.

"I endeavoured to illustrate these attributes of God, by references and allusions to the daily aspects of nature around them, and to ideas and notions with which their mode of life, and the system of superstition in which they had been trained, rendered them familiar. My especial aim was to lead them, unconsciously, as it were, and without making any direct attack upon their religion, to contrast the benignant character of Him who has permitted us to call Him 'Our Father in Heaven,' with that of the malignant beings they had been taught to worship.

"I next spoke of death, and of a future life, and assured them that the friends whom they had buried, and they themselves, and all who had ever lived, should awake as from a brief sleep, and live again for ever. But when I proceeded to declare that most awful and mysterious doctrine of our religion, and spoke of the worm that dieth not and the fire that is not quenched, of eternal happiness, and unending woe, I could see by the earnestness of their attention, and the expression of their countenances, how powerfully they were impressed.

"I cannot remember all that I said, or the language I used, but I endeavoured to set before them in a shape adapted to their comprehension, the simple elements of the Christian scheme—the great doctrines of God and immortality, of human sinfulness and accountability, and of salvation through Jesus Christ. But encouraged by the attention and apparent interest of the silent and listening circle, in the glow of the moment, I went beyond this prescribed limit, and from these vast general truths, I began at last to speak of particular acts and practices. As I thought once more of the marae in the forest, and of the unhappy Malola, I told the people that our Father beyond the sky could alone hear their prayers, and should alone be worshipped; that he desired no sacrifices of living things; that he was offended and displeased with all cruelty and bloodshed; and that the offering of human sacrifices, and the killing of aged persons, were crimes which he detested, and would be sure to punish; that he had expressly commanded children to love and honour their parents, and that it was their duty, the older, the more infirm and helpless they became, the more faithfully to cherish and protect them. In speaking on this subject, I grew earnest and excited, and probably my voice and manner too strongly expressed the abhorrence I felt for such monstrous and unnatural crimes.

"At this point, Barton, who had for some time been looking on in astonishment at the serious turn which the matter had so unexpectedly taken, interrupted me with the whispered caution—

"'Be careful, Arthur! I fear from the black looks of one of your clerical fathers here, that you are giving offence to the cloth, and trenching upon perilous ground.'

"But the warning came too late. Just as I glanced round in search of the threatening looks to which Barton alluded, a frightful figure sprang up on the outer edge of the circle of listeners, directly in front of me, and with cries of rage forced its way towards the spot where I stood. I recognised at once the old priest of the marae, but how changed since I last saw him! Every sign of age and decrepitude had vanished: his misshapen frame seemed dilated, and instinct with nervous energy: his face was pale with the intensity of his fury, and his small eyes flashed fire.

"'Perish, reviler of Oro, and his priests!' he cried, and hurled at me a barbed spear, with so true an aim, that if I had not stooped as it left his hand, it would have struck my face. Whizzing over my head, it pierced the tough bark of a bread-fruit tree, ten yards behind me, where it stood quivering.

Instantly catching a club from the hands of a bystander, he rushed forward to renew the attack. He had reached the foot of the rock where I stood, when Rokóa with a bound placed himself between us, and though without any weapon, motioned him back, with a gesture so commanding, and an air at once so quiet, and so fearless, that the priest paused. But it was for an instant only; then, without uttering a word, he aimed a blow full at Rokóa's head. The latter caught it in his open palm, wrenched the weapon from him, and, adroitly foiling a furious attempt which he made to grapple with him, once more stood upon the defensive with an unruffled aspect and not the slightest appearance of excitement in his manner.

"The baffled priest, livid with rage, looked round for another weapon. Half a dozen of the men who had arrived upon the ground with him, uttered a wild yell, and pressed forward with brandished clubs and spears. Barton and I, placed ourselves by Rokóa's side, the former handing me one of his pistols. All was tumult and confusion. The outbreak had been so sudden and unexpected, and what I have just related had passed so rapidly, that the bystanders had not yet recovered from the first shock of astonishment and terror. Of the women, some shrieked and fled from the spot, others threw themselves between us and the armed natives, or invoked the interference of their brothers and friends for our protection. Only a few, even of the men, seemed to participate in the feeling of hostility against us.

"But however inferior in number, the party of our foes far surpassed that of our friends in resolution and energy. Foremost among them were the priest and the hard-featured chief, who had been so deeply incensed by what he regarded as the wanton insults offered him by Barton. A number of the young men also, whose anger and jealousy had been aroused by his sudden popularity, and the attention which had been paid us, sided zealously with the priest and his party, and joined in the clamour against us.

"Meanwhile, Mowno, at Olla's entreaty, strove to calm the tumult, and to pacify the leader and instigator of it; but his authority was fiercely spurned, and our good-natured protector quailed before the fury of the vindictive old man. As yet, however, our enemies, conscious that the sympathies of a large number of the bystanders were with us, had offered us no actual violence, confining themselves to menacing cries and gestures, by which they seemed to be striving to work themselves up to the requisite pitch of excitement. This was likely to be speedily attained under the influence of the fierce exhortations and contagious fury of the priest. Some of the young men, in fact, now commenced a sort of covert attack, by throwing stones and fragments of wood at us from the outskirts of the crowd, and Barton was struck violently in the mouth by one of these missiles, by which his lip was badly cut. In the midst of all the excitement and tumult, Rokóa stood, with the outward appearance at least, of perfect composure. Neither the ravings of the priest, nor the menacing attitude of 'Catiline,' nor the brandished weapons of their followers, deprived him of his coolness and presence of mind. He steadily confronted them with an unblenching eye, grasping the club of which he had possessed himself, in readiness to meet the attack, which he at the same time did nothing, by look or gesture, to provoke. His calm intrepidity, while it seemed temporarily to restrain our enemies, served also to reassure and steady Barton and myself; and endeavouring to emulate his self-possession, we stood ready to act as circumstances should indicate, looking to him for the example."

Here Arthur paused, as if about to suspend his narrative. Johnny, who was now broad awake, and listening eagerly, waited patiently a few moments, expecting him to recommence. Finding, however, that he did not do so, he at length asked him to "go on."

"It is getting quite late," answered Arthur; "see, those three bright stars which were high in the heavens when we first sat down here, are now on the very edge of the horizon, about to sink behind the ocean. As we expect to be up, and on our way to Castle-hill before sunrise to-morrow. I think we should now go to rest."

"If we do," replied Johnny, "I am sure I shall not be able to sleep; I shall be thinking of that terrible old priest, and trying to guess how you escaped at last."

"I judge," said Browne, "that you are pretty nearly at the end of your adventures in Angatan, so pray let us have the remainder now."

"Do so," added Morton, "and set Johnny's mind at rest, or he will be dreaming of cannibals and cannibal-priests all night, and disturbing us by crying out in his sleep."

"I think it's quite likely," said Johnny, shaking his head in a threatening manner; "I feel just now very much as if I should."

"Since that is the case," said Arthur, "I suppose I must 'go on,' in self-defence; and as I believe that twenty minutes will suffice for what remains, I will finish it."

Chapter Twenty Three
The Flight

Te Vea—The Victim for Sacrifice—The Escape
and Pursuit—The Priest's Ambush

"For life, for life, their flight they ply,
And shriek, and shout, and battle-cry,
And weapons waving to the sky,
Are maddening in their rear."

"While the party hostile to us, thus stood hesitating, but to all appearance rapidly approaching a point where all hesitation would cease, Olla, with tears streaming down her cheeks, besought us to fly to her husband's house, where, she seemed to imagine, we should necessarily be safe from violence. But though no one yet laid hands on us, we were surrounded on all sides, and could not with any certainty distinguish friends from foes; and the first movement on our part to escape, would probably be the signal for an instant and general attack by the priest and his followers. We thought, therefore, that our best hope of safety lay in maintaining a firm but quiet attitude, until Mowno, and those disposed to protect us, could make their influence felt in our behalf. They, however, confined their efforts to feeble expostulations and entreaties; and perhaps it was unreasonable to expect them to engage in a deadly conflict with their own neighbours, relatives, and personal friends, in the defence of mere strangers like ourselves. They could not even restrain the younger and more violent portion of the rabble from carrying on the species of desultory warfare from which Barton had already suffered; on the contrary, the stones and other missiles, thrown by persons on the outskirts of the crowd, fell continually thicker and faster. At length Rokóa received a staggering blow on the back of the head, from a clod of earth, thrown by some one who had stolen round behind the rock for that purpose, and who immediately afterwards disappeared in the throng.

"'How much longer are we to endure this?' cried Barton. 'Must we stand here and suffer ourselves to be murdered by these cowardly attacks? Let us shoot a couple of them, and make a rush for the shore.'

"But a moment's reflection was enough to show the utter hopelessness of such an attempt. However much the natives might be astounded for an instant by the discharge of fire-arms, all fear and hesitation would vanish upon our taking to flight. Our backs once turned would be the mark for a score of ready spears; and except perhaps for Rokóa, whose speed was extraordinary, there would be scarcely the possibility for escape. Still it was evident that the audacity of our enemies was steadily increasing, though their attacks were as yet covert and indirect, and, as I knew that Rokóa would not hesitate to retaliate upon the first open assailant in which case we should be massacred upon the spot, we might soon be compelled to adopt even so desperate a suggestion, as the only alternative of instant death.

"At this critical moment, I noticed a sudden movement of surprise or alarm, on the outskirts of the crowd. A group, directly in front of us, no longer giving us their exclusive attention, began to whisper among themselves, glancing and pointing towards the rising ground in our rear, while a half suppressed and shuddering exclamation of 'Te Vea! Te Vea!' was heard among the people. Turning round, and looking where all eyes were now directed, I saw a tall native, with a peculiar head-dress of feathers, and a small basket of cocoa-nut-leaflets in his hand, running rapidly towards us. His appearance seemed to awaken in those around us, emotions of terror or aversion, strong enough to swallow up every other feeling, for, no sooner was he perceived, than all thought of prosecuting further the present quarrel, appeared to be abandoned. The priest, alone, evinced none of the general uneasiness or dread, but, on the contrary, a gleam of exultation lighted up his hard and discoloured countenance. The people made way to the right and left, as the new-comer drew near, and a number of them slunk away into the forest or to their homes. The stranger proceeded directly towards Mowno, and taking a small parcel wrapped in leaves, from the basket which he carried, delivered it to him: then, without pausing an instant, or uttering a word, he passed on, taking his way at a rapid pace straight through the village. Mowno received the parcel with a reluctant and gloomy air, though it seemed to consist of nothing but a rough stone, wrapped in the leaves of the sacred miro. For several minutes he stood holding it in his hand, like one deprived of consciousness. Several of those who appeared to be the principal persons present, among whom were Catiline and the priest, now approached him, and they began to hold a whispered consultation, in the course of which the priest frequently pointed towards Rokóa, as though speaking of him. Mowno seemed to be resisting some proposal urged by the others, and spoke in a more decisive and resolute manner than I had thought him capable of assuming. The discussion, whatever was its subject, soon became warm and angry: the voices of Catiline and the priest were raised, and even threatening. Every moment I expected to see Mowno relinquish his opposition; but he remained firm, and at last, with the air of one resolved to put an end to further debate, he said —

Arthur's Story.

"'No! it shall not be either of the strangers; it shall be Terano: he is an evil man, and it will be well when he is gone.' Then speaking to two of those who stood near him, he said, 'Go quickly to Terano's house, before he sees the messenger and hides himself in the mountains,' whereupon they seized their spears, and immediately set off in the direction of the village.

"Olla now renewed her entreaties for us to leave the spot, and go with her to the house; and Mowno,—by a quick gesture, meant to be seen only by us, indicated his wish to the same effect. Rokóa nodded to me to comply, and we followed Olla as she bounded lightly through the grove, no one offering to oppose our departure. But the priest's restless eye was upon us, and had we set off in the direction of the shore, we should not have been permitted to escape, without an attempt on his part to prevent it. As it was, he appeared to give some direction to those about him, and four or five young men followed us at a distance, keeping us in sight, and taking care that they were always in such a position as to enable them to intercept us in any attempt to recross the island. After having dogged us to Mowno's house and seen us enter, they withdrew into the forest out of sight, where they probably remained on the watch. Rokóa now proceeded to select from Mowno's store of weapons, a club, of more formidable weight and size, than that which he had wrested from the priest, and requested Barton and myself to follow his example.

"'We must try to get to the shore,' he said, 'there are at present, none to hinder us, but the young men who followed us hither.'

"'But that demon of a priest, and the rest of his crew, are not far-off,' said Barton, 'and they will be sure to waylay us. For the present we are safe here; and perhaps Mowno will be able to get us back to our boat without danger.'

"Rokóa shook his head. 'There are others here,' he said, 'more powerful than Mowno, and who are our enemies: we must rely upon ourselves.'

"Olla watched us anxiously during this conversation; and now, as if she understood its subject at least, she said, with an expression of intelligence and cordial friendliness in her fine eyes, 'Listen to me: the words of the priest are more powerful with the great chief than the words of Mowno: to-night, the priest will go to the great chief, and before he returns you must fly; but not now, for you are watched by the young men; you must wait until night—until the moon is behind the grove.'

"This seemed to me a wiser course than to undertake, at present, to fight our way to the boat; but Rokóa remained of his former opinion; he apprehended an attack upon our party at the shore during our absence, by which we might be cut off from all means of leaving the island. This certainly was a weighty consideration, and one that had not occurred to me. We were still hesitating, and uncertain what course to pursue, when Mowno came in, looking much troubled, and carrying in his hand the mysterious package, the object and meaning of which I forgot to explain.

"A stone, folded in the leaves of the miro, sent by the king, or paramount chief, to the subordinate chiefs of districts or villages, is the customary method of notifying the latter that they are expected to furnish a human victim for some approaching sacrifice. The principal occasions upon which these are required, are at the building of national maraes, at the commencement of a war, or in cases of the serious illness of a superior chief. The number of victims sacrificed, is proportioned to the magnitude of the occasion; as many as a score have sometimes been offered to propitiate the gods during the severe sickness of a powerful chief. The priests signify to the chief the number required; the latter then sends out his runner or messenger, (te vea), who delivers to each of the subordinate chiefs, one of these packages for each victim to be furnished from his immediate district. The odious duty of designating the individuals to be taken, then devolves upon the subordinate, and having decided upon this, he sends a number of armed men to secure the destined victims before they secrete themselves or flee into the woods, as those who have any reason to fear being selected generally do, at the first appearance of the dreaded messenger, or even as soon as it is publicly known that an occasion is at hand for which human sacrifices will be required. When secured, the doomed persons are most commonly killed on the spot by the chief's men, and the bodies wrapped in cocoa-nut leaves and carried to the temple. Sometimes, however, they are preserved alive, and slain by the priests themselves at the altar.

"Upon the arrival of the messenger, as already related, with a requisition for one victim from the village, the majority of Mowno's advisers had insisted upon selecting Rokóa for that purpose, and thus avoiding the necessity of sacrificing one of their own people. The priest had gone further still, and proposed to seize upon us all, and send Barton and myself to the two neighbouring villages, to be furnished by them as their quota of victims. To these councils, Mowno had opposed a determined resistance, and he had finally sent his followers to despatch an old man named Terano, whose death would be considered a general benefit, as he was a notorious and inveterate thief and drunkard, who, when not stupefied with ava, was constantly engaged in desperate broils, or wanton depredations upon the property of his neighbours. It seemed, however, that the old man had taken the alarm and fled; several of Mowno's followers were now in pursuit of him, and unless they should succeed in taking him before morning, another person would have to be designated, as it was required to furnish the victims at the great marae, by noon of the following day.

"I sickened with disgust, as I listened to details like these. Never before had I so fully realised the darkness and the horrors of heathenism—all the more striking in the present instance, because of the many pleasing and amiable natural qualities of the people who groped amid much darkness, and were a prey to such horrors.

"Mowno also recommended us to postpone any attempt at flight until a late hour of the night. He said that he had seen a number of men lurking in the woods near the stream, and that the priest and others had remained in the grove after he had left, probably with the intention of joining them in watching the house.

"Olla now went out into the garden, where she walked about looking up among the branches of the tree; and calling out, 'Lai-evi!' as if in search of her tame wood-pigeon. After going round the garden, she passed out of the gate, and wandered away in the direction of the brook, still looking among the trees, and repeating at intervals her call of 'Lai-evi!'

"By-and-bye she returned, and though without her little favourite, she had accomplished her real object, and ascertained the number and position of the spies. She had seen seven of them skulking in the wood along the brook, and watching the house. They seemed anxious to avoid observation, and she could not, without awaking suspicion, get more than transient glimpses of them, so that possibly there might be others whom she had not seen.

"Rokóa questioned her as to the space along the bank of the stream occupied by these men, and the distance from one another at which they were stationed. Then after a moment's reflection he turned to Mowno, and asked whether he was confident of being able to protect us, while in his house; to which the latter replied with much earnestness that he both could and would do so.

"'Wait here, then,' said Rokóa, addressing Barton and myself, 'I will return before the moon sets:' and without affording us an opportunity to inquire what he designed to do, he passed through the door, and bounded into the forest, in the direction opposite to that where the spies of the priest were lurking.

"'Is it possible,' said Barton, 'that he intends to desert us?'

"'You should know him better,' I answered, 'unless I am mistaken, he is about to risk his life in an attempt to communicate with our crew, in order to put them on their guard against a surprise, and to render our escape the more easy. If he lives, he will return, to incur a second time with us the very dangers to which this attempt exposes him.'

"Knowing as I did Rokóa's great activity, coolness, and presence of mind, I was sanguine that he would succeed in eluding the vigilance of our enemies, and accomplishing his purpose.

"Soon after his departure, Olla set out for our evening meal a light repast of bananas, baked bread-fruit, and vi-apples, fresh from the garden. But neither Barton nor I could eat anything: our thoughts were with Rokóa upon his perilous adventure. When the food had been removed, Mowno suggested that we should all go out into the inclosure, and walk a few times around the house in order that those who were on the watch might be satisfied that we were still there. This we accordingly did, and continued strolling through the garden until it became quite dark. Rokóa had now been gone nearly an hour, and Barton began to grow restless and troubled. Mowno, stationing himself at the end of the walk leading from the house, leaned upon the gate in a listening attitude. As I sat in the wide doorway, beneath the vi-apple trees planted on either side of the entrance, watching the bright constellation of the Cross, just visible above the outline of the grove in the southern horizon, Olla began to question me concerning what I had told the people in the afternoon, of God, and a future life, and the doctrines of Christianity. I was at once touched and astonished, to perceive the deep interest she took in the subject, and the readiness with which she received these truths, as something she had needed and longed for. She seemed to feel how much better and more consoling they were, than the superstitions in which she had been educated.

"I was amazed to find that this young heathen woman, growing up in the midst of pagan darkness, was nevertheless possessed of deep and strong religious feelings, which could not be satisfied with the traditions of her people. As I gazed at her ingenuous countenance, full of earnestness and sensibility, while she endeavoured to express the vague thoughts on these subjects which had at times floated through her mind, I could scarcely believe that this was the same gay and careless being, whose life had seemed to be as natural, as unconscious, and as joyous, as that of a bird or a flower. She said, that often when alone in some secluded spot in the depth of the wood, while all around was so hushed and peaceful, she had suddenly burst into tears, feeling that what she had been taught of the gods could not be true, and that if Oro was indeed the creator of so beautiful a world—if he had made the smiling groves, the bright flowers, and the multitude of happy living things, he must be a good being, who could not delight in the cruelties practised in his name. Often, when a mere girl, thoughts like these had visited her, wandering by the sea-shore at twilight, or looking up through the foliage of waving cocoa-nut-groves at the starry skies, when nature herself, by her harmony and beauty, had seemed to proclaim that God was a being of light and love, in whom was no darkness at all!

"Presently Mowno joined us, and I talked with him in regard to the intended burial of the aged woman, his aunt and endeavoured to make him see the act in its true light. But with all his natural amiability, such was the effect of custom and education, that he seemed perfectly insensible on the subject. He observed, in a cool, matter-of-fact manner, that when people got very old and could not work, they were of no use to others or themselves— that it was then time for them to die, and much best that they should do so at once; and that if they did not, then their friends ought to bury them. As to Malola, his aunt, he said that she was quite willing to be buried, and had in fact suggested it herself; that she was often very sick, and in great pain, so that she had no pleasure in living any longer; he added, as another grave and weighty consideration, that she had lost most of her teeth, and could not chew her food, unless it was prepared differently from that of the rest of the family, which caused Olla much trouble.

"Finding that argument and expostulation had not the slightest effect upon him, I changed my tactics, and suddenly demanded whether he would be willing to have Olla buried, when *she* began to get old and infirm? This seemed at first to startle him. He glanced uneasily at his little wife, as if it had never before occurred to him that she *could* grow old. Then, after staring at me a moment in a half angry manner, as though offended at my having suggested so disagreeable an idea, he seemed all at once to recover himself, remarking quickly, that *he* should be old then, too, and that they could both be buried together. This consolatory reflection seemed completely to neutralise the effect of my last attack, and Mowno's countenance resumed its habitual expression of calm and somewhat stolid placidity.

"Baffled, but not discouraged, I next strove, by drawing an imaginary picture of Olla and himself in their old age, surrounded by their grown up children, to show how happy and beautiful the relation between the child and the aged parent might be. I summoned up all my rhetorical powers, and sketched what I conceived to be a perfect model of an affectionate and dutiful Angatanese son. After clothing him with all the virtues and accomplishments of the savage character, I proceeded to endue him with that filial affection, whose beauty and power it was my chief object to illustrate. I represented him as loving his father and mother all the more tenderly on account of the infirmities of age now stealing over them. Upon the arm of this affectionate son, the white-haired Mowno supported himself; when at morning and evening he went forth to take his accustomed walk in the groves. He it was, who brought home daily to his aged mother, the ripest fruits, and the freshest flowers. His smiling and happy countenance was the light of their dwelling; his cheerful voice, its sweetest music. I was proceeding thus in quite an affecting strain, as it seemed to me, (though I must in honesty confess that Mowno appeared to be less moved by it than myself; and somewhat cooled my enthusiasm by giving a great yawn in the midst of one of the most touching passages), when Olla, who had been listening with moistened eyes, gently stole her arm around her husband's neck, and murmured a few words in his ear. Whether it was my pathetic eloquence, or Olla's caress, that melted his hitherto obdurate heart, I will not pretend to say, but it is certain that he now yielded the point, and promised that Malola should be permitted to live. 'At least,' he added, after a moment's reflection, 'as long as she can see, and walk about.'

"Several times, since it had grown dark, I had heard sounds like the distant beating of drums, mingled occasionally with the long and sorrowful note of the buccinum-shell, or native trumpet. Twice, also, while Mowno was standing at his gate, messengers had arrived, apparently in haste, and after briefly conferring with him, had posted off again. When I remarked upon these sounds, Mowno said that they came from the marae, where preparations for the approaching ceremony were going forward; but to me, they seemed to proceed from several different points, at various distances from us.

"I now began to feel painfully anxious at Rokóa's protracted absence. It was nearly midnight, and there had been ample time for one less active than he, to go to the shore and return. The terrible apprehension, that in spite of all the resources of his skill and courage, he had fallen into the hands of some of the parties of natives which seemed to be scattered about in the forest, gained every moment a stronger hold upon my mind.

"'He has either been taken, or else he finds that he cannot rejoin us, without too great risk,' said Barton, breaking a long silence, and speaking of that which each knew the other to be thinking about; 'we must start for the shore ourselves, if he does not come soon.'

"'Hark!' whispered Olla, 'some one is approaching from the wood.' Her quick ear had detected stealthy steps crossing the avenue. The next moment some one bounded lightly over the hedge at the side of the house, where the shadow of the bread-fruit trees fell darkest. Mowno started, and seemed agitated, and for an instant a suspicion that he had betrayed us, and was about to give us up, flashed through my mind. But the figure which came forward into the light, was that of Rokóa, and I felt pained at the wrong which my momentary doubts had done our inert, but well-meaning, host. Rokóa breathed quick and short. Without speaking, he pointed to the moon, now on the edge of the western horizon of forest, to intimate that he was punctual to the time set for his return.

"The sounds which I had before heard, were now borne more plainly than ever to our ears upon the night breeze. As soon as Rokóa recovered his breath, he said that we had not a moment to lose, but must commence our flight at once. He had passed an armed party of more than twenty men, coming in the direction of the house, with the purpose, as he supposed, of demanding that we should be given up to them. Mowno seemed more displeased than alarmed at this intelligence, and earnestly repeated that no harm should befall us while beneath his roof, if he had to lay down his life in our defence. But Rokóa urged our immediate departure, before the arrival of the party which he had seen. Mowno then offered to accompany, and guide us to our boat, which Rokóa firmly declined, on the ground that his presence might endanger him, and in the excited and determined mood of our enemies could be no protection to us.

"We accordingly took a hurried leave of him, and Olla. 'Good-bye, Artua,' said the latter, 'Olla will not forget what you have told her of our great Father in the sky; she will ask him for a new heart that she too, may go when she dies, to the Christian heaven,' and she pointed upward, while a happy smile lighted up her intelligent, and, for the moment, serious countenance.

The Flight.

"We sprang over the hedge, and Rokóa leading the way, proceeded swiftly but silently down the avenue. We passed some distance beyond the point where we had struck into it in the morning, to avoid the neighbourhood of the village, then turning towards the shore, descended into the valley until we reached the stream. At this point, it was deep and narrow, with a rapid current, but we had no time to look for a ford. Cries and shouts on the hill above us, showed that we were pursued, and a confused clamour from the village indicated the existence of some unusual commotion there. Tum-tums were beating fiercely, and the long dismal wail of the tuba-conch resounded through the echoing arches of the forest. We swam the stream as silently as possible, Barton holding his pistols above his head in one hand to keep the charges dry. As we climbed the further bank, and plunged into the wood of miros, we could hear the splashing of the water caused by persons fording the brook a short distance below us, and opposite the village. In the same direction a multitude of candle-nut torches gleamed through the foliage, and revealed dusky forms hurrying hither and thither. We pushed on through the wood at the top of our speed, until suddenly the outlines of the marae, illuminated by the glare of a large bonfire, loomed up before us. A score of half-naked men, were dancing around the fire in front of the inclosure, with the wildest and most extravagant contortions of body. Seen by the fitful and wavering light, their painted countenances scarcely looked like those of human beings, and the grim, immovable idols, upon their pedestals, seemed vaster and more hideous than ever.

"As we turned, and plunged into the grove again, resuming our flight in a somewhat altered direction, an eager shout announced that we had been seen. But this cry proceeded, not from the group in front of the marae, who were wholly absorbed in their savage orgies, but from a straggling party of pursuers from the village, to whom the light of the bonfire had betrayed us. The chase was now no longer random or uncertain; they came on like hounds in full view of the game, uttering yells that caused the blood to curdle in my veins. My strength began to fail, and I felt a horrible spell creeping over me, like that which often in dreams, deprives us of the power to fly some appalling danger. Rokóa restrained his superior speed, and kept beside Barton and myself. 'Courage, Artua!' he said, 'we are near the shore,' and he offered me his hand to assist me, but I would not take it. Notwithstanding our utmost exertions our pursuers gained upon us. I was very nearly exhausted when we reached the ravine which divided the miro-grove from the bread-fruit plantation, and as we struggled up its steep side Barton panted and gasped so painfully for breath, that I dreaded each moment to see him fall to the ground incapable of proceeding further. But we knew that our lives were at stake, and forced ourselves to exertions which nature could not long support; still, the cries of our pursuers, the sound of their footsteps, and the crashing of branches in their path drew continually nearer.

"At last we had nearly traversed the breadth of the plantation, and the welcome sound of the waves, breaking upon the beach, greeted our ears.

Safety now seemed within our reach, and we summoned all our remaining energies for a final effort. The trees, growing more thinly as we approached the skirt of the wood, let in the light, and between their trunks I caught a glimpse of the sea. Right before us was a thicket, tangled with fern, and scarcely twenty yards beyond it lay the beach shining in the star-light. As we turned a little aside to avoid the thicket, an appalling yell rang out from it, and half a dozen dark figures started from their ambush, and sprang into the path before us. The old priest was at their head: my heart sank, and I gave up all as host. Rokóa, swinging up his ponderous club, bounded into their midst. 'Onward!' cried he, 'it is our only hope of escape.' His movements were light as those of a bird, and rapid as lightning. His first blow stretched the priest at his feet. The savages gave way before him, scattering to the right and left, as if a thunderbolt had fallen among them. Barton discharged both his pistols at once, and with fatal effect, as was witnessed by the groans that followed. Before they could rally or recover themselves, we had burst through their midst. As we reached the shore, I looked round and missed Barton—he was no longer beside me. An exulting cry behind us at once explained his absence: at the same time we could hear him call out in a voice broken by exhaustion, 'Save yourselves, you can do nothing for me!' Without an instant's hesitation, Rokóa turned, and we rushed back into the midst of our shouting enemies. Three or four of the party which had been in pursuit of us, were just coming up. The audacity and desperation of our attack seemed to confound them, and two of their number fell almost without a struggle beneath Rokóa's rapid and resistless blows. Two more of them, who were dragging Barton away, were compelled to leave him at liberty in order to defend themselves. At that moment a sudden shout from the water raised by our crew, who had either heard our voices, or seen us when we came out upon the shore, increased their panic by causing them to suppose that we were leading back our whole party to the fight. They hastily gave way before us, and we had all turned once more, and gained the beach before they recovered from their surprise, and perceived their mistake.

"Our boat was just outside the surf; where the crew were keeping her steady with their paddles. We hailed them, and plunged in the water to swim out to them. The natives, stung with shame and rage at having their prisoner torn from them in the very moment of triumph, with such reckless boldness, swarmed down to the beach and pursued us into the water. They seemed excited almost to frenzy at the prospect of our escape. Some standing upon the shore assailed the canoe with showers of stones, by which several of our men were wounded. Others swam out after us, as if about to endeavour to board the vessel, and did not turn back until we had hoisted our sail, and began to draw steadily from the land.

"And thus ends the story of the Cannibal Island of Angatan."

"Is that all?" inquired Johnny, looking somewhat disappointed.

"Yes, that is all," answered Arthur, "it comes as near to being a cannibal story, as any thing I know. I did not see any one actually roasted and eaten, but if the savages had caught us, I suspect there would have been more to tell, and probably no one here to tell it."

"But," persisted Johnny, "the story don't end there. You haven't told us about the rest of the voyage, and whether Rokóa found his brother at last."

"O, that don't properly belong to *this* story. According to all artistical rules I ought to end precisely where I have, in order to preserve the unities. But some other time, if you wish, I will tell you all about it."

"Pray don't talk of artistical rules," exclaimed Max, "after showing yourself such an egregious bungler! You had there all the elements of a capital story, and you have just spoiled them."

"'How prove you that, in the great heap of your knowledge,'" cried Browne, "'come now, unmuzzle your wisdom,' and specify the blunders of which he has been guilty. I say, with Touchstone, 'instance briefly, shepherd; come, instance.'"

"Why, in the first place, there was a miserly spirit of economy in regard to his men. He should have invested the narrative with a tragic interest, by killing Rokóa and Barton, at least;—being the narrator he couldn't kill himself conveniently;—but he might, with good effect have been 'dangerously wounded.'"

"But suppose," said Arthur, "that I wanted Rokóa to figure in a future story, and so couldn't afford to kill him just yet?"

"A miserable apology! it evinces a lamentable poverty of imagination to make one character serve for two distinct tales."

"Well, a further instance, 'gentle shepherd,'" cried Browne, "'a more sounder instance.'"

"Then, again," resumed Max, with an oracular air, "it was a capital error to make Olla a married woman; what business I should like to know, can a married woman have in a story?—She belongs properly to the dull prosaic region of common life—not to the fairy land of romance. Now the charm of sentiment is as necessary to a perfect tale, as the interest of adventure, or the excitement of conflict, and had Olla been single, there would have been the elements of something beautifully sentimental."

"Enough!" cried Browne, "if you have not 'lamed me with reasons,' you have at least overwhelmed me with words—there now! I believe I am unconsciously catching the trick of your long-winded sing-song sentences—it must be contagious."

"Well," said Arthur, "I give over the 'materials' to Max, with full permission to work them up into a romance after his own fashion, introducing as much slaughter and sentiment as he shall judge requisite for the best effect, and when completed, it shall be inserted by way of episode in our narrative."

> Note. Upon consulting the charts we find an island called "Ahangatan", (of which Angatan is perhaps a contraction), laid down on some of them, about one hundred and fifty miles north of Hao. On others the same island is called Ahangatoff. The US Exploring Expedition visited Hae, and most of the neighbouring islands, but we have not been able to discover any mention of Angatan in the published records of the expedition.

Chapter Twenty Four
House-Building

Dawn on the Lagoon—The "Sea-Attorney"—The "Shark-Exterminator"—Max "Carries The War Into Africa."

"Another hour must pass ere day grows bright,
And ere the little birds begin discourse
In quick low voices, ere the streaming light
Pours on their nests, just sprung from day's fresh source."

After the late hours we had kept on the last evening, most of us would willingly have prolonged our slumbers beyond the time previously fixed for setting out upon our return to Castle-hill. But before it was fairly light, Arthur was up, with an unseasonable and provoking alacrity, calling loudly upon us to bestir ourselves.

In vain Browne apostrophised him in moving strains as "the rude disturber of his pillow," remonstrated against such unmerciful punctuality, and petitioned for another nap; in vain Max protested that we were not New York shop-boys, obliged to rise at daylight to make fires, and open and sweep out stores, but free and independent desert islanders, who had escaped from the bondage of civilised life, and the shackles of slavish routine, and who need not get up until noon, unless of our own good pleasure. Arthur was inexorable, and finding that further sleep was out of the question, we yielded at last to his despotic pertinacity, and groped our way into the boat, yawning desperately, and not more than half awake.

The sea-fowl had not yet begun to stir in their nests, when we pushed out into the lagoon, and commenced pulling homeward—as we had now almost come to regard it—holding a course midway between the reef and the shore. A few moments' exercise at the oars sufficed to dispel our drowsiness, and to reconcile us somewhat to the early start, which we had so reluctantly taken.

The faint grey light revealed the sleeping landscape, invested with the delicious freshness and repose of the earliest dawn in summer. The shores of the island, with their dense masses of verdure, were so perfectly mirrored in the lagoon, that the peculiar characteristics of the different kinds of foliage could be distinguished in their reflections. The drooping plumes of the palms, the lance-shaped pandanus leaves, and the delicate, filmy foliage of the casuarina, were all accurately imaged there; the inverted shore below, with its fringe of trees and shrubbery, looking scarcely less substantial and real, than its counterpart above. But as the light increased, these reflections lost their softness, and the clearness of their outlines. The gradually brightening dawn, cast new and rapidly changing lights and shades upon the waters and the shores; and the latter, which, as we moved onward, we beheld every moment from a new point of view, charmed the eye with a perpetual variety. In some places they were abrupt and bold; in others smoothly rounded, or gently sloping. Now we were opposite a jutting promontory, which, crowned with verdure, and overgrown with pendulous and creeping plants, pushed out over the narrow alluvial belt of shore, to the water's edge; now shooting past it, we caught a sudden and transient glimpse of some cool valley, opening down to the lagoon, and stretching away inland through vistas of fine trees.

Johnny expressed a fervent wish that he was a painter, in order that we might sail round the island, take sketches of the scenery, and then paint a panorama, embracing all the best views, by exhibiting which at twenty-five cents a head, we should all make our fortunes upon getting home. He appeared to have some doubts, however, whether that particular time of day could be painted, even by the most accomplished artist. The lagoon channel wound through fields of branching coral trees of luxuriant growth, among which, numbers of large fish were moving sluggishly about, as if they had got up too early, and were more than half inclined to indulge in another nap. As we passed over a sort of bar, where there was not more than a fathom and a half of water, we espied an immense green turtle at the bottom, quietly pursuing his way across our track, and though by no means a beautiful creature, looking infinitely happier and more lively than the dull-eyed wretches of his race, which I have seen lying on their backs, at the doors of the New York restaurants, ready to be converted into soup and steaks. Johnny mourned over the impracticability of making any attempt at his capture, and heaved a sigh which seemed to come from the bottom of his heart, as the unsightly reptile disappeared among the mazes of the submarine shrubbery. The hardship of the case, seemed to be greatly aggravated in his eyes, as he contrasted it with the better fortune of Robinson Crusoe and the Swiss Family, the former of whom, as he reminded us, caught "any quantity of turtles" on the beach of his island, with no other trouble than that of turning them over upon their backs; while the latter, having surprised an enormous fellow taking an afternoon nap on the surface of the water, treacherously harpooned him in his sleep, and then, steering him as easily as one would drive a well-broken nag, compelled him to tow themselves and their pinnace ashore.

A somewhat startling incident put an end to these interesting reminiscences. Johnny was leaning over the gunwale, and with his face almost touching the surface, and his hands playing in the water, was peering down into the lagoon, probably on the look-out for another turtle, when a large shark, coming as it seemed from beneath the boat, rose suddenly but quietly, and made a snatch at him. Johnny saw the monster barely in time; for just as he sprang up with a cry of affright, and fell backwards into the boat the shark's shovel-nose shot four feet above water at our stern, his jaws snapping together as he disappeared again, with a sound like the springing of a powerful steel-trap. Though baffled in his first attack, the voracious fish continued to follow us, watching closely an opportunity for a more successful attempt. He was a large brown shark, of the species known to sailors as the "sea-attorney," which designation, together with his formidable reputation for keenness, vigilance, and enterprise, shows the estimation in which the members of the ancient and honourable profession of the law, are held by the honest sons of Neptune. Max professed to recognise him, as our acquaintance of the previous evening, by whom himself and Browne had been for a time kept in a state of blockade: our present visitor certainly evinced the same uncommon fierceness and audacity which had astonished us in the individual referred to. He was a trim, round-bodied, compact fellow with a wonderful display of vigour, and even of grace, in his movements; but though not without a certain kind of beauty, I do not wish to be understood as saying that his personal appearance was upon the whole, prepossessing. On the contrary, his expression, if I may venture to use the term, (and he certainly had a good deal of expression), was, if not decidedly bad, at the least exceedingly sinister. His flattened head, and long leather-like snout together with a pair of projecting goggle eyes, so situated as to command a view both in front and rear, and which he kept turning restlessly on every side, contributed greatly to enhance this forbidding aspect. Every moment he seemed to grow fiercer and bolder, and at length he actually laid hold of our keel next the rudder and fairly shook the boat from stem to stern. To our great relief, he soon desisted from this, for such was his bulk and strength, that we hardly knew what he might not effect in his furious efforts. His next move, was to make a sudden dash at Max's oar, which had probably given him offence by coming too near his nose, and which he jerked from his hands.

Max seemed to regard this last exploit as a personal affront, and loudly declared that "this was going altogether too far, and that he should not stand it any longer." He accordingly proceeded with great energy, to lash his cutlass to the handle of one of the remaining oars, with some twine which he found in the locker, threatening all sorts of terrible things against the unsuspecting object of his wrath. Meanwhile Morton succeeded in fishing up the lost oar, which the vigilance and activity of our attentive escort rendered a somewhat dangerous undertaking; when recovered, the marks of six rows of formidable teeth were found deeply indented upon its blade.

Max having completed his novel weapon, Browne, who had been engaged in an unprofitable attempt to strike the shark across the eyes with his cutlass, inquired, "what he was going to do with that clumsy contrivance!"

"That clumsy contrivance, as you rashly term it," replied Max, with dignity, "is designed as a shark-exterminator, with which I intend forthwith to pay my respects to this audacious sea-bully. We have stood on the defensive quite long enough, and I am now about to carry the war into Africa."

He accordingly jumped upon the middle seat of the yawl, where, in spite of all attempts at dissuasion, he stood watching a favourable opportunity for a thrust. This was soon presented. All unconscious of the unfriendly designs cherished against him, the shark came propelling himself carelessly alongside, and directly under Max's nose, with his back fin quite above water. The temptation was not to be resisted. Max braced himself as firmly as possible in his position: Arthur expostulated, and begged him at least to get down and stand in the boat: Morton exhorted him to caution. But he only answered by a wave of the hand and a grim smile; then requesting Browne to lay fast hold of his waist-band, to assist him in preserving the centre of gravity, he raised his weapon in both hands, and giving it a preliminary flourish, brought it down with his full force, aiming at the broadest part of the fish's back, just forward of the dorsal fin. But the weapon was too dull, or the blow too feeble, to pierce the tough hide of the "sea-attorney," for it glanced smoothly off and Max losing his balance, went headlong into the sea. Browne, in a hasty effort to save him came near going over also, while the boat careened until the water poured in over the gunwale, and for a moment there was imminent danger of capsizing. Max came to the surface, almost paralysed with fright, and clutched convulsively at the side of the boat; when we drew him on board unharmed, but pale and shivering, as he well might be, after so extraordinary an escape. The shark had disappeared, and was now nowhere to be seen. Not being accustomed to Max's system of "carrying the war into Africa," so sudden and headlong an attack in his own element had probably somewhat disconcerted him. Max made a great effort to assume an air of composure. "Well!" said he, looking coolly around, "the enemy has, I perceive, beaten a retreat. I dare say he was quite as much frightened as I was, and that is saying a good deal."

"But what has become of that patent shark-exterminator!" observed Browne, "I don't see it anywhere: has the enemy carried it off as a trophy of victory, as conquering knights take possession of the arms of their vanquished adversaries!"

"It is much more likely," replied Max with disdain, "that he has carried it off stuck fast in his carcass."

But neither supposition proved to be correct, for we presently picked up the "exterminator," floating near us. Johnny narrowly examined the blade, and was much disappointed at not finding "any blood on it."

Max now took an oar to steady his nerves by rowing, for, notwithstanding his assumed composure and forced pleasantry, they had evidently been a good deal shaken by his recent narrow escape.

By the time we came in sight of Sea-bird's Point, the increasing light, and the rosy glow in the "dappled east," heralded the rising of the sun, and announced that the heat and glare of the tropical day, were on the point of succeeding the mild freshness of "incense-breathing morn." Nor were other tokens wanting, that the reign of night was over. A strange confusion of indistinct and broken sounds, issuing from myriads of nests and perches all along the beach, showed that the various tribes of sea-fowl were beginning to bestir themselves. A few slumbrous, half-smothered sounds from scattered nests preluded the general concert, and then the notes were taken up, and repeated by the entire feathered population for miles along the shore, until the clamour seemed like that of ten thousand awakening barn-yards. And now the scene began to be enlivened by immense multitudes of birds, rising in the air, and hovering in clouds over the lagoon. Some wheeled around us in their spiral flight; others skimmed the water like swallows, dipping with marvellous promptness after any ill-starred fish that ventured near the surface; others again, rose high into the air, from whence, by their incredible keenness of sight, they seemed readily to discern their prey, when, poising themselves an instant on expanded wings, they would pounce perpendicularly downward, and disappearing entirely in the water for an instant, emerge, clutching securely a struggling victim. But in carrying on this warfare upon the finny inhabitants of the lagoon the feathered spoilers were not perfectly united and harmonious; and fierce domestic contentions occasionally interrupted and diversified their proceedings. A number of unprincipled man-of-war hawks, who preferred gaining their livelihood by robbing their neighbours and associates, to relying upon their own honest industry, would sail lazily around on wide-spread pinions, watching with the air of unconcerned spectators the methodical toil of the plodding gannets. But the instant that one of the latter rose from a successful plunge, with a plump captive writhing in his grasp, all appearance of indifference would vanish, and some dark-plumaged pirate of the lagoon, pouncing down like lightning upon his unwarlike neighbour, would ruthlessly despoil him of his hard-earned prize. One of these piratical gentry suffered before our eyes a fate worthy of his rapacity. A gannet had seized upon a fish much larger than his strength enabled him to manage, and was struggling in vain to lift it into the air, when a hawk darted upon them, and striking his talons into the fish, put the gannet to flight. But the greedy victor had greatly miscalculated the strength of his intended prey. A desperate conflict, sometimes under water, and sometimes just at the surface, ensued. The hawk struggled gallantly, but in vain, and was at length drawn under by his ponderous antagonist, to rise no more.

We landed a short distance beyond Johnny's row of "Oyster-trees," and by the time we had climbed the hill, the sun had risen, though not yet visible above the wooded heights which sheltered us to the eastward.

We were so intent upon our house-building project that, contenting ourselves with a self-denying breakfast of cocoa-nuts, we at once set zealously to work in carrying it out.

Arthur directed, superintended, and laid out the work in detail. Morton, having fitted a handle to the hatchet-head, and laboriously sharpened it upon a rough stone, undertook to supply materials as fast as called for. While he cut down trees of the kind and size required by Arthur, Max trimmed off the branches with his cutlass, and prepared them for use. Johnny and Eiulo dragged them to the site of the building, where Browne and I assisted Arthur in setting the posts into the ground, and putting together the frame of the house. Of course, our destitution of proper tools and implements rendered all this exceedingly laborious, and, but for Arthur's perseverance and ingenuity, we should more than once have given up in despair. Instead of spades, we were obliged to use sharp bivalve shells from the shore, in digging places for the upright posts of the building, and as it was necessary that these should be set quite deep, in order to give it firmness and stability, the toil was severe. Max, who came up occasionally to see how the work was progressing, and to offer suggestions and criticisms, (more especially the latter), on finding us upon our knees, patiently grubbing up the earth with our shells, flatteringly compared us to so many hedge-hogs excavating their burrows.

Nevertheless, we persevered; and before night we had nearly completed the frame of our building, with the exception of the ridge-pole, the rafters, and cross-pieces.

The posts at the sides stood six feet out of the ground, and were stationed about three feet apart. The centre-posts, to support the ridge-pole, were nine feet high, and made from the trunks of well-grown trees, some six inches in diameter. This certainly was a good day's work under the circumstances; at any rate, we were quite unanimous in considering it so; and towards twilight we went down to the beach for our evening bath, in an exceedingly complacent and self-satisfied state of mind, Max enlarging upon the pleasures of industry, and professing to be in the present enjoyment of those feelings—

"Which follow arduous duty well performed."

Instead of repairing to our usual bathing-place, we proceeded along the beach to the north-west, until we reached the clump of trees at the edge of the water, already mentioned as being visible from Castle-hill. As we approached the spot, we found that what had appeared at a distance to be but a single group of trees, was, in fact, a small grove extending along the shore, and fringing a little cove of nearly elliptical form, which at this point set into the land. The narrow, shelving beach, rivalled the whiteness of a fresh snow-drift. The trees were mostly cocoa-palms; indeed, scarcely any others could flourish in such a spot; and there were no shrubs or undergrowth of any kind. The cove was perhaps a hundred paces long, and half as wide in the widest part; contracting to less than fifty feet where it communicated with the lagoon. The water was clear, the bottom smooth and regularly formed, and the greatest depth was only eight or ten feet. Max, after viewing the cove with the eye of a connoisseur, pronounced it a noble spot for bathing purposes, and fully equal to the basin on the reef in every respect, except in depth and facilities for diving.

The impression of his morning's adventure, however, was still fresh, and he hinted at the possibility that some shark of elegant tastes, and possessing an eye for the beautiful, might be in the habit of frequenting the cove. Arthur volunteered to keep watch at the narrow entrance, while the rest of us were bathing, in order to give timely notice of the approach of the dreaded enemy; but on walking out to the edge of the lagoon we found that this precaution would be unnecessary. A bar, consisting of a coral patch, very near the surface, stretched across the mouth of the cove, rendering it almost impossible for a shark to enter.

Johnny named the spot, "The Mermaid's Cove," but this possessive designation was merely complimentary, for so far were we from renouncing the cove in favour of the mermaids, that from the day on which we discovered it, it became one of our favourite and regular resorts.

Chapter Twenty Five
The Cabin by the Lake

A Democrat in the Woods—Echo-vale and Lake Laicomo— The "Wild Frenchman" Discovered at last

"A few firm stakes they planted in the ground,
Circling a narrow space, but large enow,
These strongly interknit they closed around
With basket-work of many a pliant bough.
The roof was like the sides; the door was low,
And rude the hut, and trimmed with little care,
For little heart had they to dress it now:
Yet was the humble structure fresh and fair.
And soon the inmates found that peace might sojourn
there."

It took us an entire week to complete the frame of our building, and this alone involved an amount and variety of labour which few of us had anticipated when we commenced it. One day was consumed in selecting, felling, and trimming a tree, tall and straight enough to serve as a ridge-pole. We next had to get out some thirty rafters of hibiscus to support the roof. Then, as we had no nails, (Max's ship with the hardware not having yet arrived), we were obliged to adopt the means used by the Polynesian builders for fastening the rafters to the ridge-pole and cross-pieces, which consists of tying them firmly in their places with sennit. To supply the place of sennit, we manufactured a quantity of cord from twisted hibiscus bark, which answered the purpose very well.

At length the skeleton of the house was completed. Twenty-seven strong posts, (including the three tall centre ones), deeply planted in the ground, supported the string pieces and the ridge-pole. Fifteen slender rafters, regularly placed at small intervals, descended from the ridge-pole to the eaves on either side, and the whole was firmly bound together with tough and durable withes of our own manufacture.

The thatching occupied another week, and but for Eiulo's skill and dexterity, we should never have accomplished this nice and difficult operation, except after a very bungling and imperfect fashion. Arthur understood very well how it should be done, but his knowledge was theoretical rather than practical, while Eiulo had acquired considerable skill in the art, by building and thatching miniature houses in the woods, an amusement which he and his young playmates had often practised at home. The only thing now remaining to be done, was to make a number of coarse mats, with which to enclose the sides of the house—as far as in such a climate it is desirable to enclose them—together with an additional supply, ready to be put up in bad weather, on fastenings constructed for the purpose. But for this, there seemed to be no immediate necessity. The sides of the building were low, and the eaves extended two feet beyond them, and as we had an excellent roof above us, we considered ourselves tolerably prepared, even for rainy weather. However, we commenced manufacturing mats, in which, with the instruction and example of Arthur and Eiulo, we were tolerably successful; but we proceeded with this very much at our leisure. One or two brief showers, like that which had exerted so sudden an influence in hastening the commencement of our building scheme, afforded us the most satisfactory evidence of the good qualities of our roof, which did not admit a drop of rain. But at the same time we became aware of another defect in our house, as a dwelling in wet weather. We had no floor but the bare earth, and though Arthur had so levelled it, and protected it by a little trench and embankment, that no water from the adjacent grounds could reach us, except by the gradual process of saturation, still it was very damp after a severe rain. To remedy this, Arthur talked from time to time of making a floor of cement, which would dry to the hardness of stone, and through which the moisture from the ground could not penetrate. When asked where lime was to be obtained with which to make his cement he assumed an air of mystery, and merely said that there would be no difficulty on that score. One day, after we had got a large supply of mats completed, and ready for use, he again recurred to the subject of improving our floor, and explained that he intended to prepare his mortar or cement, from sand and lime, the latter of which was to be procured by burning coral rock in a pit. He prevailed upon Morton, Browne, and myself to set about digging a "lime-pit" in the gully beside Castle-hill, while he took Eiulo and Johnny with him in the boat, to go in search of a quantity of the sponge-shaped coral, which, he said, was the best adapted to his purpose.

Max pronounced the whole project a humbug, and refusing to have anything to do with it, equipped himself with club and cutlass, and started off on a solitary excursion towards the south-easterly part of the island, which we had not yet explored. He returned in the afternoon with a glowing account of the discoveries he had made, among which were a beautiful pond of fresh water, a stream flowing into it, and a waterfall.

In two days we completed a lime-pit of proper dimensions. Arthur and his assistants had in the same time collected and brought to the spot a sufficient quantity of coral rock; we then covered the bottom of the pit with fuel, and laid the coral, previously broken into small pieces, upon it. The pile was next kindled, and when the fuel was consumed, we found that the coral had yielded a supply of excellent lime, fine and beautifully white. Without going into further details, it is enough to say that the rest of Arthur's plan was carried out with the same success. The cement was made, and a thick layer of it spread over the floor of the house, as evenly and smoothly as could well be done, with no better trowels than gigantic oyster-shells. In three days it was hard as marble, and our house was now as complete as we could make it. It had cost us a great deal of severe toil; we had found the construction of it no such holiday employment as we had imagined; but it was the fruit of our own ingenuity and perseverance, the work of our own hands, and we regarded it with much complacency. Johnny impartially compared it with the dwellings of I don't know how many other desert islanders, and found it superior in some point to each and all of them.

Being now in a state of complete preparation, as we flattered ourselves, for all sorts of weather, we began to feel as though a regular out-and-out storm, would be rather a luxury than otherwise. These bright skies and sunny days were very well in their way, but it wasn't in anticipation of them, that we had been planning and working for a month or more. There was no use at all for our model house in such fine weather; indeed, while it continued, our old lodgings under the green forest leaves and the star-light, were far preferable. It took full half a dozen of our sleeping-mats, (and we had but three apiece), laid upon the stony floor of our dwelling, to make a couch half as soft as those heaps of leaves, which we used to pile up beneath the trees for our beds, and which we could not now introduce into the house for fear of "making a litter." The prudent citizen—who, having at the threatened approach of winter laid in a bountiful provision of wood and coal, put up his hall-stoves and his double windows, now feels quite ready, in the strength of anthracite and hickory, to snap his fingers in the face of Jack Frost, and bid him do his worst—is not more impatient to have the thermometer fall to the neighbourhood of zero, in order that he may realise the comforts he has paid for, than were we for the advent of such a storm, as would enable us to say to one another, "Ah! is it not fortunate that we have a roof over our heads? What should we do *now*, if we had not made timely preparation?"

Well, at last we had our wish. A shower came up one day, in the afternoon, which did not cease in half an hour, as the previous ones had done. On the contrary, when darkness came on the rain still continued falling steadily, with no sign of abatement. Johnny was in ecstasies. This was evidently no night for camping out; it was a night to justify all our expenditure of labour, in planning and perfecting our dwelling. We hung up every extra mat, and fastened them securely with the store of wooden pegs and pins prepared for that purpose. To be sure, we were in complete darkness, but then we were perfectly snug and comfortable; and what a luxury, to lie sheltered from the storm, and listen to the pattering of the rain upon the root and the dismal sound of the water dripping from the eaves!

The second morning after this rain-storm, which had so pleasantly tested the qualities of our dwelling, we started, under Max's guidance, to make an excursion to that part of the island, to the south-east of Castle-hill, of which he had given so glowing an account. After half an hour's toilsome march over uneven ground, we entered a grove, which, to Johnny's great exultation, was composed almost entirely of bread-fruit trees. They grew with much regularity, at almost equal distances, so as to form broad straight avenues, overarched by a canopy of spreading branches and dark glossy leaves. Vistas of shapely diamond-chequered trunks stretched away in every direction, in long and shady perspective. Among the dense masses of foliage, hung a profusion of large globes, of a light-delicate green, or a golden yellow, the splendid fruit of this noblest and most stately tree of the tropics. The ripe and the unripe fruit hung side by side from the same branches, and Johnny could hardly be persuaded to postpone gathering a supply of it until our return. Our course had been upon the whole rather an ascending one, so that this grove must have occupied an elevated situation. The ground over which it extended was nearly level, with slight wave-like undulations. As we approached its eastern limit, Max told us to prepare ourselves for the most charming spectacle that we had ever beheld. He walked on before with the air of a cicerone when about to exhibit a *chef d'oeuvre*, and stood waiting and beckoning for us at the border of the grove. On joining him we found that he had scarcely exaggerated in his descriptions of the spot.

We stood at the top of a smooth and gradual descent. Before us lay a secluded valley, from which the land rose on every side, to about the elevation of the grove behind us. In some places it ascended in gentle slopes, in others by abrupt acclivities. In the bosom of the valley spread a little lake of oval form, fringed in some places with shrubbery, while in others, groups of casuarinas extended their long drooping boughs in graceful arches over the water. After pausing a moment we descended to the margin of the pond, which was so limpid that we could distinguish every pebble at the bottom. At the upper or northern end, and near the point at which we had come out of the grove, a small stream precipitated itself some fifteen feet down a rocky declivity, and fell into a circular basin a few yards in diameter. Overflowing this basin, it found its way into the lake by another descent of a few feet. Around the basin, and on both sides of the waterfall, were several curious columns of basalt, and irregular picturesque piles of basaltic rock. The plash of the water, falling into the rocky basin, was the only sound that broke the Sabbath-like silence that pervaded the valley. There was, or seemed to be, something unreal and dream-like about the scene, that made us pause where we stood, in silence, as though the whole were an illusion, which a word or a motion would dispel.

"How beautiful!" exclaimed Browne, at last, and a soft clear echo, like the voice of the tutelary spirit of the valley, answered, "Beautiful!"

"Hark!" cried Johnny, "what a charming echo. Listen again," and he shouted "Hurrah!"

"Hurrah!" softly responded the echo, and almost in the same breath a harsh voice, apparently close at hand, and which was evidently not an echo, cried out, "Hillioh—oh!"

We started, and gazed around us, and at each other, in astonishment, but we could see nothing from which this strange exclamation could proceed.

"That," said Johnny, in a trembling whisper, and seizing Browne's hand, "that is the voice of the wild Frenchman I heard in the woods near Castle-hill."

"Yes," answered Max, gravely, "who knows but there are cannibals here? You had better be careful, Johnny, how you hurrah in the woods." Max's manner made me suspect that he possessed some clue to the mystery which the rest of us lacked.

"I don't care," answered Johnny, stoutly, while the apprehensive glances which he cast around on every side, hardly agreed with his valiant words, "I shall hurrah in spite of all the savages on the island."

"Hillioh!—Hillioh!" yelled the same voice, more fiercely than before.

Max burst into a fit of laughter, when following the direction of his eye, we looked up, and espied an enormous parrot perched upon a purau branch, directly over our heads, from which he eyed us with a disdainful and truculent air.

"There's your wild Frenchman at last, Johnny," said Max, "I expect he'll call us to account presently for our treatment of his hat."

"Don't give up de sheep!" screamed the parrot.

"Come," said Max, "what's the use of trying to talk English: it's quite plain you're a Parly-vous."

"Vive l'empéreur!" shrieked the parrot.

"No doubt you can give us a song, monsieur," pursued Max; "favour us with 'Polly put the kettle on,' s'il vous plait."

The bird twisted his head round, as though giving earnest attention to what was said; then, after a moment, which from his wise look seemed to be occupied in profoundly considering the reasonableness of the request, he burst forth with—

"Allons enfants de la Patrie
Le jour de gloire est arrivée!"

Shrieking out the two lines as though they composed a single word. Apparently satisfied with this display of his accomplishments, he spread his wings, and flew heavily across the lake, alighting not far from the shore, whence we could hear him occasionally uttering a shrill cry.

"Do you see where the parrot is now?" inquired Morton of me, a moment afterwards.

"Yes, I see his green feathers among the foliage, but not very distinctly."

"Unless I am much mistaken," pursued he, "there is a shed or building of some kind among the trees, on the other side of the lake, where he has alighted."

On shifting our ground a little, we could all perceive between the boughs of the trees, something, that did in fact look like a low wooden building, and after a moment's consultation, it was agreed that Morton and Max should cross the stream, (which could easily be done where it poured into the lake), and reconnoitre, while the rest awaited their report.

By leaping from stone to stone, and wading occasionally for short distances, they picked their way to the other side, and presently disappeared among the casuarinas. After about fifteen minutes they returned to the shore, and called for us to come over, saying that they had discovered a building, which appeared, however, to have been long deserted. Browne took Johnny upon his back, and we forded the rapids as the others had done.

Following Max and Morton, we soon reached a kind of landing-place, half-way between the lake and the top of the ascent, in the centre of which was a low wooden building, surrounded by a rude fence of pointed stakes. Entering through a gate, hung upon leather hinges, we found ourselves in front of the hut. It appeared to be built of timber which had once composed part of a ship, and was put together with considerable skill. The yard was full of rank weeds, and damp masses of lichen and moss hung from the eaves of the house, and covered its roof. The door, which was furnished with a lock and brass-handle, was closed, but not fastened; we opened it, and entered a large square-room, lighted by four windows, two of which had evidently been taken from the stern of a vessel; the remaining two seemed to have once constituted the upper parts of sash-doors. These windows were well put into the sides of the house, and from the appearance of all the work about the room, I inferred that it had been done by persons accustomed to that kind of labour. A pine-table, which had lost half of one leg, and two chairs without backs, composed the entire furniture of this apartment. A rude shelf was fastened against the wall between two of the windows, upon which a number of earthen-ware dishes were arranged. A smaller apartment was partitioned off with rough boards from the first, with which it communicated by a simple opening or doorway, without any door.

In this second room were several low wooden frames, probably designed as bedsteads, ranged side by side, and a large chest stained or painted blue. In one corner stood a small square writing-table, of some dark-coloured wood, with several drawers. In another corner, Max discovered a rusty gridiron and sauce-pan, a small iron pot and a toasting-fork, upon which he pounced with the eagerness of a miser lighting upon hidden treasures. The chest was empty, but a small box, or till, fixed in one end of it, contained a number of vials, a cork-screw, a tin-canister, and a French Bible, upon the last of which Arthur seized with as much avidity as Max had evinced in appropriating the cooking utensils. Johnny pulled open the drawers of the little writing-table, and found a bunch of quills, a spool of green ribbon, a file of invoices and bills of lading, a bottle of ink, and about half a ream of letter-paper, which he declared was just what was wanted for the purpose of writing "our story."

The place had a gloomy and deserted air, and we unanimously agreed that neither the dwelling nor its location was nearly as pleasant as our own at Castle-hill.

There were several articles which we wished to carry away with us, but we concluded to postpone this until a future visit. Max, however, having once laid hold of the gridiron, seemed extremely loath to part with it again, and, finally yielding to the irresistible fascination which it evidently had for him, he threw it over his shoulder as we started on our return, and brought it away with him. Having been fastidiously purified by repeated scourings and ablutions, it proved very useful in preparing our meals, of which fresh fish frequently formed the principal part.

In the evening, as we sat at the terraced top of Castle-hill, Johnny took seriously in hand the important business of finding appropriate names for the discoveries of the day.

The valley beyond the grove of bread-fruit, he concluded to call "Echo Vale." For the lake itself, quite a variety of names was suggested, none of which, however, seemed to be entirely satisfactory. After puzzling over the subject a long while without any result, and working himself into quite a nervous and excited state, a happy thought seemed all at once to suggest itself and turning to Arthur, he eagerly demanded what was "the most beautiful lake in all the world?"

"Loch Katrine, to be sure!" said Browne; "some would say Loch Lomond, but that is the second:"

"Lake George!" cried Max, decisively.

"Lake Como, in Switzerland, is said to be, by the tourists and the poets," answered Arthur, to whom the question had been more particularly addressed.

The last name seemed to please Johnny exceedingly, and after repeating it several times with approbation, he inquired of Arthur, "What it was that Olla, in the Cannibal story, called her pet wood-pigeon?"

"Lai-evi," answered Arthur.

"And you said that meant Little Captive," pursued Johnny with great animation, "and the 'Lai' means 'little,' I suppose?"

"Yes, 'Lai' is the diminutive."

"Well, then, I have it at last! Our lake, though so small, is—"

"Quite a Como for its size," interrupted Max, "and *so* it shall be called—"

"Lake Laicomo!" cried Johnny, exultingly.

I am thus particular in mentioning these names, chiefly for the benefit of all persons engaged in the preparation of new editions of the school geographies and atlases; and I take this opportunity, at Johnny's especial request, to call their attention to the matter, in order that our island and its geographical dimensions may be accurately laid down and described in future works of the kind referred to.

Chapter Twenty Six
The Removal

Preparations for the Rainy Season—Going into Winter-Quarters—"Monsieur Paul"—The Patriarch of the Lake

"Now Winter comes to rule the varied year,
Sullen and sad, with all his gloomy train
Of vapours, clouds, and storms."

We had now been several months upon the island, and notwithstanding our constant watchfulness, we had not, during all this time, seen a single sail. Of the vast multitudes of vessels that track the ocean in every direction, not one had visited the solitary sea that lay within the boundaries of our horizon; or if any had crossed the verge of the wide circle, her coming and departure had been alike unobserved by us.

And now, by a variety of indications, it was manifest that the winter of the tropical year was at hand. The steady easterly breezes, which, with occasional variations of south-easterly, had hitherto prevailed, were succeeded by violent and fickle winds, blowing sometimes from a dozen different and opposite points of the compass in the course of twenty-four hours. The brief and sudden showers which we had had at intervals for some time past gradually became more heavy and frequent. At length, one calm, sultry day, about noon, a storm, accompanied by thunder and lightning came up, with so little previous notice, that although Arthur and myself were at the time scarcely two hundred yards from the house, we were thoroughly drenched before we could reach it. And this proved to be no mere thunder shower, such as we had already been two or three times surprised by. Scarcely had we got under shelter, when the air grew so dark that it would really have been difficult to see one's way through the grove. I had never before witnessed any thing like this, and I began to fear that we were going to be visited by one of those terrible hurricanes which sometimes devastate tropical countries. The wind soon commenced blowing with such violence, that the largest and sturdiest of the old trees that surrounded our house, bent and swayed before its fury. Their tops lashed each other overhead, and filled the air with clouds of leaves, whirled away upon the tempest. Large boughs were twisted off like twigs, and strewed the ground in every direction. The creaking and groaning of the trees; the loud flapping of the palm-leaves, like that of a sail loose in the wind; the howling and shrieking of the gale, as it burst in quick, fierce gusts through the forest; with the almost total darkness that enveloped us, were truly appalling.

The strength of our dwelling was now put to a severer test than its builders had ever anticipated, and it yielded to the force of the wind, so that at times the side-posts stood at an angle of forty-five degrees with the floor; had they been of any material less tough and pliant than the hibiscus, they must have snapped off in an instant. It was well, too, that they had been deeply and firmly planted in the ground, or the whole fabric would have been lifted bodily into the air, and swept away like a withered leaf. As it was, though wrenched and twisted woefully, it stood firm. The thatch, of which Arthur was so proud, and which had hitherto been storm-proof, now opened in many places, and a dozen little streams began to pour in upon us.

Before night, the sound of running waters without was like that of a great spring freshet. Cataracts were leaping on every side from the edges of the height, and a raging and turbid torrent filled the gully that separated the forest from Castle-hill.

The tempest continued for nearly forty-eight hours. By the time it was over, we had quite come to the conclusion, that if this was to be regarded as a foretaste and specimen of what we had to expect during the rainy season, it would never do to think of remaining in our present habitation. Considering this as a timely warning, we resolved, after a formal consultation, to put the deserted cabin by the lake, forthwith into tenantable condition, so as to be ready to take up our winter-quarters there, if we should find it expedient to do so.

On the first fine day, we commenced carrying this resolution into effect, knowing that we had now but little time to lose. The cabin had originally been built substantially, and with a good deal of skill, and it had suffered but little from decay. We had, in fact nothing to do in the way of repairing it, except to rehang the door, which was loose, and partially unhinged, and to mend the roof, which leaked in one or two places. We then cleared the yard from the rank weeds by which it was overgrown, aired the house thoroughly, by setting door and windows open for a day or two, and swept out both apartments with cocoa-nut brooms.

We next, under Arthur's direction, commenced laying in a stock of provisions. Abundance of ripe bread-fruit could now be procured. We gathered a considerable quantity, which Arthur and Eiulo baked and pounded, and prepared, by burying it under ground, wrapped in leaves, in such a manner that it would keep, as they said, for several months. We also piled up in one corner of the small room, a great heap of cocoa-nuts, with the husks on, in which way they can be preserved fresh a long while. A bushel of candle-nuts, and about the same quantity of taro and patara roots, completed our winter supplies.

Johnny was much dissatisfied with the poverty of these preparations for the rainy season. He thought we ought to have laid in a large stock of salted or smoked fish, besides catching a score or two of turtle, and depositing them safely upon their backs in some convenient place, ready to be converted into soup, at any moment by the magic of Max's culinary art.

Arthur thought that we need not anticipate a season of continuous storms or steady rains—that though the prevailing weather for some months would be tempestuous, there would nevertheless be some fine days in nearly every week, during which we could venture forth.

Another storm, as violent as the last, fully decided us to make the contemplated removal to the cabin, and that without further delay. Johnny transported thither his entire collection of shells, corals, etcetera, which had now grown to be quite extensive. Arthur carried over an armful of specimens of plants and flowers, which had long been accumulating for an "herbarium." Max, however, averred that they were a part of the materials for a treatise on "The Botany of Polynesia," which Arthur cherished the ambitious design of composing, and which was to be published with coloured plate, simultaneously with the history of our adventures. In order that he too might have some indoor occupation during the anticipated bad weather, Max provided himself with a huge log, hacked and sawed with great labour, from a bread-fruit tree, blown down in the last gale, out of which he declared it to be his purpose to build a miniature ship, destined to convey the aforesaid history, together with Arthur's botanical treatise, to America.

The day fixed for our final migration to "Lake Laicomo," at length arrived, and taking a farewell for "the season," of our deserted tenement at Castle-hill, we set out for the cabin, to spend our first night there. It was not without some feelings of regret that we left a spot now become so familiar, to bury ourselves in the woods out of sight of the sea. It seemed almost like going again into exile. Johnny, in particular, felt greatly humiliated, at being obliged to abandon the house which had cost us so much toil, to take refuge in one constructed by others. He seemed to look upon this as a kind of tacit admission of our own utter incapacity to provide for ourselves in that respect.

On arriving at the cabin, we were somewhat surprised to see our democratic friend the parrot, perched over the door, as if waiting to welcome us to our new quarters. He appeared to be in no degree disturbed at our approach, but greeting us with one or two boisterous "Vive Napoleons!" maintained his position until we had passed into the house, when he flew in also, and alighting on the shelf against the wall, seemed to feel as much at home as any one. Johnny sagely suggested that he knew that the rainy season was coming on, and was anxious to establish himself in comfortable quarters until it was over: possibly this supposition did our visitor injustice, by ascribing to him motives more selfish and interested than those by which he was really actuated. It is more charitable to believe, that having been once accustomed to human companionship, and being weary of his solitary life in the woods, where his vocal accomplishments were wasted on the desert air, he now sought our society, as being more congenial to his tastes and education, than that of the feathered denizens of the forest. Be this however as it may, "Monsieur Paul," (as he called himself), from that time took up his abode with us, and though he would sometimes disappear for days together, he was sure to come back at last, when, if he found the door and windows closed, (as sometimes happened), he would scream, and hurrah for "Sheneral Shackson," until he gained admittance. One circumstance, which I am sorry to say throws some shade of suspicion upon the pure disinterestedness of his motives, is, that he generally went off at the commencement of fine weather, and returned a little before a storm. This was so uniformly the case, that Max used to prophesy the character of the weather by his movements, and often, when to our eyes there was not the slightest indication of a change, he would say— "There comes Monsieur— look-out for a storm presently"—and it was rarely that he proved mistaken in such predictions.

The second day after our removal, there was a gale, in which great trees were blown down or torn up by the roots. Though shaken by the force of the wind, the cabin was too firmly built to permit any apprehension of its being overthrown; and there were no trees of large size near it, by the fall of which it could be endangered: but we should scarcely have felt safe in our former dwelling.

We now improved every pleasant day to the utmost, in completing our preparations for the period of heavy rains, which Arthur declared to be close at hand. Browne and Morton made a fish-pond by building a dam of loose stones across the rapids below the fall, just where the stream entered the lake. It was soon well-stocked, without any trouble on our part, with fish resembling roach and perch, numbers of which were carried over the fall, and prevented by the dam from escaping into the lake. We also collected a large quantity of bread-fruit bark, and of the fibrous netting which binds the stalk of the cocoa-nut leaf to the trunk, to be worked up in various ways. This singular fabric, which in texture somewhat resembles coarse cotton cloth, is often obtained from the larger trees in strips two or three feet wide. It is strong and durable, and is used by the natives for making bags, and for other similar purposes. Garments too, are sometimes made from it, though for that purpose tappa is preferred. While the leaves are young and tender, this remarkable substance is white and transparent, quite flexible, and altogether a delicate and beautiful fabric, but not sufficiently strong to be put to any useful purpose: as it becomes older and tougher, it assumes a yellow colour, and loses much of its flexibility and beauty. A quantity of hibiscus bark was also collected, to be used in the manufacture of cord for fishing-lines, nets, etcetera.

While the rest of us were actively engaged, under Arthur's direction, in accumulating a stock of these materials, Max devoted all his energies to the task of capturing an enormous eel which frequented the upper end of the lake. But he exhausted all his ingenuity in this endeavour without success. The monster had a secure retreat among the submerged roots of an old buttress tree, beneath an overhanging bank, from which Max daily lured him forth by throwing crumbs into the water; but, after devouring the food that was thrown to him, he would immediately return to his stronghold under the bank. Max was at great pains to manufacture a fish-hook out of a part of a cork-screw found in the till of the blue chest, by means of which he confidently expected to bring matters to a speedy and satisfactory issue between himself and his wary antagonist. But the latter would not touch the bait that concealed the hook. Driven to desperation by this unexpected discomfiture, Max next made sundry attempts to spear and "harpoon" him, all of which signally failed, so that at the end of the brief interval of fine weather, this patriarch of the lake, whose wisdom seemed to be proportioned to his venerable age and gigantic size, remained proof against all the arts and machinations of his chagrined and exasperated enemy.

Chapter Twenty Seven
Winter Evenings at Home

Amusements and Occupations—Story-Telling—The South-Sea Lyceum

"When the winter nights grow long,
And the winds without blow cold,
We sit in a ring round the warm wood fire,
And listen to stories old."

Having now brought my story down to the period of our getting into winter-quarters at Lake Laicomo, (where, during the last few weeks, the foregoing portion of this narrative has been written), I shall change my tenses, for the present chapter at least, while I sketch the occupations and amusements by which we endeavour to fill up the time of our imprisonment.

The rainy season is now nearly over, and we have got through it much more comfortably and pleasantly than we anticipated. The few fine days during which we finished our preparations for it, as mentioned in the last chapter, were succeeded, in accordance with Arthur's prediction, by more than a week of steady rain, and for several weeks there was not a day without rain. During this time, of course, we were thrown entirely upon our indoor resources, and, thanks to the forethought which had provided an abundant store of materials, upon which the ingenuity or industry of each of us could be variously exercised, we have thus far managed to keep pretty busy.

We have twisted a great store of cord for fishing-lines, nets, and other purposes, from the supply of hibiscus bark previously laid in. We have also manufactured more than a dozen pairs of serviceable moccasins, with no other materials than cocoa-nut cotton and bread-fruit bark. Browne has made a chess-board, and rudely but elaborately carved a complete set of men, of gigantic size, in which he has evinced much skill and ingenuity, and a vast deal of perseverance. The castles are mounted upon the backs of elephants, which Johnny innocently mistook for enormous swine with two tails apiece. The knights are provided with shields, bearing Saint Andrew's cross and the thistle for a device, and would have been arrayed, without doubt, in kilt and tartan had it been possible. The bishops wear grotesque-looking cocked hats, intended for mitres, and their countenances are so singularly truculent and unprepossessing, that Max accuses the artist of having in this petty way, evinced "his Scottish and Presbyterian spite against Episcopacy."

Morton has, among other things, made a couple of nets, and a mortar and pestle for pounding bread-fruit and taro.

Max's time and attention have been chiefly devoted to the manufacture of a variety of warlike weapons, among which are four or five formidable bludgeons, which he styles "Feejee war-clubs," made from the hard and ponderous wood of the casuarina. He has also worked a good deal, at intervals, upon the huge log, out of which the "Messenger ship" is to be constructed.

Arthur has been more usefully employed in contriving two frames or stands, designed as candlesticks for holding the native substitute for candles, which substitute consists simply of a cocoa-nut stalk, some eighteen inches long, strung with candle-nuts. These nuts are of about the size of a horse-chestnut, and contain a considerable quantity of oil: they are the fruit of one of the largest and most magnificent trees of our island. One nut will burn from five to ten minutes, according to its size, and if they are pressed closely together upon the stalk, the flame communicates readily from one to another, affording a tolerably clear and steady light until the entire string is consumed.

To supply the place of Johnny's jacket and trousers, which are completely worn out, Arthur has made, from two or three large strips of cocoa-nut cotton, a garment resembling the South American "poncho," being a loose wrapper, with a circular aperture through which the head of the wearer is to be thrust. It is by no means an elegant article of apparel, and Johnny was at first inclined to look upon it with disfavour. But upon being informed that it was in all respects, except the material of which it was made, like the "tiputa," formerly worn by the Tahitian chiefs and men of note, he became fully reconciled to it.

These, (which I mention merely as a sample of our industrial labours), and similar tasks, furnish us occupation during the day. As soon as it gets dark, we set out the broken-legged table in the middle of the room, and lighting three or four skewers of candle-nuts, amuse or employ ourselves in a variety of ways. Browne and Morton frequently sit down to a game of chess, or seizing a couple of Max's "Feejee war-clubs," practise the broad-sword exercise, in which Browne, who has some skill in fencing, occasionally gives lessons to the rest.

Arthur has opened an evening-school, in which he teaches Eiulo reading and writing, and gives Johnny instruction in botany and conchology, using his "herbarium," and Johnny's collection of shells, for the purpose of illustration. He also writes a good deal, and asks Eiulo many questions respecting the customs, ceremonies, and traditions of Tewa. Occasionally, during such conversations, when he makes a note of something new or striking, Max laughs, and says, that in addition to the great work on the botany of Polynesia, Arthur designs to enlighten the world with a learned treatise on the "Traditions and Superstitions of the South-Sea Islanders."

Johnny either re-arranges his "collection," or plays jack straws with Eiulo, or devotes himself to the education of the parrot.

As for me, I have hitherto amused myself during the evenings in writing up "the narrative," and occasionally reading portions of it aloud, claiming, however, the privilege of skipping such passages as I think proper. It having been solemnly resolved that the "history of our adventures" must be written in the form of a "regular desert island story," to use Johnny's expression, and divided into chapters, Max insists that the commencement of each chapter should be furnished with a poetical motto, and offers, in the capacity of a dictionary of quotations, to furnish scraps of rhyme for that purpose, to order, in any quantity required, and at the shortest notice, upon merely being informed of the sentiment with which the motto is desired to harmonise.

After hearing the narrative thus far, with the exception of such portions as I have thought proper to omit, Max expresses strong distrust of my fairness and impartiality as a historian. He accuses me in particular, of having done him injustice by omitting some of his most remarkable exploits, as well as many brilliant sayings upon a great variety of subjects. He declares that I do not understand and appreciate him—that I am incapable of doing so; and that I have unjustly, though perhaps unintentionally, represented him as a trifling, light-minded sort of person. I have, therefore, felt bound to record this protest of the injured party, but having just read it to him, he pronounces it unsatisfactory, and an aggravation of the original wrong.

Sometimes, as a variation of our evening amusements, we put out the lights, and sit and tell stories in the dark. Browne's memory is stored with an unfailing supply of marvellous tales and legends, founded upon Scottish history and tradition, or the habits and superstitions of the people; some relate to wraiths, warnings, second sight, etcetera; some illustrate the prowess of Scottish heroes and worthies, from Bruce and Wallace, right down to Johnny Armstrong and Rob Roy Macgregor; others, again, are wild and tragical tales of covenanting times, or of the sufferings endured, and the dangers encountered by his countrymen, for their religious faith, from the time of the murder of "holy Patrick Hamilton, the first Scottish martyr," to the forays of prelatical moss-troopers, and the butcheries of Claverhouse, in later days.

The chief point of all Browne's narratives, however various their subjects, is to illustrate the superiority of Scotland, and every thing Scottish, from martyrs to mendicants, and from heroes to highwaymen, over all the rest of the world in general, and the sister kingdom in particular. I was greatly amused by one of his stories, which related how a Scottish border-robber outwitted and plundered an English professional brother. In his patriotic resolution to uphold the superiority of his country in all respects, Browne was not even willing to allow that the pilferers and marauders south of the Tweed, could at all compare in address and audacity, with those who enjoyed the advantage of having been bred to the north of it.

Max, too, was, (at least in Johnny's estimation), a famous story-teller, almost equal in fact to Schehezerade, of the Thousand and One Nights. His stories, however, were of an entirely different character from those of Browne. They had no savour of historic or traditionary truth,—no relation to actual life,—and in this consisted their great charm. Their subject matter, was the wonderful exploits of bold knights-errant, sallying forth, attended by their trusty esquires, in search of high adventures; their chivalrous encounters with other knights in mortal quarrel, or for the honours of the tourney; their incredible feats of strength and valour in the rescue of captive maidens, wandering princesses, and distressed damsels, from all sorts of unheard-of perils, and in the redress of all manner of grievances, by whomsoever suffered. In his more romantic flights he described exploits yet more perilous than these,—conflicts with giants and ogres,—the storming and demolishing of enchanted castles, defended by scaly griffins, and fire-breathing dragons, backed by the potent spells and incantations of some hostile magician. To such narratives Johnny would willingly listen by the hour. Any trifling anachronisms or inconsistencies, which sometimes occurred, never troubled him in the least. If some of Max's knights, equipped with sword and shield, and sheathed in mail, were also expert at fire-arms, and handled a rifle or a revolver, like a Kentuckian, Johnny respected and admired them all the more on account of these varied accomplishments, and never troubled the narrator with any vexatious demand for explanations.

At first Max had been greatly piqued at the slight interest which Johnny seemed to feel in the fate of his heroes. The fact was, that he had become so familiar with that department of literature, and was so accustomed to see the hero come safely out of the most horrible and unheard-of dangers, that he regarded it as quite a matter of course, and there was now no such thing as alarming him for his safety. It was to no purpose that Max surrounded his heroes with fierce and numerous foes; Johnny took it quite coolly, expecting him to cut his way out as a hero should. It was in vain to cover him with wounds—a hero's wounds are never mortal. Cast him away upon an iron-bound coast in the midst of a hurricane—Johnny knew that *one* would escape: drown a hero! who ever heard of such a thing! Max at length resented this indifference, by suddenly becoming quite tragical, and actually despatching two or three heroes with very little ceremony. The first of these unfortunate gentlemen perished, if I remember correctly, by "a tremendous backstroke of a two-handed, double-edged sword, that severed his head from his body." At this sentence, which seemed pretty decisive, Johnny was somewhat staggered, but, immediately recovering himself, he bade Max "go on," expecting, I verily believe, that it would turn out that the head was not in fact *quite* cut off or that if it was, it would, like that of the physician Dubin, in the Arabian Nights, be again set upon the shoulders, and life restored by the healing virtue of some potent medicament. Great was his astonishment and consternation, on being made at last to comprehend, that the hero was actually dead; which fact he did not, however, appear fully to realise, until Max, to put the matter beyond doubt, buried him with great funereal pomp and ceremony, and erected over his remains a splendid monument, with an inscription recording his exploits and his valour. This method of proceeding, Max judiciously followed up, by giving a tragical termination to his romances, often enough to keep Johnny reminded that *his* heroes at any rate were mortal.

In addition to these resources for our evenings, we have the semi-weekly meetings of "The South-Sea Lyceum," which was organised soon after the commencement of the rainy season, and of which Arthur is the president having been twice unanimously elected to that dignified and responsible office. Recitations or declamations, essays, and debates upon questions previously selected, constitute the regular exercises at these meetings. Browne possesses quite a talent for dramatic recitation, and he has Shakespeare almost by heart, which circumstances, early on the voyage out, earned for him the nickname of "Shaks." At nearly every session of the "Lyceum," he is either among the regular appointees for a recitation, or is called out by acclamation for a voluntary one. Max shines chiefly in debate, in which he is always ready to take either side, of any question. Indeed he sometimes speaks on both sides of the same question, and displays his ingenuity by refuting his own arguments.

These meetings have thus far been exceedingly pleasant, and on many a night when the driving rain was beating upon roof and window, and the wind was howling dismally around our solitary cabin, all has seemed bright and cheerful within, as Max and Morton carried on a spirited debate, or Browne declaimed Wolsey's soliloquy, or "To be, or not to be, that is the question."

The minutes of one meeting of the Lyceum may answer as a sample of their entertainments: —

Recitation, (by Johnny), Lines supposed to have been written by Alexander Selkirk, "I am monarch of all I survey," etcetera.

Recitation, (by Browne), Clarence's Dream.

Essay, (by the President), on the traditions of a Deluge, to be found among the Polynesian tribes.

Essay, (by myself), The theory of the formation and structure of Coral Islands.

Debate. Question: Is childhood the happiest period of human life?

Affirmative maintained by Max, negative by Morton.

Summing up of the arguments by the President and decision by him in the negative.

Reading of the Polynesian Intelligencer, by the Editor, (Max).

Recitation, (by Eiulo), a Tewan War-song, in the original.

After the first protracted rain was over, there were frequent intervals of fine weather, which lasted sometimes several days. But we found on going forth, that a change had taken place in the condition of things, which rendered any long excursion, even during these intervals, entirely out of the question.

Considerable streams poured down from the higher ground toward the interior, and traversed the island at short distances, presenting formidable barriers to all travelling. The ground was everywhere so miry that it was difficult to avoid sinking above the ankles at every step.

As the season advanced it became still worse, and at length we confined ourselves almost entirely to the house. Lately, however, there has been a very perceptible improvement; the rains have become lighter, and less frequent, and the season is evidently drawing towards its close. We are already discussing our plans for the summer, and have resolved upon a thorough exploration of the island, as soon as the fine weather has been long enough established to remove the effects of the heavy rains.

Chapter Twenty Eight
The Separation

Our Seclusion Invaded—Spring in the Tropics—
The Excursion and its Consequences

"Reviving Nature bounds as from her birth:
The sun is in the heavens, and life on earth;
Flowers in the valley, splendour in the beam,
Health in the breeze, and freshness in the stream."

I resume my narrative, under circumstances widely different from those in which the preceding chapter was written. The events of the last few days have completely changed the aspect of affairs in our little world. The peace, the seclusion, the security, with which in our minds it had hitherto been invested, exist no longer. Our quiet life, so free from vicissitudes and alarms, as to seem almost monotonous, has been rudely broken into, and in a few days we are to take a step which cannot fail to be attended with consequences momentous to us, but whether fraught with good or evil, it is impossible to foresee. This, however, is anticipating the regular course of events.

It is scarcely credible, how short a time after the cessation of the rains, sufficed to remove every trace of their effects. Three or four days of sunshine seemed to restore things to nearly the condition in which we found them on first reaching the island.

It is true the vegetation now had a fresher look than before, and slender brooks still murmured through ravines usually dry; the lake, too, formerly so limpid, was somewhat discoloured by the turbid streams running into it from the surrounding heights; but the standing pools of water had evaporated, and the ground had, in most places, become once more firm and dry.

As soon as the weather was fairly established, we made several excursions in various directions, though not to any considerable distance. On visiting Castle-hill, we found nothing left of our house there, except the foundation; the entire framework, having been swept away by the wind. A large candle-nut tree, just before the door, had been struck by lightning, and the blasted and blackened trunk, sadly marred the beauty of the spot.

Arthur had selected a favourable location on the margin of the lake near the fish-pond, for a taro and patara patch; and we spent several days in ransacking the neighbouring woods for roots with which to stock it. Yams, we had not yet succeeded in finding, though they are indigenous in most of the Polynesian islands, and we had made diligent search for them in the localities where they are usually found.

One fine morning, soon after the cessation of the rains, Arthur proposed an expedition into the interior, following the course of the stream upward towards its source. In addition to the general object of exploration, he had in view the discovery of the much-coveted vegetable last-mentioned, there being one large variety of it, which is found growing wild among the mountains, or upon the sides of the hills of the interior. All received the suggestion with cordial approval, being particularly pleased with the proposed route, along the banks of the brook. Johnny, exulting in his recovered liberty, after the long imprisonment of the winter, and anticipating all sorts of wonderful discoveries in the vegetable, floral, and ornithological departments, at once enlisted Eiulo and himself as members of the party of exploration.

As we were about to enter a region with the resources of which, in the way of provisions, we knew nothing, we considered it a measure of wise precaution to fortify ourselves against the fatigues of the journey, by a hearty breakfast of broiled fish and roasted taro. This important duty having been conscientiously attended to, our remaining preparations occupied but little time, and we set out at an early hour.

Johnny, equipped with his longest bow, and an abundant stock of arrows, in readiness for the appearance of anything in the shape of a jackal or a tiger-cat, marched valiantly in advance, while Eiulo, in the capacity of armour-bearer, or trusty esquire, followed, carrying his cutlass. Next, carefully surveying the ground we passed over, came Arthur, with a bag upon his arm, and a basket of cocoa-nut leaflets in his hand, ready for the reception of the yams, when found, and of all sorts of roots, plants, and botanical specimens, that might be discovered in the meantime.

Max was armed to the teeth, as though in preparation for a pitched battle. By his side, in a belt of hibiscus bark, was stuck his cutlass: in one hand he carried a "spear," and in the other, one of his "Feejee war-clubs." Morton and myself were provided with a cutlass apiece; and Browne, without having encumbered himself even to that extent, strolled leisurely along with his hands in his pockets, whistling "blue-bonnets over the border."

It was now the spring of the tropical year: the deciduous trees were renewing their verdure, and were covered with young shoots, and bursting leaf-buds. Even the evergreens—though they change but little throughout the year, and the old leaves and the new, the blossoms and the ripe fruit, may be seen upon the same tree at almost every season, looked brighter and fresher than before the rains. The earth was carpeted with beautiful grasses, mingled with tufts of moss, and bunches of fern. Blue and white flowers were scattered about almost as profusely as the "pinkster blossoms," in April, in the woods at home; and in sheltered places, the modest cape-jasmine was beginning to unfold its fragrant leaves. A delightful freshness filled the air, and there was as yet, at this early hour, nothing to remind us that we were beneath the fervent skies of the burning zone.

Rejoicing and exhilarated at finding himself in the woods once more, Johnny ran furiously hither and thither, closely attended by Eiulo, gathering wild-flowers, ferns and mosses; chasing bugs, beetles, and butterflies; and letting fly his arrows at every unfortunate member of the feathered community that came within the range of his archery. In every thicket and almost at every step, he came upon something to call forth the most boisterous exclamations of surprise or delight. He was manifestly in the state of mind declared by the poet to be so eminently happy and desirable—

"To all exhilarating influences,
Of earth and heaven alive!"

Scarcely a moment passed, that he did not come running all aglow and out of breath to Arthur, with eager questions about something or other which he had just seen, and then dash off again into the forest without waiting for a reply, where fresh explosions of admiration or wonder, would soon announce new, and if possible, still more astounding discoveries.

The shores of the stream were picturesque and varied. For the first half-mile from our starting-point, it wound between smooth grassy banks, adorned with scattered clumps of trees. It then entered a dense wood, where its channel was a rugged ravine, inclosed between steep rocks of black basalt. Here, the scraggy, ill-conditioned trees were crowded together, and overgrown with gigantic creepers. The branches, reaching across from the opposite shores, were interlaced and matted into thick masses, almost excluding the light of day. Max here displayed his agility, by laying hold of a long bough which extended from bank to bank, and walking "hand over hand" across the stream that flowed darkly and sluggishly some twelve or fifteen feet below.

We were an hour at the least, in toiling through this tangled wood, though it did not extend more than half a mile. After leaving it behind us, frequent rapids showed that we were steadily ascending as we proceeded. Birds, such as we had not before seen on the island, and which reminded me of some of my old acquaintances of the New England woods, perched upon the trees, or flew familiarly around us. One or two, of the woodpecker tribe, looked wonderfully natural and home-like, as they sat industriously drumming upon hollow logs. Another, a small, brown bird, with modest plumage, surprised and delighted me, by a clear, full whistle, that sounded not unlike that of our own robin redbreast. We also saw numbers of a species of pigeon with black bills, slate-coloured bodies, and a ruff of white feathers about the neck. One of these Johnny brought down with his bow, besides wounding very seriously, (as he alleged), a considerable number of others. The woodpeckers and whistlers enjoyed a temporary immunity from his formidable shafts, reluctantly granted them at my intercession in their behalf, on the score of old associations.

About an hour before noon we reached a spot where the stream was divided by a rocky islet, around which it spread out like a small lake. A grove, of a very peculiar appearance, and seeming to consist of a single tree, sheltered and overspread the entire spot.

Here we concluded to halt, beginning by this time to feel quite tired, and inclined to rest. The water was shallow at this point, and Max wading over to the little island, presently called upon us to follow him if we wished to behold "a veritable banyan tree." Whether a banyan or not, (Arthur pronounced it to be a species of barren fig), it was certainly a wonderful specimen of vegetation. The main trunk, springing up in the centre of the islet, was nearly three feet in diameter. At the height of some fifteen feet from the ground, large branches extended horizontally in every direction. From these branches, at regular intervals, pendulous, vine-like shoots sprouted and grew downwards until they reached the ground, where they took root, and gradually increasing in size formed new trunks or pillars, to support a further extension of the branches. This process of growth had gone on until the tree had overrun the entire island, resembling a flat roof of green branches, resting upon rows of columns. Some of the perpendicular shoots had not yet reached the ground, others had just taken root, and were slender and flexible, while many of the older ones rivalled the parent stem in size, and could not easily be distinguished from it.

While we rested here, a pair of the little brown songsters alighted among the branches of the "banyan," and entertained us with a vocal performance, in which they took up the strain alternately, responding to each other, and occasionally uniting in a chorus.

Max now declared himself savagely hungry, and commenced exploring the neighbourhood in search of something eatable. But no fruit-bearing trees were to be found, and he returned from his foraging expedition protesting that the country was a perfect desert, and declaring that he for one would not proceed a step farther until he took up the line of march for home. We were all of the opinion that we had done enough for one day, and it was agreed that after resting ourselves a short time we should commence our return.

Meantime, Arthur caught sight of some trees upon a ridge of land a short distance further up the stream, whose foliage resembled, as he thought, that of the "auti," or cloth plant. Saying that he would return in a few moments, he walked along the west bank of the brook in the direction of the ridge, followed by Johnny and Eiulo, who seemed as animated and unwearied as ever. Presently they turned a bend in the stream, and we lost sight of them. For lack of more interesting occupation, I began to count the stems of the grove-tree. There were seventeen, of large size, and a great number of smaller ones. Max discovered a deep pool at the lower end of the islet, in which were a number of fish, marked like yellow perch: and as he had a fishing-line of Eiulo's manufacture, in his pocket he amused himself by angling, using wood-beetles for bait. Morton and Browne hunted up four flat stones, and commenced pitching quoits.

After half an hour passed in these various ways, we began to wonder at Arthur's long delay, and to grow impatient for his return. I had counted every stem of the banyan-fig, great and small. Max had become quite disgusted with angling for fish, which were too wary, or too well-fed, to favour him with even a nibble. Browne, after being beaten for five successive games, had very naturally lost his interest in the sport, and tossed his quoits into the brook.

Another half-hour passed, and still the absentees failed to make their appearance. Max now professed to be suffering from the pangs of hunger, and longed for the sight even of the much-abused cocoa-nut tree. At last our patience being utterly exhausted, we resolved to go in search of Arthur and his suite, whose protracted absence greatly surprised us.

On reaching the point, or bend, behind which they had disappeared, we hallooed loudly, but there was no answer. As we proceeded, the ground became very rough and broken, and the bed of the brook was full of loose rocks. A little further on, the noise of a waterfall was heard, and after one or two more turns, we reached a spot where the stream leaped down a precipice some twenty feet. Our further progress in the direction we were pursuing was barred by a wall of rock; an active and fearless climber might, it is true, have scaled it by the aid of the stunted shrubs and jutting crags upon its face, but we knew that Arthur accompanied by Eiulo and Johnny, could not have passed on by any such route.

Proceeding to the left, along the foot of the precipice, and pausing at short intervals to repeat our halloos, we at last reached a wide fissure in the rock, by scrambling through which we gained the higher level. This was in all probability a part of the ridge which Arthur had seen from the islet. We now returned along the brow of the precipice until we came to the waterfall, where we shouted again, but still without getting any answer. To push the search further in this direction seemed useless, for it was morally certain that Arthur would not have continued beyond this point up the stream; the understanding with which he had left us, forbade any such supposition.

We began now to feel alarmed, and to fear that some accident had befallen them, though of what nature we were at a loss to conjecture. Morton suggested the possibility that they had taken the opposite bank of the brook, and that while we were looking for them, they might have returned to the islet. This seemed not improbable, and striving hard to convince ourselves that it must be so, we regained the lower level by the same pass through which we had ascended, and hastened along the base of the height, and down the shore of the stream till we reached the islet again. But our companions were not there. Still, they might have returned during our absence, and supposing that we had started homeward, proceeded after us. We were greatly perplexed what course to pursue. If we delayed our return much longer, we should not be able to reach the cabin before night set in: the wilderness around seemed to contain nothing that could serve as food, and we should have to fast as long as we remained in it. Then, too, our waiting longer could be of no benefit to the others, even if they had not yet returned to the islet. Upon finding us gone, they would know at once that we had set out for home, and there was no possibility of their mistaking their way thither.

We concluded, accordingly, to return without further delay. Browne cut a stout stick, and planted it in the sand at the margin of the brook, arranging a number of large pebbles at its foot, in the form of a hand, with the index finger pointing homeward. We then set out at a brisk pace, with some hope, but little actual expectation, of overtaking our companions on the war.

We soon reached the thick wood with its matted undergrowth, and the old and knotted vines twining like enormous reptiles around the trunks of the trees; and so slow was our progress through it, that when we emerged into the open country it was nearly sunset. The remaining distance was more rapidly accomplished. As we drew nigh to the cabin, I began to look anxiously for the appearance of the missing ones. Each moment I expected to see Johnny rushing towards us with a laughing boast of having "beaten us home." But no one came forth to meet us, and I thought that the valley had never before looked so lonely.

It was not, however, entirely deserted. The parrot was perched in solitary state upon the eaves of the cabin, and as we opened the gate, he flapped his wings, and croaked forth in dismal tones a sentence which Johnny, little dreaming of its present application, had been at much pains to teach him:— "Poor Paul's lonesome!" he cried, "they're all gone—all gone!"

Chapter Twenty Nine
The Search

Home Sweet Home—Max on Moonlight—
Following a Trail—The Concealed Canoe

"Where'er thou wanderest, canst thou hope to go
Where skies are brighter, or the earth more fair?
Dost thou not love these aye-blue streams that flow,
These spicy forests, and this golden air?

"O yes! I love these woods, these streams so clear,
Yet from this fairy region I would roam,
Again to see my native hills—thrice dear!
And seek that country, of all countries,—Home."

Max hastened to collect fuel, and kindle a fire, in order to prepare some food. Assuming, as usual, the entire superintendence and control of the culinary department, and every thing connected therewith, he set Browne to work washing and scraping tara-roots, despatched me after a fresh supply of fuel, and sent Morton with the hand-net down to the fish-pond to take out a couple of fish for a broil. But while thus freely assigning tasks to the rest of us, with the composed air of one accustomed to the exercise of unquestioned authority, he by no means shrunk from his own fair share of the work; and having got the fire burning cleverly by the time that Morton returned with the fish, he rolled up his sleeves, and with an air of heroic fortitude, commenced the necessary, but somewhat unpleasant process of cleaning them.

Night had now set in, but the sky being perfectly clear, and the moon at her full, it was scarcely darker than at early twilight.

Max seemed to prolong his culinary operations to the utmost, either from pure love of the employment, or with the still lingering hope, that our companions might yet arrive in time to partake of our supper.

At last however, it became apparent that the cookery could not, without serious detriment, be longer protracted. The bursting skin of the taro revealed the rich mealy interior, and eloquently proclaimed its readiness to be eaten. The fish were done to a turn, and filled the cabin with a savoury odour, doubly grateful to our nostrils after a twelve hours' fast. Max declared with a sigh, that another moment upon the gridiron would ruin them, and he was reluctantly compelled to serve up the repast without further delay, when, notwithstanding our growing anxiety on account of Arthur's absence, we made a hearty meal. After feeding Monsieur Paul, and setting by some food in readiness for our companions when they should arrive, as we still hoped they would do in the course of the evening, we went out to a spot above the cascade, where Morton and Browne had arranged some rude fragments of basalt, so as to form a semicircle of seats, which, if less comfortable than well-cushioned arm-chairs would have been, might at any rate be considered in decidedly better "rural taste," and in more harmonious keeping with the character of the surrounding scene.

From this point we could trace the windings of the brook for some distance in one direction, while below us, in the opposite one, spread the moonlit lake, reflecting in its mirror-like surface the dark masses of foliage that fringed its shores. It was one of those tranquil, dreamy nights, known only in tropical countries. A subtle fragrance of fresh buds and blossoms filled the air. The light streamed in a silvery flood upon the tufted tops of the groves; while in the solemn shade beneath, the serried trunks reared themselves in long ranks, like the grey columns of some Gothic ruin.

As we sat listening to the murmur of the waterfall, the rustling of the trees, and the distant and muffled booming of the surf, I fell into a dreamy reverie, which was at length dissipated by Browne's voice—

"Can any thing be more beautiful than this scene at this moment!" exclaimed he, "and yet I do not know when I have experienced such a weariness of it all—such an intense longing for home, as I feel to-night."

"I shall begin to believe in mesmeric sympathy," said Morton, "I was myself just thinking of home. Home, sweet home!" and he heaved a long-drawn sigh.

Yes! the charm and illusion of our island life had long ended. We were tired of tropical luxuriance, and eternal summer. Glowing skies, and landscapes like a picture, had almost ceased to gratify even the eye. I longed for a glimpse of a rugged New England hill once more. A gnarled New England oak, though stripped by wintry winds of every leaf, would be a sight more grateful to me, than all those endless groves of waving palms.

"I cannot believe," resumed Browne, "that we are destined to waste our days in this lonely spot, elysium as it is, of external beauty. We have faculties and desires, which can find no scope here, and which are perishing for lack of exercise. Still it is possible. But it is a dreary, dreary thought! I can now feel the pathos of the words of the ancient mariner on coming in sight of his native land—

"'Oh dream of joy! is this indeed
The light-house top I see?
Is this the hill? is this the kirk?—
Is this mine own countree?

"'We drifted o'er the harbour bar
And I with sobs did pray—
O let me be awake, my God!
Or let me sleep away!'"

Browne recited the lines with a power and feeling, that affected even the matter-of-fact Morton; Max hastened to show that he was above being so easily moved.

"All this comes," cried he, "of lying here under the trees in the moonlight. Moonlight certainly has a tendency to make people melancholy and sentimental; it also makes them do foolish things. The most absurd and unreasonable notions I ever entertained, came into my head by moonlight, and wouldn't go away. Only twenty-five minutes ago, we were quite a rational, practical set of persons, eating our supper, (a well-cooked supper, too, though I say it myself), with a keen appetite, like Christians. And now, we have fallen to sighing and quoting poetry, and Browne waxes quite pathetic at the touching thought of getting a glimpse once more, of the smoky chimneys of Glasgow! Finally, I have nearly caught the infection myself, and unless I escape out of the moonlight presently, I dare say I also shall become quite lack-a-daisical, and commence a poetical apostrophe to my native village of Hardscrabble—or rather to plump little Susan Somers, my first love, at the 'madam's' school, who affected my weak mind and susceptible heart to that extent, that in her bewildering presence my tongue clave to the roof of my mouth, while I grew red in the face like a perplexed turkey gobbler. But what *can* have become of Arthur and the rest? Unless something had happened to them, they must have returned before now."

A little before midnight we retired to the cabin to sleep, having first agreed, that in the morning three of us should proceed up the stream again, to make a thorough search for our companions, the fourth remaining behind until near noon, when, if the absentees had not yet returned, he should set out to join the others at the islet below the falls, which we fixed upon as the rendezvous.

In the morning, lots were drawn to determine which of us should remain at the cabin, and that duty fell to Morton. The rest of us, having armed ourselves, and prepared a supply of taro and bread-fruit, sufficient, as we supposed, for several days, set out, soon after sunrise. Our progress was much more rapid than it had been when we first went over the ground, as we now had a definite object in view, and pressed steadily forward, without allowing any thing to interrupt or delay us. In an hour and a half after starting, we came in sight of the islet. Opposite it was the stake which Browne had planted in the sand, just as we had left it. We pushed on up the stream to the cascade, and crossing to the right bank, we began to skirt the base of the rocky wall on that side, looking carefully around for some traces of our companions.

We had proceeded in this way, about one hundred yards from the brook, when I picked up one of Johnny's arrows in a tuft of fern. This was conclusive evidence that we were upon the right track. A little farther on, was a piece of marshy ground, and here we made a startling discovery. In the soft soil, several foot-prints could be plainly distinguished. Some were coarse, shapeless impressions, precisely such as would be made by the rude moccasins worn by Arthur and Johnny. Others were the prints of naked feet, and some of these were of far too large a size to be made by either of the three. This discovery affected us for the moment like an electric shock, and we stood looking at one another without speaking, and scarcely breathing, while the very beating of our hearts might be heard.

Browne was the first to recover himself, when he commenced a close examination of all the tracks. The piece of ground upon which they could be traced, extended some thirty yards, and after a careful scrutiny of the whole of it, we became convinced that at least four persons, besides our three companions, had recently passed over it. All the tracks were not in the same direction, and from finding those of precisely the same size lying in opposite directions, we inferred that some of these persons, at least, had passed and repassed the spot.

The most distressing surmises as to the cause of the disappearance of our companions, now began to suggest themselves. We were so astounded by this decisive evidence of the presence of strangers upon the island, that we scarcely knew what to do next, but at last concluded to return to the islet and await Morton's arrival, being anxious to avoid the risk of any further division of our numbers. We accordingly retraced our way thither: supposing that Morton would have set out before we could reach the cabin, and that we might pass each other on the way without knowing it, if we should proceed down the stream to meet him, we remained quietly at the islet, keeping a vigilant and somewhat nervous look-out on every side.

He arrived about noon, having started rather sooner than had been agreed upon. On being informed of the tracks which had been discovered, he said that we ought at once to trace them as far as we were able. "We must not rest," said he, "until we know something more of this, even if we have to traverse every inch of ground on the island."

Browne was inclined to infer from the foot-prints, that the interior, and the eastern part of the island, of which we as yet knew nothing, were inhabited, and that our companions had fallen into the hands of the natives.

"Let us, in the first place, find, if possible, where they are. We can then judge what is to be done, if indeed we can do any thing," said Morton, "and now for the place where the tracks you speak of are to be seen."

Grasping our weapons, which were no longer to be regarded as a useless incumbrance, we once more proceeded up the brook, and soon reached the piece of low ground before mentioned. We again narrowly inspected the tracks: Morton measured them with a twig, and concluded, as we had previously done, that these were the foot-prints of at least seven persons— there being that number of clearly different sizes. Three of these were without doubt the tracks of Arthur, Johnny, and Eiulo. The impressions made by the moccasins of the two former led only in one direction, (*from* the stream), while those of the naked feet, (or of some of them), were in two opposite directions. Following these tracks eastward along the rocky ridge, we soon came to firm dry ground, where footsteps could no longer be traced. But by a minute scrutiny, we were still able to detect slight but decisive indications of the course of the party whose trail we were endeavouring to follow.

In one place, a bunch of spreading ferns had been trodden down, and the long graceful fronds bruised and broken: in another, a cluster of crushed wild-flowers betrayed a recent footstep. A little further on, we came to a wide, meadow-like expanse, where the grass and weeds grew rank and tall, and through this the path of a considerable party could be readily traced. Gradually becoming accustomed to this species of minute investigation, as we continued carefully to practise it, we soon grew so expert and skilful, that things very slight in themselves, and which would ordinarily have altogether escaped notice, sufficed to guide and direct us.

The path trodden through the meadow, led to the foot of an ascent, up which we followed the trail slowly and with difficulty, the soil being hard, and the vegetation scanty. On gaining the top, we found that we had reached the eastern, or south-eastern extremity of the island, and the sea spread before us, almost at our feet. The trail led directly towards the edge of a steep bank, just above the shore, near which we lost it altogether. Morton leaped down the bank some ten or twelve feet, while the rest of us were looking round for easier and more gradual means of descent. Finding a stunted tree springing from the lower ground, close against the bluff, I leaped among its spreading branches, and climbed down its trunk to the shore, where I found Morton searching for some traces of the party which we had tracked almost to the edge of the height.

In a moment we were joined by Max and Browne, who had clambered down the face of the bank by the assistance of the shrubs and bushes growing upon it.

"It is useless," said Browne, "to look here for the trail we have lost. If they descended to the shore, it must have been in some place where Johnny and Eiulo could have got down."

"The track seemed to lead directly to the sea," said Morton, "and you must consider that a party of savages would not find much of an obstacle in such a bank as this, and would scarcely be as careful as ourselves of the safety of Johnny and Eiulo. In fact, I suppose they would hand or drop them down such a height, without scruple or ceremony. What I now begin to fear is, that our unfortunate companions have fallen into the hands of a party of savages, landing here for some transient purpose, and have been carried off by them."

At this moment an exclamation from Max, who had walked a little way along the beach, announced some discovery, and turning round we saw him beckoning to us.

"What is that?" said he, when we had joined him, stooping down, and pointing towards a clump of stunted trees, growing in an angle or indentation, where the bluff fell back for a short distance from the shore, "is it not a canoe drawn up under the trees?"

It was not easy to distinguish the object clearly, on account of the thickness of the foliage. After waiting a moment, and looking carefully about, being satisfied that there was no one in the vicinity, we approached the spot. Max was not mistaken; a large canoe, capable of holding fifteen or twenty persons, was lying among the bushes, where it had evidently been placed for concealment. In the bottom were a number of carved paddles, a mast wound about with a mat-sail, several calabashes containing water, and some cocoa-nuts.

Having hastily noted these particulars, we withdrew to a short distance, behind a rock detached from the bank, and surrounded by a dense growth of tangled shrubbery, to hold a consultation.

From the position in which we found the canoe, with no dwelling near that we could see, and from the circumstance of its containing water and provisions, we inferred that it did not belong to persons inhabiting the island, or this portion of it at any rate. There was at least a probability of its belonging to the party which we had tracked so nearly to the spot, and that they were now somewhere in the neighbourhood.

"This canoe must be destroyed," said Morton, after a moment of silence, "and we had better set about it at once."

This proposition seemed a bold and a somewhat strange one. Browne demanded the object of such a proceeding.

"Unless we do this," answered Morton, "our companions, if they are still alive, and in the power of the savages, may be carried away from the island before our eyes, and separated from us for ever. As long as they are here, within our reach, there is hope of our being able to rescue them; if not by force, then by some device or stratagem. At the worst, we only run some unnecessary risk, by what I propose. Could we ever forgive ourselves if Arthur should be carried off through our having omitted a precaution calculated to prevent it?"

Morton's decision and earnestness prevailed; while he undertook the work of destroying the canoe, Max, Browne, and I, stationed ourselves at different points around the spot, so as to give timely notice of the approach of any person. He devoted himself to his task with such vigour, that in a very few moments he had completely broken up the bottom of the canoe, by repeated blows of a stone as heavy as he could lift in both hands. Not content with this, he disengaged the outrigger, and threw it, together with the mast and sail, into the sea.

Chapter Thirty
The Rencontre

The Two Leaders—An Unexpected Meeting—
The Council of War—And what followed

"Now screw your courage to the sticking point."

"With many a stiff thwack, many a bang,
Hard crab-tree and old iron rang;
While none who saw them could divine
To which side conquest would incline."

I had climbed to the top of the bank as my look-out station, while the work of demolishing the canoe was going forward, and on perceiving that Morton had accomplished his task, I was about to descend again, when taking a final sweeping glance to the north and east, I observed several figures moving rapidly along the beach, at a point somewhat less than a quarter of a mile distant, of which my position commanded a view, and coming towards us. In consequence of the indented character of the shore, and the height of the bank bordering it for some distance, they passed out of sight almost instantly.

Without losing a moment, I sprang down to the shore to communicate what I had seen. Max, who had been posted upon the beach to keep a look-out northward, ran up at the same time, having also caught sight of the persons approaching us, as they came round a projecting point.

We now looked hurriedly around for some place of concealment, and Morton pointed out a cluster of shrubs and rank weeds upon the verge of the bluff just above us, from which, without any risk of being seen ourselves, we could command a view of the shore and those passing along it. There was but little time for deliberation or choice, and hastily summoning Browne from his post, where he was still on the watch, we scaled the almost perpendicular face of the height, with an ease and celerity which would have been impossible under circumstances of less excitement.

In the spot which Morton had designated, tall grass and flaunting weeds fringed the edge of the bluff, and we threw ourselves down among them, and awaited, with almost suspended breath, the approach of the persons I had seen.

We were scarcely settled in our hiding-place, when a half-naked figure, swinging a short club in one hand, rushed into view. Another, and another followed, until I had counted seven of them. They were well-made, athletic men, of a fine olive colour, with long straight hair falling over their shoulders. The maro, which is a sort of fringed belt, was their only clothing, and they carried spears and clubs of some dark-grained wood.

Among them was one striking figure. It was that of an old man, of large and powerful frame, and a marked and resolute countenance, the expression of which reminded me of an old lion which I had seen in some itinerant menagerie, years ago. His massive head was covered with a tangled mass of iron-grey hair that streamed like a mane over his broad shoulders. The club which he carried might have served Hercules himself; it certainly would have severely tasked the strength of an ordinary man to wield it. I observed that all of them seemed to breathe quickly as though they had been running, or exerting themselves violently in some way; and the old man, who came last looked backward once or twice, as they came opposite us, in a way that caused me to suppose that they were pursued. The one who had first come in sight, went towards the spot where the canoe was concealed, and upon seeing its condition, uttered an exclamation of surprise that quickly brought the others around him, when they all commenced gesticulating, and talking in a low key, looking cautiously about every moment, as though apprehensive that the perpetrators of the mischief might still be lurking near.

The old man, however, neither talked nor gesticulated, but stooping down, he examined the canoe narrowly, as if to ascertain the precise extent of the injury done, and whether it admitted of any remedy. When he had completed his inspection he arose, and shaking his head sorrowfully, uttered some expression, which, accompanied as it was by a threatening gesture with his ponderous club, sounded much like an emphatic imprecation. Morton, who was crouching close beside me, peering cautiously through the tufts of grass, at what was going on below, gave a nervous start, as though the consciousness of the leading part he had taken in the mischief so recently wrought, made him consider himself the special object of the old giant's fury. One of them having gone back a little way along the beach, as if to reconnoitre, now returned in haste, and made some announcement, upon hearing which the old man waved his hand, and the others immediately started off upon a full run along the shore towards the south-west; he then followed them at a somewhat less hurried pace.

"They are certainly pursued, judging from their actions," whispered Morton, "let us keep quiet, and see what comes next."

But a few minutes had passed, when half a dozen savages, resembling in their appearance and equipments those we had just seen, came in sight, running at full speed, but with the air of pursuers rather than of fugitives. Straggling bands of two or three each followed at short intervals, all probably belonging to the same party, but scattered in the heat of the chase. Altogether, there must have been as many as fifteen or twenty of them. A tall, wild-looking savage, large-framed, but gaunt as a greyhound, and with a kind of fierce energy in all his movements, seemed to be the leader of the pursuing party. Just below us on the beach, he turned and gave some order to a portion of his followers, speaking with great rapidity, and pointing towards the bluff; after which he darted off again along the shore at a speed that seemed really marvellous. Those to whom he had spoken, immediately began, as if in obedience to the order just given, to climb the bank, not a dozen yards from the spot where we were lying.

The object of this movement undoubtedly was, to anticipate and frustrate any attempt on the part of the fugitives, to escape, by quitting the shore and making towards the interior. The party thus detached had probably been directed to continue the chase, keeping to the higher ground. If so, they would pass quite near our place of concealment, and there was some danger of our being discovered, to avoid which, we crouched close to the ground, and remained perfectly silent and motionless. The point where the savages were attempting to ascend was steep and difficult, and several of them, apparently to disencumber themselves for the effort of climbing, threw their clubs and spears before them to the top. One of these weapons, a short, heavy club, fell near me, and fearing that the owner might come to seek it, I hastily cast it to a conspicuous place, free from vegetation, a little distance from the bank, and nearer the spot where they were scaling it. But the savage had probably noticed where it first fell, for the next moment some one came running directly towards the place, and just as I was expecting to see him stumble into the midst of us, a deep guttural exclamation announced that we were discovered. Any further attempt at concealment was clearly idle, and we sprang up at once; the man was within three yards of us; he seemed quite as much startled as ourselves at so sudden a rencontre, and after standing for a minute looking at us, he turned and ran off to his fellows.

"They will be back directly in a body," said Browne, "and we must decide quickly what we are to do—whether to trust ourselves in their power, or to make such resistance as we can, if they undertake to meddle with us."

"I doubt if it would be safe to trust them," said Morton, "at any rate I don't like the idea of risking it. There are but five or six of them; the rest are far enough off by this time."

"I wish Arthur were here," said Browne, anxiously; "he understands them and their ways, and could tell us what we ought to do. I don't know what the probability is of their injuring us if we throw aside our arms and submit ourselves to them, and therefore I am loth to take the responsibility of deciding the matter."

Meantime the savages appeared to be also holding a consultation. They stood at a short distance talking rapidly, and pointing towards us. At length they began to approach the spot where we stood, but slowly, and with some apparent hesitation.

"Well," said Browne, "we must come to a decision quickly."

"I distrust them entirely," exclaimed Morton, "I am for acting on the defensive."

"And I also," said Max, "I have no faith in them: but perhaps they won't stop to interfere with us after all."

"Very well, then," said Browne, "we will fight if we must. But let us stand strictly on the defensive, and offer them no provocation."

I could not help regarding this determination as unwise, but it was the mind of the majority; and the present was no time for divided or uncertain counsels. I therefore kept my thoughts to myself, and grasping my cutlass, prepared for what was to follow.

Browne and Max were armed with the "Feejee war-clubs," of the latter's manufacture: they were long, heavy bludgeons, of the wood of the casuarina, rather too ponderous to be wielded with one hand by a person of ordinary strength. Morton and I were provided with cutlasses, which we had preferred as being lighter and more convenient to carry.

The savages were armed with spears and short clubs, the former of which they presented towards us as they advanced.

I confess that my heart began to thump against my breast with unwonted and unpleasant rapidity and violence. I dare say it was the same with my companions; but externally we were perfectly composed and steady.

"There are just five of them," said Browne, "two antagonists for me, and one apiece for the rest of you. If any one interferes with my two I shall consider it a personal affront."

"Confound those long spears!" exclaimed Max, with a disturbed air, "they have a mighty uncomfortable look, with those fish-bone barbs at the end of them."

The still more "uncomfortable" thought that those fish-bone barbs were perhaps poisoned, suggested itself to me, but I considered it expedient to say nothing on the subject at the present juncture.

"Pshaw!" cried Browne, "the long spears are easily managed, if you will only remember my fencing-lessons, and keep your nerves steady. It is the simplest thing in the world to put aside a thrust from such a weapon: depend upon it, those short clubs will prove much more dangerous."

The savages, having now had a sufficient opportunity to note our equipments, and our youthful appearance, quickly lost all hesitation, and came confidently forward until they stood facing us, at the distance of but ten or twelve feet. Then, seeing that we maintained a defensive attitude, they paused, and one of them, stepping a little before the rest, spoke to us in a loud and authoritative voice, at the same time motioning us to throw aside our weapons.

"Can't you muster a few words of their heathen talk, Archer?" said Browne, "perhaps if we could only understand one another, we should find there is no occasion for us to quarrel. It seems so irrational to run the risk of having our brains knocked out, if it can be avoided."

I shook my head: the few phrases which I had picked up from Arthur and Eiulo, could be of no use for the present purpose, even if they should be understood.

The spokesman, a sinewy, hard-favoured savage, whose native ugliness was enhanced by two scars that seamed his broad squat face, repeated the words he had before uttered, in a higher key, and with a still more imperative air, accompanying what he said, with gestures, which sufficiently explained what he required.

"If I understand you, my friend," said Browne, appearing to forget in the excitement of the moment that what he was saying would be utterly unintelligible to the person he addressed, "If I understand you, your demand is unreasonable. Throw away your own weapons first; you are the most numerous party:" and he imitated the gestures which the other had made use of.

The savage shook his head impatiently, and keeping his eyes steadfastly fixed upon Browne, he began to speak in a quiet tone. But I saw that though looking at Browne, his words were addressed to his companions, who gradually spread themselves out in front of us and without making any openly hostile demonstrations, handled their weapons in what seemed to me a suspicious manner.

"Be on your guard," said I, speaking in my ordinary tone, and without looking round, "I am sure they are meditating sudden mischief."

Scarcely were the words uttered, when, with the quickness of lightning, the spokesman hurled his club at Browne, narrowly missing his head, then bringing his spear into a horizontal position, he made a thrust full at his chest with his whole force.

Browne, however, was on his guard, and knocking aside the point of the spear, he swung round his long club; and, before the other could draw back, brought it down with such effect upon his right shoulder that his arm fell powerless to his side, and the spear dropped from his grasp. Browne promptly set his foot upon it, and the owner, astonished and mortified, rather than intimidated at his repulse, shrunk back without any attempt to regain it.

This attack was so sudden, and so soon foiled—being but a blow aimed, parried, and returned, in a single breath—that no one on either side had an opportunity to interfere or join in it. The other savages now uttered a yell, and were about to rush upon us: but the leader, as he appeared to be, motioned them back, and they drew off to a short distance. If we were for a moment inclined to hope that we should now be left unmolested, we soon learned the groundlessness of such an expectation. The discomfited savage, instead of being discouraged by the rough treatment he had received, was only rendered more dangerous and resolute by it; and he prepared to renew the attack at once, having taken from one of his companions a club somewhat heavier and longer than his own.

"I wish," said Max, drawing a long breath as he eyed these ominous proceedings, "that we had a few of Colt's revolvers, to keep these fellows at a respectable distance: I confess I don't like the notion of coming to such close quarters with them as they seem to contemplate."

"A genuine Yankee wish!" answered Browne, grasping his club with both hands, and planting himself firmly, to receive the expected onset; "to make it completely in character you have only to wish, in addition, for a mud breastwork, or a few cotton bags, between us and our friends yonder."

"Which I do, with all my heart!" responded Max, fervently.

"Let Kaiser Maximilien represent the high Dutch on this occasion," said Morton, edging himself forward abreast of Browne, who had stationed himself a trifle in advance of the rest of us; "he has no claim to speak for the Yankees except the mere accident of birth. Archer and I will uphold the honour of the stars and stripes without either revolvers or cotton bags."

"Fair play!" cried Max, pushing Browne aside, "I won't have you for a breastwork at any rate, however much I may desire one of turf or cotton bales." And we arranged ourselves side by side.

"Really," said Morton, with a faint apology for a smile, "it appears that we have to do with tacticians—they are going to outflank us." This remark was caused by our antagonists separating themselves; the leader advancing directly towards us, while the others approached, two on the right and two on the left.

"Well," said Browne, "we shall have to form a hollow square, officers in the centre, as the Highlanders did at Waterloo, and then I shall claim the privilege of my rank."

But our pleasantry was, as may easily be imagined, rather forced. Our adversaries were now evidently bent upon mischief, and thoroughly in earnest. We were none of us veterans, and notwithstanding an assumption of coolness, overstrained and unnatural under the circumstances, our breath came thick and painfully with the intense excitement of the moment.

At a signal from their scarred leader, the savages rushed upon us together. I can give no very clear account of the confused struggle that ensued, as I was not at the time in a state of mind favourable to calm and accurate observation. A few blows and thrusts were exchanged; at first cautiously, and at as great a distance as our weapons would reach; then more rapidly and fiercely, until we became all mingled together, and soon each of us was too fully occupied in defending himself to be able to pay much attention to any thing else. At the commencement of the attack I was standing next to Browne, who being evidently singled out by his former opponent, advanced a step or two to meet him. He skilfully parried several downright blows from the heavy club of the latter, who in his turn dodged a swinging stroke which Browne aimed at his head, and instantly closed with him. The next moment they went whirling past me towards the edge of the bank, locked together in a desperate grapple, which was the last that I saw of them. I was assailed at the outset by an active and athletic savage, armed with a short club. He was exceedingly anxious to close, which I, quite naturally, was as desirous to prevent, knowing that I should stand no chance in such a struggle, against his superior weight and strength. While I was doing my best to keep him off with my cutlass, and he was eagerly watching an opportunity to come to closer quarters, Morton, locked in the grasp of a brawny antagonist, came driving directly between us, where they fell together, and lay rolling and struggling upon the ground at our feet. My opponent, abandoning me for a moment, was in the act of aiming a blow at Morton's head, when I sprang forward, and cut him across the forehead with my cutlass. The blood instantly followed the stroke, and gushing in torrents over his face, seemed to blind him: he struck three or four random blows in the air, then reeled and fell heavily to the ground. Throwing a hasty glance around, I perceived Max among some bushes at a little distance defending himself with difficulty against a savage, who attacked him eagerly with one of those long spears, towards which he entertained such an aversion. Browne was nowhere to be seen. Morton and his strong antagonist were still grappling on the ground, but the latter had gained the advantage, and was now endeavouring, while he held Morton under him, to reach a club lying near, with which to put an end to the struggle. Another of the enemy was sitting a few steps off apparently disabled, with the blood streaming from a wound in the neck. I hastened to Morton's assistance, whereupon his opponent, seeing my approach, sprang up and seized the club which he had been reaching after. But Morton gained his feet almost as soon as the other, and instantly grappled with him again. At this moment I heard Max's voice, in a tone of eager warning, calling, "Look-out, Archer!" and turning, I saw the savage I supposed to be disabled, with uplifted arm, in the very act of bringing down his club upon my head. I have a confused recollection of instinctively putting up my cutlass, in accordance with Browne's instructions for meeting the "seventh" stroke in the broad-sword exercise. I have since become convinced by reflection, (to say nothing of experience), that the principles of the broad-sword exercise, however admirable in themselves, cannot be applied without some modification when iron-wood clubs, with huge knobs of several pounds' weight at the ends of them, are substituted for claymores. However, I had no time then to make the proper distinctions, and as instead of dodging the blow, I endeavoured to parry it, my guard was beaten down—and that is all that I can relate of the conflict, from my own knowledge and personal observation.

Chapter Thirty One
Reconnoitring by Night

The Search Renewed—The Captives—Atollo and the Tewans

"Trembling, they start and glance behind
At every common forest-sound—
The whispering trees, the moaning wind,
The dead leaves falling to the ground;
As on with stealthy steps they go,
Each thicket seems to hide the foe."

From the moment when startled by Max's warning cry, I turned and saw the uplifted club of the savage suspended over my head, all is blank in my memory, until opening my eyes with a feeling of severe pain, and no distinct consciousness where I was, I found Browne and Max bending over me, my head being supported upon the knee of the former.

"Well, how do you feel?" inquired he.

I stared at him a minute or two without answering, not understanding very clearly what was the matter with me, though having at the same time a vague impression that all was not quite right. Gradually I collected my ideas, and at length, when Browne repeated his question the third time, I had formed a pretty correct theory as to the cause of my present supine attitude, and the unpleasant sensations which I experienced.

"I feel rather queer about the head and shoulders," I said, in answer to his inquiry: "I must have got a pretty severe blow. I suppose!"

"Yes," said Max, whose uneasy look ill agreed with his words and manner, "see what it is to be blessed with a tough cranium; such a whack would have crushed mine like an egg-shell; but it has only enlarged your bump of reverence a little."

"Nothing serious has happened, then—no one is badly hurt," said I, trying to look around; but the attempt gave my neck so severe a wrench, and caused such extreme pain, that I desisted.

"No one has received any worse injury than yourself," answered Browne—"at least, none of us."

"And the savages—what has become of them?"

"We have nothing to apprehend from them at present, I think—they have been gone but a short time, and Morton is in the tree yonder, keeping watch for their return—do you feel now as if you can stand up and walk?"

"Certainly, I can; with the exception of the pain in my head, and a stiffness about the neck and shoulders, I am all right, I believe." And in order to convince Browne, who seemed somewhat sceptical on the point, notwithstanding my assurances, I got up and walked about—carrying my head somewhat rigidly, I dare say, for it gave me a severe twinge at every movement.

"Well," said he, "since that is the case, I think the wisest thing we can do is to leave this neighbourhood at once."

While Max went to summon Morton from his post of observation, Browne gave me a brief and hurried account of what had occurred after I had been felled, as related.

He, and the leader of the savages, whom I had last seen struggling upon the brink of the height, had gone over it together; the latter, falling underneath, had been severely bruised, while Browne himself received but little injury.

Leaving his adversary groaning and, as he supposed, mortally hurt by the fall, he had climbed again to the higher ground, and reached it at a very critical moment.

Morton was struggling at disadvantage with the same formidable antagonist from whom he had before been for a moment in such imminent danger; and Max was dodging about among the bushes, sorely pressed by another of the enemy with one of those long spears against which he entertained so violent a prejudice. I had just been disposed of in the manner above hinted at, by the savage who had been wounded in the neck by Morton, at the very commencement of the affray, and he was now at liberty to turn his attention either to Max or Morton, each of whom was already hard bested.

Browne immediately fell upon my conqueror, almost as unexpectedly as the latter had attacked me, and by a sudden blow stretched him senseless upon the ground. He next relieved Morton, by disabling his adversary. The two, then, hastened to Max's succour, but the savage who was engaged with him, did not deem it prudent to await the approach of this reinforcement, and made off into the forest. They then gathered up all the weapons of the enemy, permitting Morton's recent antagonist to limp off without molestation. The man whom I had wounded was by this time sitting up, wiping the blood from his face and eyes; the other, also, manifested signs of returning consciousness; but having been deprived of their clubs and spears, no danger was apprehended from them. My three companions had then carried me to the spot where we now were, from whence they had witnessed the departure of the rest of our foes. Even the man whom Browne had left dying on the shore, as he supposed, had managed to crawl off at last.

As soon as Max and Morton returned, we set out at once, weary as we were, for the islet in the brook, without any very definite notion as to what was to be done next. The prudence of removing from our present neighbourhood was obvious, but we were still too much discomposed and excited by what had just taken place, to have been able to decide upon any further step, even had not the momentary apprehension of the return of the savages in greater numbers rendered every thing like calm deliberation entirely out of the question.

We took the precaution to choose our path over the hardest and dryest ground, in order to afford the savages the fewest possible facilities for tracing our course. By the time we reached the islet, we were completely out by the fatigue and excitement of the day; we must have walked at least twelve miles since morning.

After partaking sparingly of the food which we had so fortunately brought with us, accompanied by copious draughts of water from the brook, we began to feel somewhat refreshed. Still we were greatly disheartened by the gloomy and distressing circumstances in which we found ourselves so suddenly involved; the great uncertainty as to the fate of our companions, and the danger that threatened our own lives from the vindictive pursuit of a numerous body of savages. All our energy and courage seemed for the present, at least, to be completely broken. Browne laid down upon a couch of dry fern beneath the many-pillared Aoa. He looked pale and ill—more so, I thought, than the mere effects of excitement and over-exertion could account for.

Morton soon revived the question of what was now to be done.

"I suppose we must remain here for the present, at least," said Browne, "and defend ourselves, if attacked, as well as we can."

Max suggested Palm-Islet as a place of greater security and one where we should run less risk of discovery.

"And meantime," said Morton, "are we to give up all attempt to find Arthur and the rest?"

"I hardly know what we can do," answered Browne, with a perplexed and discouraged air; "we have no clue to guide us in a fresh search. If these savages inhabit the island,—or if they remain here,—we cannot hope to escape them long, after what has taken place; we must fall into their hands sooner or later, and if they have captured our companions, I am willing for my part, that it should be so. I doubt if we acted wisely in resisting them at all,—but it is now too late to think of that."

We continued to talk the matter over for some time, but without coming to any definite resolution, and at length Browne dropped asleep, while we were still discussing it.

As it began to grow dark, Max became disturbed and excited. He was possessed by a vague conviction, for which he was unable to account, that our lost companions were in some imminent peril, from which it was in our power to rescue them. He was anxious to do something, and yet seemed uncertain what to propose. Morton was equally desirous of making a further effort to discover our lost friends; he was also quite clear and explicit in his notion of what ought to be done. His theory appeared to be, that they had fallen into the hands of the natives, whose encampment or place of abode, (temporary or otherwise), was on the north-eastern side of the island. He further supposed that some feud or quarrel having arisen among themselves, the worsted party had fled along the beach as we had witnessed, pursued by their victorious enemies,—that in the meantime, their captives had been left, (perhaps unguarded), at the encampment or landing-place of the natives. Morton was as minute and detailed in stating this hypothetical case, as if he had either actually seen or dreamed the whole. He proposed that as soon as the moon rose, some of us should set off for the shore, and proceed along the beach, in the direction from which we had seen the natives come, by pursuing which course, he was confident we should be able to learn something respecting our companions. This he wished to undertake alone, saying that one person could prosecute the search as well as four, and with much less risk of discovery: if successful in ascertaining any thing definite, he should, he said, immediately return and apprise the rest of us. Max eagerly embraced this suggestion, and wished to decide by lot, which of us should carry it into execution, insisting that, otherwise, he would either set off at once by himself, or accompany Morton.

At length Browne awoke; he said that he had derived much benefit from his two hours' sleep, and was now ready for any necessary exertion.

He also approved of Morton's plan, but objected to his going alone, and was at first in favour of setting out all together. At last it was settled that the search should be undertaken by two of us, the other two awaiting the result at the islet. Browne then prepared four twigs for the purpose of deciding the matter by lot, it being agreed that the one drawing the longest, should have the choice of going or remaining, and should also select his companion. On comparing lots after we had drawn, mine proved to be longest; and having decided upon going, I felt bound to name Morton as my associate, since he had been the first to suggest, and the most earnest in urging the adventure.

An hour after dark the moon rose, and soon lighted the forest sufficiently to enable us to see our way through it. We then armed ourselves with a cutlass apiece, and taking leave of Max and Browne, proceeded up the brook to the fall, where we crossed it, and, following the rocky ridge, which ran at right angles with it, we endeavoured to hold, as nearly as possible, the course we had taken in the morning. After leaving the stream, a good part of our way was through the open country, where there was nothing to prevent us from seeing or being seen at a considerable distance in the bright moonlight. But the only alternatives were, either to creep on our hands and knees, the whole distance from the edge of the forest to the shore, and so avail ourselves of such concealment as the rank grass and weeds afforded,—or to push boldly and rapidly forward, at the risk of being seen: we preferred the latter, and soon got over this dangerous ground, running part of the time, in the most exposed places. On reaching the bluff, over the beach, we lay down among the bushes a few moments to recover our breath, and reconnoitre, before taking a fresh start. All was perfectly silent around us, and no living thing could be seen. When sufficiently rested, we proceeded cautiously along the edge of the height, where we could command a view both of the beach below, and of the open country inland. The bluff extended about a quarter of a mile, when it gradually sunk to the level of the beach, and was succeeded by a low, flat shore, lined with large trees. We had gone but a little way along it after this change, when we came quite unexpectedly upon an inlet, or salt-water creek, setting in to the land, and bordered so thickly with mangroves, that we narrowly escaped going headlong into it, while endeavouring to force our way through the bushes to continue our course along the beach.

It was some twenty yards wide; but I could not see how far inland it ran, on account of the immense trees that overhung it on every side, springing up in great numbers just behind the low border of mangroves. Holding fast by one of these bushes, I was leaning forward over the water, looking hard into the gloom, to gain, if possible, some notion of the extent of the inlet and the distance round it, when Morton grasped my arm suddenly—

"What is that, under the trees on the opposite shore?" whispered he; "is it not a boat?"

Looking in the direction in which he pointed, I could distinguish some object on the opposite side of the inlet, that might from its size and shape be a boat of some kind, as he supposed, and, continuing to gaze steadily, I made out quite plainly, against the dark masses of foliage on the further shore, what appeared to be a white mast. A profound silence reigned all around us, and while I was still peering into the heavy shadow of the trees, I heard a sound which resembled a deep, and long-drawn sigh, followed by an exclamation, as of a person in bodily pain.

"We must get round to the other side," whispered Morton, "and see what this means."

We backed out of the mangroves with the utmost caution, and inch by inch: when we had got to such a distance as to render this extreme circumspection no longer necessary, we commenced a wide circuit around the inlet, which proved to be only a small cove, or indentation in the shore, extending less than a hundred yards inland. In approaching it again on the opposite side, we resumed all our former stealthiness of movement, feeling that our lives in all probability depended upon our caution.

When, at last, we had got, as we supposed, quite near the place where we had seen the boat, we proceeded, by creeping on our hands and knees through the bushes for short distances, and then rising and looking about, to ascertain our position.

It was so dark, and the undergrowth was so dense—the moonlight scarcely penetrating the thick foliage—that nothing could be distinguished at the distance even of a few yards, and there was some danger that we might come suddenly, and before we were aware, upon those whom we supposed to be already so near us. While thus blindly groping our way towards the edge of the inlet, I heard a voice almost beside me, which said—

"Will they never come back?—Are they going to leave us here to starve?"

The voice was that of Johnny's beyond the possibility of mistake. Turning in the direction from which it proceeded, I saw a little to the right three figures upon the ground at the foot of a large casuarina. Another voice, as familiar, almost immediately answered—

"I only fear that they will return too soon: have patience! in a little while I shall have gnawed through this rope, and then I do not despair of being able to get my hands free also."

This was enough to show how matters stood.

"Are you alone?" said I, in a low voice, but loud enough to be heard by those beneath the casuarina.

There was an exclamation of joyful surprise from Johnny; then Arthur answered, "If that is you, Archer, come and help us, for we are tied hand and foot. You have nothing to fear; our captors have left us quite alone."

We now came forward without further hesitation. They were all bound fast, their hands being tied behind them, in addition to which, each was fastened to the tree by a rope of sennit. It would be difficult to say which party seemed most rejoiced at this sudden meeting. As soon as they were liberated, we embraced one another with tears of joy.

"Let us leave this place as fast as possible," said Arthur, as soon as he became a little composed, "I expect the return of the natives every moment,—and we have more to dread from them than you can guess. But I find I am so stiff after lying bound here all day, that I can hardly walk. Now, Johnny, take my hand, and try to get along. How is it with you, Eiulo—do you feel able to travel fast?"

The latter appeared to understand the drift of the question, and answered by frisking and jumping about in exultation at his recovered liberty.

Instead of returning by the way by which we had come, along the shore, we pushed on in a straight line, in the supposed direction of the islet, in order to avoid the risk of meeting the natives. After toiling for an hour through the woods, we emerged into the open country to the east of the rocky ridge that traversed the course of the stream. During this time, we had been too fully occupied in picking our way with the necessary caution, besides the constant apprehension of suddenly encountering the natives, to ask for any explanations. But now we began to feel somewhat reassured, and as we hastened on towards the islet, Arthur very briefly informed us, that they had yesterday been suddenly surprised by a party of six natives, soon after leaving us at the islet, and hurried off to the shore: that they had been left by their captors this morning, secured as we had found them, and had remained in that condition until released by us. He added that he had more to communicate by-and-bye.

The joy of Browne and Max at our return, accompanied by the lost ones, may be imagined—but it can scarcely be described. In fact, I am obliged to confess that we were such children, as to enact quite "a scene," at this unexpected meeting. Heartfelt and sincere were the thanksgivings we that night rendered to Him, who had kept us in perfect safety, and reunited us, after a separation made so distressing by our uncertainty as to each other's fate.

After Arthur, Eiulo, and Johnny, had appeased their hunger with the scanty remains of our supply of provisions, the two latter lay down upon a bed of ferns beneath the Aoa, and were soon sleeping as soundly and peacefully, as though all our troubles and dangers were now at an end. How easily they put in practice the philosophy that vexes itself not about the future! Exercising the happy privilege of childhood, they cast upon others, in whom they placed implicit confidence, the responsibility of thinking and planning for them—free from all care and anxiety themselves.

Arthur now gave us a more detailed account of what had occurred since our separation.

"Do you remember," said he, when he had finished, "hearing Eiulo, in talking of affairs at Tewa, make mention of a person named Atollo?"

"Atollo?" said Browne, "was not that the name of an uncle of his whom he made out to be a strange, unnatural sort of monster, even for a heathen, and who concocted a plot for the murder of his own father and brother, and afterwards attempted to kill Eiulo by rolling rocks down a precipice after him in the woods!"

"The same," answered Arthur. "I hardly supposed that you would have remembered it, as no one but myself seemed to take much interest in Eiulo's reminiscences of Tewa, the rest of you being obliged to get them at second-hand, through me as interpreter. Well, that Atollo has reached this island in some way, with a band of followers: it was by them that we were captured yesterday; it is from his power that we have just escaped."

"What is this Atollo like?" inquired Browne. "Is he a tall, large-framed man, but gaunt and spare as a half-starved hound?"

"Yes, with sharp features, and a wild, restless eye."

"Why, then," continued Browne, turning to me, "it was he, who was at the head of the second party of natives that we saw this morning by the shore."

We now gave Arthur an account of our rencontre with the savages; but no particular mention was made of the destruction of the canoe, or of the lion-like old man who seemed to be the leader of those who fled.

"And little Eiulo's dread of this strange uncle of his," said Browne, "is then so great, that he preferred running away to us again, to remaining with his own people?"

"Incredible as it may seem," answered Arthur, "I am convinced that his fears are not without foundation, and I even believe that this man intended to take his life, and would have done so, had we not escaped."

"Incredible, indeed!" exclaimed Browne, "and what could be the motive for so atrocious a crime?"

"I know of none that seems sufficient to account for it fully, and I am therefore almost forced to regard the man as a monomaniac."

Arthur thought that Atollo had probably made some further desperate attempt against his brother at Tewa, and, having failed in it, had fled hither with a part of his followers, among whom some quarrel had since arisen, in the prosecution of which they had been engaged, when we witnessed the flight and pursuit along the shore. This, however, was mere conjecture: they had talked but little in his presence, and he had not been able to learn any thing from the conversation which he had overheard, as to the cause of their coming hither. Eiulo had been questioned minutely by them, and from him they had ascertained that there were four more of us upon the island.

Morton inquired of Arthur, whether he apprehended that any serious effort would be made by the savages to find us, and what kind of treatment we should probably receive in case we should fall into their power.

"That search will be made for us," answered the latter, "I have not the slightest doubt; and I do not think that we can look for any mercy, if we fall into their hands, since to-day's affray and escape."

"This feud among themselves," said Browne, "may keep them so busy as to afford no leisure for troubling themselves about us. I have some hope that they will use those ugly-looking clubs upon one another, to such purpose, as to rid us of them altogether."

"That old giant," said Max, "who ran away, with such an awkward air, as if he wasn't at all used to it, will certainly do some mischief if they once come to blows."

"Ay," pursued Browne, "though he didn't look quite so wicked and like a warlock, as the gaunt, wild-eyed heathen that led the chase, I will warrant him his full match in fair and equal fight, man to man."

"Well," said Arthur, who during the latter part of this conversation had been apparently engaged in serious and perplexed thought, "for to-night, at least, we are in no danger. Let us now take our necessary rest, and to-morrow we shall be fresher and better prepared to decide upon the course of action to be adopted."

Chapter Thirty Two
The Single Combat

Preparations for Defence—A Demand and
Refusal—The Two Champions

"On many a bloody field before—
    Man of the dark and evil heart!—
We've met—pledged enemies of yore,
    But now we meet no more to part—
Till to my gracious liege and lord,
    By thee of broad domains bereft,
From thy red hand and plotting brain,
    No fear of future wrong is left."

The sense of surrounding danger with which we laid down that night upon our beds of fern beneath the Aoa, continued to press darkly upon our minds even in sleep, and awake us at an early hour to confront anew, the perplexities and terrors of our situation.

Arthur, in whose better understanding of the habits and character of the savages we confided, far from affording us any additional encouragement, spoke in a manner calculated to overthrow the very hopes upon which we had been resting.

We had supposed that they could have no motive but the desire of revenge, for seeking or molesting us, and as none of their number had been killed, or in all probability even dangerously injured in the rencontre with us, we trusted that this motive would not prove strong enough to incite them to any earnest or long-continued search. But Arthur hinted at another object, more controlling in the mind of their strange leader than any desire to prosecute a petty revenge, which would impel him to seek for and pursue us, for the purpose of getting Eiulo again into his power. This enmity—so fixed and implacable—against a mere child, seemed incredible, even after all that had been said or suggested in explanation of it, and the explanations themselves were far-fetched, and almost destitute of plausibility.

Taking possession of the Frenchman's Hut.

And how could we hope to escape a pursuit so determined and persevering as Arthur anticipated? Whither could we flee for safety? To think of successful resistance to Atollo and his band, if discovered by them, seemed idle. Max suggested Palm-Islet as the most secure retreat with which we were acquainted. But Arthur now broached a more startling plan. "Nowhere upon this island," said he, "can we longer consider ourselves secure. The only step that holds out any prospect of safety is to leave it in the yawl, and sail for Tewa."

"Is there any certainty," said Browne, "that we can find it? Do we even know positively where, or in what direction from this place it is; and shall we not incur the risk of getting lost again at sea?"

"I would rather take that risk," said Max, "than remain here, within reach of these savages—any thing is preferable to falling into their power."

"I confess," said Arthur, "that we know nothing certainly in regard to the distance, or even the direction of Tewa, but I think we have good reason to believe that it lies about forty or fifty miles to the northward."

We could not, however, bring ourselves thus suddenly to adopt a resolution so momentous, and it was at last tacitly decided to continue for the present, at least, at the islet.

"If we are to remain here," said Arthur, on perceiving that there was no disposition to act immediately upon any of the suggestions which had been made, "let us make such preparation as we can, to defend ourselves if it shall be necessary."

This surprised us all; it seemed worse than useless to think of forcible resistance to a party as numerous as that of Atollo; coming from Arthur such a suggestion was to me doubly surprising.

"I see," said he, "that the notion of attempting to defend ourselves, if discovered, seems to you a desperate one—but I believe it to be our only course—we can expect no mercy from Atollo."

"Surely," said Morton, "they can have no sufficient motive for murdering us in cold blood. But, fresh from another conflict with them, we could not perhaps look for forbearance, if in their power. Against *us* they cannot now, it seems to me, cherish any feelings so vindictive as you imply."

"And suppose it to be so? Suppose that they merely aim at Eiulo's life, without wishing to molest us?"

"I don't fear that I shall be misunderstood, if I speak plainly," answered Morton, after a pause. "It seems, from what you have intimated, that for some reason they wish to get Eiulo into their hands; they are his own people, and their leader is his own uncle; have we any right to refuse him to them?"

"Why, Morton!" interposed Browne, warmly, "what cold-blooded doctrine is this?"

"Have patience, a minute, and hear me out—I cannot bring myself to believe that they actually intend him harm; I think there must be some mistake or misapprehension in regard to this alleged design against his life, utterly improbable as it is in itself."

"But Arthur understands all that, far better than you or I," interrupted Browne, once more, "and it is clear that the poor child stands in mortal dread of this man."

"I was going to add," resumed Morton, "that even if this danger does exist, it is entirely out of our power to afford him protection against it: we should merely throw away our lives, in a desperate and unprofitable attempt. It may seem unfeeling to talk of giving him up; but will not these people be far more likely to act with cruelty, both towards him and us, after being excited and enraged by a fruitless opposition? I have spoken frankly: but whatever is soberly determined upon, however unwise in my view, I will abide by."

"I admit," answered Arthur, "that there is little prospect of success in a conflict with them: but I regard our fate as certain if we submit, and we can but be slain in resisting. I am so fully satisfied of Atollo's designs in respect to him, that I should feel in giving him up, as if I were an accessary to his murder."

"Let us rather defend ourselves to the very last extremity," said Browne, earnestly, "if we are so unfortunate as to be found."

"If," said Max, with an excited air,—"if I really believed they would kill Eiulo, I should say, never give him up, whatever the consequences may be;—and I do think this Atollo must be an incarnate fiend. I don't believe it will make any difference in their treatment of us whether we resist or not."

"O no!" cried Johnny, who had been listening eagerly to this conversation, while Eiulo stood looking wistfully on, as if he knew that it concerned him. "O no! don't give him up to that wicked man. I would fight, myself, if I had my bow and arrows, but they took them away from me: can't we hide ourselves in the banyan tree?—they never will think of looking for us there?"

"That is not a bad suggestion," said Morton, "and if we should be discovered, it is a strong place to defend. We can move easily and quickly about on that strong horizontal framework of branches, and it will be a hazardous undertaking to climb those straight smooth trunks, in our faces."

It seemed, in fact, as if a party stationed upon the roof, (as it might be termed), of this singular tree, would occupy a vantage-ground from which it would require strong odds to dislodge them, and the assailants, unless provided with fire-arms, or missile weapons, would labour under almost insurmountable difficulties.

Arthur discovered a place where it was easy to climb quickly into the tree, and requested us all to note it particularly, in order that we might effect a retreat without loss of time, if it should become necessary. Johnny and Eiulo were to take refuge there at the first alarm.

Browne proceeded to cut a number of bludgeons from stout saplings, which he then deposited in different places among the branches, ready to be used, in defending ourselves, if pursued thither. Max collected a quantity of large stones, and fragments of rock, along the shore, and from the bed of the brook, and wrapping them in parcels of leaves, he hoisted them into the roof of the grove-tree, and secured them there.

Morton surveyed these preparations with a grave smile, and none of us, I think, placed much reliance on their efficacy. We trusted that there would be no occasion to resort to them.

The supply of provisions which we had brought with us was exhausted, but the painful suspense, and constant apprehension incident to our present circumstances, long prevented any thought of hunger. It was not until the day had passed without any alarm, and it was beginning to grow dark, that we experienced any inclination to eat. Arthur and I then went in search of food, but could obtain none, except a quantity of pandanus cones which we gathered from a group of trees near the waterfall. The kernels of these were the only food that any of us tasted that day.

At night, it was deemed best to keep a watch, in order to guard against any surprise. As we made our arrangements for this purpose, my thoughts reverted to the time of our sufferings at sea in the boat. But in our present position, sought and pursued by malignant human beings, bent upon taking our lives, and who might at that moment be prowling near, there was something more fearful than any peril from the elements, or even the dread of starvation itself.

But the night passed without disturbance or alarm of any kind, and in the morning we began to indulge the hope that Arthur had overrated the strength of the feelings by which Atollo was actuated, and to shake off in some degree the profound depression of the preceding evening.

With the abatement of our fears and the partial return of tranquillity of mind, we became more sensible to the demands of hunger. Max and Morton ventured a little way into the adjoining forest in search of birds, and returned in less than half an hour with about a dozen pigeons, which they had knocked down with sticks and stones. Arthur had in the meantime caught quite a string of the yellow fish which had so perseveringly rejected all Max's overtures a couple of days since. Morton then kindled a fire to cook our food, though we felt some hesitation about this, being aware that the smoke might betray us to the savages, if they should happen to be at the time in the neighbourhood. But Max declared that falling into their hands was a fate preferable to starvation, and that rather than eat raw fish and birds, he would incur the risk of discovery by means of the fire. In the absence of cooking utensils, we hastily scooped out a Polynesian oven, and covered the bottom with a layer of heated stones, upon which the food, carefully wrapped in leaves, was deposited: another layer of hot stones was placed on top, and the whole then covered with fresh leaves and earth. This is the method adopted by the natives for baking bread-fruit and fish, and with the exception of the trouble and delay involved, it is equal to any thing that civilised ingenuity has devised for similar purposes, from the old-fashioned Dutch-oven to the most recent style of "improved kitchen ranges" with which I am acquainted. The heat being equally diffused throughout the entire mass, and prevented from escaping by the wrapping of leaves and earth, the subject operated upon, whether fish, fowl, or vegetable, is thoroughly and uniformly cooked.

Max had just opened the oven, and was busily engaged in taking out and distributing the contents, while the rest of us were gathered in a group around the spot, when Eiulo suddenly uttered a shrill cry, and springing up, stood gazing towards the west side of the brook, as if paralysed by terror.

Looking up, we saw two natives standing at the edge of the wood quietly watching us. One of them I at once recognised as the lithe and active leader, whom I had seen upon the shore in swift pursuit of the fugitives.

Our first impulse, was to spring at once into the Aoa, according to the understanding to which we had partially come, as to what we were to do if discovered. But a second glance showed that there were but two enemies in sight, and as Arthur, to whom we looked for an example, gave no signal for such a retreat, we hastily snatched up our weapons, and placed ourselves beside him.

Atollo's quick eye—for it was he—ran from one to another of us, until it rested upon Eiulo, when coming down to the margin of the brook, he pronounced his name in a low, clear voice, and beckoned him with his hand to come over to him.

Pale and trembling, like a bird under the charm of the serpent, Eiulo made two or three uncertain steps towards him, as if about mechanically to obey the summons: then, as Johnny seized the skirt of his wrapper, and called out to him, "not to mind that wicked man," he paused, and looked round upon us with a glance, half appealing, half inquiring, which said more plainly than words—"Must I go?—Can you protect me—and will you?"

Arthur now stepped before him, and addressed some words to Atollo in his own language, the purport of which I could only guess.

The other listened attentively without evincing any surprise, and then made answer, speaking rapidly and by jerks as it were, and scanning us all the while with the eye of a hawk.

When he had finished, Arthur turned to us. "This man requires us, he said, to give up Eiulo to him; he claims him as his brother's son, and says that he wishes to convey him home to Tewa. He promises to leave us unmolested if we comply, and threatens us with death if we refuse: you see it concerns us all—what do you say?"

Arthur was very pale. He looked towards Morton, who said nothing, but stood leaning against one of the pillars of the Aoa, with his eyes steadfastly bent upon the ground.

"Ask Eiulo," said Browne, "if this man is his uncle."

The question was accordingly put, and the trembling boy answered hesitatingly, that he did not know—but he believed that he was.

"Ask him," pursued Browne, "if he is willing to go with him."

Arthur put the question formally, and Eiulo, grasping his arm, while Johnny still held fast by his skirt, answered with a shudder that he was afraid to go with him.

"Ask him why he is afraid," continued Browne.

The answer was, that he believed his uncle would kill him.

These questions were put loud enough to be easily heard by Atollo, and Arthur deliberately repeated the answers first in Tahitian, and then in English.

"Well," said Browne, "I am now quite ready with an answer, as far as I am concerned. I never will consent to give up the poor boy to be murdered. He is old enough to choose for himself and I think it would be right to resist the claim even of a father, under such circumstances."

"Is that to be our answer?" said Arthur, looking round.

It was a bold stand to take, situated as we were, and we felt it to be so; but it seemed a hard and cruel thing to yield up our little companion to the tender mercies of his unnatural relative. Though there were pale cheeks and unsteady hands among us, as we signified our concurrence in this refusal, (which we all did except Morton, who remained silent), yet we experienced a strange sense of relief when it was done, and we stood committed to the result.

Arthur now motioned Johnny and Eiulo to climb into the tree, then turning to Atollo, he said that as the boy preferred remaining with us, we were resolved to protect him to the extent of our ability.

By this time we had somewhat regained our self-possession, and stood grasping our weapons, though not anticipating any immediate attack. Much to my surprise, Atollo had during the conference manifested neither anger nor impatience. When Arthur announced our refusal to comply with his demand, he merely noticed with a smile our belligerent attitude, and advanced into the brook as if about to come over to the islet, swinging a long curving weapon carelessly by his side, and followed by the other savage.

Browne, holding his club in his left hand, and a heavy stone in his right, stood beside me, breathing hard through his set teeth.

"The foolish heathen!" exclaimed he, "does he expect to subdue us by his looks,—that he comes on in this fashion?"

It did, in fact, seem as though he supposed that we would not dare to commence an attack upon him, for he continued to advance, eyeing us steadily. Just as he gained the middle of the brook, three or four more savages came out of the forest, and one of them ran towards him, with an exclamation which caused him to turn at once, and on hearing what the other eagerly uttered, with gestures indicating some intelligence of an urgent and exciting character, he walked back to the edge of the wood, and joined the group gathered there.

A moment afterwards, Atollo, attended by the messenger, as he appeared to be, plunged into the forest, first giving to the others, who remained upon the shore, some direction, which from the accompanying gesture, appeared to have reference to ourselves.

Johnny and Eiulo had already climbed into the Aoa, whither we stood ready to follow, at a moment's notice. The group of savages opposite us seemed to have no other object in view than to prevent our escape, for they did not offer to molest us. Soon after Atollo disappeared, two more of his party came out of the wood, and I immediately recognised one of them, who walked stiffly and with difficulty, seeming but just able to drag himself about, as the scarred savage with whom Browne had had so desperate a struggle. We now thought it prudent to effect our retreat into the tree without further loss of time, but at the first movement which we made for that purpose, the natives set up a shout, and dashed into the water towards us, probably thinking that we were about to try to escape by getting to the further shore.

They pressed us so closely that we had not a moment to spare, and had barely climbed beyond their reach when they sprang after us. One active fellow caught Browne, (who was somewhat behind the rest), by the foot, and endeavoured to drag him from the trunk he was climbing, in which he would probably have succeeded, had not Max let fall a leaf-basket of stones directly upon his head, which stretched him groaning upon the ground, with the blood gushing from his mouth and nose.

At this moment Atollo himself, with the rest of his party, joined our besiegers below, and at a signal from him, the greater part of them immediately commenced scaling the tree at different points. Our assailants numbered not more than thirteen or fourteen, including Browne's former foe, who did not seem to be in a condition to climb, and the man recently wounded, who was still lying upon the ground, apparently lifeless. We felt that we were now irrevocably committed to a struggle of life and death, and we were fully determined to fight manfully, and to the very last. We stationed ourselves at nearly equal distances among the branches, armed with the bludgeons previously placed there, so as to be able to hasten to any point assailed, and to assist one another as occasion should require. The savages yelled and screeched hideously, with the hope of intimidating us, but without any effect, and we kept watching them quietly, and meeting them so promptly at every point, that they were uniformly obliged to quit their hold and drop to the ground before they could effect a lodgment among the branches. Occasionally we addressed a word of encouragement to one another, or uttered an exclamation of triumph at the discomfiture of some assailant more than ordinarily fierce and resolute. But with this exception, we were as quiet as if industriously engaged in some ordinary occupation. This lasted for full fifteen minutes, without our enemies having gained the slightest advantage. Atollo himself had not, thus far, taken any part in the attack, except to direct the others.

At length, he fixed his eye upon Browne, who stepping about in the top of the tree with an agility that I should not have expected from him, and wielding a tremendous club, had been signally successful in repelling our assailants. After watching him a moment, he suddenly commenced climbing a large stem near him, with the marvellous rapidity that characterised all his movements. Browne had just tumbled one of the savages to the ground howling with pain, from a crushing blow upon the wrist, and he now hastened to meet this more formidable foe. But he was too late to prevent him from getting into the tree, and he had already gained a footing upon the horizontal branches, when Browne reached the spot. Atollo was without any weapon, and this was a disadvantage that might have rendered all his strength and address unavailing, had not the foliage and the lesser branches of the tree, interfered with the swing of the long and heavy weapon of his adversary, and the footing being too insecure to permit it to be used with full effect. As Browne steadied himself and drew back for a sweeping blow, Atollo shook the boughs upon which he stood, so violently, as greatly to break the force of the stroke, which he received upon his arm, and rushing upon him before he could recover his weapon, he wrested it from his grasp, and hurled him to the ground, where he was instantly seized and secured by those below.

While Atollo, armed with Browne's club, advanced upon Max and Arthur, who were nearest him, several of his followers, taking advantage of the diversion thus effected, succeeded in ascending also, and in a few moments they were making their way towards us from all sides. Leaving them to complete what he had so well begun, Atollo hastened towards the spot where Johnny and Eiulo were endeavouring to conceal themselves among the foliage. Though now outnumbered, and hopeless of success, we continued a desperate resistance. The ferocity of our adversaries was excited to the highest pitch. There was scarcely one of them who had not received some injury in the attack, sufficiently severe to exasperate, without disabling him. We had used our clubs with such vigour and resolution in opposing their attempts at climbing, that every second man at least, had a crushed hand or a bruised head, and all had received more or less hard blows. Smarting with pain, and exulting in the prospect of speedy and ample revenge, they pressed upon us with yells and cries that showed that there was no mercy for us if taken. But even at that trying moment our courage did out fail or falter. We stood together near the centre of the tree, where the branches were strong and the footing firm. Only a part of our assailants had weapons, and, perceiving the utter desperation with which we fought, they drew back a little distance until clubs could be passed up from below, and thus afforded us a momentary respite. But we well knew that it was only momentary, and that in their present state of mind, these men would dispatch us with as little scruple as they would mischievous wild beasts hunted and brought to bay.

"Nothing now remains," said Morton, "but to die courageously: we have done every thing else that we could do."

"It does appear to have come to that at last," said Arthur. "If I did unwisely in advising resistance, and perilling your lives as well as my own, I now ask your forgiveness; on my own account I do not regret it."

"There is nothing to forgive," answered Morton, "you did what you believed was right, and if I counselled otherwise, you will do me the justice to believe that it was because I differed with you in judgment, and not because I shrunk from the consequences."

"I never did you the injustice to think otherwise," answered Arthur.

"If our friends could but know what has become of us," said Max, brushing away a tear, "and how we died here, fighting manfully to the last, I should feel more entirely resigned; but I cannot bear to think that our fate will never be known."

"Here they come once more," said Arthur, as the savages, having now obtained their weapons, advanced to finish their work, "and now, may God have mercy upon us!"

We all joined devoutly in Arthur's prayer, for we believed that death was at hand. We then grasped our weapons, and stood ready for the attack.

At this instant a long and joyous cry from Eiulo reached our ears. For several minutes he had been eluding the pursuit of Atollo with a wonderful agility, partly the effect of frantic dread. Just when it seemed as though he could no longer escape, he suddenly uttered this cry, repeating the words, "Wakatta! Wakatta!"—then springing to the ground, he ran towards the brook, but was intercepted and seized by one of the savages below.

There was an immediate answer to Eiulo's cry, in one of the deepest and most powerful voices I had ever heard, and which seemed to come from the west shore of the stream. Looking in that direction I saw, and recognised at once, the lion-like old man, who had fled along the beach, pursued by Atollo and his party. Several men, apparently his followers, stood around him. He now bounded across the stream, towards the spot where Eiulo was still struggling with his captor, and calling loudly for help.

Atollo instantly sprang to the ground, and flew to the spot; then, with a shrill call, he summoned his men about him. Eiulo's outcry, and the answer which had been made to it, seemed to have produced a startling effect upon Atollo and his party. For the moment we appeared to be entirely forgotten.

"This must be Wakatta," said Arthur eagerly, "it can be no other. There is hope yet." With a rapid sign for us to follow, he glided down the nearest trunk, and, darting past Atollo's party, he succeeded in the midst of the confusion, in reaching the old man and his band, who stood upon the shore of the islet. Morton and I were equally successful. Max, who came last, was observed, and an effort made to intercept him. But dodging one savage, and bursting from the grasp of another, who seized him by the arm as he was running at full speed, he also joined us, and we ranged ourselves beside Wakatta and his men. Browne, Eiulo, and Johnny, were prisoners.

It now seemed as though the conflict was about to be renewed upon more equal terms. Our new and unexpected allies numbered seven, including their venerable leader. On the other hand, our adversaries were but twelve, and of these, several showed evident traces of the severe usage they had recently received, and were hardly in a condition for a fresh struggle.

There was a pause of some minutes, during which the two parties stood confronting each other, with hostile, but hesitating looks. Wakatta then addressed a few words to Atollo, in the course of which he several times repeated Eiulo's name, pointing towards him at the same time, and appearing to demand that he should be released.

The reply was an unhesitating and decided refusal, as I easily gathered from the look and manner that accompanied it.

Wakatta instantly swung up his club, uttering a deep guttural exclamation, which seemed to be the signal for attack, for his people raised their weapons and advanced as if about to rush upon the others. We had in the meantime provided ourselves with clubs, a number of which were scattered about upon the ground, and we prepared to assist the party with whom we had become so strangely associated.

But at a word and gesture from Atollo, Wakatta lowered his weapon again, and the men on both sides paused in their hostile demonstrations, while their leaders once more engaged in conference.

Atollo now seemed to make some proposition to Wakatta, which was eagerly accepted by the latter. Each then spoke briefly to his followers, who uttered cries of the wildest excitement, and suddenly became silent again. The two next crossed together to the opposite shore, and while we stood gazing in a bewildered manner at these proceedings, and wondering what could be their meaning, the natives also crossed the brook, and formed a wide circle around their chiefs, on an open grassy space at the edge of the forest. We still kept with Wakatta's party, who arranged themselves in a semicircle behind him.

"What does this mean!" inquired Morton of Arthur, "it looks as though they were about to engage in single combat."

"That is in fact their purpose," answered Arthur.

"And will that settle the difficulty between these hostile parties?" said Morton, "will there not be a general fight after all, whichever leader is victor?"

"I rather think not," answered Arthur, "the party whose champion falls, will be too much discouraged to renew the fight—they will probably run at once."

"Then our situation will be no better than before, in case the old warrior should prove unfortunate. Can't you speak to his followers and get them to stand ready to attack their enemies if their chief falls."

"I will try what I can do," answered Arthur, "and let us be ready to act with them."

Meantime the two principal parties had completed their preparations for the deadly personal combat in which they were about to engage. Atollo took from one of his followers a long-handled curving weapon, the inner side of which was lined with a row of sharks' teeth, and then placed himself in the middle of the open space, first carefully kicking out of the way a number of fallen branches which strewed the ground. His manner was confident, and clearly bespoke an anticipated triumph.

Wakatta was armed with the massive club, set with spikes of iron-wood, which he carried when I first saw him upon the shore. He advanced deliberately towards his adversary, until they stood face to face, and within easy reach of one another's weapons.

The men on both sides remained perfectly quiet, eyeing every movement of their respective champions with the intensest interest. In the breathless silence that prevailed, the gentle murmur of the brook sliding over its pebbly bed, and even the dropping of a withered leaf, could be heard distinctly.

Glancing over to the islet, I saw that Browne, although his hands appeared to be bound behind him, had rolled himself to the edge of the brook, from which he was watching what was going forward.

Each of the two combatants regarded the other with the air of a man conscious that he is about to meet a formidable adversary; but in Atollo's evil eye, there gleamed an assured and almost exulting confidence, that increased my anxiety for his aged opponent; his manner, nevertheless, was cautious and wary, and he did not suffer the slightest movement of Wakatta to escape him.

They stood opposite each other, neither seeming to be willing to commence the conflict, until Wakatta, with an impatient gesture, warned his adversary to defend himself, and then swinging up his ponderous club in both hands, aimed a blow at him, which the other avoided by springing lightly backwards.

And now the fight commenced in earnest. Atollo made no attempt to guard or parry the blows levelled at him—which would indeed have been idle—but with astonishing agility and quickness of eye, he sprang aside, or leaped back, always in time to save himself. He kept moving around the old man, provoking his attacks by feints and half-blows, but making no serious attack himself. There was a cool, calculating expression upon his sharp and cruel countenance, and he did not appear to be half so earnest or excited as his antagonist. I saw plainly that the wily savage was endeavouring to provoke the other to some careless or imprudent movement, of which he stood ready to take instant and fatal advantage.

At length some such opportunity as he was waiting for, was afforded him. The old warrior, growing impatient of this indecisive manoeuvring, began to press his adversary harder, and to follow him up with an apparent determination to bring matters to a speedy issue. Atollo retreated before him, until he was driven to the edge of the brook, where he paused, as if resolved to make a stand. Wakatta now seemed to think that he had brought his foe to bay, and whirling round his club, he delivered a sweeping blow full at his head with such fury, that when Atollo avoided it by dropping upon one knee, the momentum of the ponderous weapon swung its owner half round, and before he had time to recover himself, his watchful adversary, springing lightly up, brought down his keen-edged weapon full upon his grey head, inflicting a ghastly wound.

And now Atollo's whole demeanour changed: the time for caution and coolness was passed; the moment for destroying his disabled foe had come. While his followers set up an exulting yell, he darted forward to follow up his advantage: the triumphant ferocity of his look is not to be described. Wakatta was yet staggering from the effect of the blow upon his head, when he received a second, which slightly gashed his left shoulder, and glancing from it, laid open his cheek. But to my astonishment, the strong old man, cruelly wounded as he was, seemed to be neither disabled nor dismayed. The keen-edged, but light weapon of Atollo was better calculated to inflict painful wounds than mortal injuries. Either blow, had it been from a weapon like that of Wakatta, would have terminated the combat.

Before Atollo could follow up his success by a third and decisive stroke, the old warrior had recovered himself and though bleeding profusely, he looked more formidable than ever. He at once resumed the offensive, and with such vigour, that the other, with all his surprising activity, now found it difficult to elude his rapid but steady attacks. He was now thoroughly aroused. Atollo seemed gradually to become confused and distressed, as he was closely followed around the circle without an instant's respite being allowed him. At last he was forced into the stream, where he made a desperate stand, with the manifest determination to conquer or perish there. But Wakatta rushed headlong upon him, and holding his club in his right hand, he received upon his left arm, without any attempt to avoid it, a blow which Atollo aimed at his head: at the same instant he closed, and succeeded in seizing his adversary by the wrist. Once in the old man's grasp, he was a mere child, and in spite of his tremendous efforts, his other hand was soon mastered, and he was thrown to the ground. It was a horrible scene that followed. I wished that the life of the vanquished man could have been spared. But his excited foe had no thought of mercy, and shortening his club, he held him fast with one hand, and despatched him at a single blow with the other.

Chapter Thirty Three
The Migration

A Tewan MD—Exchange of Civilities—Max's
Farewell Breakfast—A Glance at the Future

"We go from the shores where those blue billows roll,
But that Isle, and those waters, shall live in my soul."

As the victor rose to his feet, his followers uttered a fierce yell, and precipitated themselves upon the opposite party, which instantly dispersed and fled.

Wakatta cast a half-remorseful glance at the corpse of his adversary, and raising his powerful voice recalled his men from the pursuit. Then wading into the brook, he began to wash the gore from his head and face: one of his people, who from his official air of bustling alacrity, must have been a professional character, or at least an amateur surgeon, examined the wounds, and dexterously applied an improvised poultice of chewed leaves to his gashed face, using broad strips of bark for bandages.

Meantime Arthur hastened over to the islet, and released our companions from the ligatures of tappa which confined their limbs. Eiulo was no sooner freed, than he ran eagerly to Wakatta, who took him in his arms, and embraced him tenderly. After a rapid interchange of questions and replies, during which they both shed tears, they seemed to be speaking of ourselves, Eiulo looking frequently towards us, and talking with great animation and earnestness. They then approached the place where we were standing, and Wakatta spoke a few words, pointing alternately from Eiulo to us. Arthur made some reply, whereupon the old warrior went to him, and bending down his gigantic frame gave him a cordial hug; his fresh bandaged wounds probably caused him to dispense with the usual ceremony of rubbing faces.

"I expect it will be our turn next," said Max, with a grimace, "if so, observe how readily I shall adapt myself to savage etiquette, and imitate my example."

It proved as he anticipated, for Wakatta, who must have received a highly flattering account of us from Eiulo, was not satisfied until he had bestowed upon each one of us, Johnny included, similar tokens of his regard, Max rushing forward, with an air of "empressement," and taking the initiative, as he had promised. The "surgeon," who seemed to think that some friendly notice might also be expected from him, in virtue of his official character, now advanced with a patronising air, and in his turn paid us the same civilities, not omitting the rubbing of faces, as his chief had done. Another one of our "allies," as Max called them, a huge, good-natured-looking savage, picked up Johnny, very much as one would a lap-dog or a pet kitten, and began to chuck him under the chin, and stroke his hair and cheeks, greatly to the annoyance of the object of these flattering attentions, who felt his dignity sadly compromised by such treatment.

As soon as these friendly advances were over, Arthur entered into a conversation with Wakatta, which, from the earnest expression of the countenance of the latter, appeared to relate to something of great interest. Presently he spoke to his men, who seized their weapons with an air of alacrity, as if preparing for some instant expedition, and Arthur, turning to us, said that we must set out in a body for the inlet where we had seen the canoe of the other party, as it was thought of the utmost importance to secure it if possible. We started at once, at a rapid rate, Wakatta leading the way, with tremendous strides, and the big, good-natured fellow, taking Johnny upon his back, in spite of his protestations that he could run himself, quite as fast as was necessary. But on reaching the inlet we found that the other party had been too quick for us; they were already through the surf, and under sail, coasting along towards the opening in the reef opposite Palm-Islet, probably with the intention of returning to Tewa.

It is now eight days since the events last narrated took place. On the day succeeding, we buried Atollo on the shore opposite Banyan islet, together with one of his followers, who had also been killed or mortally wounded in the conflict with us. Two others of them, who were too badly hurt to accompany the hasty flight to the inlet, are still living in the woods, Wakatta having strictly forbidden his people to injure them.

I ought here to explain the circumstances, as Arthur learned them from Wakatta, which brought the natives to our island. A civil war had recently broken out in Tewa, growing out of the plots of the Frenchmen resident there, and some discontented chiefs who made common cause with them. One of the foreigners, connected by marriage with the family of a powerful chief, had been subjected by the authority of Eiulo's father, to a summary and severe punishment, for an outrage of which he had been clearly convicted. This was the immediate cause of the outbreak. Atollo and his followers had issued from their fastnesses and joined the insurgents; a severe and bloody battle had been fought, in which they were completely successful, taking the chief himself prisoner, and dispersing his adherents.

Wakatta, attended by the six followers now with him, was at this time absent upon an excursion to a distant part of the island, and the first intelligence which he received of what had taken place, was accompanied by the notice that Atollo, with a formidable band, was then in eager search of him. Knowing well the relentless hatred borne him by that strange and desperate man, and that Tewa could furnish no lurking-place where he would be long secure from his indefatigable pursuit, he had hastily embarked for the island where he had once before taken refuge, under somewhat similar circumstances. Hither his implacable foe had pursued him. This statement will sufficiently explain what has been already related.

All our plans are yet uncertain. Wakatta meditates a secret return to Tewa, confident that by his presence there, now that the formidable Atollo is no more, he can restore his chief to liberty and to his hereditary rights, if he yet survives.

An experiment has been made with the yawl, in order to ascertain whether she can safely convey our entire party, savage and civilised, in case we should conclude to leave the island. The result showed that it would scarcely be prudent for so great a number to embark in her upon a voyage to Tewa, and Wakatta and his people have now commenced building a canoe, which is to be of sufficient size to carry twenty persons.

Browne's prejudices against the "heathen savages," have been greatly softened by what he has seen of these natives, and he says that, "if the rest of them are equally well-behaved, one might manage to get along with them quite comfortably." Max has taken a great fancy to Wakatta, whom he emphatically pronounces "a trump," a "regular brick," besides bestowing upon him a variety of other elegant and original designations, of the like complimentary character. This may be owing in part, to the fact, that the old warrior has promised him a bread-fruit plantation, and eventually a pretty grand-daughter of his own for a wife, if he will accompany him to Tewa and settle there.

As the preparations of our allies advance towards completion, we are more and more reconciled to the thought of embarking with them. Johnny has already commenced packing his shells and "specimens" for removal. Max has ascertained, greatly to his relief, for he had some doubts on the subject, that the gridiron and other cooking utensils can be stowed safely in the locker of the yawl, and he anticipates much benevolent gratification in introducing these civilised "institutions," among the barbarians of Tewa.

The intestine feuds which still rage there, and the probability that "our side," will find themselves in the minority, furnish the chief grounds of objection to the step contemplated. But we would cheerfully incur almost any danger that promises to increase our prospect of ultimately reaching home.

There is some talk of a preliminary reconnoitring expedition, by Wakatta and two or three of his people, for the purpose of getting some definite information as to the present position of affairs at Tewa, before setting out for it in a body. Max, yesterday, finished his miniature ship, and exhorted me to "wind up" our history forthwith, with a Homeric description of the great battle at the islet, and our heroic defence of the banyan tree. He declares it to be his intention to enclose the manuscript in the hold of the vessel and launch her when half-way to Tewa, in the assured confidence that the winds and waves will waft it to its destination, or to use his own phrase,—"that we shall yet be heard of in Hardscrabble."

Five days ago, the canoe was completed, and on the succeeding afternoon, Wakatta, accompanied by "the doctor," and two other of his people, sailed for Tewa, for the purpose of endeavouring to learn whether it would be prudent for us to venture thither at present.

We have been living of late at the cabin, and our "allies" have made an encampment by the lake, within a hundred paces of us. The state of feverish expectation naturally produced by our present circumstances, prevents any thing like regular occupation. We do nothing all the day but wander restlessly about among the old haunts which were our favourites in the peaceful time of our early sojourn here. Max has endeavoured to relieve the tedium, and get up an interest of some sort, by renewing his attempts against the great eel. But the patriarch is as wary, and his stronghold beneath the roots of the buttress tree as impregnable as ever, and all efforts to his prejudice, whether by force or stratagem, still prove unavailing. To escape in some measure the humiliation of so mortifying a defeat, Max now affects to be convinced that his venerable antagonist is no eel after all, but an old water-snake, inheriting his full share of the ancient wisdom of the serpent, and by whom it is consequently no disgrace for any mortal man to be outwitted.

For several days past we have even neglected preparing any regular meals, satisfying our hunger as it arose with whatever could be most readily procured.

Max pronounces this last, "an alarming indication of the state of utter demoralisation towards which we are hastening, and, in fact, the commencement of a relapse into barbarism."

"One of the chief points of difference," he says, "between civilised and savage man, is, that the former eats at stated and regular intervals, as a matter of social duty, whereas the latter only eats when he is hungry!"

Two days later. Wakatta has returned from his expedition, full of hope and confidence, and actually looking ten years younger than when I first saw him. He says that the position of affairs at Tewa is most promising. The recently victorious rebels have fallen into fierce contentions among themselves, and a large faction of them, with the leaders of which he has entered into communication, is willing to unite with him against the others, upon being assured of indemnity for past offences. Eiulo's father still lives, and has already gathered the nucleus of a force capable of retrieving his fortunes.

All is now finally determined upon, and we only wait for a favourable breeze to bid adieu to these shores.

The morning of Wakatta's return, also witnessed another event of nearly equal importance. I allude to a great farewell breakfast, given by Max in celebration of our approaching departure, as well as for the purpose of stemming the current of the demoralising influence above alluded to. The "founder of the feast," together with Eiulo and Johnny, was up preparing it with his own hospitable hands, a full hour before the rest of us were awake.

It consisted of all the delicacies and luxuries that our island can afford: there were roasted oysters fresh from the shore, and poached eggs fresh from the nest, (Max had despatched one of the natives to Sea-birds' Point after them before daylight); then there were fish nicely broiled, and mealy taro, and baked bread-fruit hot from a subterranean Polynesian oven.

In the enjoyment of this generous fare, our drooping spirits rose, and Max, as was his wont, became discursive.

"What a humiliating reflection," exclaimed he, "that we should have permitted ourselves to be so disturbed and fluttered, by the prospect of a slight change in our affairs! Why should we distrust our destiny, or shrink from our mission? Why these nervous apprehensions, and these unreasonable doubts?"—(Hear! hear!)

"'There *is* a providence that shapes our ends,
Rough-hew them how we will.'

"Let us accept, then, the belief which all things tend to confirm, that a glorious future awaits us in our new sphere of action at Tewa!"

"Ah!" sighed Browne, after a momentary pause, "Tewa may be a fine place—but I doubt if they have any such oysters as these there." The action accompanying these words must have given Eiulo a clue to their purport, for he hastened eagerly to protest, through Arthur, as interpreter, that the oysters at Tewa were much larger and fatter; he added, "that since we liked them so much, he would have them all 'tabooed,' as soon as we arrived, so that 'common people,' wouldn't dare for their lives to touch one."

"I used to regard the 'taboo,'" said Browne, "as an arbitrary and oppressive heathen custom. But how ignorant and prejudiced we sometimes are in regard to foreign institutions! We must be very careful when we get there about introducing rash innovations upon the settled order of things."

"We will establish an enlightened system of common schools," said Max, "to begin with, and Arthur shall also open a Sunday-school."

"And in the course of time we will found a college in which Browne shall be professor of Elocution and Oratory," said Morton.

"And you," resumed Max, "shall have a commission as Major-General in the Republican army of Tewa, which you shall instruct in modern tactics, and lead to victory against the rebels."

"In the Royal army, if you please," interrupted Browne; "Republicanism is one of those crude and pestilent innovations which I shall set my face against! Can any one breathe so treasonable a suggestion in the presence of the heir-apparent to the throne?—If such there be, Major-General Morton, I call upon you to attach him for a traitor!"

"And I," cried Johnny, "what shall I do!"

"Why," answered Max, "you shall rejoice the hearts of the Tewan juveniles, by introducing among them the precious lore of the story-books. The rising generation shall no longer remain in heathen ignorance of Cinderella, and Jack of the Bean-stalk, and his still more illustrious cousin, the Giant-killer! The sufferings of Sinbad, the voyages of Gulliver, the achievements of Munchausen, the adventures of Crusoe, shall yet become to them familiar as household words!"

"And Archer's mission shall be no less dignified and useful," resumed Browne, "he shall keep the records of the monarchy, and become the faithful historian of the happy, prosperous, and glorious reign of Eiulo the First!"